King Death

The hall was hung with purple, scarlet, magenta and gold. Candles bloomed, the floor was laid with mosaics of dragons, and golden lamps hung down between the pillars of carved and gilded cedarwood. The roof was a cupola of a million fragments of translucent jewels, blue and red and green and violet, and black and white striped doves flew about under it, turned to flying rainbows from its colors. On tables of painted glass lay a feast of food and drink.

Death had not moved from the stone chair, but now it was a chair of gold. A bloody banner hung behind him. The many lights gleamed on his collar and rings of gold and all his white garments glinted with silver and gems. A circlet of rubies held back his long white hair, and across his knees rested a sceptre of ivory whose head was a silver skull.

King Death he surely was.

DEATH'S MASTER

by
Tanith
Lee

DAW BOOKS, INC.
DONALD A. WOLLHEIM, PUBLISHER
1633 Broadway, New York, NY 10019

FIRST PRINTING, FEBRUARY 1979

3 4 5 6 7 8 9

 DAW TRADEMARK REGISTERED
U.S. PAT. OFF. MARCA
REGISTRADA. HECHO EN U.S.A.

PRINTED IN U.S.A.

TABLE OF CONTENTS

Book One

Book Two

BOOK ONE

PART ONE

Narasen and Death

1

Narasen, the leopard queen of Merh, stood at her window and watched Lady Plague walking about in the city. Lady Plague wore her yellow robe, for the sickness was a yellowish fever, yellow as the dust that swirled up from the plains and cloaked the city of Merh and choked it, yellow as the stinking mud to which the wide river of Merh had turned. And Narasen, powerless and angry, said within herself to the Plague: "What must I do to be rid of you?" and the dimly seen yellow woman bared her teeth and grimaced as if she answered: "You know, but cannot do it." And then the dust storm folded her away and Narasen slammed the window-shutters closed.

The bedchamber of the queen of Merh was this way: Burnished weapons of hunting and war hung upon the walls which were painted with scenes of hunting and war. The floor was carpeted with the spotted and striped skins of beasts Narasen had slain, and in the bed by night there often lay a pretty girl, the current love of Narasen. The king of Merh, Narasen's father, had trained and raised her as if she were son rather than daughter, preparing her to rule after him, and this had fitted her inclination very well. Yet she had a woman's beauty.

One noon, a year before this, Narasen had ridden with her chosen companions over the plains, to hunt the leopard. Her hunting gear was of gold and white and her white hounds ran beside her chariot like snow on legs. A headdress of gold wires and pearl kept back her rose-red hair from her face and her eyes were like the eyes of what she hunted. But there were to be no leopards speared that day. The chariots reached a curve of the river, then cool and dark and with the great trees growing on its banks. As the hounds drank, the companions of Narasen discovered a young man sitting beneath a tree. He was handsome and pleasing to look at,

9

and though he sat alone there with neither attendant nor guard yet he was richly dressed, and at his side rested a staff of white wood with two green emeralds in the pommel.

"Bring him to me," said Narasen when they told her, and the young man was not slow in coming. "Now, what is this?" she said. "You are within the limits of Merh yet not a citizen of Merh, I think, and you sit alone in your finery. Has no one warned you, wild beasts come to drink at the river and have a nose for human flesh, and robbers live in this land, as in all lands, and they have a nose for jewels."

The young man bowed, and he gazed at her in a certain way which she had occasionally seen before, which there was no mistaking, and his eyes darkened. But he spoke politely.

"My name is Issak: I am a magician and the son of magicians. I fear neither beasts nor men, for I know spells to charm them."

"Then you are fortunate. Or boastful," said Narasen. "Come, show me proof."

The young man bowed again. Then he lifted the staff, and it changed to a white snake with green eyes, which looped itself three times round his neck. After that, he whistled, and suddenly the water of the river was cut by a thousand bright blades, all its bright fish leaping. And then again he whistled, differently, and birds fell from the trees like leaves and settled on his shoulders and his hands.

Narasen's companions were diverted and applauded him. But Narasen said, seeing how he still looked at her, and not liking it:

"Now fetch me a leopard."

At once the birds flew away and the fish sank like stones. The young man named Issak fastened his gaze to hers, frowning, and he whistled a third time. Through the shadow of the trees, ten golden leopards walked, spattered with the shadow and their own shadowy freckling, and each had the eyes of Narasen. Narasen smiled and called for her spears. But as she drew back her arm to make the cast, the young man pulled the snake from around his neck and threw it from him. At once the snake became a staff, fixed point downwards in the soil of the river bank. The ten leopards vanished.

"So it was only an illusion," said Narasen, "a trick. I do not like to be cheated by trickery."

Then Issak smiled too. Very gently he said: "Whatever it was, most beautiful queen of Merh, I think you could not do it."

This Narasen did not take to, being told what she could

and could not do. She turned away, and to one of her guard she said, "Give the showman some coins. He has a famished air, and probably his finery is an illusion too."

Issak refused the money. He said: "No coin will suffice. I desire another reward, for it is another thing I hunger for."

"And what is that?"

"The queen of Merh."

Never in her life had any man dared speak to Narasen in this fashion. It angered her, and somewhere at her roots it made her uneasy.

"Well," she said however, lightly, "since you are clearly of barbarous people, and do not understand our civilized manners, I will not have you beaten."

"Narasen may beat me," he said, "but no other."

One of the hounds of Narasen, sensing her anger, began to snarl at Issak. But Issak the magician stretched out his arm toward the hound, and instead it immediately lay down and fell asleep.

"And now," said Issak, "Narasen the beautiful must learn this. She also might be charmed as easily as her dog. Despite your words, lady, and what you are, love stirs in me at the sight of you. Tonight we shall lie together, and there is no way you can prevent it." When he said this, rather than arrogance or lust, the young man's face took on a look of sadness and pain.

Narasen snapped at her guard, who leapt forward to seize Issak the magician. But somehow, where their hands fell, he was not—he seemed to vanish as the leopards had done, and though the guard of Narasen thrust about along the track a good while, he was not to be found.

Narasen returned to the city in an unsettled mood. She was not unjust, though she could be cruel; now she hankered to exact payment for the insolence of the stranger. She believed too, he was intent upon his promise to her, and perhaps had some chance of success, seeing he was so skilled in magic. There was no love in her for the bodies of men, yet, had he approached her another way, she might have commiserated with him. Then she recalled the bizarre tragedy which showed on his face, the expression of despair and hurt. . . . Narasen flung open her bronze doors with a crash, and shouted for her own sorcerers.

Night opened its black flowers; the flower-garden windows of lamplit Merh bloomed below. In the palace of Narasen the guard was doubled at the gates, with orders to watch for foreigners. Outside the apartments of the queen two giant men stood with clubs of brass, leering at each other, hoping there would be trouble that they might commit violence. On the inner door there hung the skull of a hyena and other unsavory amulets devised by the palace sorcerers. Within the rooms, obscure aromatics smoked.

But Narasen, as the night progressed, growing deeper and more still, grew also still and began to doubt herself. From the high windows, she watched the flower lamps of Merh go out, now a scarlet flower, now a gold, plucked by blue fingers of the peaceful dark. She thought of the sorcerers fumbling their spells and chanting in an antechamber. She thought of the dinner she had sent away with a curse, and of the girl with flax-pale hair who this month shared her bed. And then she thought of Issak the magician, and she laughed to herself and at him, his clever illusions, his boasts, his lust. Almost, she pitied him.

So she went out into the antechamber, and through the purple smoke of the braziers, she saw the sorcerers had fallen asleep at their work, and the floor all littered with their instruments, their bits of bone and silver flails and strings of polished beads. Then she crossed to the bronze doors and opened them, and there the two giant men stood, rigid as old trees, and though their eyes were wide, they saw nothing. In the passageway a green bird was flying up and down. A moment after Narasen had opened the doors, the green bird flew by her, and straight into the antechamber. And there it shed its feathers and became a green jewel which fell to the floor, and the jewel cracked open and out of it burst a shining ray. When the ray faded, there stood Issak the magician.

He looked at Narasen and his face was pale. In his hand he carried one rare blue rose, of the kind that was often spoken of but seldom seen, and this he offered to Narasen, and when she did not take it he said, "If you would prefer sapphires, then so be it."

Narasen was near speechless, but she made speech nevertheless.

"Your magic is truly remarkable. Am I to be ensorcelled next?"

"If you will not yield in love to me."

Narasen considered him, his white face and his hand which trembled about the stem of the rose.

"I do not lie with men," said Narasen.

"Tonight you shall."

"Perhaps and perhaps," she said. "Drink with me and we

12

will discuss it." Then, because he made no move to stop her, she went to a cabinet of wines, and poured for him a generous measure, but she filled her own cup with a harmless sherbet of dates. "Now," said Narasen, watching him as he slowly drank, "tell me one thing. Your sorcery is vast, yet, rather than use it, you cajole me. You speak of desire, but you have the pallor of a man in fear or sorrow. You woo me with gifts, yet mean to force me if you are able. Why not one thing or the other?"

Issak drank deeply, and his pale face flushed.

"I will tell you, Narasen the fair," he said. "I am a magician, as you know very well, and I have had traffic with demon-kind, particularly with the Drin, the ugly dwarf-folk of the Underearth. I wished to increase my powers, and these Drin led me to the house of a special mage, far older and more cunning than I, saying he would teach me. But the Drin liked this wretch the better, for he was more the villain. He made a bargain with me for my tuition, that every night he would lie once with me. Now I was young and stupid and anxious to be powerful and wise, and it seemed to me that the delights and abuses of the flesh were nothing compared to this power and wisdom. So, though he was foul, old and bestial, I agreed. Each night I endured him then. One whole month I was his pupil by day, his doxy after dark. It seemed a high fee enough, but I did not know how high a fee. For each time his weapon sheathed in me, his lechery and his sin went with it, passing with his seed into my vitals and thence into my unrealizing flesh, my body and my soul. And every time that this was done, a year of his evil existence was hung on me and in return he drew from me a year of my life to increase his own. Such was the nature of his spell, and so he told me, when at length I would accept no more. 'You go from me, Issak,' said he, 'a magician gifted now with some portion of my brilliant art. But, though you may appear a wholesome youth and your inclination is to be one, my whims and vices are in you, and you will from time to time, indulge in the deeds that I have pleasured in, become a forcer of maidens and a plunderer of men. Yet, do not lament, you shall not long be troubled. Thirty years have you added to my span; just three years of life are left to you. Only be sure, they will be merry.' And thus," said Issak, letting fall the cup of wine half full, "it is with me as he said. Having seen you, it is the legacy of his hot zeal brings me here. The blue rose alone is my guest-gift at the visit." Then he leant his head upon his arm like a child, and wept.

13

Narasen said sternly: "You must resist this bewitchment."

"I have tried," Issak groaned. "It has availed me nothing."

"Come, do not weep," said Narasen. Compassion and contempt were mingled in her, and she had forgotten danger. She went to him and laid her hand on his shoulder in a brotherly fashion. Too late, she saw his tears were suddenly dry, and in that instant he seized her.

Narasen was no weakling, and she was limber, but the youth was exceedingly strong. He bore her to the ground. His face was changed, infused with blood, inflamed as a drunkard's or a madman's face, and through the clear eyes there seemed to glare the eyes of another.

With one iron hand he held her, and with the other hand he ripped the garments from her as if they had been paper. And now he panted like a dog and his saliva dripped upon her breasts.

But Narasen had not been as innocent at the cabinet of wines as she had appeared to be, for inside the cabinet she kept a sharp little knife with which she would break the seals of the wine jars. And, as the young man lurched upon her body, striving to gain access into her, Narasen altered herself as if she had melted.

"Ah, but I like you better so," said she, "not whimpering but masterful. Come, master me, my darling. Only let go my hands and I will help you to the gate."

However, Issak freed only her left hand, holding the other fast. Then she kissed his face and caressed him, so that presently he forgot to keep hold of her. At that, she drew the knife from her sleeve, and she stabbed him through the ear.

Screaming in agony, he tumbled aside from her, but Narasen had no mercy now. Running to the wall, she snatched one of her hunting spears, and this she plunged into his heart with such force that the point ran through his body into the floor beneath.

He did not die outright. Instead, an unpleasant alteration overcame him. He grew withered and carious, and his handsomeness ran away like water from a broken vessel. This was what his mentor had reduced him to; only the cunning spells Issak had learned had kept for him the semblance of the youth and beauty which should have been his by right. And now that he was vile to look at, the vile nature of that other seemed to possess him entirely. As if he had no pain, he grinned and he crowed at Narasen:

"So, my three wretched years end on your palace floor. You are an unkind dealer of fate. And now I will tell your own fate, Narasen of Merh, for I have just the strength to put my curse on you, and you may not silence me. You do not like to lie with men, and great joy that aversion shall bring you. Indeed, inside the year, the land of Merh shall know many joys. First shall come the storm winds and into Merh they shall blow the three droughts humanity fears the most; drought of the waters, drought of the milk of the herds and drought of the womb's richness in every female thing. An infertile place shall this be then, starved and dry, its rivers gone to mud and the yellow dust upon the lips and in the eyes, and no child born and no beast born. Barren as the womb of the queen shall Merh become. Famine and plague shall sit dicing in the streets for mortal lives. The people will cry for omens, cry to the gods to relieve them, to instruct them on how they may avert the ailments that beset them, to tell them when the blight will end. And the oracle will answer them: Merh shall be Narasen. When Narasen the fair brings forth a child. When Narasen ceases to be arid, so shall the land become lubricous. When Narasen is fruitful, then shall the land bear fruit. And then, O queen, they will come and hammer on the palace gates and demand that you lie with men. And then, O queen, to your humiliation and your shame and your disgust, you will lie beneath all the men, you will give yourself, in your desperation, as a whore does, to any man, the prince, the commoner, the drover of swine, the stranger passing. All will come to your door and enter there, but leave no token. For here is the sting in the tail of this curse. Your reluctant womb will never quicken from the seed of any man living. Barren you shall stay, and barren shall the land stay with you. Never from the seed of any man alive shall you bear fruit, and your kingdom shall perish. Merh shall be Narasen. And if your people do not slay you, then you will wander an outcast over the earth. And, as you wander, think of Issak."

Then he seemed to sink backward into the floor itself, and in his eyes there stirred an unexpected bitterness, and he whispered: "Yet it was my old teacher's venom made me curse you. Issak alone would never have cursed you, beloved, even with your spear in his heart."

At that, blood ran from his lips instead of words, and his life after it.

When first the bane was spoken, Narasen was chilled through. But soon enough she buried the recollection of the curse within her, as the corpse of Issak was soon buried in the earth. That was an unmarked grave, in a plot beyond the city walls where the bodies of felons were thrown. But the burial of the curse in the soul of Narasen had its markers, some part of her did not forget, and presently she had good reason to remember.

In a month the wild winds arrived, garbed in the ochre dust of the plains, and the city of Merh became a little hell. And after the winds, the drought drank up the river, and the herds could not be watered there, and the udders of the female beasts became slack. And next, the women could not give milk to their newborn, and then there were no longer any to need the milk, for all that were delivered were still-births, and after these, no woman grew round bellied in the length and breadth of Merh. Nor was there any rain. The heat of the year swelled and the crops failed. Famine entered, and plague danced in Merh, now in her red robe, now in her black.

The people entreated their gods, as Issak had foretold. And as he had foretold, the gods appeared to answer, but maybe it was only the instinctive divination of the priests. Eventually the oracles spoke from their caves of smoulder or from the dry wells, where once the water had run, green and sinuous. The oracles said: "Merh shall be Narasen. When once the queen of Merh brings forth a child, the blight shall end. When Narasen is fruitful, then shall the land have fruit, but while she is dry, dry as a bone the land shall be, and drier than a bone."

So the people hammered on the gates of the palace, and their faces were like hot stones, and they bared their teeth like wolves.

It was a curious thing, some part of the malediction itself, perhaps, that the punishment must be exactly as Issak—or the entity which had possessed him—had predicted. She must do it all. Partly, she believed some chink remained in the curse if she could only find it out, some tiny flaw by means of which she might deliver herself from the death of her land and the hatred of her people. For if she loved anything, it was to be the queen of Merh. If she must be shamed in order to hold Merh, she would be shamed, and not be shamed by that shame.

Narasen opened her doors. No giants stood at the portal now to guard her person. A line of men stood there, some striplings, some in their prime, and some were abashed and some were bold and looked her over as the bull looks at the cow. Fit punishment indeed, but she would not meditate on it. She nodded to them courteously. Each had a reputation of a singular sort. She led them in, and into the room they came and into Narasen they came. She suffered it, and her people praised her, and when she did not conceive, they sent from among themselves their most potent and their best to serve her. Later, strangers were admitted.

The year scorched to a yellow husk. And Narasen, twisted in the flame of that year, grew also scorched and wizened. But only her soul was burnt. Her beauty stayed; she chained it to her. How could she entice the seed of men without her beauty? And her pride remained. She was proud, though in far lands now they spoke of her, the Harlot of Merh—for none believed she did not revel in her task, or at least take payment. The pains which had torn her faded. She was made of bronze. She clothed her bronze in black for it was like shadow from an unrelenting sun. "Beware," the travellers said, "when you pass through Merh, or the Harlot will eat your phallus. It is well known," they said, "she is always hungry, and the land starves too."

Winter came. It was a brown hard winter. The country all about seemed like the wreck of some lost place, cast up by a sea of fire and left behind. The snow lay high upon the mountains, but the snow turned black. Even the winter fell sick in Merh.

Narasen walked on the highlands. She lay with the shepherds and the men of the herder-folk. When she stood bare before them, her honey flesh and her rose-red hair entranced them. They imagined a goddess had come to call, and dreamed of sons made in her loins. There were no sons, but they did not know it. She lay with robbers. One cut her with his knife, and she slew him. It did her some good to be revenged on this solitary man. No women in her bed now, no leopards on her spear. Men in her bed, she the leopard to their spears. She felt nothing of them. She lived in a trance. She was only this: pride, beauty, the shameless bearing of shame. But also she was barren, and the land died.

Winter left Merh, and glad to go. The spring was storms, the summer yellow dust. Plague, who had slept a little, put on a dress of yellow fever and walked up and down the streets, knocking on the doors.

And then it was one day, for no reason that she knew, that Narasen woke from the trance which had bound her. She stared from her windows at the horror Merh had become, and she thought: *Everything I have done is nothing. I might have kept my body to myself for all the good it has achieved to lease it out. I have been the quarry, now I must go hunting.* And she looked plague in the face, and she thought: *What must I do to be rid of you?* And plague said: "You know, but cannot do it." At which Narasen slammed close the shutters on the dust and stench of Merh.

And she did so, she heard a woman begin to cry and shriek somewhere within the palace: "Oh, my beloved is dead of the fever! My beloved is dead!"

When she heard this, Narasen felt bruise her the sharp bright fragments of what she had been, and she clenched her fists, for she had seen at last the chink through which she might pass.

2

By night, the Lord Uhlume strode across a battlefield. It was mostly a quiet place, the battle long concluded (as all games, even the best, must finally be), the victors ridden northward with their spoils, only the dead left behind. Mostly quiet. After the battle had come the rear guard; in the dusk the crows had mustered. Now the jackals ran to begin their own war among the heaps and dunes and the piled mountains of speechless and unmoving flesh. Here and there a little patch of fire lit up the blackness, but these haphazard lanterns were dying too. Only the stars gave their fixed, seldom varying shine. Thick were the stars upon the plain of night, and still, and silent. As if, up there too, there had been a battle and the corpses lay about, save that these corpses were beautiful, and they glowed.

It was the stars showed the battlefield to the Lord Uhlume, and revealed him also, if any were left to see.

He was black, was Uhlume, satin black like panther skin, or polished black like a burnished black gem. And from very blackness he seemed carved, to the shape of a tall and slender man. But his hair was long and white as ivory, and his clothes were ivory, and his white hair and his white cloak furled and flickered behind his blackness as he strode, like smoke behind a thin black flame. His face was rare, inexplicable and desolate. His eyes, which were the color of a gleaming nothingness, were desolate. Men looked in his desolate face, and could not afterwards remember it. It slipped from their minds like water through the fingers, like surf from a beach at the tide's turning. Yet whoever saw him, not remembering, somehow remembered there was something they had forgotten. The Lord Uhlume.

On the battlefield there was a place where a shallow stream wandered. Here some of the wounded had crawled to drink before they died, and lay now with their faces and their hands in the water, and the stream was dark with the blood they had spilled in it. A few feet from the stream one warrior lay who was not dead. It had been his goal to reach the water and to drink, but he had not the strength. Glimpsing, through the blur of his pain, Uhlume's tall shadow pass between him and the stars, this warrior called out. His voice was more slight than any noise of the plain, yet Uhlume turned aside at it.

The last warrior was very young; his sight had been guttering but he seemed to see Uhlume well and clearly. The young warrior whispered his entreaty, and Uhlume bent close to hear.

"If you are compassionate, bring me water."

"I am not necessarily compassionate," answered Uhlume. "Besides, the water of the stream is foul."

"Is it some kindred of yours you search for?" whispered the youth. "The women will come in the morning, weeping, and search among us. Our enemies will allow them then. My mother will come, and my sisters. They will take up what the jackals have left of me and bear it home. I shall not live to see the harvest."

"The harvest is here," said Uhlume. His great eyes were melancholy, their pale brightness was like a well of unshed tears.

"Bring me water," said the youth, "or any drink, sweet or bitter."

"I have one drink I may give you," said Uhlume gently, "but it would not perhaps be to your liking. Only think. Maybe you will live till morning."

"The night is cold and I am thirsty."

"Well, then," said Uhlume. From within his cloak he took a flask and a cup of yellow-white smooth bone. Into the cup he poured a drink. It had no color and no smell, nor any definite taste. Uhlume rested the young man's head on his arm, and he showed him the cup. "In three hours," said Uhlume, "it will be morning."

"The beasts would find me," said the youth, "and I cannot endure this thirst."

"Drink then," said Uhlume, and he set the cup against the young man's lip.

19

He drank, the warrior. He said, "It has the taste of summer grass." And then he said, "I am not thirsty now." And he shut his eyes forever.

As Uhlume was walking on, a small band of women came over a hill. They carried no lamps, for they had stolen out early, in fear of the northern enemy and in despite of his decree. They had huddled the darkness round them like their cloaks, and when they saw Uhlume they shrank together, moaning. But, as he went by, one woman lost her terror, and she cried after him: "I know *you*, you jackal!" And she spat on the ground where he had passed.

3

Five miles to the east of the city of Merh was a wall of mountains; to travel over them took seven days. Beyond, lay an infertile valley and, at the valley's end, a forest of ancient dead cedars. This part of the journey took two days. Beyond the forest opened a feral country, where many things grew, but out of control and out of a pure determination to be born. Here the huge-thorned roses bloomed spotted as cats on the briars, the apples were salt, and the fruit of the quince tree was like wormwood. Bright birds lived in the thickets, but they had no song. The native beasts were savage, but they did not often hunt men, for men did not often come there to oblige them. Three miles eastward into these parts, there was an orchard of wild pomegranates. The fruit was toxic, and had the hectic color of red poison, and in the midst of the orchard stood a blue house. This dwelling, which was known as the House of the Blue Dog, was a witch's mansion.

Narasen, seeking particularized knowledge, had questioned her own sorcerers and any of that profession who entered her city. Her people had lost patience with her. They, too, had begun to name her the Harlot. "She cannot conceive because her lusts have burnt out the ability of her womb." Some ran like hyena packs in the streets of Merh, some printed her name up in foul slogans. Some broke into the palace by night and tried to slay her. But Narasen took up her sword and slew them instead. At length, when she saw she must seek outside the city, she went disguised and by obscure routes, taking a guard only of ten men, the rest left behind to keep order in Merh and to hold the palace secure. With her small escort, she crossed the mountains, the valley of stone, and rode through the petrified cedar forest and into the riotous country beyond. On the eleventh day of their journey they reached the meadows that bordered on the orchard. At this spot, Narasen dismounted, and went on alone. She walked half a mile over the rank grass and through the pomegranate trees till she came to the witch's mansion.

Although it was the afternoon, the orchard was dim with shade. The House of the Blue Dog rose suddenly from this gloom, as if it had been sleeping there. Two pillars of indigo fronted a brazen door, before which burned a tall lamp of blue glass with a pink fire in it.

Narasen went to the door and knocked with her riding crop. At once the door opened. There in the doorway stood a dog. Seven hands high, the dog was, and made of blue enamel. It opened its jaws and barked at her, but its bark was speech.

"Who are you?" barked the dog.

"One who has need of your mistress," answered Narasen.

"That is self evident. But I deal in names."

"Deal in this one, then. I am Narasen, the queen of Merh."

"Those that lie here, sometimes die here," snarled the dog.

"Then tell no lies and live," snapped Narasen. "Come, bring me to your witch-mistress. I will not be questioned by a cur."

At that the dog wagged its tail as if her hauteur pleased it, and it licked her hand with a tongue like dry hot glass.

"Pray follow," said the dog, and scampered into the house.

All was blue inside. Up a stairway of azure stone the dog led Narasen, and into a room of many blue lamps with pink fire in them.

"Be seated," the dog said. "Shall I bring refreshment?"

"I will eat nothing here and I will drink nothing," said Narasen. "Those that mention your mistress say she is so wise that few dare to enter her house. But more enter than come out of it."

The dog laughed at this, an odd noise to be sure, like ceramic bricks rattling in a chimney. Just then a piece of drapery blew aside, and into the room came the witch herself.

Now Narasen had spoken to many concerning the lady of the blue mansion, for many knew of her, but rarely had any seen her. One said she took on the form of a basilisk and her eyes were flints, another said she was a crone a thousand years old and older. But this was what Narasen saw: a young maiden of fifteen of less, slender as a silken rope, and clad only in her malt-brown hair which fell to her ankles, though

21

occasionally, as it must, a slim white arm would appear from this veil of hair, or a white foot or thigh, or two breasts like the buds of a water flower. And though Narasen understood that this might only be a spell she was seeing, yet she was stirred despite herself. And the young witch crossed the chamber and sat down at the feet of Narasen, and gazed up at her, smiling, with a mouth like the first rose ray of dawn.

"Now tell me everything, elder sister," said the witch, "for you have travelled some distance to find me."

So Narasen steeled herself. She ignored the blue dog, which ridiculously champed upon a blue porcelain bone in the corner with apparent relish; she ignored the silver flesh of the witch winking at her from the veil of hair. Narasen spoke of her trouble, of Issak and the lust of his mentor, and of the curse and the plague and the barren death of Merh, of how Merh could not bear fruit again till she herself, who had no wish for it, bore a child.

"But then, you will have lain with men in order to procure the child," said the witch.

"I have indeed, though I am no lover of the arms of male animals. I have given myself to the man-bull and the goat-man, to the wayside oaf, the stinking robber—all I have lain down with, and not spared myself. But I am barren still. For the scorpion's tail of the curse was this: that my womb shall never quicken from the seed of any man living."

"Why," said the witch, "that is a clever curse. To show the road, and then to bar the way to it. But curses are curses, and the curse of such a magician as this Issak would be hard to break. Why seek me, O queen?"

Narasen saw, despite the words of the witch, a sly glint in her eyes. *She thinks as I do,* Narasen said to herself. And to the witch she said: "I sought you because I heard that the lady in the House of the Blue Dog had converse sometimes with a mighty personage, one of the Lords of Darkness, no less."

"And if I do, what help is that to Narasen of Merh?"

"This help: It has come to me that, since to save Merh for myself I must be got with child, I must lie again with a man. But that it need be only for one single time and with one solitary man. Providing merely that he is not living."

For a while the witch did not speak, but again she smiled.

"The queen of Merh is also wise," said the witch eventually. She got to her feet and put back her hair, and revealed to Narasen the entire pale loveliness which had hidden in that hair, and showed, too, that round her waist was a girdle of little white finger bones strung on a chain of gold. "Now," said the witch, "I acknowledge I may entreat a Lord of Darkness, one who could aid you, if he wills. I can entreat, and he may come, or he may not come, for he is not at the beck and call of me, I am no greater than his servant. Yet, he might come. If he does, be prepared for your own fear, for those who are far from him generally fear him. It is no tiny thing that he should be invited in and that he should comply. Also, as you will suppose, there must be a bargain struck."

"I have heard something of it," said Narasen.

"You may refuse," said the witch, "even to his face you may refuse him. He forces no one. But, even so, it is not easy to refuse. Do you wish me to call him still?"

"I wish it," said Narasen.

Then the witch trembled, whether with terror or joy was not clear, maybe with both or neither. She whistled and the dog ran away and the fires sank in the lamps. Then she went to a table and opened an ivory box which stood there. Inside the box was a drum, as small as the drum a baby might play with. But the drum was made of bone and the skin that was stretched over it had been taken from the body of a beautiful dead virgin girl.

The witch seated herself once more at the feet of Narasen, and she began to tap in quick little patterings on the girl-skin of the drum. This was how Narasen noticed, as she had not till now, that the third finger of the witch's left hand had been severed at its top joint. And Narasen remembered the finger bones about the waist of the witch, but exactly then the fires went out in all the lamps.

What came down was more than darkness in a house. It was the darkness of a vast black shell within the earth, a hollow dark. And it rang with hollow whispers, with breaths and sighs and with the relentless tapping of the witch's drum.

It was sunset, and in the red light of it, Uhlume stood beside the door of a hovel, and a young woman curtsied to him.

"Please make free of my home," said she. But there was not much there for any to make free of. A wretched hole it was, and on one patchwork bed sat several infants, solemn as owls. On the other bed lay a female child about three or four. "I sent my man for a doctor," said the young woman, "but my man has not returned. Did you come on ahead, sir?"

"I did," said Uhlume as he crossed the threshold. He

seemed to bring a huge quiet with him. It fell upon the sick child, and the lids of her eyes relaxed. But the mother shivered.

"I regret," she said, "we have nothing to pay you with. But I promise you all the money from the sale of the piglets, when they are sloughed from our sow."

Uhlume bent above the sick child. The stale and pitiable room was full of a sort of chill ambience, like gray twilight, but the sky through the door was red.

"Wait," said the mother. "Tell me, sir, who are you?"

"You know," said Uhlume.

The mother clasped her hands.

"I thought you were the doctor. I was mistaken," said she. "I beg you to go."

"But you do not," said Uhlume. "For these three nights you have prayed that you be relieved of one at least of these several mouths which must be fed, and these several miniature bodies which must be clothed and warmed."

"So I did," murmured the mother. "The gods will destroy me for my wickedness."

But she wept and hid her face. And Uhlume leaned close to the child on the bed, and he lightly touched her heart and turned away. And as he left the hovel, two passionless icy tears fell from his white lashes on the wild flowers that grew beside the door, and the wild flowers died.

But most of the children chattered to each other, for it seemed to them the evening wind had come into the room and gone more cold than it came. The sick child was silent.

Uhlume followed the sun, moving after it as it sank. His was not always the hour of darkness, despite his dominion and his lordship. Fast he strode, faster than a man. His strides ate up the land, so the sun was forever sinking before him, forever going down, red as henna, on the world's brink, but not quite gone. Yet, the earth being at that time flat, in the end, though after a long while, the sun outdistanced him, and fell beyond sight.

Uhlume paused, as the night gathered from the corners of the earth. And as the night reached him, a sound evolved from it, a soft scattering of sound, now like beads of rain tossed upon sun-baked ground, now like a moth's wings clapping together in flight—a sound too faint for mortal ears, yet Uhlume heard it. But now the sound was like two thumbs and seven fingers fluttering on a drum-skin.

Uhlume stood considering. His eyes, with their store of emotionless tears, turned eastward. You could read nothing from his face. He had no expressions. His whole person, rather, expressed his mood, his role. The gods perhaps had made him, once, long ago in the days of unformed things and chaos. Or perhaps he had only come to be since there was a need for him, or for his name. Yet here he was, and he stood there on the world's back, listening to that which pleaded, considering.

The young witch caught her breath, but she did not stop her work upon the drum. Round her narrow waist the bones began to click upon their chain. Then, into the lightless hollow that the House of the Blue Dog had become, poured a shadow-glow which lit up everything, but which warmed nothing.

At the chamber's farthest end stood a lean pallid dog, in color bluish-white. So Narasen beheld what the mansion was really called for.

The witch set by her drum. She rose, and the bones rattled at her waist. She kneeled to the dog, and her hair spread on the floor.

"My Lord," she said, "forgive your handmaiden that she asked for you."

The dog padded close. It was noble but ghastly. Some had met this hound and been afraid, but Narasen did not fear it. Then it was gone, and in its place was a man more beautiful than any man Narasen had ever seen, and stranger than any man, wrapped in a white cloak, white haired but black skinned and with eyes like phosphorous. And Narasen grew afraid. Not of the man, not specifically of him. Nor was the fear like another. It was like the dreary sadness that comes in the ebb hours of the night, fear that was rather despair; an abyss, unavoidable, all-pervasive, painless.

He did not glance at Narasen, he gazed down into the face of the witch. Somehow he had a blind look. He said in a quiet, quiet voice:

"I am here."

"My Lord," said the witch, gazing back at him, "I have one in this room who has a need to make herself supplicant to you."

"Bring her," he said.

The witch got up again. She beckoned to Narasen, and Narasen left her seat and went forward until she was very near to the man in the white cloak. And then she stared at him boldly even though his bottomless eyes, settling on her, seemed to draw her and drink her in.

25

"As you perceive, sir," said Narasen, "I do not cower at confronting you, for in the end, there is none who can avoid you. Honor and greetings, Lord Death."

Death—whose seldom-spoken name was Uhlume—one of the Lords of Darkness, said merely: "Tell me what you want."

Narasen told him: "To keep my land and crown, I must bear a child. I have been cursed, I can conceive the child of no man living. I must conceive from the embrace of a dead man. And the dead are your folk, my Lord."

The witch clapped her hands once. A chair of stone appeared, draped with white velvet. The arm-rests were of gold, and where the hands lay grinned two dogs' skulls, but they were gold too, with pearls in the eye sockets. Death sat in this chair. He seemed to reflect on what Narasen had told him. Presently he said: "It can be done. But can you endure such a couching?"

"To lie with any man is abhorrent to me," said Narasen. (She said this even though Death was formed in the shape of a man.) "To lie with a dead one makes no odds, and may be better."

"And do you know the price?"

"That when I die, I must become, for a space, your slave. I had believed the whole of humanity fared thus."

"No," said Death, the Lord Uhlume. "I am the king of an empty kingdom. But I will show you as much. This you shall learn immediately: That you must remain with me a thousand mortal years. I ask no more, and no less."

Narasen paled, and she was pale already. But she said grimly:

"That is indeed some little while. And what is it that you want me for, that a thousand years are required to satisfy you?" Death looked at her. The heart of Narasen shrank, but she was not actually afraid of him, though her fear was absolute. "Well," she said, "pray do not be reluctant, my Lord, to inform me."

Something went over the face of Uhlume, Lord Death; not an expression, not a shadow, yet something.

"Life has not trampled you," said Uhlume. "Most who seek me are the victims of their life, and yield to anguish before they will yield to me. But you have burned up through the dirt and harm that was cast upon your fire. I should be glad of your companionship. For that is what you sell me, woman, for my thousand years. Not your flesh. Your flesh is mine in any case, once you are dead. It belongs to me, your flesh, and in the earth it lies till it becomes the earth. Nor do I want your womanhood, for I love neither man nor woman. Death does not couch, Death does not couple. Think, lady, of the jest there would be in that if Death were to spawn out procreative seed. No. It is your soul I would keep, your soul I would hold back in your body, and retain the two with me for my thousand years. And when the thousand years are done, your soul is free to leave me."

"To go where?" asked Narasen, fierce and quick.

"Do not ask for news of a life-beyond-life from me," he said.

Narasen said, "Show me your kingdom, and show me a way to get a child in me, and I will tell you whether or not I agree to your terms."

From the shade behind the chair, the voice of the witch hissed out:

"You are too exacting! Correct yourself."

But Uhlume murmured to her some words Narasen did not catch, and the witch sighed and said no more.

Then Uhlume rose from the chair of stone. His white cloak seemed to billow out like a white wave and Narasen was wrapped in it. The chamber of the witch fell away. Narasen found herself, furled in the white leaf of the cloak of Death, hanging in black air above the earth. The lights of mankind burned below, and the lights of stars above. The cloak of Death was vast. It held her close, yet she had no contact with the person of Death.

"Where now?" asked Narasen.

"To the Innerearth," said Death, "which is my kingdom."

Death and his cloak swirled toward the ground. A wide valley lay before them, rushing up in the darkness, and as they plunged, Death stretched out his hand, and the valley parted before him. This much was true, that wherever Death had once been, there he could return, and there he could command. And the whole world was a graveyard, for on every inch of it, at one time or another, something had died, bird or beast, man or woman, or a tree or a flower or a blade of grass. Even in the seas, which had their own laws and rulers, and would not aid, without recompense, the most accomplished magicians of the land, even there things died, the fish of the high ocean levels and the monsters of the deep, and so there also Death could come or go as he pleased, and none gainsay him. Accordingly, the valley obediently gaped and the rock strained wide, and Death sank through with Narasen of Merh folded in his cloak.

The way was invisible, and partly like the passage into sleep, for faces and illusions floated across the brain of Narasen, though not across her eyes. Yet once, it seemed, the waters of a leaden river roiled about her, and in the water, crowds of phantom creatures swam and jostled each other, but this impression faded, and the cloak of Death bore her farther and farther down, till softly she slid to rest, and there was only silence and no light.

Narasen's fear, to which she had almost grown accustomed, lashed out at her and became definite.

"Is this some tomb I am in?" she cried harshly.

"Be patient," said Uhlume, Lord Death. "You will see presently and hear whatever is to be seen and heard in this domain of mine. It is because you enter the place alive that for the moment you are blind to it. As a dead man's spirit which cannot free itself from the world, goes back to visit the earth and has no substance there, thus here you are a ghost in the world of the dead."

At which Narasen regained her sight and that other sense, of hearing. But she could not smell anything, nor feel it with her hands, nor, had she put it in her mouth, would she have tasted. She was, as he said, a living ghost in the dead lands.

But to Narasen it was enough that she saw and heard, and too much. She shuddered to her heart's core, she who had held leopards on her spear, she who had fought battles unafraid in the realm of men.

They stood upon a cliff, and about the cliff were rolling plains and hills, with here and there another cliff, and on the left hand a dim range of mountains. The color of this land was gray; the cliff resembled lead, and from it gray tufts of verdure grew that were not like grass, being thin and brittle as an old woman's hair, while mosses of a darker gray had risen from crevices. The plain below was a desert of gray dust, the hills were stone, and where their shadows fell they were black. Above, the sky of Innerearth was dull white and comfortless. No sun or moon or stars were lit here. It did not change, only occasionally a cloud blew over it like a handful of cold cinders. That was for sight. For sound, there was a deaf blankness, troubled in fits by a thundering wind. And though the wind thundered and pushed the clouds before it, it had no power, for the clouds went slowly and the grasses never stirred, and even the great cloak of Death hung slack as if its folds were full of weights.

Seeing her shudder, Death said to Narasen: "This is not your land. Why fear it?"

"This is where you would have me come. This is where all humankind must come when they die."

"Walk with me through this land," said Death, "and if you see any man, tell me."

Death descended from the cliff and Narasen with him. Death cast a shadow black as pitch, but Narasen did not. They moved across the dismal country, through the dust desert, over the stone hills. A forest appeared on the other side, but the trees were pylons of gray slate. Mosses dripped from them. The wind rattled by, disturbing nothing. They came to a river. It reflected the sky and was white, and Narasen could not see into it, only its surface, but nothing ruffled the surface or agitated the depths.

They walked a long while. The sky did not alter, there was no specific time. Narasen, a ghost of life, felt no tiredness. Still, they walked a long while, and longer. And everywhere she looked and peered and listened, but she heard no cry of man or animal. The stone trees had no birds. The wind carried no voices. Patently, undeniably, no one dwelt here.

"One," said Uhlume, for he had read her thought. "I. Sometimes, others. Others who have made the bargain with me, a thousand years in exchange for some favor only Death can grant."

Narasen regarded Death.

"It is true then that the souls of the dead travel elsewhere, and cannot be constrained. This being so, I pity you," she said frostily, "for even Merh is not worth this prison to me."

"Wait," said Uhlume, "till you have seen everything."

They walked on, and Narasen, the leopardess, the daring, despite her terror of the aura of Uhlume, watched him with contempt and scorn.

There was a palace of granite. It had no beauty. Tall columns of rock upheld a roof of shadow. There were no windows and no lamps, but it was not dark within, at least, only a tepid darkness. In a hall, a granite chair, without ornament, waited for Death to sit in it. Death sat. He leaned his chin upon his hand. He stared into the hall's void, and, without sorrow or any noise, the tears dropped from his lashes. This was the symbol of himself which he had become. So the gods, or the nightmares of humanity, had made him. Melancholy despair amid the waste of stone.

And then Narasen heard music. It startled her; she spun about. Through the many archways into the hall, men and women were advancing and the music stole in with them, drowning the roars of the feeble wind. As the men and women filled the hall, a change occurred there in the blink of an eye, and nothing was the same.

The hall was hung with purple, scarlet, magenta and gold. Candles bloomed, the floor was laid with mosaics of dragons, and golden lamps hung down between the pillars of carved and gilded cedarwood. The roof was a cupola of a million fragments of translucent jewels, blue and red and green and violet, and black and white striped doves flew about under it, turned to flying rainbows from its colors. On tables of painted glass lay a feast of food and drink. Death had not moved from the stone chair, but now it was a chair of gold. A bloody banner hung behind him. The many lights gleamed on his collar and rings of gold and all his white garments glinted with silver and gems. A circlet of rubies held back his long white hair, and across his knees rested a sceptre of ivory whose head was a silver skull. King Death he surely was. Narasen took him in, and he said to her and to her alone, and only she heard him: "It is the illusion they make, these men and these women. They pretend they are my court and I am emperor. None of it is real, bits and pieces of their memories of the world and the world's riches, which they recreate here by their presence and because they cannot bear the Innerearth as it is."

"And how can they work such magic?" asked Narasen coolly.

"Because their souls live, though their bodies are dead, and the souls are yet in the bodies. All these are they who have made the bargain with me to remain a thousand years. The soul is a magician. Only living flesh hampers it."

"And you, Lord," said Narasen with sharpness, "who keep them here to make this entertainment for you. Can you not find such stuff on the earth?"

"The earth is not mine," said Uhlume, "though I am the earth's. I am often there, but on business."

Narasen turned aside, and she moved through the men and women whose bodies were dead, but whose souls Death had trapped in them. The bodies had remained entire since even the worm, decay, which ate dead men in their graves, did not dare venture into Death's personal territory. The bodies had kept their years also, what age they were at the moment of death, though this did not seem to hinder them, and they were sprightly enough. Some, too, were young, had died young of a malady, and some had died young of a wound— and these wounds were still to be seen, though excellently camouflaged. A young soldier who had perished at a sword's end, wore a golden rose over his heart. Another who had expired when a stone pierced his eye, had an eye of sapphire—and seemed to see as well with it as with the other. Beneath a pillar sat a woman who was very pale, for she had lost her life in childbirth and much blood had left her. In her lap she nursed a little tiger, no larger than a child, and presently she gave it her breast and it sucked gently and she smiled. At the center of the floor, two old men with grizzled beards had crouched to drink and throw dice; their laughter was that of young men.

Uhlume had come to Narasen's side.

"There is no pain here, and, despite the age of the body, no sense of age and no weariness. Neither is there wine; they have invented it, yet they taste the wine and enjoy it and will shortly be drunk. This land is a blank parchment where anyone may write what they wish."

Narasen believed him. The wine and the food were not real, neither souls nor dead bodies had need of it, and the glamourous furnishings were not. The birds under the rainbow cupola did not exist, the tiger cub was the fantasy of she who mourned her child, left behind in life.

"And do you reckon me," said Narasen, "such a soft fool as these? Do you think I shall sit and pine for the world I have lost, and make its images come to intoxicate me or to amuse you till my thousand years are done? No. I will tell you now, for all your dreary kingdom, when I am here, you will get no pretty mirage from the mind of Narasen."

"You could not bear it otherwise," said Uhlume.

"We shall see," said Narasen. "Perhaps you will turn bored with me, with your performing bird which will not sing. Perhaps you will set me free before my thousand years are done."

"Never dream it," said Death.

"I dream as I please," said Narasen, "and never for your entertainment, my Lord."

The face of Death had no expressions. However, as once before, something seemed to journey across that face.

"Yet I perceive you have agreed to the bargain," said Death.

"This much the illusion did; it reminded me of Merh and the beauty of kingship. Yes, I have agreed."

Narasen beheld a hallucinatory window. It revealed a park of flowers and trees and evening hills and shining rivers under a new moon like a pale green bow. And Narasen laughed, remembering the barren deadlands as they actually were, which now she foresaw she could tolerate, seeing that would be to fight the will of Uhlume, Lord Death, who was formed as a man.

Next second, all was gone like smoke into the dark. Death and she were returning swiftly to the earth.

4

The witch had left her mansion, and slunk about the orchard of poisonous pomegranate trees. She was restless with envy of Narasen, for her high-handedness, and because at this moment Narasen journeyed with Uhlume.

At the age of twelve, this witch with the blue house had been adept and sly. She learned from mages and sorcerers two years, selling her body in the streets to get coin, or to the sorcerers themselves. None tricked her as Issak had been tricked, she was devious and quicker than foxes. She took the name of Lylas. When she was fourteen, wandering home late from some orgy of an obscure sect over the hills in the hour before dawn, Lylas the witch had met Death. It was at a place where the ground was unloved, a place of thorns, and nearby three men had been hanged. Lylas had been well schooled, and she knew a thing or two more than most. She paused under the creaking gallows when she recognized the ebony Lord in his white clothes, and into her shrewd and youthful brain there came an inspiration. It was an inspiration of the sort to set heart banging, teeth jittering, hands cold and mouth dry. It was of the sort which comes only once, and must be harkened to and acted on—or let go and ever regretted. Lylas chose not to regret. So she went up to Death and addressed him humbly.

They talked a little while, she and he, till the sky burned at its eastern edges, and the swinging shadows of the hanged men turned to a brackish red on the path below. Then Death and the maiden concluded their bargain, and he took something from her which was her pledge and he promised her another thing, and then she went on a journey in his name, and afterwards she did as she pleased with time to spare. For the witch in the blue house had lived well over two hundred years, and she would live for many more, and she had aged not a day, not an hour, not a minute beyond her fifteenth birthday.

But now, in her jealousy, she prowled about, and tore the fruit from the wild trees. Till abruptly a tree to the right of her cracked open as if a huge axe had split it, and out stepped Uhlume with Narasen at his back.

The witch bowed to Uhlume till her hair swept over and over the roots of the pomegranates.

"It is agreed," said he. And to Narasen he said, "You understand the token I must be given."

Narasen did not answer, and the witch said, sweetly, to conceal her spite, "My honoured elder sister must give me in keeping for this mighty Lord the third finger of her left hand, or at least what is severed at its highest joint."

"I am ready," said Narasen, and she drew off the rings from her finger.

Indeed, she had noted among the soul-inhabited corpse people of Death's court, that each was missing this portion of a member, as the witch of the blue house had been. (Lylas wore each finger bone about her waist on her golden chain, and when the debt was paid, and the soul and the body had gone down into the Innerearth, then the witch was free to take that particular bone and grind it in powder and drink it in wine. It was the magic property of these ivories, these binding seals on Death's treaty with decay and incarnation, which had preserved the witch's youth so long. And for her part, she acted as the intermediary, drumming up, as it were, custom for Death's secret trade.) She ran forward eagerly to take the bone of Narasen.

Uhlume touched the third finger of Narasen's left hand, and the finger lost its feeling to the second joint. When the knife of the witch flashed greedily in the gloom, Narasen experienced no pain. And no blood left the wound.

"It is done," said Lylas.

"So it is," said Narasen. "And now, how long must I wait?"

"How impatient she is, my Lord," sniggered Lylas.

Narasen said: "I have paid for the wares and now I seek delivery. And I will ask one further thing, mighty Lord of the Dark. That he should not have been too long in the ground, this bed-mate I am to have."

"I am just in such matters," said Uhlume, "and have marked down your preference. Return to the edge of the cedar forest, no farther. Tomorrow night our bargain will be kept." Then Uhlume glanced toward the witch, where she leaned on a tree, grinning behind one hand, with the bloodless finger of Narasen pinched in the other. "Instruct the royal woman in the lore of what she must do, as you have been tutored."

Lylas bowed down again to the soil of the orchard.

"Your handmaid obeys you, Lord of Lords."

Death turned and vanished, sinking in the earth like steam.

Lylas crept forward and pressed her lips to the spot where he had stood, taking care Narasen saw her. Narasen gave no heed, for her limbs were suddenly water, and her brain full of beating wings, and, iron—cold to her spirit, she chafed her seven-fingered hands for warmth.

5

The sun had risen above the forest of petrified cedars. Its arrows had not pierced the black spreading canopy; the sun had gone away, and the blue dusk had followed. And the dusk permeated the forest as the sun had not been able to.

The crimson pavilion of Narasen was erected on a rise among the outlying trees. A torch flared before the pavilion, and a short way off burned the camp fire of her soldiers. Here six men sat. The fire glinted on their eyes and teeth, and on the games they played with small plaques of painted wood. They were not easy. Their curses were soft and they seldom spoke otherwise. Two more of their number, sentries, patrolled around the perimeter of the camp. But the last pair of the ten had deserted the night before, sneaking off from the meadows about the orchard of the witch, not liking the glimmers and whispers that came from there.

Inside the pavilion, Narasen waited. She had everything in readiness. Even her own self she had made ready, casting dread aside, and fixing her thoughts on Merh. Before her was a cup of strong dark liquor, but she had scarcely tasted it. Beside the cup was a wooden box.

In the cedar forest, a sentry started, and stared about. But it was three black lizards running.

Before the fire, a soldier muttered:

"I am not sure I reckon her my queen and ruler. First she acts the man and lies with women, then she is a whore and spreads her legs for all the rams of Merh. Now, she courts the *dead*."

But the captain of these soldiers struck this one in the mouth and bade him shut it.

"She has done as she must," said the captain, "to save our land."

His eyes said: She is a bitch and a harlot and a sorceress, but she pays me still my wages.

The youth was barely sixteen when he died. His brother killed him on the very day that Narasen was riding back, toward the cedar forest. The blow had been an accident; the brothers were quarrelling. The elder was sturdy and rough, and worked hard as an ox in their father's tannery. The younger was lazy, the elder said, and preferred to wander by the river where the flowers hung over, gazing at their faces in the water, showing the young brother how he also might gaze at himself. "You are a girl, and have a girl's silly ways," bellowed the elder brother, and forgetting—or maybe not—that in his hand he held a sharp knife for cutting hides, he struck his kinsman on the arm. The knife went deep and unbarred the vital vein. Blood poured on the tannery floor; the younger brother shut his eyes at once and fell down, and very soon he was dead and white as cold marble.

The village wives sobbed as they prepared the tanner's son for the grave. There had never been a youth so handsome, they said. They washed his bloodless body and combed his yellow hair. They hid the wound in his arm by binding it with a silk bandage. "Death is cruel," said the women, inaccurately.

The villagers carried the youth to the walled yard of stone tombs on the hillside. The elder brother tramped behind the bier. He had rubbed lemon in his eyes to make them redden and water. No one had seen him strike the blow. He had told the village the younger brother had stumbled against a bench and cut himself this way on the knife which had been lying there.

They laid the youth on his bier inside the tomb, and shut the door. The priest and the kinsfolk stayed to keep one night's respectful watch.

Two hours before midnight, the tomb door opened and out came the tanner's dead son. Bloodless he still was, and on his head the wreath of flowers the women had made him. Glancing neither left nor right, he trod the path between the horrified watchers. Right to the stone wall of the graveyard he went, and there a white gust of wind whipped from the black night and bore him away. The kindred prayed, the priest fainted. The elder brother flew howling, and drowned himself in one of the tannery vats.

35

It was midnight. The soldiers sat like rocks now, as if petrified along with the cedar trees. The fire had sunk, and the
torch was smouldering before the pavilion.

A wind blew through the forest, out of the forest and
through the camp, scattering the rosy clinker of the fire, giving back movement to the garments and hair of the petrified
men. Then the wind was gone.

Out of the forest, after the wind, a figure came walking.

Slowly, as slowly as the figure walked on its road toward
them, the soldiers rose. They moved back, but the way they
made was wider than it needed to be to let pass this slight
boy with the garland about his head and silk about his arm.
The soldiers moved backwards till their spines met the cold
spines of cedar trunks or till they lost their footing. And
there, where they were stopped, they froze. The boy stepped
on till he reached the queen's tent.

Narasen, seated before the scarcely tasted cup and the box
of wood, looked up at a stir of the crimson cloth entrance to
the pavilion. But she kept where she was, and narrowed her
eyes to see what Uhlume, Lord Death, had sent her.

After a moment, she let out her breath and smiled.

She left her seat then and, going to the apparition, observed him minutely, and next touched him.

"Why," said Narasen, "your master deals well with me."

She led him to the tent's center and, malleable as a very
small child, he let her lead him. He had no will, save Death's,
and now her will, who had bargained with Death. Narasen
gazed at him again, and circled about him, and gazed once
more.

Certainly Uhlume had noted her preference, as he said,
and certainly he had been just. There was no appearance of
the dead here. All was sweet and whole, indeed pleasing to
each sense, of touch, smell or sight. The blue eyes were open,
somewhat glazed, but only as if with sleep or wine, swimming
rather than vacuous, and the movements were like those of
one in a trance, languorous and extremely pliant. But not in
that alone had Uhlume been just. This youth, who in life had
been more girl than man, had had a girl's beauty. His contours were slender, but rounded rather than angular; no
harshness intervened. Despite the mortal pallor, the two buds
on his breast were faintly colored still, the color the witch's
mouth had been, dawn's first warm shade, which was the
color of his mouth also. His face was fully a maiden's, a virgin's face, beardless-smooth, delicately shaped as something
fashioned rather than born. And about the face the long hair

was spun, a topaz flowering from his ivory flesh, and the flowering hair was crowned with flowers as if for a feast or a wedding.

Narasen persuaded the body of the youth, by pressure and by direction, that it must lie on the rugs. This done, she took up the wooden box the witch had given her, and opened it. Within was coiled a plaited cord, and this cord Narasen now drew across the quiescent male flesh before her, over shoulders and torso, between the fingers of the slim hands and over the passive loins. After that, swiftly she threw the cord aside.

The cord struck the tent's floor just beyond the lamps, and from the half glow there, came a flicker like an unsheathed blade.

Narasen stretched herself beside the body of the beautiful young man, and set her lips to the face that was like the face of a virgin girl.

"If your body remembers anything," said Narasen, "suppose I am some man you have loved. Suppose I am he. I do not abuse you. It is your lover who kisses you thus."

Then she kneeled above him and leaned and caressed his body, her hands and mouth upon his skin that was scented yet with clean unguents and incense and the lingering fragrance of life itself.

In the half glow beyond the lamp, something tensed and trembled. Muted light licked over a network of small fires. A snake with amber scales, spent, on its belly, head in the shadow—a snake, the cord from the box of wood.

Narasen made the movement of a river with her palms across the body of the youth. Her red hair, loosened, hung about them, enclosing them with crimson, as the crimson pavilion enclosed them. Her hands slipped into the shallow river-bed, between the fine golden reeds. Her hands traced the course of the river, had a river come there.

In the half glow beyond the lamp, the amber snake shivered the length of its long shimmering, shivered off the light, though its head remained in shadow.

Narasen's fingers clasped the root of the river, its source. She lowered her head to sip from its waters, had there been waters.

In the half glow, the snake jerked. It rippled. The snake became a river, the river which swelled and sluiced under the river-bed. The snake's head lashed upon the floor. From the shadow, the head of the snake rose. Straight the snake's head stood. The snake danced upon its tail.

Narasen lifted herself. She enclosed the youth in a third pavilion of crimson. The light slid on her back like silver daggers, as it slid on the back of the writhing snake. Narasen stared into the face of a maiden, the phallus of a man within her, and she thought of Merh. And Merh was a leopard and the struggle of the leopard on the spear. And Narasen arched her back with the pleasure of the slaughtering of this leopard, and she felt its death like her own.

And the snake reared up its head and gasped wide its jaws and hissed forth a rain of fiery needles.

PART TWO

The Crying Child

1

Merh was green again with spring, green and gold. Her broad river, like dark jade, wound cool and clear beneath the great trees. The herds of Merh drank at the margins of the water, the long-legged birds waded there. Young grain ripened in the earth, young fruit swelled unseen within the blossoming orchards. Plague had taken her leave and barrenness had fled. There was water in the wells, and milk in the round breasts of the women and in the rich sacs of beasts. Young animals cried from the stalls now, and babies cried from the houses. So many young things were born that spring after the barrenness, they called it later the time of the Crying Child. And for another reason also, it was called that.

Narasen had come back from the east, across the mountains, into Merh. She had seen the land was altered, already healing, putting on again its sheen of health. Narasen had waited a month and a little longer in the cedar forest. Returning, she knew why Merh was fecund once again, for Merh was Narasen, and the queen of Merh had cancelled the bane of Issak: she was with child.

The people knelt to her on the country paths. They brought her wild flowers and jars of wine; they brought her baskets of corn seed to bless. She was their fertility goddess, she who had been prince and king here. In the city they lay down in the roadway before her. They poured perfume on the street before her where they did not lie down. In the square below the palace gate, they had taken some men and hanged them for reviling her name in the days of the plague—choosing to forget how they had, everyone, reviled her then. The commander of Narasen's guard, who had held the palace safe for her in her absence, and a semblance of order in the streets, came swaggering out and bowed and kept his eyes from her belly.

Narasen endured the pregnancy stubbornly as she had endured all she had undertaken in order to retain Merh. But she was a slave chained to a millstone, and the millstone was in her womb. Nor was the child eager to leave her. It curled in her, asleep, and its soul did not quicken it to be going at the proper season.

Narasen thought of the child with distaste. It was a sluggard, this dead man's babe. Perhaps it too was dead. She could not ride or hunt; she had no appetite for food or drink or exercise. She had no love for her women. Fat as a great whale stranded aboard the pitiless land, she must note that all but she were lithesome running deer. "Come, millstone, free me. You have done your work." She considered she might kill it when it was born. She was a warrior and a man who had been forced to play at motherhood. Yes, she might well kill this child.

The child seemed to hear her at last. It pierced her with a sword.

I will not make lamentation for you, thought Narasen. *You shall screech, not I*.

And Narasen did not cry out, though the child ripped and rent her like a cloth.

"She will die," the physicians murmured dolefully above Narasen, "Even her womb refuses to believe itself a womanly thing, and will not let the child out. Ah, she will die."

"I will not," replied Narasen, through hurt and rage. "But I shall remember each who told me that I should."

Two days passed, two nights. The days were molten silver and the nights were hot black blood, both poured upon Narasen. She recollected Issak, how he had spoken of his misguided traffic with the Drin, the dwarf-folk of the demon lands. She came to believe these Drin had taken up their abode within her belly, and hammered there and had their forges going, for they were metalsmiths, but here the red metal they forged was agony and the jewels they set in it were the diamonds of unuttered screams.

"Yes," said the physicians, "she will die."

Narasen could no longer speak. She thought: *Not I, but all men I will kill tomorrow. All men, who with their lusts cause this.*

The third day came. It rushed on slippers of silk this gentle day, in at the palace door. And just behind the day rushed another, less gentle, and through another door.

"Bless the gods, lady, for it is a son," a girl's voice cried.

Narasen whispered: "If it is a man, take it and throttle the thing."

40

"Tut," said the chief physician, "the girl is a dolt, majesty. It is a female child."

Narasen recalled herself. She was made of pain, but she lay in the bed beneath the burnished weapons and the painted scenes of war and hunting. She was Narasen of Merh, and she was alive.

The chief physician and his attendants had drawn aside to hold up an infant before a window in apparent wonder. But a solitary doctor remained at Narasen's pillow, who bent and put a little cup to her lips. Fluid ran into her mouth. She swallowed. The doctor with his cup unbent and slunk away and out at the door.

Narasen felt, unlooked for, a spider biting at her heart. She opened her eyes, and saw, between the ripplings of a scarlet veil, a woman in a blue robe grinding something in a pestle. The veil eddied, not gauze but wine, and Narasen floated, a ground bone in that wine, and somewhere a blue dog laughed.

Am I not strong enough to survive this idiot act of birth? Narasen demanded of herself, of her body and her fate. But she felt a cold tide rising, a cold tide which washed away her stamina and her hope.

She thought of the cup against her lips, of this one physician who had slunk away and taken the cup with him. She had enemies, many who were covetous of her high place, several who hated her. Vulnerable, rejoicing in her grasp on life, had she let it go in the unguarded moment, drinking without protest that single mouthful? No. Yet the cold tide in her blood, rising, sang like the sea, yes, and yes.

The physicians chattered at the window. The child they held up shone like a milky glass, and the light of day seemed to pass through its limbs. It kicked but did not cry. *You also keep silent,* Narasen thought. She was angry. She had reckoned to reign in Merh for sixty years or more, and to secure these sixty years she had undergone whoredom, sorcery, the bondage of her soul, and last, this birth, which she had determined to survive. Now all was taken from her. She would reign a day, or less, the fruit of her struggle was sour. Yet even her anger was faint and sullen. She had no energy left to give her fury. Even wrath was denied her.

Then she glimpsed a shadow, between the air and the wall of the chamber. Black the shadow was, not Death, but the forecast of Death.

"So," said Narasen within herself, "I have been cheated."

"Not so," the shadow seemed to answer. "Uhlume does not

41

ordain the hour of your death. Your destiny ordains it. Your
adversaries or your misfortune claim you. Death is like the
night. He comes when he must, but he does not choose the
moment of his coming. He is a slave, too."

Narasen smiled bitterly.

"I am too weak to rail," she said. "Tell your master to beware of me when I am with him and strong again, in his
wretched country of dusts."

"That will be soon."

"I know it."

The physician who had poisoned the queen of Merh,
scuttled through the by-ways of the palace, entered the bar-
racks of the soldiers, and passed presently into the chamber
of the commander of the guard. The commander reclined
upon a couch. He was indolent and handsome, and he ate a
purple fruit.

"My lord Jornadesh," said the physician, "the queen, alas,
is very sick."

"Alas indeed," said Jornadesh, the commander, eating his
fruit.

"Such travail," said the physician, "such loss of blood and
strength. Besides, a child conceived by witchcraft, by acts of
perversity and necrophilia—we must grieve, for death is inevitable."

"And when, to the hour, is this sad, inevitable death to be
expected?" inquired Jornadesh.

"Sunset," said the physician. "I will respectfully remind
your lordship that the draught I have so cleverly procured is
of great accuracy and efficiency. I will bring to your lordship's mind, most courteously, that I have also been very diligent on your behalf in applying this drug. No trace will be
discovered, providing the queen is promptly buried."

"And the child?" impatiently asked Jornadesh. "Dead too?"

"Not dead, but reportedly a freak," said the physician,
"Best buried with the mother."

"Doubtless so," said Jornadesh, spitting out the seeds of the
fruit.

He had always abhorred the man-queen of Merh, and marvelled that the throne should be hers. His days as sole lord in
the palace when the leopardess was away, had moved him to
meditation. Now Narasen was stretched on her death-bed and
his men waited in readiness to seize Merh. Thereafter Jornadesh would rule by right of his cunning and the favor of
the gods. In order not to anger these same gods, he did not

42

mean to kill the newborn infant. There was a stigma, even to a man of blood, in spilling the blood of a child. To bury it alive, however, was another matter. It gave the gods an opportunity to intervene, if so they were minded, which they would not be. Jornadesh was delighted at himself. He had thought of everything. He paid the physician and sent him out, then sent another to pay the physician in different currency—a knife's end. And then Jornadesh called for a jug of yellow wine and a girl with wine-yellow hair, and thus he waited for good news.

When the sun fell from the sky's brink, Narasen fell into death. Shadows came and went about her chamber, but in the streets red torches flamed and horses galloped. Three hours before midnight, Jornadesh was the king of Merh, and Narasen queen only of a silver bier.

They took her, by way of the river, in the dark.

It was a moonless night. The dim lamps dripped dim color in the water, the priests whispered their dirges, the muffled oars folded the current aside like velvet, and the great barge went by the banks like a phantom, wrapped in a pall. Few saw the slow ship pass, for word of Narasen's demise had travelled as slowly. Some that saw it, took it for a supernatural thing. For out of the obscure darkness of it, borne on the same wind, which blew shorewards the smell of the incense of the rites for the dead, there came a thin crystal crying, white blades of sound, horned to pierce the skin of the night.

The child had not cried when it was born. It entered the world unafraid, with little to weep at save the loss of its unloving cage. But now freedom turned to threat. The child sobbed and none quieted it. They feared it, either to kill it or preserve its life. They had put it in a round bowl of beaten copper, and here it crawled, trying to get some purchase on the smooth sides, trying to discover the mammalian mound from which it might suck milk. But the bowl was less loving even than Narasen, and more dry. And beyond the bowl, the black rain of night dropped in the child's eyes, and the river rocked it harshly, ironically.

A tributary of this river ran northward through Merh. The silken trees swept down about the funeral barge, inky willows, their hair twined with the green jewels of fireflies. And from the black lawns above the river there presently loomed a wall of stone with gates of bronze.

They went ashore. The priests swung their censers, the soldiers bore the bier of Narasen and the bowl with the baby

43

crawling helplessly in it. They marched through the bronze gates and through the streets of a city where no lights were ever lit, not being needed, and where none looked out or called a greeting: the necropolis of Merh. And beyond an avenue of trees they climbed a marble platform to a mausoleum of red stone, and here the rulers of Merh had been laid for three centuries, and here Narasen was laid on her silver bier.

The priests hurried to get the rite done. All about, heaps of bones gleamed dully from the lamps, and sometimes a gem glittered; but if the proceeding disturbed them, these denuded kings, their bones gave no sign.

And still the child cried, as if purposely to disturb them, as if to wring some response from the deaf blind dark. A weasel of hunger gnawed its vitals and between the loud cries, it whimpered. Easily, its noise drowned the muttering of the priests. It stretched its hands and its legs and tried to grip some reassuring thing, but only the chill and the shadow were near, and even the black nurse who had rocked it so harshly had left off her rocking. At length, the vague light, the vague susurration which, till now, had constantly been about it, were also withdrawn. There came the clanging shut of a vast door. And the child conceived through death was alone with death in the place of death.

And in that moment, Death came.

The eyes of the baby were unfixed and weak, but in those days of the earth's flatness, even the newborn could recognize Lord Death. So the child stared and saw and knew him.

Death bent close. His slender long hand, like a black bird flying, hovered above the child, but Death did not touch. Something in the eyes of the child, which were of a curious bright yellow-green color, like certain stones found deep in the loins of mountains, deterred Death, put him off. Something in the eyes leapt with a pathetic, feeble yet unrelenting urge to live, and Uhlume was then no cutthroat and no robber.

Shortly, he turned away. He turned and lifted from her silver bed the body of Narasen of Merh. They had dressed her in a black robe belted with a girdle of rubies and on her arms and round her neck they had put gold bands, and earrings of topaz in her ears, because she had been the ruler of Merh and Jornadesh had left her uneasily a portion of state. But her hair had not been dressed and it fell about her like a lank red garden of weeds, and its tint had changed, its red more blue from what she had drunk. And her skin, too, bore the soft blush of this blueness, and even the whites of her golden eyes, which now snapped open at the touch of Uhlume's hands.

"I do not resist," said Narasen in a voice that was no longer a voice at all. "See, I am ready, and may you get much joy of me." And she put her own hands on the shoulders of Death, and so the child perceived them sink straight through the floor of the tomb, the black man and the blue skinned woman, and they were gone.

Then the child began to shriek. Its cries were terrible. From some psychic source it dredged up an ultimate strength to scream, as if it understood these screamings alone remained to mark it out from the dead.

But who, hearing wild roarings from a graveyard at night, would hurry there to look?

Below the city of tombs, the other side from the willow banks of the river, there was a wood. On this night of no moon, it was a dancing-ground of black shade, where night flowers bloomed the color of pale yellow papers, and minute glowing insects spattered like hail across them. And into this midnight room of trees two demon Eshva had wandered, and were in fact dancing there to music the leaves made in the wind.

The demon country of Underearth had three classes: the dwarfish Drin, who made things, the princely Vazdru, the elite, and the Eshva who served the Vazdru, and who dreamed of dreaming and lived in a dream and liked to walk the world by night in this dream, unspeaking, beautiful and oblique.

The two Eshva in the wood were female. In their black hair silver snakes wound languorously, and two black cats, attracted to the Eshva magic, circled about their feet, dancing too.

Till, clear through the stillness, broke the wild spikes of the child's screaming.

The Eshva paused, balanced on air. They had no compassion, but they had great curiosity, a bottomless, limpid well of desire to meddle in human affairs.

Together, as one, they skimmed between the trees, and the two black cats ran after. They came to the slope above the river, came to the wall of stone. Eshva went where they wished; they flew over the wall and drifted along like a pair of leaves. Among the streets of the dead they drifted, following the cries of the child, which now were growing fainter, guttering out. The Eshva did not fear death. Only sunlight was to be avoided, that, and the displeasure of their Vazdru Lord,

Prince of the Princes of Underearth. They reached the platform of marble and floated up it to the door in the mausoleum of red stone.

One of the Eshva breathed on the door and stroked it with her fingers, and the door groaned softly to itself. The two black cats prowled on the marble stairway and played with a flower-from-the-wood they had brought with them for the purpose. The second demon woman sighed and shut her eyes.

Then the door opened, unable to resist the caress of its inmost locks.

The child had screamed and wept itself dumb. It lay in the copper bowl and did not move, not even to try to wriggle aside from the weasel of hunger that bit on its vitals. The Eshva who had opened the door, glided up and put her hand on the child to feel its warmth and humanness. And in this way she found the child's strangeness.

The Eshva leaned near, and her snake-wound hair brushed the child, so it shivered. Fascinated, the Eshva licked the eyelids of the child, tasting the salt of its tears, and she breathed in its nostrils the demon-breath which was like a perfumed drug. Then the child caught her hand and putting one of her fingers in its mouth, sucked on it.

The demon woman laughed with her eyes. She drew the child up and carried it outside, wrapped in her arms and her hair, and the snakes unwound themselves and peered into the child's face, but it took no notice of them.

Eastward the demoness sped then, on to the plains of Merh, and after her the other Eshva came, and the cats ran till they could no longer keep up.

A leopardess had her lair in a cave above a high ledge, half a mile from the river. Narasen had never hunted this leopardess, though her mate she had slain. Now the leopardess had coupled elsewhere and given birth out of season, for when the barrenness that had fallen on Merh lifted, it had changed the times of such things. The leopardess slept in her cave and her young slept beside her. It was two hours past midnight, two hours before the sun rose and before she must rise with the sun and go hunting. Yet into her sleep stole a thing which shone and teased and troubled her pleasantly, till she woke.

The Eshva women called the leopardess from her cave, and when she came slinking out into the starlight, they breathed on her eyes and ran their hands over her freckled pelt until she sank down between them. Then they laid the child against her belly, and put the amber beads of her dugs

46

into its mouth one after another. The child sucked and clung. Its body writhed gently, tightening and relaxing with each drawing motion of its mouth. The musk-sweet milk filled it, and when it was full, it rolled aside and slept.

2

Though the demons might occasionally reproduce, their methods were unusual. Love was their pleasure and their art but their seed was sterile and demon women had no wombs, though all else they had and to spare. Perhaps it might be said, this being the case, that the Eshva who took the child of Narasen from the mausoleum felt some maternal stirring. But maybe it was only as a plaything they took it, as they would steal the panther's child or the serpent's. Whatever else, many months they spent with this human baby, these two weird guardians, and though the time of demonkind is not of the same duration as that of mortals, and in the Underearth the world's years went by in days, or less, or possibly a very little more, even so, it was a long while, the Eshva being as they were.

By day they left the child, but always in some safe spot, or what to them was safe—the high deserted houses of owls, the hollows beneath trees. However, leaving it, they drugged their charge asleep with their pervasive magic, the brushing wings of their hair and their sighs. The child never stirred and no one found it. If a beast chanced on the place, it scented darkness there and went away. At night the Eshva carried the child with them. They fed it on the milk of leopards, foxes and wild deer, and later on herbs and flowers and things that sprang from the earth. And the child, born so strangely, began to grow amid equal strangeness, privy to the wild wanderings and flights of the Eshva, and their wordless language which seemed written on the air in somber lights. In this atmosphere the child's own eerie peculiarity took on a normalcy, or at least a rightness. Before it could chatter out one word of human speech, the child could charm the bird from the cloud and the snake from under the stone. And though no mortal brain could ever quite fashion the sibilance of demon musings, yet this mortal baby had a knowledge of them, while of its own miraculousness it was in command, and feared nothing of itself. Had it been reared among men there would have been another story to be told.

47

The child had mingled both parents in itself, an alchemy of the bizarre. The colors of these parents' hair had been mixed, the red and the blond, to give the child hair the shade of apricots ripening on the tree. The colors of the parental eyes had also mixed, tawny with azure, and made the eyes of the child a saffron-green. Beautiful it was, its mother and its sire having been beautiful. But Narasen, the man-queen of Merh, had lain with a fair, dead and effeminate youth, a match not generally achieved, and here too there had been a mingling, for in its body the infant was neither a man-child nor a girl, but both. A fitting toy for the Eshva to play with.

It was not that they tutored it, the demon women, for they set themselves to teach it nothing. Yet it learned from their proximity. Instinct, the father of all human sorcery, rose untrammelled to the surface of its soul like bubbles from a lake's floor. All the while, its days were inchoate wakings, dreams and sleep, its nights volatile excursions through the shadows of the world and the burning dream of the Eshva folk. It glimpsed cities spangled with lights and seas of glass beneath a moon of white salt; it observed a desert like snow under this same enchanted moon, it watched a mountain which painted the moon red with its fire. (They had gone far from Merh. It was a much-travelled baby.) It caught brief flickers also from the haphazard areas of men, but it saw men through demon eyes, or very nearly. It danced its own tumbling dance with the black velvet sons and daughters of the panther, in the midnight glades where the Eshva swayed to the music of leaves and wind.

They would have tired no doubt, the demon women, of their charge, Or they would have forgotten it. One night, caught by some other whim, they would not have remembered to return to the cover where they had left the child—though they loved it, it was not the sort of love that lasts, the Eshva being the Eshva. Yet, before that inevitable forgetting came, some prince of the Vazdru called them instead to do his errands in Druhim Vanashta, the demon city underground. There many mortal nights could pass in an hour, or less, or a little more. Or, if the errands were complex, the quick years of earth might drift by like sand along a beach. Now even the dreamy Eshva realized they could not abandon a human child so long, for it would die, and since they still cared for it, this moved them.

They had concealed the child recently in an ancient garden. In the blue dusk, white blossoms drifted from the trees to powder the face of the pool. The child sat beside the mossy statue of a boy. Under the moss, this boy of stone played on a pipe, but the ants had nested in his stone hands and walked up and down the pipe, insolently taking the air. The child, intrigued by the stone boy, had assumed its female sex, in order to complement him. A small girl now, the child rested her head on the hip of the stone boy and her apricot hair curled round his feet.

"Now look at this," said some of the ants, and the child almost heard them, "here is another one of these statues. It is drier, too. But it moves."

Just then there came from the blossoming trees beside the pool a hideous dwarf. Its bow legs gaped so its belly almost brushed the ground between, and about its loins was a great boastful guard of shining metal set with gorgeous jewels. Its face meantime was like some dreadful mask that had been smashed and re-established without due care. Only its sable hair was beautiful. Now any mortal child, clapping eyes on this horror, would have fled wailing, and no wonder. But this child, being raised differently, had no fear. For the monster was none other than one of the lower demons, a Drin.

"Ha!" said the Drin, smacking his lips at the ants, "if you were down below with me and something larger, we should have a fine time, you and I, you pretty harlots." (For the Drin enjoyed much love with the insects of Underearth.)

But the Eshva women were coming. They slid across the pool like two dark swans. Seeing them, the child altered itself once more. Its minute organs reversed themselves, one giving way to the other. The process was swift, as a chameleon would rearrange its colors, or a flower fold itself shut at the going of the sun; not, however, quite comfortable, but the initiation was to the child a natural and reflexive sympton of change, no worse than the action of yawning or sneezing.

The Drin, though, took in the child's exchange of the female for the male with mad ribald laughter. He bowed low to the Eshva and licked their ankles, congratulating them on their unusual find, commiserating with them that they must give it up.

The child did not know the speech of the Drin, but yet it sensed something of what was said. The child became aware its companions were to leave it. Human sorrow it had temporarily lost track of. It had mislaid the responses of fright and sobbing. But it stared with its gold-green eyes till the dwarf came and put round its neck a silver chain with a gem set in it that was the match for these eyes.

"See, mistresses," said the Drin to the Eshva women, "a

perfect resemblance. Now it has three eyes, this brat of yours. And there I carved the name, as you instructed me."

The child looked at the symbol chiselled in the brilliant jewel. It could not read the demon writing, one of the seven languages of the Underearth, nor could it pronounce the name in any language of the earth or under it, yet still it comprehended the name. Simmu, it was, which in the demon tongue meant Twice Fair.

The Eshva came to the child and kissed it. Their kisses were like soft fires and the child's head swam and it shut its eyes. The Drin leapt about shouting: "Kiss me! Kiss me too!" But the Eshva paid no heed. They bore the child away, leaving the Drin grunting and hopping in the garden.

Some miles westward a temple stood. All around were groves and pastures; within the high walls were gardens and many courts. White birds nested on the roofs, and these birds would fly up at dawn, like smoke from the burning sun. A priesthood served the temple. Their ideals were poverty and modesty, but the building had yellow pillars ringed with gold, and here and there were statues of gods and wise men, with ivory hands and faces and ornaments of silver.

On the steps of this place, in the hour before sunrise, the Eshva women set the child. Somewhile they smiled, thinking their misty wicked thoughts of mischief brought here in the child's person. Then they gazed at the child, and wept their beautiful Eshva tears, a farewell.

Seeing them weep, for the first time since it had cried in the tomb at Merh, the child began to weep too.

But the east was paler than it had been, the coming of the light was written there, and birds wings opened and closed on the roofs like fans. The Eshva drew away from the crying child. They swirled into a flurry of dark patterns, the patterns of hair and garments, and dissolved themselves and were gone back to the Underearth before the final star melted from the sky.

The sun rose. Presently, four young priests came from the temple and found a child seated on the steps, a naked male child, not quite two years old, with a green jewel round its neck. And the child wept. Nor did it cease crying to look at them, nor respond when they spoke to it, and when they took it into the temple, still it cried. And for days after, it shed water from its eyes and would not be comforted.

PART THREE

The Master of Night

1

For Simmu there began then a time of near humanness, a time of near forgetting. As the tree was dormant in the winter, empty of fruit and leaves, so was Simmu. Spring woke the tree; a spring would come also to wake Simmu, but Simmu's spring was yet far off.

The Eshva had gone. Their memory followed them, out of the child's brain. Unremembering the Eshva and the months he had travelled with them, one with them almost, caught up in their dusky glamour, the child unremembered much, though not all, of what he had been and could be. He became apparently simply mortal because all he saw about him now were simply that. He had become already a male and remained so, because all about him now were male. And he mislaid the knowledge that he could be other than male. He was a human little boy, if an unusual one, shed by folk he had no recollection of, as unwanted babies often were, an extra mouth that could not be fed. For sure, the demon name he forgot. The symbol on the Drin jewel was a character unknown among the tongues of men. The priests, who from pious charity took him in, called him a name which meant Shell, because they said he had been found in a sea of tears. They were fanciful, these priests. They had a fancy for the bright green jewel, and accepted it graciously as the fee of those who had abandoned the child. They put it in the temple treasury, among the other loot.

Thus Shell, who was Simmu, grew up in the temple, a foundling. Several were, for the priesthood would take in any that had no blemish and were fair to look at, (the gods could not be expected to adopt the crippled or disfigured), and providing some token payment had been left with the infant, in order to show proper respect and gratitude. And all these young were dedicated immediately to the service of the gods, and to the ideals of poverty and humility, among the pillars ringed with gold.

The children of the temple had their own courts. Here the small ones played and cried and ran about, tended by various lay brothers whose duty it was to watch over them, for no woman was permitted inside the holy precincts. Despite the extreme youth of this nest of babies, particular disciplines were enforced, such as the hours of bedding, rising and feeding, and even the tiniest was taken before the images of the two gods who presided over the children's courts, and taught to kneel down there and bow their heads, and those who sobbed or giggled were scolded. The two gods were rather alarming to the children. One had a blue face, the other a red face. They wore silver diadems and their lower parts were bestial, the blue one being a tiger from the hips down, the red one a ram. The function of these gods was to do with the weather. The blue tiger controlled the storm winds and the red ram the summer heat. They belonged to an older pantheon than that now generally venerated in the temple, and had been retained as guardians of the children out of an odd mixture of cautious respect and scorn.

The older boys dwelt in the upper section of the children's courts until they were twelve and initiated into the priesthood. From six years on they would learn to read and write. At ten years they would study from the brown scrolls and dusty books of the great library. Much learning these young priests acquired, concerning histories of the earth, of wars and sagas; of the being of the earth, its strange flatness, like a dish of mountains and seas, ringed by an uncharted substance—ocean or air; of the minerals of the earth and the laws of the earth and its peoples and its creatures. At least, each of these things, in the manner in which the books reported them, they learned. The ritual and lore of the temple they studied also. They read the testaments of revered prophets and messiahs, how they must strive to be modest before the might of the gods, how they must value every man and be kind to him.

Half a mile east of the temple enclosure was the House of Service. Here women were allowed; they came to wash the robes of the priests and to sew new ones, to cook and bake for them. Nearby stood the House of Gifts. Through its gate hunters brought a tenth of what they had trapped or killed, and farmers a twentieth of the land's yield, and merchants a fifth of the revenue obtained from their goods. Sometimes the rich would bring a gift in order to get a prayer said in the temple, a malachite dish or a chain of pearls. Whenever a wealthy girl was to be married, she sought the blessing of the gods in the Sanctuary of Virgins in a grove half a mile to the west of the temple, and the price was the weight of her right hand in gold. Whenever a woman was to bear a child, the husband came and thanked the gods and brought them a jar of wine, and when the child was born, if it lived and was a man, the father would, if he could, dedicate a little shrine to heaven in the child's name, and the cost of the shrine was a bag of silver, or seven sheaves of wheat or three sheep.

At the five festivals of the year, some of the younger priests would be elected to journey here and there about the countryside. They would bless whoever came to them and heal the sick, and two or three wagons would travel behind them to hold the presents they were given. In the festival at the time of harvest, the high priest himself would go out, riding in a chariot under a canopy and drawn by four white oxen. On that occasion, five wagons would travel behind.

The robes of the high priest were of yellow silk. This signified the power of light and the clarity of day. On the robes were sewn rubies and emeralds, which signified wisdom and love. The younger priests had garments of fine yellow linen, every day a fresh one. In winter they put on outer vestments of wool, lined and trimmed with the yellow furs of desert foxes. They wore their hair long, for they believed it a sin to cut off the hair of either sex, and for a man to shave his face was a worse sin. But they trimmed their beards and used the scented oils from the jars which piled up in the House of Gifts. Each evening the huge inner hall of the temple was laid as if for a feast. The priests would eat and drink, meat and wine and white bread and sweetmeats. Their religion forbad them only one pleasure of the flesh—to lie with woman or man. Anything else they might indulge in. Still, they were esteemed that they ate but a single meal a day, and merely a portion of fruit and bread in the morning and at noon. And once a year, at midwinter, they fasted on fish and cakes, and drank no red wine, only white.

Now and then, one who was sick was brought to the temple, to the Outer Court if he were a man, to the Women's House by the Sanctuary of Virgins if not. These sick the priests would see to, and their grasp and application of healing was excellent. However, it might be in the middle of dinner that the sick one arrived, and then there might be some delay, and maybe the sick one would die. "Alas, the gods are stern and exacting," the priests would say. And twice a day the priests would kneel to the gods, and worship them for their generosity and forgiveness.

It was a rich land, and a religious land, and as well, for the temple milked it as a cow is milked.

And amid the richness and the ritual and the religion, Simmu, who was called Shell, grew, almost forgetting, dormant, but beautiful and protean as the winter tree.

2

When Simmu called Shell was ten, another entered the courts of the children, a year older than he, and this boy had been sent here by his father, one of the nomadic kings of a far desert country to the south.

The boy's name was Zhirem, and he was the king's son by his most favored wife, but there had been discord over him.

They were a brown people, the nomads, with clay-colored hair and russet eyes, but the boy the woman birthed was dark haired, dark as the shadow of early night, and his eyes were the color of green water reflecting a blue sky.

"Now what is this?" roared the king, striding about his scarlet tent. He thought his woman had been playing games with a foreigner, but she had not, and told him as much, and besides asked her husband if he had ever seen such a foreigner in those parts. "My mother was dark," said she, "and my grandmother had such eyes."

"Am I to believe a male child is nothing but a patchwork of his mother's female ancestors?" demanded the king.

"Well, at least," said the woman humbly, "he is handsome, as his father is."

The king relented somewhat at that, and said no more on the matter, not then. And the child was a handsome child for sure, and became more handsome. The women of the tents loved him for his rarity and for a certain grave sweetness in his manner, and for his beautiful green-blue-water eyes. But the old men avoided glancing at him. "Such darkness is unlucky," they said. "The dark haired ones are marked, as a goat bears the brand of the king to set him apart from other herds; marked and branded and already promised to demonkind and to the Black Jackal, the Master of Night." When they spoke this way they spat afterwards to clear the words from their mouths. The one they called Black Jackal and Master of Night had many names and titles, and the more

54

abstract and less familiar the naming, the better. His true name they did not speak though they knew it, Azhrarn, the Prince of Demons, a Lord of Darkness.

The king's favorite wife, however, loved her son, the king's youngest, fiercely, and as he grew older and more fair, so she grew more afraid.

"On all sides are enemies," she whispered to herself in her heart. "The young men envy him already, and the old men hate him. Well, we know that demons roam by night, but does my son roam? What is there in him but goodness and innocence? And presently the young men will take him hunting with them, and they will lead him where lions are, and leave him without spears, and he will be slain. Or else someone will cut open his veins when he sleeps in the palm shade at noon. Or else he will wed some bitch, and her brothers will hiss in her ears that she has coupled with evil and she will put poison in his cup." Then the woman wept, but she could tell no one and ask help from no one, and even her husband looked unlovingly at Zhirem.

One day, when Zhirem was five years old, the men were away hunting and a weird crone came into the place of tents. She was dressed in stinking pelts and her matted hair was tangled with metal rings and polished bones. But around her arm was twined a living golden snake, and her eyes were keen and clear as a girl's.

The women were afraid and would not approach her, but the king's favorite wife, who had too much trouble to take on fear as well, went out to her and asked her what she wanted.

"To sit in the shade and drink cool water," said the crone. Then she caught sight of the boy child Zhirem, and she said, "And there are both."

The king's wife frowned. She brought the hag into her own tent and sat her down. With her own hands she gave her food and liquor, the best from the king's store, and a dish of milk for the snake. Then the king's wife went to a chest of red sandstone and brought out her earrings of turquoise, her bracelets of gold and her anklets of amber, and an onyx bird which had been her mother's, and three great pearls, and she put them beside the crone.

"Very pretty," said the crone, blinking her clever youthful eyes.

"Take them," said the king's wife.

The crone smiled with the nine black teeth she had left.

55

"There is nothing for nothing in this world," said she. "And what is it *you* want?"

"The safety of my son and his life," said the king's wife, Zhirem's mother, and she poured out her story as she had poured out the jewels.

When the story was finished, the hag said: "You think me a witch, and you think cleverly. I will do what I can for your boy, but he may not thank me as you do, for there is no benefit which has not a sister in misfortune. When it is dusk, bring your child, and go with him to the far purple ridge and wait there. One shall come for you and conduct you to me."

"Suppose I cannot do it?"

"Then neither can I do anything," said the hag, and she got up, creaking in her joints. The king's wife pointed to her jewels and the witch said: "I want none of those. I will tell you my price tonight."

When the king and his warriors returned, his favorite wife went to him and kissed him, and she said: "My lord, pardon me if I do not stay here with you tonight, but all day my head has pained me and I crave to lie down alone in my tent in the silence of night."

The king was lenient with her, for he still liked her well. So she took Zhirem secretly to her tent, and when the dusk came down she stole away with him through the grove of palms which stood there, and they ran together to the far purple ridge, the boy laughing, for he thought it was a game.

They had not been there long, and the horizon was yet green from the afterglow, when a cloud blew out of the west though there was no wind. This cloud fell down from the sky and covered Zhirem and his mother. The woman was alarmed and clutched her child to her, but next moment all was motion and the moment after all stillness, and the cloud had faded. The woman and her son found themselves in another spot altogether and did not guess how they had come there.

It was a garden of sorts. High stone walls showed nothing but the sky, which was darkened with starless black. Fine green sand lay underfoot and four brass lamps were lit at the garden's four corners, exaggerating the trees of black wood with orange fruit and the shrubs which gave off a strange scent, and highlighting too a well of stone in the garden's center. Nervous though she was, the woman felt drawn to look into the well. But fire rather than water seemed to glow deep down in it. Just then the witch appeared through a narrow door in the wall and closing it carefully behind her, she came up to the king's wife.

"Well, here you are," said the witch. "Now I will tell you a few things. Down in the well where you were staring is an old fire of earth. Should you leap into the fire you would burn to a cinder, and so would any but a little child, for this fire burns strongest when it has knowledge and wickedness to feed on, and we soon learn to be cunning and to be cruel in this world. But a child does not know much and is not very wicked usually. And the younger the child the better. Now the virtue of the fire is that it makes proof what burns in it against all harm. No weapon and no ailment can damage what has once endured the fire. Only age and natural death can take, and then they come slowly. One who rises from this fire may live two hundred years, or longer." The king's wife listened, her eyes wide and her face pale. The witch said: "I will say this, your boy is four or five years. It would have been better if he had been less, a baby newly born. As he is, the fire will pain him. Can you bear to hear his screams when he is in the well, in order that he emerge invulnerable and never to be hurt again?"

The king's wife trembled. She clasped her child tight, and he, not understanding what was said, gazed round the garden, surprised at everything.

"I can bear it," said the king's wife, "but if you trick me and he does not benefit, I will kill you."

"Oh, kill me, will you?" cackled the hag, vastly amused.

"Yes, despite your magic and everything you may do. I will tear you apart with my bare hands and rip out your throat with my teeth."

The hag grinned.

"No tricks," she said, "but I am glad you mentioned your teeth." She sidled up to Zhirem's mother, and the witch's luminous eyes shone brightly. "See here," she said, pointing at the eyes. "My sight failed me, because I was a crone, so I bought a new pair of eyes with a spell. These eyes belonged to a young man who was to die, and, in order to be free, he gave them me. 'Better be blind and live,' he said. 'Quite so,' affirmed I. Now behold how beautiful my eyes are. But oh, my wretched teeth, which ache and turn black and fall from my mouth. Your teeth, I note, are sharp and white and sound. Sharp, white and sound enough to tear out a poor old woman's throat, indeed. Give me your lovely teeth. That is my price for this service to your son."

The king's wife shuddered. But she glanced down at

Zhirem and she kissed his face and said: "Agreed. Such a charge must mean fair dealing."

Instantly the witch snatched the child. She tied a cord into his dark curling hair, and she lifted him up on to the lip of the well. Zhirem turned round desperately in fright, but before he could escape, the witch, keeping fast hold of the cord, pushed him over the well's brink. Thus, holding the cord which bound the hair of Zhirem, she dangled him into the terrible fire of invulnerability, for every part of him must be laved in the flames.

But in the well, he screamed, as the witch had said, and his cries were worse than the foretelling. The king's wife covered her ears and she screamed too, till her throat was raw, for every agony of her child seemed to pierce her.

And then at last the awful noises stopped, and the witch drew up by the cord, out of the well, a burnt and blackened, unrecognizable thing, and laid it on the green sand of the garden.

When she saw it, the king's wife snarled like a beast and ran at the witch. But the witch only laughed. "You have no fangs now to bite me with," and she showed how her mouth was abruptly full of white teeth, and the king's wife checked, finding her own mouth whole but empty. "A moment's patience," said the witch. And, just as she spoke, the burned thing on the ground began to twitch and wriggle, and the blackness of it flaked off like dirt from an ivory vessel. And presently the ivory vessel of the child lay entire and unburned there on the sand, and only the lustrous dark hair was left of the blackness, and the black lashes of the eyes. There was, too, a sort of glow about him, a kind of sheen like light on gold.

"Is he dead?" whispered the mother, for the boy was motionless.

"*Dead!*" crowed the witch. "Look where he breathes." She took the king's wife close to her son, and suddenly the witch drew a knife and plunged it, with all her strength, in Zhirem's heart.

Zhirem's mother shrieked.

"What a fool you are," said the witch, showing the king's wife how the blade of the knife had buckled and broken as if on a wall of steel, and how there was no wound in the invulnerable flesh of Zhirem.

She had been very careful, the mother of Zhirem, in leaving the camp of the scarlet tents. But, as they said among the

58

desert people, there is no jar so closely sealed that a single grain of sand cannot enter. The king had other wives and these wives other sons. One of these sons had gone out from supper to make water up against a palm tree, and while he was doing his deed, he caught sight of Zhirem's mother slipping by in the dusk with her child. There was a deal of jealousy between the wives and between the sons of the king, and this boy was no exception. He therefore took it on himself to keep a watch, and dallied near the woman's tent, and about midnight he saw her come back, and the look of her scared him. Her face was white and her hair ragged, and she hurried along with Zhirem in her arms, apparently asleep. And as she hurried she breathed through her mouth, and it seemed to the spying boy there were no longer any teeth in her gums. No sooner was she inside her tent than he ran to tell the tale to his own mother, and this wife made haste to tell the king this: That Zhirem's dam went out to sport with demons in the evening, and carried with her her demon son, and she sold her teeth for spells.

The king was made uneasy. He feared witchcraft at once, for he had never been happy about dark-haired Zhirem. The king paced about, and when the dawn swept night from the desert, he went to the tent of his favorite wife.

There he spoke harshly, accusing her with what he had heard, and when he had finished, he said he would see the inside of her mouth.

Zhirem's mother realized no lie could save her, nor the truth, but she mixed them together swiftly, and to give herself a little time to do it, she wept.

"My lord," she said, "I am afraid to say what I have done, but I see I was stupid to imagine I might hide anything from your wisdom. Be merciful to me. When I complained to you I suffered from a pain in my head, it was in fact a dreadful aching of all my teeth. I have had this affliction some while, and striven to keep it secret, and begged the gods to relieve me of it, but it was no use. At length a woman came here who was intelligent with herbs, and I let her know my anguish. And this woman said there was no help for me unless all my teeth were drawn, for, though they appeared sound, they were diseased at the roots and would eventually poison my whole body. Thus, my lord, I stole out covertly in my shame to this same woman, and let her do her work, and your son I took with me, as my only comfort in the night. And now you will cast me off because I am ugly, and I shall die of misery."

59

The king was moved with pity, and believed everything. He assured his favorite wife that he would love her still, that her beauty was not only her teeth. He chid her gently for thinking to outwit him and for risking herself and the child alone in the desert. Later, he sent for his spying son and thrashed him, and the wife who had told him the tale he gave to another king as a token of friendship between them, but adding as a proviso: "Beware this vixen's mouth, which has both teeth and falsehood in it."

Five years passed, for years will always pass, no matter what else remains. The people of the tents moved across the desert, feeding their herds at the green places, and journeying on when the green withered. Sometimes there was a dry lean season and they prayed for the rains, and sometimes the rains came in abundance, and the arid slender rivers of the desert swelled and overflowed their banks, and it was a season of plenty, for a while.

Zhirem, who had been the king's youngest son, was ten and no longer quite the youngest, though the favorite wife had borne no more. Truth to tell, she was not the favorite wife any more. A woman had been married to the king; her eyes were like rufous amber and she knew several arts and bore several sons, and she was now the favored one. But the king had no son to rival the looks of Zhirem.

The old men had given over saying his darkness was a brand of night and Night's Master, the Demon. They even talked to the boy. They were getting senile. Yet, behind their faces, there was still a shadow, something unsaid but ready, a rusty knife that could be cleaned.

Among the man children of the king mulled envy and dislike for Zhirem, also unvoiced, also ready. One who had been thrashed was fifteen now, and he went hunting. "Let this young cub come hunting too," he said, caressing the hair of Zhirem. "We will take care of him. He is too often with women, and he has never seen lions."

Zhirem was solitary, a dreamer. Once, five years before, his mother had rocked him and her tears had fallen on him. "What do you remember, beloved?" she had asked. "Do not remember anything. No fire, no pain, no garden of green sand. And even if you think of it, say nothing, nothing."

It was her sorcery that she made him forget. He had this dim memory, less than a memory, more an illusion of scalding light and scalding agony. It was a nightmare of his babyhood. He had sloughed it. Yet, impossibly, he knew it had

60

left its mark on him, it set him apart more than his coloring, more than his beauty—of which he was not aware. He understood himself as different, and did not question why, for he supposed no answer existed. He dwelt in a country where all were strangers. He met those who named themselves his brothers and his kin, but he met no one there who was like himself or who spoke the language of his soul. And so the villainies and inconsistencies of those about him did not unnerve him or even really distress him. He anticipated nothing else in this alien land.

They went to hunt lions, three of the king's sons, their three friends, and Zhirem.

Up in the rocky hills the lions were lying, golden-eyed, their bodies the color of the dust in the afternoon sun. Four of them there were, three she-cats, and a male whose mane was black as if the heat of the day had singed it. They had tasted men, all this pride, and when they smelled him on the wind, their nostrils curved open and their eyes narrowed and they rose and lashed with their tails.

What had happened was this.

The hunters had come to a spot in the rocks where a fig tree leaned by a pool of water. They knew lions were near, since this was a run for lions.

"Now you go that way with the dogs," said the thrashed son of the king, whose mother had been given to another king as his slave. He was speaking to the three friends, and he directed them off to the north. The three king's sons next pondered together. "It is a pity," said the thrashed son, "that we do not have a nice tender baby goat, a yearling, to tempt the lions this way." He and his two brothers bemoaned their lack and smote their brows at their own foolishness in not providing one. And then they seemed to have an idea. "How would this be," they said, "if we took young Zhirem here and left him where the lions would notice him? Succulent and pretty as any yearling is our darling Zhirem. Come, you would not mind it, would you, brother Zhirem? We should be close by with our spears."

Zhirem only gazed at them. The brothers laughed, and conducted him up the rocky paths.

"Now," they said, "you shall not be sad to be bound to this stone, dear little brother Zhirem?" And they bound him fast and left him there, and went to watch from a safe distance high among the rocks.

Presently four pale golden shadows crept down the hills.

61

The lions were coming with their lashing tails and their thin hot eyes.

Zhirem watched the lions. He was not afraid, yet he could not have said why he was not, for the lions were very terrible to watch, and all he had ever been told of them was to their extreme discredit.

The male lion ran to him first. It leaped like a bow or an arrow from a bow, and its claws raked him. There was a sound like tearing paper, as if the air itself were torn. Nothing but the air was torn. The lion roared and growled and jumped aside. It altered its shape in defeat and amazement, no longer a leaping active thing but planted like a marble animal, its massive head hanging. It did not try again. But the female cats made several sorties, darting, slashing. Their breath seemed red as it gushed from their red mouths, and had a red stink. At length, they also withdrew, all but one who paused to snuff at Zhirem and to lick his flesh. He felt her rough tongue but not her teeth or her claws. Her eyes seared holes in his body, but she could not. She licked him vigorously, lusting to devour, licking and sucking at him, tasting what she could not eat.

From a distance, unexplained, this licking seemed to the appalled brothers of Zhirem like an act of homage. They shook with fear. Not only did the lions not obligingly kill Zhirem, they adored him, made love to him.

The three brothers lay abject on the rocks, observing the lions conclude their worship and crawl back up the hill with their bellies low and their tails trailing. Then they rushed to Zhirem and dragged him on a horse—which sweated and rolled its eyes, for the stink of lions was thick on him—and raced homeward to the tents of their father.

It was the moment of the sun's death, and the whole camp bloody with it. In the red glow, the three brothers hastened to find their father the king, and they threw the child smelling of lions before him.

"In the hills," the brothers cried, "this Zhirem wandered away, and when we went after him, we found four lions licking him and fawning on him. Surely the demons are friends to him for his dark hair. Surely he is protected by the Master of Night as our wise men have always murmured."

The king's superstitious inclination was to credit this; simultaneously he felt he should not, for he was familiar with jealousy.

"And what do you say to this?" he shouted at Zhirem. "Do lions not harm you?"

"It is true," said Zhirem, "though I do not know why not."

These words the king interpreted as insolence. He raised his arm and struck Zhirem in the mouth. Or would have done, but the blow went nowhere, or into some other place, and the king's hand scorched him as if he had struck fire. That was enough. He needed no more.

The king called a council among the tents, his warriors, the sages of the nomads and the old ones whose age must be honoured. They sat down about the tent of the king, and the king sat on a chair of black wood set on a carpet of red and yellow, and they discussed Zhirem and how he had become. The three brothers came and told of the lions, and they constrained their three friends to speak too, as if they had witnessed it, which they had not. Then the old men cleaned their rusty knives of malice, and spoke of shadowy hair and ill-luck and the Prince of Demons. Zhirem's mother they did not call to tell them anything; she was a woman and they forgot her. Nor did they ask Zhirem to speak, only they stood him on the edge of the carpet and one threw a clod of earth at him and it fell aside without touching him, and then one threw a stone, and this too fell aside. And in the end the king took up a spear and cast it at Zhirem, and the spear splintered into a hundred fragments on the air. They all sighed then as if with relief and pleasure. Zhirem alone stared at the shattered spear with horror in his eyes.

3

A band of holy men lived in the desert at a watering place. Their house was a ruined fortress which they shared with hawks, owls and lizards.

The king had put his son Zhirem on a black horse and tied him to the saddle, and he hung bells and amulets on it to restrain the evil spirit which Zhirem contained or had been altered to. Then the king and some of his warriors set off through the early dark for the ruin, driving the black horse before them.

Zhirem, tied to the horse, had lapsed into a wild silence in which he would say nothing, but in which his eyes screamed. No longer was he merely surrounded by strangers and enemies, he had also become an incomprehensible stranger and enemy to himself. They called him demon, and demon he must

63

be. More than the casting of the spear, he recoiled from its failure to wound him. Even at this hour he did not recall the well of fire. At five years all things are wonders and mysteries, and that only one savage miracle the more. Now, driven before his father's men, glimpsing their grim hatred, in sympathy with it, it was as if he had glanced idly in a mirror and seen himself changed, with no warning, into a beast.

They reached the ruin under a moon-bright sky. Owls sat in their white rags on the towers and the holy men sat about below in their brown rags. Pride was a sin, they said, and they wore tattered garments and did not wash themselves, to prove they were not proud, but when they spoke to others they said: "We are the pure children who earn for ourselves eternal life, and whom the gods value. When you are dust, we shall stand in glory." And if any offered them gold, the ragged men would glower down their noses till the gold withered in the giver's hand. "We are too humble," said the ragged men arrogantly, "to take the riches of earth. Build no palace in the world," they bellowed, trampling through their filthy ruin. "Amass treasure in the land of the gods." And whenever they fell sick, or knew pain, they declared: "The gods have chosen to test me," as if the gods thought only of them and were constantly devising methods to be sure of their virtue. But if another, not of their order, was ill, they shouted: "This is the punishment for your abysmal wickedness and you must repent."

Yet despite this, or because of it, they claimed to be magicians and had a reputation for duels with demons—or with certain bizarre apparitions which men took to be demons.

The king went to the steps of the fortress and declared at random, for the holy men had no leader:

"Here is my son. A devil possesses him, which will not let him be hurt, and makes even lions render him homage."

Then the ragged brown owls got up from their perches and advanced on Zhirem without a word. Without a word they cut his bonds and took him down, and without a word, only his eyes calling for help or explanation, Zhirem let them take him.

"He shall stay with us one month," said a voice from among the holy men.

"Come back when next the moon is full," said another voice.

The king nodded grimly and rode away with his warriors. Zhirem was borne into the ruin.

First, they questioned him, and when he would or could not answer, they burned a blue incense which loosened his tongue. Into this answering of his, because of the incense, there filtered some reference to the well of fire. Zhirem, drugged, barely grasped what he had said, neither did his interrogators grasp it, but they thought they smelled demons. For this reason they locked Zhirem in a tiny cell without windows, and left him there for seven days without food and only a crock of scummy water to drink from. "If a common devil inhabits him and the habitation lacks comfort, then it will depart," they said. But when they dragged Zhirem from the cell on the eighth day, they perceived in his eyes the same madness they had witnessed earlier. So they scourged him to make the possession more uncomfortable, but the scourges frayed and broke in their hands. It was a pernicious devil indeed.

After this, the holy men practiced cunning. They fed the boy and let him roam where he would about the ruin and the oasis, keeping watch on him to see what he or any demon might do.

But Zhirem went to the green bank of the pool and sat there, staring blindly in the water. For fourteen or fifteen days Zhirem did simply this. When they called him to eat he came obediently; when they locked him in the cell to sleep, he made no protest. Free, he sat by the pool, and a picture more innocent or more beautiful would be hard to come on.

The holy men were moved by what they saw, despite themselves. It dawned on them, as the day dawned on the dark, that there seemed nothing evil in the male child who meditated in the bright day—which day, in any case, demons avoided.

Finally, some of the holy men went to the boy and set out before him various articles which reputedly had the knack of affrighting the powers of the night. Zhirem showed no fear; he handled the magic items and put them down. Even his eyes were quiet now, the madness and the anguish driven too deep to show. When they spoke to him, he replied gravely.

"The devil is gone," said the holy men. "Now, king's son, you have only to remain true to the gods. Remember, the world is folly, vanity and sin. The way to the gods is up a steep and slippery stair, beset with traps, with stones and naked blades."

"Do the gods then," said Zhirem quietly, "desire men should not reach them, that they litter the way with snares?"

"It is men themselves who make the snares," said the holy

65

men. "And one follows with his black and red dogs to devour those that tumble. Beware the Master of Night, the Beguiler. Remember he is ever close and has nearly taken you already."

Then a bleak swirling panic rose in the face of Zhirem.

"There, trust in heaven," said the holy men, stroking him, unmindful of their own lusts which the weeds of piety had choked but not altogether slaughtered. "Beware of the flesh and its appetites. It is women you must be careful of. Your own mother has brought you into danger, meddling with the dark. Devote yourself, body and spirit, to the gods, and the gods will save you from he that hunts in the night."

When the king rode back to the ruin, the holy men told him all they had discovered, and pronounced that the boy should be dedicated to some religious order to ensure his safety.

"But is he cured of this invulnerability, this thing which sets him apart from humanity?"

"No," said the holy men. "He is proof against weapons, perhaps proof against all unnatural forms of death. This is a facet of the spell his mother made which may not be eradicated. Yet he himself does not properly understand how he is. If he lives humbly, he may never learn and so may never seek profit or unwholesome gain from the gift. Leave him among us and we will teach him the path."

But the king, to their dejection, would not. Conscious of his royalty among the tents of the desert races, he sent Zhirem instead a year's journey to the north, to the great temple there. And with him were two horses with coffers of pearls on their backs and gold and other things which the temple liked to receive and the holy men were too humble to accept.

"If he must be a priest, he shall be a fine one, for men may know he is my son," said the king.

But Zhirem's mother, the king's wife, he cast out into the desert for her part in the spell making. Some say another people took her in, and some that she died there and a tree grew out of her bones in the middle of the empty dunes.

One day, a merchant and his servants happened to rest under this tree where they had hoped to find water, but there was none.

"Now how can a green tree grow here and no water within three miles?" the merchant asked of the air.

66

He turned pale when the air answered: "I am nourished by my own tears."

"Who says this?" demanded the merchant. Looking round, he saw his servants some way off and only the tree was left to have conversed with him. "Now, is it you?" he asked, "and if it is, then you must be a sprite."

But the tree whispered in the wind and all it said was:

"Give me news of my son."

"Tell me his name," said the merchant.

But either the tree did not recall, or it would not say any more.

Years after, it was related, another man, finding the tree, dug down to come at its source of moisture and found at last a little water, but it was salt.

4

"Pay heed, O adopted of the gods," cried the fat priest who brought Zhirem into the upper section of the children's courts. "Here is one, by name Zhirem, formerly a king's son, now dedicated to the temple, and thus your brother."

The children gawped, as children of any race or time or age will do. Thin and dark, the new child stared back at them, with a curious, gleaming, melancholy stare.

The fat priest was ugly. Like Zhirem, his place here had been bought, so he had not needed to be without blemish as the foundlings did. Now his ugly gaze was attracted from the shadowy child standing by him in the sunlight, to a child like a bit of sunlight glinting in the shadow across the court. It was the boy with reddish-yellow hair, the strange boy called Shell, an unblemished foundling.

The fat priest did not like Shell.

The glances of Shell were like bright green slivers shot from the eyes of a lynx. Very silent was Shell, hardly a word came from his mouth, only laughter sometimes, sometimes a wordless commanding yell or a melodious whistling. Crying and bawling Shell had been as a baby, when he was found on the steps and taken in. But the folk who had abandoned him had taught him no speech and no desire for speech. Half a year had elapsed, the priests said, before the brat deigned to talk at all, and now, though he read swiftly from a book in his own brain, he would not read aloud—they had beaten him and still he would not—nor pray aloud, and rarely did he answer more than "yes" or "no" or "maybe." At the same time, the whole entity of this Shell was a sort of speech. His limbs and body spoke in their movements; he ran like a deer, walked like a dancer with a balance and a grace beyond his years. He could leap high enough and snatch quick enough to steal damsons from the twisting tree above the Jade Court, and no child had ever managed that before, but had to be content with the fruit which fell or was shaken down. Even in repose, Shell's body communicated. Even with just one lynx eye, a twitch of the mouth or nostril, a flicker of the hands, like an animal or an instrument that played by itself. And there were other things. Though the temple gates were bolted and barred by night, yet Shell would get out. Somehow, over the tall sheer walls he went, into the groves beyond. The night seemed to summon him, the night and the moon, and nothing could keep him in. Even two priests acting guard by the dormitory had missed his passing and only found the empty pallet. When Shell remained indoors it was not obedience or because they had out-guessed him, merely that, for this night, he felt no urge to wander.

And when he wandered, what did he seek?

A rumor: Shell lay along the bough of a tree and whistled, and nightingales began in the wood. Another rumor: Shell ran with foxes and showed them how to get into the yards of the farms. A fact: a black cobra entered the schoolroom, inspiring terror, but Shell reached out and picked it up, making the while a sizzling noise, and the cobra lay on his shoulder and they rubbed their faces together with affection until the boy carried his pet outside and courteously directed it away among the summer grasses. One creature alone Shell seemed to fear, that was any creature which was dead. The corpse of the lizard and the mouse he fled, but did not seem to know why, and never mentioned the fear aloud. He had never seen a man's death or a woman's.

The priests viewed Shell with sensual unease, anger and disquiet, but since it was beneath them to consider such intensity might be sprung in them by a rootless child, they translated their sensations as indulgence and disapproval.

To the rest of the boys of the children's courts, Shell might easily have become victim or hero, one or the other. Yet his obliqueness, his actual *unhumanness*—which they were able perfectly to sense, as the adult and clouded priests were not—set him too far off to fit a role. Shell was enigma. The children hovered at the edges of his life and his aura, poised to adore or to hate, never quite achieving either, in limbo.

And now the children beheld another rite of which they could not partake, beheld unerringly as they beheld the oddity of Shell. In truth, the ugly priest noticed too, and did not warm to the vision.

There was one like a flame, and here was another like a darkened lamp, the lit child and the shadow child. As two opposing poles exert magnetic influence between them, so these two opposites seemed held in a tension of unseen rope which bound one to the other.

"Now," said the priest, ordering this and that done. "Attend!" snapped the priest, his weighty orders tossed like bits of paper by a heedless gale. "Behave," commanded the priest. "Venerate the gods."

The face of the shadow child, Zhirem, fixed and closed. He had been reminded of who hunted at his heels.

5

It was sunset, the sun a jar of pink bronze oil poured on the temple roofs. The older boys sat at supper in the highest court where the weather gods stood, the blue tiger and the red ram. The babies had been brought up to worship an hour before and hauled away. Now the table was there, and the older boys squealed and jabbered as they fed like a tribe of monkeys, and sometimes a lay brother tweaked their ears to obtain more ruly manners. All this the blue tiger and the red ram observed impassively, and the cool of the evening sank down with the going of the light and there came a scent of trees and incense.

Shell sat beneath the red ram. It was always now his place and none dared challenge it, though they did not exactly fear Shell. The seat of the red ram was against the wall of the court where there was a broken brick. Looking through you could see the rose sky smoking out in the groves half a mile off, and the lamps lighting in the Sanctuary of Virgins and the Women's house. The point of which being that maybe, squinting that way, you might catch a forbidden view of a woman, if you had a hawk's sight. Shell, however, always seemed inclined to watch the night coming and nothing more. He ate fruit and little else at supper, but had been known to eat, on different occasions, grass, leaves and flowers from the temple ponds. At the low table's opposite end, eating nothing, sat Zhirem.

Zhirem's head was bowed. He gazed into his water cup. His dark hair curled round his face like secrets.

"Well," said a boy close by, "if you are a king's son, why are you here? Does he not love you then, your father?"

"His mother danced with a snake in a cave," said a second boy. "She held up her skirt and the snake wriggled inside. A month later, she dropped an egg, and there was Zhirem." The boy giggled. The lay brothers were some distance from him or he would not have cared to invent such a tale out loud.

"It is worse than that," said the first boy, "I heard gossiping. Zhirem's mother sold her body to demons. Zhirem they left behind. The Prince of the Demons had no liking for him either."

Zhirem did not raise his head. Somehow, and quite quickly, he had come to comprehend at last the true maleficence of others. He thought vaguely of his mother, whom he supposed still among the tents of the king. He thought of his brothers who had left him as a snack for lions. While he was thinking, one of the boys surreptitiously tried to kick the newcomer, and this boy squealed, kicking instead—he believed—some hot adamance he had not reckoned on being under the table.

Shell rose. A sort of noisy silence descended at once—the chatter and the activity going on, yet muted, watchful. Even the adults watched, perturbed, pretending otherwise.

Shell went to the far end of the court. He reached up to the wall which sloped there and scooped something from it. He walked directly as a cat, back to the table, and the boys shuffled aside, one nursing his leg. Shell leaned past Zhirem and placed before him a white bird which had been sleeping on the wall. The bird ruffled its feathers; it whistled a single note, and bent its head to peck the bread on Zhirem's plate.

"Shell is a magician," murmured the boy who had kicked, slyly.

Shell turned and looked at this boy, looked and looked at him, until the boy's face curled up, and he stamped and ran away.

Zhirem looked only at the white bird. Shell dipped his fingers in the water bowl, and with these wet fingers he patted at the face of the other taunting boy. The boy flinched, meant to howl but reconsidered. Shell did not generally make such moves. (Once a bullying child had thrown a stone at him and Shell had found the stone and carried it about with him, and followed the bullying child wherever he went, constantly showing him the stone, saying nothing. In the end the

70

bullying child had grown hysterical, but this was two years before.) Now, the boy with the wet face also ran away, and Shell then returned to his seat by the red ram god.

Presently the white bird finished Zhirem's bread and flew off into the deepening sky.

No one spoke to Zhirem any more, for good or ill.

Three days were born and three days died in the temple after that. In the Court of Wisdom in the morning the boys bowed before the altar and tended the fires of the images there. (No longer weather gods to hold them in awe, they were for eating under when you were nine or older.) Later they learned from the books of the library or sat under the red-flowering trees to chant the rituals of the temple. They fed the fish in the Sacred Pond and trouped to their noon meal. In the afternoon they walked about the inner lawns with their teachers.

"Do not let the richness of the temple confound you," instructed the teachers. "A lily must be beautiful in order that the bee visits her, and the temple must be fair to attract the favor of gods and men alike. Dress in good linen and wear rings, but be humble. Humility is in the heart not on the hand."

Two lines carved themselves between the brows of Zhirem, but the teachers did not reckon that children of ten and eleven should debate, and feigned unnotice.

Shell patrolled the lawn, lynx-like. He ate a flower in a cruel, loving, beautiful way, as if he ate some small animal he had caught. Sometimes he moved by Zhirem and sometimes not. Zhirem glanced at him. The superstition of the desert nudged him. He looked swiftly to see if Shell had a shadow. Shell had. Shell saw, and laughed like a fox laughing.

Dusk came to the third day and killed it with a blue sword. Always it was the same, and the day, always taken by surprise, never escaped, but bled and swooned and shut its eyes in blackness.

Zhirem woke because a shape had touched his forehead with two fingers, and said: "Come."

"Where?" said Zhirem, who, even in sleep, had somehow anticipated this.

"Into the night," said Shell.

Zhirem considered night. A dull blade grazed his mind: a journey to a garden of sand, a terrible something without name, a journey back in a woman's arms, and night in all of it, like poison in a cup.

71

"No," said Zhirem.

And Shell turned without a sound, and went away. And then, before he reasoned, Zhirem was on his feet and going after.

Shell moved soft, but Zhirem not much less so, for the desert too had taught him lessons.

Outside, the court was dim, though the moon was rising, a huge late low yellow moon with a single veil of cloud it had thrown back from its face. None kept guard any more. They ignored Shell's wandering for they could not prevent it.

Up the wall they slid, the amber cat and the shadow cat, up by way of tiny faults, tiny loops of creeper strong enough to aid a thin agile child, over the top where iron dragons aided them further, and leaped out, winged with hair, into the velvet nothing of dark.

They dashed onto the black carpet and through the curtaining of leaves.

"I will show you a fox's house," said Shell.

They roamed the groves and the woods. Only they and the night things were about. To Zhirem it was curious, eventful, but to Shell it was oddly and obviously familiar as the day.

They sat under a tree and ate its fruit which had a taste of night, a black hidden taste.

"Night is best," said Shell, "and better when the moon rises." He rarely, rarely spoke so much. "But I do not remember why."

"I too have a memory I cannot remember," said Zhirem. "I feel it will be safer to forget."

"I should like to remember," said Shell, "and when I saw your hair, which is dark, I almost did remember."

"The priests are liars?" asked Zhirem.

Shell laughed softly. "Yes."

"All men, perhaps."

"All."

They drank at the stream, and each noticed the other reflected as they drank, each looking at each rather than himself, for the first time truly aware of another human in the world apart from themselves, another human who was as real as they.

6

Years, which in childhood and youth seemed the longest, brought in that slow season rapid changes to flesh and heart and brain. Six years to the elderly priests were static yet passed swift as adders. But in those same six years a child could alter to a man.

The old priests sat in the afternoon court. They ate one meal and dreamed of the next. When it arrived, there was always something amiss; too much red pepper, too little black, the walnuts were improperly stewed and the fowl over-rich. It was a love affair between each man and a full dish. But to the young men, the food was allayed hunger, was fuel, and to some, not even that.

The old priests squirmed and muttered to themselves as one of the young priests went by, censorious as they always were of the young, but especially censorious of this one.

The youth was seventeen, straight and lean among the well-fed bodies of his brothers. You could not miss him, for his dark hair hung curling down his back over the yellow garment. Besides, he went barefoot, soles hard from a desert, but disdaining the sandals and slippers of the temple, aping the wretched poor outside. When he turned, his face was like a god's head on a coin, copper-gold as a coin from the sun, and his eyes were like cool water, a color to quench thirst.

"They say," said one of the old priests, "he will accept only three robes, and washes them himself."

"They say," said a second, "the silver torque the High Priest presents to all the boys when they are initiated, this ingrate gave to an idiot farmer who had lost his hand and was begging at the gate."

"*I* say," said a third, "he is immodest with his extravagant ways. He takes it on himself to do heaven's work."

"Just so," said the first old priest, "and he has been reprimanded. 'Do not presume to do heaven's work which will be carried out in due course,' they tell him. And the upstart answers: 'If heaven is lazy, I am not.' "

"Ah!" cried the old priests, and, "Shameful! And there is the other mischief," they added.

The other mischief had just come from the Hour of Duty that all young priests of sixteen must offer each day to the gods—burnishing their statues and the statues of their prophets, fair-copying scrolls and books, overseeing the gods' cooks or gardeners, trimming the sacred thousand candles of the Shrines. The other mischief was also barefoot, also slight and straight of build. The yellow robe and the yellow-red hair made a shining fire elemental of this youth, who truly was brighter than any of the jewels he did not wear.

The old priests licked their dry old lips watching the two young priests meet and walk on together on their bare hard feet.

"There is something should be looked into," grumbled the old priests, brief coals smouldering in the musty chambers of appetite as they haphazardly conjured up for themselves the phallic notions of what went on between Zhirem and Shell, those sinful and prohibited things the temple denied to its sons. Of which, in fact, neither was guilty.

Strange, perhaps, with two so beautiful and at that age of mutability, shut in a kind of prison with no women, with none, even if there had been women, to be fairer than they. They loved each other, yes. But it was this way with them: they had grown from children to men in constant company with each other. They were at ease with each other and with no one else, and currently asked no more of each other than that. In addition, neither Zhirem nor Shell was quite human.

For Shell, it was, paradoxically, the wicked innocence of the Eshva still on him and in him that kept him from the temple's form of sin. To the Eshva everything was sensual, sexual; moonrise was an orgasm of the heart, the eye. A touch was love, was fire. Besides, everything was of interest, part of the dream. They had desire, but did not only live through this. Eshva lusted after the music of a look, and they never questioned nor sought to analyze the sensations that poured over them, only to prolong and enjoy. If flames woke in the vitals of Shell, and probably they did, untroubled and unhurried, he did not seek to quench them or find out their actual source. Time had no proper meaning to the Eshva; Shell had not yet recollected that to men, time was everything.

And for Zhirem, it was his own beginning that walled him off. The unremembered pain and screaming, the broken spear, the month with the holy men; their counsel. He feared to remember. Someone hunted at his heels, must not catch up. Pleasure of the flesh, any pleasure, daunted him, though he did not completely know this. The opulence of the yellow priesthood he rejected with a contempt born of that concealed fear. He wanted to be angry, to cleanse himself

74

with anger and denial, he wanted also sometimes to be quiet, to drop down like a stone into the dark pools of his own thought and to lie there, drowned and at peace, without the words and customs of men to remind him he too was a man. And both these things, the forum for anger and action, the quiet peace, both Shell gave him. Shell who seldom spoke, but Shell who listened, Shell who could not be constrained but found for them the shades of the nights to be free in and to be silent in. Shell, who gave so much, could not be metamorphosed into the antithesis of Zhirem's wish—a symbol of the slippy stair into the mouth of hounds where the Master of Night, that Lord of Darkness, the Demon, waited.

"Tomorrow is the first day of the Festival of the Spring Moon," said Zhirem as they walked through the colonnades. "I have been elected one of those who are to make the journey to the eastern villages. I think they dared not refuse me. I mean to do some good, and said so. Why should I have had all this mage-training and apothecary training if I am not to use it? What is this place," he added, "but a house for rich men to wallow in like swine? And do the gods resemble the men?"

Shell opened his fist and showed the red bead which meant he also had been elected for the eastern journey. His eyes, meeting Zhirem's, said, with irony: "You and I outside the temple? They have never kept us in."

Another strolled by, a fat young man named Beyash, who wore an earring of jasper he had been given for making twenty fair copies of a holy text.

"Eastward? I too," he said. "We shall see some women at last, if only the sick ones. But then, you pretty birds have flown out and seen women before. Whom do you meet in the groves at night? That is, when you do not invent tunes for each other."

Zhirem stared him down, a glower of steel fathered in him by the holy men of the desert. He said nothing—when not alone with Shell, like Shell, Zhirem seldom talked. His angry tirades were shut within his skull, expressed in cold and level tones if ever spoken. Probably he did not, even now, believe in those about him. He had got the habit, in defense, of blaming them for their alienness to himself, of being angered by them in order to react to their existence.

But fat young Beyash, lowering his eyes, said: "Pardon me, Zhirem, I only joked with you. But you had better be warned. They tell of a dreadful woman who has come to live in the eastern villages. A woman who sells her loins for money."

75

"Then I pity her," said Zhirem.

"Oh, do not. She is an enticer and a blasphemer. She paints her face. And she loves to tempt the young and the fair. Ah, Zhirem, Zhirem—"

Unnoted, Shell had made a small sound between his lips. A bird passing in the air suddenly opened its bowels over the startled head of the fat young priest.

Leaving him squawking, Zhirem and Shell moved on.

"What gives you power over beasts?" Zhirem said. They were walking along the road east in the forenoon, in a cloud of white dust raised by the wagons and the donkeys the other young priests rode. Here and there a youth was on foot, but only to loosen his stiffness. The two barefoot mad ones alone meant to walk all the way. "But no," said Zhirem, "I always ask you this, and you do not properly know why or how."

Shell smiled, dreaming Eshva smile. He looked at Zhirem with the innocent yet brimming total of love in his eyes. The eyes said: "If I knew, you I would tell."

Soon after, the first village came in sight.

The workers ran from the fields and vineyards and the women and children from the houses. They bowed low to the young priests. They brought them wine with honey in it and white bread baked specially. They had pinched and saved and bought a silver dish for the temple. The priests received everything with lordly grace. They blessed the village desultorily. Were there any sick? No, praise the gods, only the old man with sores. These would heal. They did not expect the young priests to deal with so irksome a chore.

Zhirem strode like wind-blown smoke through standing corn.

"Where is this man?" he asked in a voice of iron.

Nervously, two or three women directed him.

"Look, the dog, he wants to get among the bitches," crowed the young priests behind their hands. But the women were no beauties. Hard work and hot summers and cold winterings had seen to that. For the girls, they were kept from the sight of the young priests by order of the temple.

Zhirem entered the hut where the old man lay, crying in his hurt. Zhirem absorbed this hurt into himself. It moved him. He too had a memory of harm, though harm no longer came to him. He set to work with gentleness and intelligence, exhilarated by reality, determined to be one with it.

Shell had not followed him. Shell was no healer. Shell sat beneath a tree, playing a wooden pipe he had made, eyes half shut. A new feeling arose in him also, as he gazed through his lashes at the hut. Shell, Eshva-fashion, swam in the new feeling, basked in its bitter-sweetness. Jealousy.

The young priests departed, garlanded with the flowers of the first village. Zhirem had not emerged from the hut, so they left him. When he came out, only Shell remained, with the amazed children staring at him from the shrubs as he played the pipe; the men had returned to their work and the women were too awed to speak to the priest alone.

Zhirem and Shell continued along the road, following the dust cloud in front.

Zhirem brooded, his eyes luminous. Presently he said, "I consider I must leave the temple. I think I have found what I must do." Shell watched him attentively. "When I had done what I could for the old man," said Zhirem, "I felt a shadow fall behind me, a burden leave me. And something passed between us, the sick one and I."

"Yes," said Shell aloud.

An hour later they reached the second village where the rest of the priests had already been welcomed. A noon meal was being served, fruit and cakes, and more wine going round. A woman had brought her child which had fits, but she had had to wait. Shortly, from being made to sit in fright and the sun, the child had a fit. The priests, displeased, looked away. Zhirem, who had just come up, went straight to the child, and put his forefinger between its teeth so it should bite him in the spasm rather than its own tongue. When the fit passed, Zhirem picked the child up and rocked it. There was a strange tenderness on his face. Not actually feeling for the child, but at something waking in himself. Part astonishment, past laughter, partly pain. He took the mother aside and instructed her in the value of herbs, and then to the wagons where he had the temple servants parcel these commodities up for her. The mother, dry and brown like the other women, started to cry. As if some well-spring in himself filled from her emotion, tears dropped from the eyes of Zhirem.

The remaining sick of that village were brought to him.

And at the next three villages, were brought to him.

The young priests mocked him, but the people ran to him, ran to him before even he talked to them or stepped forward, as if they sensed or beheld some sign on him that he had come for them, and not simply on a journey to get veneration and gifts.

In the dusk, the priests entered the day's last village, where they were to be housed that night in a little shrine. Lamps

77

shone from every lintel and men with torches and bells escorted them. The shrine had been swept clean and adorned with flowers, incense burned and embroidered carpets hung on the wall. The herdsmen had killed a sheep and a cow to be the young priests' dinner, and now roasted this meat in the court-yard under the cinnamon trees. The red fires leapt toward the blue night, and the village people were singing over the wall as if they were glad their food was to be eaten and their gold coins taken away.

In the street, in the light of the lintel-lamps, Zhirem had carefully cleansed the lids of several children with sore eyes. An old woman shambled to him with an ache in her back. She told Zhirem it was better the instant he touched her. Perhaps it was.

Shell, playing the wooden pipe, watched Zhirem return slowly into the temple court. He had bathed in the river, and water drops hung in his hair.

"Yes," Zhirem said, sitting by Shell under the cinnamon trees. "Yes."

"Now I wish," said Shell, speaking, unexpected as his speaking always was, "now I wish I had fallen sick."

Zhirem sighed and closed his eyes.

"I will sleep three nights in this one night," he said, as if he had not heard.

Just then there came a commotion at the shrine gate, a sound of male altercation, while over the wall the village women stopped singing and bawled curses. The herders shifted at their roasting fires. The priests stared.

For into the courtyard came a woman. She wore a dress of crimson and saffron, a necklace of white enamel, and on her arms were bangles of glass, red and green and pale purple, but on her ankles were bangles of gold. Her hair was the color of new bronze and curled as a fleece, and it fell to her waist; brown and slim she was as the women of the villages, but beautiful as they were not. In her ears were bells of silver which chimed lightly as she moved. She had rouged her face to a young sunrise, and her eyes were darkened with kohl. Many village men, inside the court and out, were shouting, but none tried to stop her. presently, even the shouting ended.

Then she looked about at the young priests who stared, and she swayed herself a little so she caught the firelight, and the flames shone through her thin garments showing how her breasts were fashioned, and they were fashioned well.

"I am the harlot," said she. "Who will buy?"

78

Not a word. Though the herders and the men in the gate were savage and sullen. Though the young priests paled or flushed or fidgetted. Eyes grew hot, not only from reflected fire.

"See," said the harlot, showing herself some more. "Like the temple, I too have homage paid me and rich gifts given me." Then she walked up to the young priests, and along the line of them and through the groups of them. They smelled the incense in her dress, not like the incense of the shrine. "Ah," said she, "for shame, I thought the priests would bless me. I thought they were healers, and would heal me of the wounds I receive at the hands of these village clods when they lie down with me. Behold, all are afraid to touch me now. One touch brings desire."

Someone got to his feet and shouted. It was Beyash, the fat young priest with the jasper earring. "Harlot you call yourself, and harlot you are."

"So I am," smiled the harlot. "I have ever been truthful."

"Then, harlot, take yourself away," ranted Beyash. His face and his lips were moist; he breathed fast, and glared at her with all his sight, and breathed faster, and said: "You profane the sacred court."

"No, no," said the harlot. "I am here to be healed." And slowly she slid down the thin silk of her dress and bared one burnished shoulder and one wicked breast. There, on the swelling ripeness of her breast was a dark blue bruising made by some man's teeth.

"Note how it is with me," said the harlot. "Take pity—will you not smooth into this mark a salve, will you not rub me with your holy fingers, charitable priest?"

Beyash's eyes were popping in his fat.

The harlot laughed.

"But no. I have heard there is another here who is more kind than you. A dark-haired man, slender and beautiful as the new moon's shadow on the earth. This man I will entreat. This man will be gentle to me."

She had already discovered where Zhirem sat under the trees and fixed him with her gaze. Now she went to him and stood over him, and next she kneeled before him and shook her beautiful hair about her.

"Indeed," she murmured, "they say the brushing of your hand alone is a cure, beloved. Let us discover." And she took up his hand and laid it on her breast. "Ah, beloved," said the woman, "men bring me gold, but you I would pay to lie with. And if I lay with you, I would give over my sinful ways.

79

Your eyes are level as pools at dusk, but you tremble. Tremble for me, then, tremble for me, my heart's darling."

Zhirem took his hand from her. There was something terrible and desolate in his face she did not properly see, though his eyes had altered their shape to the shape of yearning. He said softly to her: "You are too fair to live as you do. What devil drove you to this life?"

"A devil called man," said she. "Come, change me then."

"You must change yourself."

"Into whatever it pleases my lord." And she leaned close and whispered: "Two hundred paces south beyond the village, the poplars grow by the old well. My house is there. I will leave a lamp burning and watch for you. Bring me nothing but your beauty and your loins."

Zhirem did not answer. The harlot rose and drew together her dress. Shaking her mane, she crossed back through the court; smiling she went out through the gate. The din began again outside, then faded away.

"This is a foul negligence!" screamed Beyash. "This village will be called to account for permitting such a she-beast to dwell here."

"Her house is two hundred paces from us," the herders excused themselves. "The rich men come to her, and it is hard for us to fight the rich men."

"The temple shall fight them. Her house shall be burned and the woman stoned. She is an abomination."

In the black shadow of the cinnamon trees, Shell's pipe went on a moment, playing, as it had continued to play the whole while. All had grown accustomed to it, as to the sound of the night breeze in the foliage. Now, the pipe abruptly ceased.

"When do you go to her?" a voice asked from the shadow, Shell's voice for Zhirem alone. But maybe it was no voice, only the silence, only the rustle of leaves.

Zhirem answered, "I do not."

He rested against a tree. His eyes were yet that particular shape. His hand, which had lain on the woman's breast, lay wooden on the ground.

"Beyash will go," said Shell, or the leaves.

"One should go and lift her from the pit she is in, not lie down with her in the pit."

"Go then, lift her."

Zhirem turned, but Shell sat immobile, his lips closed like the carved lips of an image which never speaks, never meddles.

A herder brought a dish of food. Zhirem ate listlessly and sparingly, as always. Shell ate the red fruit in the dish, biting the pith of it cruelly.

Beyash was not done with complaining but his complaints were more distant. The other young priests drifted into the shrine, tired by food and wine and travelling, eager to be supine and there consider the woman . . .

Zhirem and Shell remained alone, and the roasting fires sank into red cinders and into gray smoke; the herders slunk away. A night bird sang in the eaves of the shrine. The crescent moon rose like a broken ring.

"I remember," said Zhirem, "how we climbed the wall when we were children and ran about in the night. In the desert, the night is a naked thing as day is naked, but here everything is secret between the trees and the grasses."

Zhirem set off for the courtyard gate. Shell got up, paused in a feline stretching, and followed him.

In the village nothing stirred. The windows were black and no one looked out. The villagers were afraid to see any going by, any young men in yellow temple robes going by on the track toward the old well where poplars grew.

Where the village ended a track turned south before the road began. At this spot, Zhirem said: "Why will you lead me this way?"

Shell glanced at him. The glance said, "No one leads; you are already on this way."

"No," said Zhirem. And he turned and walked northward up the hill above the village, among the wild flowering olives there.

Shell did not travel with him. Shell loped along the track toward the well.

It was not that he desired the woman. It was that he had seen that Zhirem desired her, that the man's lust in Zhirem, smothered all this while, had woken.

Shell burned. The soft flames which had always lapped him, unanalyzed, now gored and snapped. Eshva-like still, he ran to the fire rather than away. Envy was a green blade in his side; he twisted to enjoy the piercing of it. Love was a violet veil over his eyes, sadness changing the color of the world. First the weakness and illness of men had been able to draw the beloved away, now a woman could do it. But a woman was less abstract, easier to contend with. Then, go and watch the woman, twist the green blade in the wound, learn it all and more.

Her house, near to the well, was finer than the village

81

houses. It was built of stone and the door was wood. Through the ornate iron lattice of the lower window came the faint glow of a lamp.

Shell slid from the shadow to the window, noiseless, and stared unblinking at the lattice with his lynx's eyes.

The beautiful harlot sat at her cosmetics table, before a bronze mirror, combing scent through her bronze hair, and she yet smiled to her reflection in the mirror, lulled by the combing and by what she thought of.

The flame gnawed in Shell. He saw how the lamp painted the woman, the quiver of the slender muscles of her arms, the glint of gold falling from the golden comb into the fleece of her hair.

Shell left the window. He circled about the house. Once, twice, three times he circled it, as the animal circles the human dwelling, cautious, curious, fascinated, meaning no good yet with no actual plan of wrong-doing.

Now the harlot did not hear him, nor did she glimpse him. But she sensed that he, or someone, was there.

She came to the wooden door and opened it, and stepped out boldly with the lamplight.

"Who is there?" she called. "Approach. I will do you no injury."

Shell was a shadow, a tree, invisible.

But from the poplars, another answered. "It is I," and into the lamplight sneaked Beyash.

"Oh, is it you?" said the harlot. "I had hoped for another. Well, what do you want? To upbraid me some more?"

"I was too harsh," said Beyash, edging closer. "How do I know what has forced you to this sin? Perhaps the gods sent you to me in order that I might redeem you."

"Thus and so," said the harlot. "My price is high. Do you have my price?"

Beyash came edging on. He edged right to the harlot.

"Let me see," he whispered, "let me see your breast again."

"What, only one breast? I have two."

"And are both of them hurt?" whispered Beyash, shuddering and licking at his lips.

"Depending on what you will give me, they may be."

Beyash fumbled in his sleeve. He brought out a shiny thing—a silver cup one of the villages had presented to the temple, and in the cup was a handful of small jewels another of the villages had given.

"Offerings," said the harlot, "will these not be missed?"

"There are so many offerings," hoarsely murmured Beyash.

"I can intimidate the clerk who keeps tally. He has committed a sin with his sister and is in my power, for I know of it."

"So many offerings, you say," mused the harlot. "You shall bring me something else tomorrow, perhaps."

"If you will," said Beyash.

The harlot pointed to her door.

"Enter then."

Beyash did as she said, stumbling as if drunk.

When the door shut on them, Shell stole again to the window. Beyash had seized the breasts of the harlot, and grasped them and felt of them as if he would commit their form to his recollection. Presently, she put him from her and slipped off her dress. The color of her was like dark honey, and she knotted up her tresses with enamel pins, and all her body was to be seen, her narrow waist and her wide hips which were strong and smoothly hard as the quarters of a lioness. She took from a chest a switch of horsehair, and opening the robe of Beyash she tickled him with this switch and then smote him with it. Beyash cried out, and his member rose from his loins like a pole. Then the woman made him sit upon the couch, and she split her thighs to kneel with her legs either side of him and sat upon his lap in such a way that she took him inside her. After this, she danced on him as a snake dances, and Beyash kneaded her with his hands and writhed as if he could not be quiet, till suddenly his face appeared over her shoulder like the face of one who has gone mad, very red, with just the whites of the eyes revealed and the mouth wide open and the spit running out, and from this mouth came a burst of howling. Having howled, Beyash fell back as if dead on the couch. The woman instantly left him and went away out of sight, and there was the sound of water being used in a basin.

Shell leaned on the wall, trembling with an odd revulsion and with the lasciviousness which now had found a name within himself. He made no move to leave the window. He observed Beyash as he recovered, now sitting up again, now fastening his robe. The face of Beyash had turned from its congested excitement to a nervous pallor. At length, he said:

"You will not tell?"

"I?" said the woman, out of sight of the window at her washing. "Whom could I tell but your temple? What could I tell but that you came here to redeem me?"

"You must not," said Beyash.

"I will not," said the woman, "if you go to the treasure

83

wagons and bring me something of gold, which does not weigh less than your two great fatty hands."

"Not gold," said Beyash, "I dare not take gold."

"You dare," said the woman, "you are very brave. You dared steal silver and gems. You dared come to the harlot's house and put up your tool inside her. You will bring me gold, brave priest."

Beyash got to his feet.

"You are a whore and full of vileness," he said. "You led me here. I never meant to visit you. You are a sorceress and have bewitched me. I am not answerable."

"If I could witch one here," said she, "it would have been another than you, you hog. Tomorrow, I go to the temple."

Through the window, Shell perceived how Beyash crept to the cosmetics table, how he caught up the bronze mirror there and, turning about, ran with it across the room and out of sight of the window. Out of sight, there came a sound, dull and indescribable, then a clatter of light objects falling, and then another fall, like heavy silk thrown on the ground.

A moment more, and Beyash reappeared. His face was once again excited, though still pale. He no longer had the mirror, but he picked up the silver cup and the jewels he had given the harlot, and returned them to his sleeve. He gazed about as if to be sure he had not forgotten anything. Then he opened the door and came out stealthily, and shut the door stealthily. And then he saw Shell leaning by the window.

Beyash cried out to the gods. His legs loosened and he sank to his knees.

"Ah, my brother, Shell—did you see? She was a sorceress. The gods directed my arm, I had no choice. I was possessed by the vengence of heaven. Ah, Shell, say nothing. We have been friends—for our friendship's sake, say nothing." Shell only looked at him, impervious, it seemed, dreadful, pitiless. "Where is Zhirem?" chattered Beyash. "Yes, he will be near if you are about. Do not tell Zhirem. Tell no one."

Shell, his caution put aside, aroused and simultaneously drained by the act he had witnessed, confused and alerted by the act he had not, looked implacably back at the quivering jelly of Beyash, till it dragged itself up and tottered away.

When he had gone, Shell went into the house of the harlot, turning toward the fire, rather than away, inquisitive as the Eshva, yet, at last, dimly afraid, as a man would be.

There was a screen of painted wood, and behind the screen a scatter of enamel pins on the rugs. Among the pins lay the woman, and in her hair lay the mirror with which Beyash had broken her neck.

Shell stood there, looking at death. Shell feared Death, who did not know? The live cobra he caressed, the dead mouse he avoided. Never before had Shell seen a human corpse. But no, that was not true. *Once* before he had seen. She had lain straight and cold in her black dress. Her skin had turned azure, and she had not heeded the child who had been locked up with her in the tomb. The child had wept, and Death had come in person. The child had seen Lord Death. The child had screamed.

Shell remembered. His eyes were sprinkled with blackness and his soul with terror. Half blind he ran from the house and cleaved the night with his passage, trying to lose himself. He had forgotten everything but Death. He ran by the village and up the hill, crazy as the beast which flees from fire.

7

A pool gleamed among the wild olive trees. Some of the green-white flowers had rained into it. Attracted by water, as were many born of a desert people, Zhirem had come to the pool and sat down there. Staring into it, between the flowers, Zhirem thought of the ruin and the holy men and the pool he had sat by then, struggling with his spirit, struggling to erase memory or to recapture it, struggling to be free of a darkness or a light. He thought of the woman too, and of the thing he must not have and of the Master of Night—who no longer was real to him, only a symbol of the blackness that crouched within his own ego.

Abruptly a figure rushed from the trees on the other side of the pool. It appeared very nearly noiselessly, doubly startling because, known as it was, it gave no sign of knowing. Shell, confronting Zhirem, regarded him with wide open eyes that had no sight in them. Zhirem got up, the mantle of self briefly dropping from him. "What is it?" Zhirem asked. As with the sick ones in the villages, this air of helpless panic moved him. Shell, who had always been real to him, became more real. "What is it, my brother?" said Zhirem gently.

"Death," said Shell. The word shattered some vessel within him. He put his hands over his face and screamed.

This was not Shell. The aura of Shell had been always one

of volatility, or of an unhuman introspection, sufficiently re-mote it could not weep or despair or rend itself.

Zhirem went around the pool.

"After all," he said, "perhaps there are demons abroad tonight."

Shell took his hands from his eyes. He wept, in everything else, as the Eshva wept, even now with their sensuous surrender. Instinctively Shell sensed how he was gliding toward some goal; he let the tears continue and did not speak.

"You say death," Zhirem said. "Whose death?"

"Death is everywhere," said Shell. He approached Zhirem and rested his head on the shoulder of Zhirem, among the dark curling hair which, as it had the desert people, had re-minded Shell from the first of demon kind. Even now, the presence of Zhirem consoled Shell. He felt terror let him go, felt Death withdraw with the swirling of a substance like white wings. Here was life. Shell put his arms about Zhirem. The contact of their bodies, similar in their male construction, was familiar to each without familiarity.

Zhirem did not embrace him. They had seldom touched, when they had the touches had been Shell's, generally the Eshva caress of eyes or breath. To Zhirem, this sensation of flesh on flesh was a threat and only that. He had touched the ill ones more readily. They had not seduced, were not able to. He had been safe with them. He thought of the woman, the flesh of Shell seemed to become her flesh, and nails of cold or heat shot through him.

"Enough," Zhirem said, and drew away. Am I a vine-stock for you to hang on? Will you tell me who scared you, or will you not?"

Shell blinked. Recognition was back in his eyes, and more than that.

"I will tell you—later," Shell said. He turned. He walked toward the trees again. "Wait for me," he said. He vanished between the shadows. Zhirem would wait, waiting as he was, perpetually, for his own soul to find him.

Among the trees, Shell ran. He leaped and stretched him-self. Death and fear had become subsidiary. He was brimmed with a wonderful insanity of life and of knowing. He knew he had reached a brink of magic, of marvel. He had only to fling himself forward and he must tumble into it. Forward he flung himself then. He ran, and he caught up with the Eshva among the olive trees, caught up with their wraiths and the months he had spent with them. Caught up, as Zhirem had not, with himself.

The figure clung to the tree. Spring was in the tree and in the clinging figure. The bark was wet from tears the figure had shed, for there had been pain this time, after so long, pain in the changing, yet pleasure too.

Gradually, sighing, the figure unwound itself from the tree.

The moon was down, yet the stars gave light.

Hair the color of apricots, the eyes of cats, they were the same. The young beard had shed itself in a pollen of fine gold. The face was smooth now, smooth as if without pores. The hands dipped, alighted, slid across the silver skin. Different now, this body. Not the body of a youth. The loins were indrawn and passive, the torso, rising from the slender indentation of the waist, had flowered into the shallow beautiful high breasts of a maiden. A girl's body and a girl's face.

The girl bent and took up the yellow priest's garment she had discarded as a man, and folded herself into it like the white tongue in the flame's heart.

It was spring, and Simmu had remembered.

Hours had elapsed. Zhirem slept between the roots of the trees beside the pool, and when the soft wind blew, the green-white flowers rained also on him. He was accustomed to sleep out of doors. Among the tents, and with Shell, he had rarely done otherwise. Accustomed he was, too, to the light step of Shell, for Shell came and went in the night as did the others who were night creatures. So, Zhirem did not wake.

He woke, disturbed yet lulled, when a cool mouth came to drink at his.

Then a second waking dawned upon the first. Zhirem lifted himself to his elbow and stared. A girl lay naked beside him, also on her elbow, gazing back at him. A girl made out of silk and summer grass and polished ivory, but a girl with eyes and hair that belonged to another. Zhirem was afraid. Yet he was stirred, she had stirred him before he woke—his flesh asked for her even as his mind denied. And now she set her hand lightly on his ribs, a touch unmoving and almost guileless, but it sprang through him like a spear.

"I am a dream," said the girl, in a girl's clear voice. "I am *your* dream. How can I be otherwise, seeing I am the youth, Shell, and also a maiden. Seeing I come to you as the woman did, yet I am not she. Thus, then, Zhirem, take what is yours. Men cannot order their dreams. The gods do not blame you. You cannot sin with a dream, there is no evil."

Then she lay back, and lowered her lids and said no more, nor touched him again.

87

Zhirem could not look away. He had been parched and now here was drink. One of the green flowers drifted over them and settled on her breast. Zhirem put out his hand to brush the flower aside, but his hand lay presently where the flower had lain. He saw she was Shell and also a maiden, and he felt the beat of her heart beneath his hand, and it spoke his name to him and called to him. So he knew she was a dream, and he put from himself all the dry counsel and the warnings, and he set his mouth on hers.

And the maiden circled his waist with her arms, and drew him down.

8

In his distraction and fright, Beyash had lurched quite a way toward the village, before he thought better of it.

The shrine was no longer a sanctuary to Beyash, Beyash who had coupled with an unclean woman, Beyash who had slain that woman. Beyash, whose deeds—worse than all—had been witnessed.

However, Beyash reasoned with himself, there had been one witness and no more, and that witness the oblique and much mistrusted youth, Shell.

Beyash had found it effortless to kill the woman; natural, almost. He had struck her with a sense of righteousness and power, silencing her puny threats. He had never before realized that he was capable of such swift decision, such unhesitating ruthless action. He wondered what it would be like to kill Shell. After all, Zhirem had not been with him, and was probably not very near. And Shell wandered aimlessly about in the night. Yes, it was expedient and the gods were counselling Beyash. Find and slay Shell—a fragile strengthless boy he looked, and nothing but a pest, good riddance—then maybe conceal the body. Tomorrow, with Shell gone and the harlot dead, the conclusion would be obvious to all. Shell had lain with the bitch and slaughtered her and then fled.

Thus, Beyash retraced his steps.

Some while he searched, unavailingly. Then, in the moist earth beyond the well, he made out the mark of Shell's bare foot pointing northeast. Now Shell could not have returned to the village, or he would have passed Beyash. Therefore Shell had run up the hill among the wild olives. Beyash accordingly started that way, as noiselessly as he was able.

It was the starlit gleaming of the pool which made him look. More than the pool he saw. Yet he saw from a distance, and distance hid a great deal from him. Change it hid, and the impossible. Beyash crouched among the trees, imagining he spied on Zhirem and Shell, and thought Shell was no longer alone and convenient prey, yet he was very vulnerable. It took only a few moments for Beyash to reorganize his plan. He liked the second plan better, he considered it was more subtle.

Presently Beyash hurried down to the sleeping village, and into the wagon where the clerk of the tally was snoring, who had once sinned with his sister.

When Zhirem woke, it was with a sense of consolation and of ease. The pale new sun rayed green and greenly gold between the olive boughs, the world smelled fragrant. At first Zhirem did not remember his dream. But the dream came drifting to him, from the morning rather than his own brain. Remembering, he sat upright, his eyes wide, a kind of nausea overcoming him. Yet it had been a dream and simply that, of this much the bizarre details of the dream—which had seemed so real—assured him. And no one, not even Shell, lay beside him now. Beautiful the earth was, and fresh and perfect. Superstitiously, his soul told Zhirem that if he had broken all his vows in the night, some blemish would have shown itself to him in the landscape, on the spring air.

Calmed, yet not entirely himself again, Zhirem set off for the shrine. He did not discover Shell on the way, and partly hoped he would not happen on him. Shell had been the pivot of the dream. Zhirem did not suppose he could meet the eyes of Shell. The shame of self the holy men of the desert had planted in Zhirem had come to flower.

So Zhirem walked down into the village, and this is what he confronted there in the cool golden morning: a blemish after all.

The young priests were milling in the street by the shrine gate, and the temple servants who had ridden with them. The villagers were close at hand, their faces sharp and eager and fearful, as if they waited for some miraculous show. At the front of the crowd, in a space on the earth track, stood the tally clerk who kept account of the gifts presented to the temple by the villages. The clerk shook and shivered and wrung his hands. His eyes were large with sorrow. Not far off, Beyash was conversing with his brother priests, but seeing Zhirem coming, Beyash ceased talking. And the face of Beyash was like the faces of the villagers, eager and afraid. It was another who spoke first, a red-headed young priest a year older than the others, who fancied he should take charge of them, and to whom Beyash had gladly and flatteringly deferred.

"Zhirem," called the red-headed priest, "here is a strange thing. An item has been stolen from the wagons of gifts."

Zhirem stopped walking. He stood in the street, saying nothing, looking at them.

"It is well known," went on the red young priest, "that even the robbers of this pious land reverence the gods and dare not steal from the temple. Who then, Zhirem, do you guess would commit such a blasphemy?"

Zhirem went on saying nothing. But now, abruptly, he felt a stone at his back, and ropes tying him to the stone, and he smelled lions.

"He will not answer," concluded Beyash.

"The clerk shall speak," said the red priest.

The clerk hung his head.

"Do not tremble," coaxed Beyash. "It is your duty to the honesty and religious devotion of your family, your aged father and your modest sister. Tell everything."

"I," began the clerk. His gaze flickered over Zhirem, pleading. Then he shut his eyes and blurted: "I woke to see one at the entrance to the wagon where I slept. He had got a silver cup, an offering, and he made away with it. I followed, but timorously kept some paces between us. The man—who was a priest without mistake—went from the village and westward to the old well. A house is there. So I hear since, the house of a woman—a woman who is no better than she ought to be. By the house there was another man, and the two men embraced and kissed each other on the lips, and it was a long kiss. And as they kissed, the light from the woman's window shone on them, and I beheld one had foxy yellowish hair and the other was dark. Then the dark one knocked, and the woman opened her door and they went inside."

"There, be comforted," murmured Beyash, patting the clerk's shoulder. "I will tell the rest. This poor man," said Beyash, "came running to me and recounted what he had seen. And, though I know him to be virtuous and holy, yet I doubted what I heard, and who shall blame me. In great trepidation, not waking another, so vast was my alarm and uncertainty, I let this clerk conduct me to the house of the wicked woman. As we were approaching, we both of us, the clerk and myself, beheld the two youths come out of the house and

90

walk off laughing among the olives on the hill. And to my dread and misery, I recognized each. Yet we tracked them a short space more, the tally clerk and I. And in among the trees we saw—oh, be pitiful to us, lordly gods—that not content with their connection with the woman, these two lay down with each other and undertook the art of congress."

A dry rustling breath rose from the villagers.

"But are you assured of it?" demanded the red priest, skillful as any showman.

"Alas, quite assured," moaned Beyash, hiding his eyes, "for they rose and sank together like the wave on the beach till both swooned with their ecstasy and were motionless."

"And the names?" cried the red priest.

"Woe and wretchedness. None but Zhirem and Shell."

It had already become noticeable to the watchful eyes of priests and villagers that Zhirem, who had stood impervious as a rock at the beginning, had, toward the end, gone white as bone.

"What do you say?" shouted the red priest.

"I say nothing," said Zhirem. But the slight lines of his youth were suddenly deep and ragged in his face.

"Where is your fellow, Shell?"

But Zhirem had said all he would say, and was silent once more.

"Perhaps," ventured Beyash, "we should send to the woman's dwelling and ask her if she knows."

So a group of villagers ran, and pounded on the door of the harlot's house and, getting no reply, they broke in the door and shortly learned she was dead. Despite their harsh comments, many had considered the lady very appetizing and useful, and they did not relish her death. It was all very well if a common man should scrimp and go short in order to get money to lie with a pretty whore—this one would not let a man touch her breasts unless he brought three silver pieces with him. But these priests, vowed to celibacy, thieved their fee from the gods, and then they slew the woman. Jealous and angry, none had any doubts that Zhirem and Shell had been the murderers.

And when Zhirem would not speak, and Shell would not be found, nor the silver cup of gems, priest and villager alike ceased to have doubts on the matter.

Even those the sore eyes of whose children had been bathed by Zhirem, came and spat at him. Even the old woman said the pain was in her back again, and cursed him.

And where was Shell?

Shell-Simmu, a girl, a maiden, had woken in the hour before dawn. She had raised herself to observe the unconscious handsome face of her lover. She had traced with her tongue's tip the lids of his eyes, where the lashes lay among their shadows, black and long as if a brush had drawn them there. Her joy and her delight in him had become so magnified as she gazed that she no longer needed him to share emotion with her. She had gone away among the trees to revel in her joy alone.

There was no thought in Simmu, (magic, a female, brought up in her formative years by demons,) no thought of logic or the set pattern of things. She had been a youth and a young priest. Well, that was done. She dismissed it all. Later, when she had savored this lonely passion to its full, she would go back to Zhirem and he would go with her, or she with him, wherever it pleased the two of them to go. Instinctively, having remembered her past and her potential, and that she had grown as a baby with those compulsive wanderers, the Eshva, she visualized existence thereafter as a permanent wandering.

Beyond the wild olives, the slopes gave way to woods of taller, darker trees, where pallid flowers dappled the grass— memory indeed of Eshva haunts. When the sun rose, amused by the other memories of the baby stowed in high branches, Simmu coiled herself up one of these tall trees, lithe as a cat, and hung herself in the black-green chambers above. Here she reclined, musing only on Zhirem, not yet quite ready to return to him, tantalizing herself by her absence from him. At last, recollecting, the sorcery of Eshva-given sleep which had held the child safe from dawn to dusk, stole over Simmu. She had not reckoned on sleeping, but she slept. When Zhirem was opening his eyes, setting aside his misgivings, turning toward the village and its trap, Simmu lay in the arms of the tree, dreaming of love.

What roused her was the brutal cacophony of a hunt below.

Simmu responded to the surrounding din as an animal would do; she froze to soundlessness, to immobility, became part of the tree, but a part which watched and listened.

Several rough men of the village thrust about and swore and went by below. Two remained, leaning on the tree's trunk.

"I think it is no use," said one, "the villain has already escaped. By every account he was strange in his wits. The

92

temple should look to itself, accepting such to serve the gods. I should not be surprised if some divine retribution follows, a famine or a plague."

"Oh, hold your noise," said the other. "We have trouble enough. In any event, the dark one is in safe custody and already on the road to the temple—they say he went meekly. But to lie with a whore indeed, and then slay her—no doubt to keep her mouth fast shut. And if she was no good, they say she was excellent at her trade. What other village had such a fine whore as ours, that rich men would travel seven miles or more to make merry with? And now these two priests have snapped her neck, and the yellow haired one has got clean away, and the other one, dark as a demon, he will get some penance from the temple—to eat only cakes three days a week or some such—"

"No, no," said the first, with somber glee. "Because he has lain with a brother priest he will be scourged. And I heard a man who is a temple servant say that since the dark one also killed, it will be a whipping to the death."

"And would I held the whip," lowed the other.

Then, having refreshed their spirits, they went on in their search for Shell among the woods.

An indescribable wash of confusion and anguish blinded Simmu. A whole minute it blinded her. But, noticeably, she had not lived with demons and gained nothing. Her mentality recovered quickly, filling her mind with pictures. Almost at once, chaos was replaced by understanding and order, and her eyes were cold as shards of chill green frost, thinking of those who would harm Zhirem.

For Beyash's plot and his lies, she knew it all, as if she had read his brain. She recalled his mention of a clerk who feared him—everything was accurately solved in seconds, for her reasoning could race when it must. For the dead woman she spared nothing. Demon-like, there was no room in Simmu save for who she held dear.

She slipped down from the tree and picked a clandestine path from the woods and among the olives. On the lower southern slopes sheep were pastured, for she had seen their droppings in that direction. Soon she came on the flock, and, humming to them, walked through their midst with no more disturbance than a summer breeze. A shepherd girl of fifteen or so sat among them. Simmu stole up on her from behind, and lightly clasping her about the forehead before she could cry out, worked on her a tactile charm of the Eshva. The girl's head drooped. She smiled foolishly and made no complaint when Simmu took her homespun dress and the cloth with which she had bound her hair.

Presently, on the westward road which, in a day's travel, would lead to the temple, there appeared a barefoot village maid. Her hair was hidden in a patchwork scarf; she walked with her head bowed. After an hour she reached a field where young horses were grazing. She stood by the wall and whistled. A horse came trotting. Without words, Simmu spoke.

"Bear me, brother, bear me, for I must be swifter than my own two feet."

The horse nuzzled Simmu and leaped the wall.

Something rushed through villages and by farms, the white dust veiling it. The village people gaped: "Who rides so fast?"

The dust blurred also the sky, the sun. Simmu rode in a dazzle of lights, and the impressions of things passed her but did not impede or snare her eye. So it was with her attention, focussed entirely on one goal.

She could not catch them on the road, the priests and their entourage, she had been too late in pursuit. Yet the horse bounded under her, galvanized by her crooning. She would not be far behind in achieving the temple.

When dusk came, Simmu saw the temple lands below, flecked with lights, and the great temple itself, a palace of lamps. She let the horse free; it was weary but not broken. It turned away into the gathering indigo of night, tossing its mane and blowing softly.

Simmu ran, fleet as a leopard.

There were more lights than usual, along the roads, among the groves—so much she saw as she ran. Many had gathered to be told of Zhirem the wicked one and his fate. Simmu learned everything in snatches as she sped by the doors of small wine shops and among the tasselled spears of the fields, where even lovers, who had hidden there for their own irreligious sins, made their after-talk of Zhirem's profanity. The High Priest had judged Zhirem and reviewed the evidence of his fault. The High Priest had collapsed with horror. Zhirem neither defended himself nor asked for mercy. Revived, the High Priest had pronounced that Zhirem must expire beneath the whip at sunrise tomorrow.

Simmu had arrived at the farthest ground she might tread lawfully in her woman's form, the Sanctuary of Virgins, half a mile westward of the temple.

Women and girls were clustered on the lawn before the

Sanctuary, dissecting the news and exclaiming. In their unlovely life, the downfall of a man pleased them, but they did not bother to think why.

Simmu went out of their sight. She stood beneath a tree. A bird fluttered suddenly from the tree into Simmu's hands.

"See Zhirem with my eyes, and know him. Fly over the temple wall, search the courts, take in the words of those that go about there. Find Zhirem. Come back to me, and tell me of it."

The bird flashed up into the darkness.

Simmu sat beneath the tree, wrapped in black shade. She watched the stars weep their light between the branches. A star fell into her lap: the bird, returning.

Simmu read the bird, a small mosaic book of macabre bird-craziness currently mingled with a bird's-eye view of the temple.

Here is a fat waddler, let fall upon his robe. There is another, dot him too. Cold is the stone beneath my feet with the sun's heat sunk away. Listen! A worm sliding under the turf. Tap with my beak! No, he is gone. Ah! A bird in the air, a bird painted on the window—I! But there is a court where a twisted dead tree grows and in a room of stone one sits. No lamp to bring the pretty moths so I might eat them. He sits with his head in his hands. It is the one. When he is dead I will bring my cousins and we will pull out his hair and line the nests with it. My near relative, the crow, would like his eyes which are like two jewels. But the crow is in the north, paying his respects at a king's funeral.

Hush, Simmu's mind to the bird. *Is Zhirem bound? Who guards him?*

No bindings. A locked door, iron at the window. Outside, these three. They have a lamp but its scent drives insects away. They juggle with six-sided white slugs which rattle. Once, I saw such lying in the grass. I pecked, but they were hard. I think, after all, I will eat the eyes of Zhirem. Why should the crow have everything?

From Simmu's mind there came then a dart of malice that sent the bird whirling up in fright.

The women by the Sanctuary heeded it this time. They pointed.

"A sparrow by night—it must be an omen."

Simmu they did not see, a white glimmer slipping through the groves, naked as in the old days with the demons, only the cloth to bind up her hair.

For some hours Simmu waited near the wall of the temple. The deep of the night drew close and closer like a gloved hand squeezing out the breath of earth, replacing it with the purple breath of a mystery. Once a lay brother passed. He urinated, embarrassed, in a bush. He clucked a holy chant of apology to the gods. Simmu hated him, and hate stuck like a blade between his shoulders, and he ran off about his errand, whatever it was, not realizing why he ran.

When the night was ready, Simmu rose up into it, and at some point Simmu had altered again to become a man. He put his hands and his feet upon the wall, climbing, as, man-shaped, he had so often climbed.

You imprisoned in the temple, beloved? When have they ever kept us in?

9

Simmu did not know that Zhirem was invulnerable and could not be killed. Zhirem did not know it either. The lions, the broken spear, the import of those things had faded from him, even though the terror associated with them remained. Zhirem, therefore, as he sat solitary in the unlit room of stone, believed in his death in the morning. Believed in it with a sort of loathing. But he had become again a dumb child, unable to express its bewilderment at the false accusations, and the awful uncomprehended crime of which it felt itself truly guilty.

In the yard of the dead tree, (this was the Court of the Felon, rarely used, nasty in its symbolism,) two lay brothers, assigned to keep watch, were dicing. A priest in his middle years looked on. The game was permissable, for the stakes were not coins, but sweetmeats. The priest, however, was too laden with care to dice. The evil of Zhirem had torn him with inner tragedy. The priest had attempted to wring from the heart of Zhirem some cry of regret, some contrition to offer the gods along with his blood. But Zhirem's heart did not respond.

In the morning, this priest intended to say to the whip men: "Strike sternly. Strike for his very soul. The worse the agony, the more likely the pardon of the gods." There were three whips. One had teeth of iron and one of bronze; the third was all metal strips, and was heated in a brazier before it was used.

The lay brothers diced. He at the table's left whispered:

"The candied quince is for Zhirem's cries. Six says he will scream at the first blow. He has no flesh to cushion him."

"I say he will cry only at the tenth blow. He will faint at the fifteenth."

The dice rattled. The blank side of the dice showed, where the four was rubbed away: "At the fourth stroke, then." "Or not at all."

The priest shifted his gaze and supposed for a moment something crouched on the wall, a lean pale cat with glinting eyes. But he could see nothing thereafter.

"Now what is this you have wrapped about my ankles?" grumbled the lay brother at the table's left.

"I was about to ask of you the same thing."

Each peered under the table. In the dim glow of the scented lamp each deciphered a rope which tightened, a rope with diamond scales. Both opened their mouths to shriek that a snake bound them in its coils, but their laments were still-born when they saw the cobra which swayed before them on the table.

"Never move," hoarsely instructed the priest, whose feet were also secured. "It is the abomination, Shell, who works this ill upon us."

And, clammy with their plight, the three jailors now discerned Shell, his hair bound in a rag, step lightly over the courtyard toward them. He spared only one glance of dislike and aversion for the dead tree. Then he glided about the table, and in three straining ears he hissed. The mesmerism which fell on the devout men was like a muddy doze, a doze full of vile dreams.

As they lay twitching and moaning and impotent, Simmu caressed, in the Eshva manner, the lock of the door of the room of stone, and charmed it open.

Zhirem did not raise his head. He did nothing. Simmu went to him and put his hand into the dark hair, and pulled the head up by this hair in a cruel hurting grasp till Zhirem must look into his face. Zhirem had been held by the hair before, inside a well of fire.

A transformation in Zhirem. No melting, no joy. It was a mask of rage and torment that Zhirem's face had been transformed to. His eyes blazed in the gloom. He leapt up, and prized off the hand of Simmu with a grip of steel. And when the power of words overtook Zhirem, they were not words of gratitude or love.

"You have sold out my life, you have killed what is good

97

in me or might have been. You foul and filthy one, you have dragged me into the slime. I did not grieve that you had deserted me after the act. I did not grieve at the lies of men, neither at death. But you, you accursed and crawling thing, I do not know how you deceived me, but I know this—I will not have you near me." And then he sat down once more and lowered his head, and he murmured: "But not only you. The fault was also mine. Leave me, let me be. The old men said I should belong to a Demon of Darkness, to a Master of Night."

"Be happy then," said Simmu, Eshva-foundling, with an edge in his voice like a polished knife. "Demonkind are to men as the sea is to the sand. And he who is the Lord of Demons, Azhrarn, he is the leaven in the world's bread."

Zhirem stared when he heard this. A new torment displaced the first.

"Are there positively such as demons, then?"

"Believe it."

"And you I regarded as friend, you are their messenger. Scant wonder that you dragged me into a cave of night."

Simmu abandoned speech. His eyes began to speak instead. Tears burst from them, but his face was contemptuous and cold. He went away into the shadows beyond the room, as once before.

And Zhirem, after he had sat staring there at the unlocked door, the court with just the three oblivious men in it, as once before, felt drawn to follow.

Yet Simmu was gone. Zhirem climbed up the wall and over it alone. He fell into the shade at the wall's foot, weak from what had been done to him, now also weeping.

"It is evidently not my hour to die," he said, "yet I am fit for nothing. Though perhaps, as the creature tells me, I am fit to be the slave of demons. I will seek him, then, this Master of Night. If he is real, let him hire me, for I am done with all else."

And Zhirem went away also into shadows, not keeping any watch for danger, yet not confident, not glad, but desolate and without hope.

Simmu was not actually very distant. He had paused to reclaim a property of his, or send another to reclaim it.

The yellow-green gem the Eshva gave to Simmu, the gem with the character on it which was Simmu's name in the Demon Tongue, lay in a coffer in the treasure room of the temple. Here was piled much wealth, gold and silver and varieties of jewels. Yet Simmu knew where the green gem lay, for he had seen it in his childhood and been told by the priests: "With this paltry but pleasing stone were the gods thanked for your place among us."

All the coffers of the treasure room were open that every man that came there could feast his sight on the temple's riches. On this occasion it was a rat who saw. It scuttled pink-eyed from the high window and down the wall-hanging and into the coffer. It dug with its paws and seized the Eshva gem and bore it to Simmu.

Simmu hung the gem by its Drin-worked silver chain around his neck. Naked but for the cloth about his hair and the gem about his neck, he went away then after Zhirem, knowing the direction by supernatural clues and by plain love.

Yet, walking, he recalled he roamed the country of men. Soon he came to a herdsman's hut. Outside, garments hung on a bush to dry after their washing, and Simmu clad himself in one of these.

Zhirem strode south. He did this with no scheme in mind and with no purpose, however obscure, of reaching the far-off southern desert. The road of Zhirem was random, and he journeyed there blind and deaf and almost dumb, and that Simmu followed he was unaware, and if he had become aware he would have turned and cursed him, as later he did.

When the sun lifted in the east, miles lay between Zhirem and the temple. Enough miles that the people who saw him pass, though they had been informed of his transgression and recognized his dark hair, had not heard of his escape from bondage.

"There is the priest who lies with harlots and slays them!"

"It is as I told you. The temple will not execute him, they have only cast him out."

"Come, let us do the work for them!"

But, though they named him an exiled priest, yet priest he still was and the travel-worn yellow robe still on him. They did not have the courage quite to try to kill him, and the stones they threw glanced off from him as if the gods protected him, and he was not hurt, which set these people wondering.

Later, another came by, but this was a girl, for they eyed the shape of a maiden's high breasts through her poor garment.

Simmu, (a girl, altered cunningly to outwit humankind) gathered information of Zhirem's passage through the land.

The bruised flowers mentioned how his feet had crushed them. The dust carried the scent of him, the trees which had reflected his shadow revealed as much to Simmu's hand.

At noon, a black bird on a stone, receiving the unspoken question Simmu asked: "Has Zhirem walked this way?", screeched out in a loud harsh voice: "Has Zhirem walked this way?" voicing the unvoiced. And Simmu hesitated and called the bird and held it some minutes against her throat, teaching it, before she went on.

Of all the demons, the Eshva were not much given to revenge, their cruelties were of the instant, and the past forgotten. But Simmu was also a woman and a man, and he had remembered Beyash.

10

For days after the temple had discovered that sorcery had visited it, it had wailed and roared to itself and demanded sacrifices and prayers from the whole country. It had despatched bands of men from the farms and vineyards, armed with knives and bearing the temple insignia, to catch up with and bring back Zhirem, but these bands were terrified of coming anywhere near Zhirem—patently a magician and in absolute league with devils—and never tracked him down. At length the temple, in a vast ceremony, conjured upon him and upon Shell an eternal bane by proxy for the gods. Then peace was permitted to creep home, and they set themselves to mislay their failure and their fear.

It was the month after that Beyash roused in the dawn because a harsh and awful voice was crying:

"Beyash slew the harlot. Beyash and no other."

Now Beyash slept in a cell alone, as did all the priests, and nobody was at hand. But looking up in terror, he perceived a big black bird hopping about the sill of the window. And again the bird shouted:

"Beyash slew the harlot. Beyash and no other."

Beyash was convinced the whole temple heard, though none heard but he. He buried himself in his pillows and waited for arrest. But no one entered, and when he peeped out the fearsome bird was gone.

"A bad dream," said Beyash. "I have committed a wrongful deed, and I must placate the gods who see everything. I must convince the gods that what I did was right."

100

So he got up early for Beyash and took his share of breakfast and put it on the altars of several gods and prayed to them and kissed the ivory feet of the statues. But when he glanced upward, he found the black bird, no dream, was perched on the head of a silver prophet. And the bird bellowed: "Beyash slew the harlot. Beyash and no other."

Beyash grovelled on the ground and then he fled. And flying, he collided with some of his fellow priests who held him and asked what was the matter. While he jabbered nonsense, up flew the bird, and it settled on Beyash's shoulder. Beyash turned white as chalk, and waited in despair for the bird to speak. But this time it did not, only watched him with a single eye. When he attempted to shake off the bird, it would not go. It clung to his shoulder as if it loved him.

"Beyash has a pet," joked the priests.

And then, the bird would not leave Beyash.

All day it sat on his shoulder. At mealtimes it pecked from his plate and sipped from his cup.

"Look how this bird adores Beyash," marvelled the priests.

At night it rode with him to his cell. It sat on his pillow, he could not dislodge it. He lay stiff and sleepless, respectful of its beak and its talons. When, exhausted, he slumbered despite himself, then the bird would shriek in his ear: "Beyash slew the harlot. Beyash and no other."

Yet, in company, it did not accuse him.

Perhaps it never will, thought Beyash.

But the bird's eyes, now one, now another, beadily savored his nervousness. *Perhaps*, suggested these eyes, *on some day, I will*.

Beyash could not eat. He grew lean and his skin hung slack on him, a second yellow robe. Beyash sought solitude very much; when he must be with others, the sweat streamed from his face.

"Now, Beyash my son," chided the High Priest gently, "it is not seemly you carry this bird with you before the gods. You must put an end to your foolish behavior."

"I cannot, Father," muttered Beyash. And the High Priest deprived him of his jasper earring for being insolent.

Ten suns rose and ten suns set, and yet the bird perched on the shoulder of Beyash. And if he was able to thrust it off, it flew back immediately, and pecked him for good measure.

On the eleventh morning, Beyash, stupid with fright and weakness and sleeplessness, ran suddenly into the Court of the Salamander where many steps led down into a water garden, and Beyash seized a large stone jug that stood on the

101

stair head. Striking at the bird so it momentarily flew upward, Beyash flung the stone jar after it. But the bird dashed aside, the stone jar crashed upon the skull of Beyash, and, in falling down the steps, his neck was broken.

11

Zhirem strode south till he came to a wide green river. Men did not live nearby, and there was no bridge nor any other way to cross. He took that as a bitter sign, and turned west along the river's bank. He had walked two months alone, not looking behind him, nor properly anywhere. The stones had ceased to pelt about him. He barely noted none struck him—maybe had not been meant to. Later, where they did not know him at all, yet slightly recognized that his garment meant a priesthood of some kind, strangers would now and then give him food or shelter. Zhirem took everything and nothing with equal courteous indifference. This world was mist to him, and through the mist he advanced, searching for a black shadow which would claim him, the shadow of night men called Azhrarn. And even as he searched he did not really believe. And even as he was skeptical, his blood ran cold in case it should be true.

The bed of the river rose toward its source, and narrowed high among stony uplands. Zhirem climbed with it, and the air became clear as crystal, and yellow eagles swirled in the sky over his head and the land was yellow too, and only the river green.

In the day's climbing, Zhirem passed through four villages. People saw him and pointed. Anything was sensational there, for seldom did anything happen. An hour after Zhirem's passing, the villagers were able to point again, for a girl went by with apricot hair, eating a handful of river grass, setting her feet in the dust where Zhirem's footprint was still marked.

Near sunfall, a woman ran to Zhirem out of a lighted door in the fourth village.

"Go no farther, traveler. Beyond is a wild strange place and no one ventures there after dark."

Zhirem stopped. He looked at the woman. Her words seemed to have struck some chord within him. She, moved by his look and his beauty, entreated him to enter her father's dwelling and eat with them. Like a blind man guided, Zhirem let her take him into the house.

There was little enough. Stewed fish from the green river, black fruits from the grudging trees. The father was aged and liked to talk, and the woman gazed at Zhirem with her hungry soul in her eyes. They were kind to him for their own selfish reasons.

Zhirem scarcely ate at all. He listened to the elderly man rambling. Presently Zhirem asked why they feared the ground west of the village.

"Grim things are said of it," intoned the ancient, "and grim things go there. The beasts are unnatural. In the time of my father's father, a child strayed into that place and three men went to find it. Night came and night departed, and only one man returned, and he was an idiot thereafter till the day of his death."

"It is a terrain of pitfalls and marshes," said the woman. "There is a lake, they say, all salt. And the horned horses go to dance there; but that is many miles' journey on. Besides, there is a wall, and none can scale it, save demons."

"Demons," said Zhirem, so soft only she heard him, for she hung on his words.

When Zhirem would leave, the woman tried to keep him. In the door of the house, she promised him many things, but he put her aside and went on into the night. As she sobbed against the doorpost, another slipped by, one who had sat in the street all this while, gazing at the lighted window. Simmu who, for two months, had similarly watched, from a distance, Zhirem within the houses of men, or Zhirem when he lay asleep on the ground.

No track led from the village. Only the thin remnant of the river continued, and this soon reached its terminus, or rather its beginning, which was three slender falls above the rock. The moon had not yet risen, and beyond this spot all was uncertain, a jagged plain which fell away before and away again to a distant sky like black blood.

Confronting this, without even a moon, Zhirem hesitated. The mist faded from his inner eye; he began to realize how far he had come, and to what end. The lightless country in front of him seemed abruptly like the gate to some hell, to Underearth itself, the domain of the demons.

And, as he hesitated, Zhirem sensed another near him. He turned and saw, behind him on the higher ground, a shape with a girl's form and a girl's hair.

Zhirem was angered. He assumed the woman had dogged him from the village. He made a rejecting gesture with his hand that said, "Go back and leave me." But the girl's shape

103

did not move. Then Zhirem retraced his steps and went up the ridge to tell her to take herself home. In the sluggish darkness, he drew very close before he recognized that the cascade of hair belonged to one he knew better.

"I trusted myself rid of you," said Zhirem. "I made no jest when I bade you choose another road than mine. I cannot breathe the air if you are near, all winds that blow become a poison. You are my shame and my defeat. I will not see you. I will offer myself to corruption, but I will not suffer you as my reminder. May the maleficent gods blast you, for they have venom to spare if they exist. If not gods, then carry my everlasting enmity. Shrivel and be damned and get from my sight."

All this while, speaking these things with dismal violence, Zhirem saw only what he reckoned to see, which was the enigmatic face of Shell.

But just then an amber moon began to come up, and Zhirem became aware it was a woman before him, the actual maiden he had lain with among the flowering olives, the maiden of the dream of sin, who was also Shell.

Zhirem was afraid, afraid since he could not understand. He snarled with his fear, and ran away toward the gate of hell.

There was a wall. It lay three miles into the curious dead-lands beyond the river. The blocks of the wall were dressed stone. A lord had built it in an age past reckoning, and here and there a skull was set in between the stones, for the lord had been of that order of lords who liked such decoration and killed his slaves to obtain it. The unwholesome aspect of the wall had done nothing to lessen the reputation of the area.

Hundreds or thousands of years ago, a blight had burnt up the landscape till it was black. Black by day, blacker by night. Fogs meandered here, coming and going from the marshes, but farther in, some eight miles westward, a lake of salt lay pink-glittering under the rufous moon. Here grew exotic malformed trees with fruits that shone like brass, and here, on the wide melanotic shore of the lake, unicorns had been known to dance, to fight and to couple. And this night the unicorns came, as if they were the sigils of a man's terror and craving, aspects only of Zhirem and his febrile surrender to darkness.

The unicorns were savage, not white as doves, but the colors of scarlet gum and old yellow bone, with twisted horns of tarnished swarthy gold. There were three. They emerged from the gruesome woods where the metallic fruit clinked. A hare started from a thicket and a unicorn tamped it to the earth with its forefoot, ripped and shredded with the serrated oblongs of its golden teeth, then kicked the carcass aside and stalked on.

On the lake shore the unicorns ran and circled, their hooves crunching the glittering charcoal sand. One had a silver scar on his flank as if a star had burnt him. He flung about and clashed his single horn against the single horn of another. Lowering their heads these two, pawing the sand, glaring from their eye sockets at an impossible angle, began to duel. The whorled horns came together, smote, screeched, struck sparks, scraped off, returned, like two smoky swords. The third unicorn, partnerless, reared to lash and thrust at the moon.

Zhirem sat on a rock not a hundred paces away.

He stared at the unicorns, hypnotized by their intrinsic terribleness.

The skull wall, crumbling, had been easy to scale after all. Directionless, he considered something had led him here to the unicorns' dancing floor. After he had come here, they had come. He wondered idly, uninvolved, if they would scent him and gallop to rend him as the leader had rent the hare. Yet he knew also some dark entity kept him for itself. Or thought he knew it.

The star-burned unicorn had risen now, prizing its battle companion up with it from the earth. They leaned together on the sky, their blades locked and their eyes rolling. The third unicorn screamed, prancing through the arch their bodies made, swerving to gore, with the awful horn, the side of each. Yet the stabbings were light, caressive almost. In that second, as the black blood ran, a fourth figure appeared on the lake shore.

Simmu walked there naked save for her hair and the green fleck of fire in the hollow of her throat. She walked like one of the wandering marsh fogs, that pale, seemingly as weightless.

The unicorns, untangling from each other, poured about to challenge what came. They dug up the black sand, lowering again their heads with the swords held ready to slash and pierce. The smell of their own blood excited them, the vision of the dismembered hare was fresh. But the girl who stepped toward them stepped nearer, and the wind lifted strands of her long hair over the moon, and she raised her arms as if the wind also lifted those, and she danced. Not the dance of unicorns, but of the Eshva. A wondrous dancing.

Not a sound on the shore now but the wind-strummed grasses. Simmu danced, and the unicorns melted, like red wax and golden wax, into shapes of tranquility. Presently they kneeled and rested their heads in the sand, their cruel mouths slid ajar, their fringed lids shut. Still Simmu danced.

She danced till the lake and the sky and all the world blurred before her eyes. She danced in the veils of her hair. She had not known this charm, this Eshva dancing, not till this moment. It came from the green gem, it came from her loins and her heart.

At last she was weary, and could dance no more, yet, even now, the dancing lingered within her. She went between the unicorns, but only their eyelids stirred, like leaves. She went to the place where Zhirem sat, motionless, on the rock. He did not seem to remember her, yet he looked only where she stood.

"I have bound you," she said, "by sorcery. Shall I let you go?"

Slowly he shook his head.

"No. Keep me bound."

"When you saw me, you hated me," she said, "but when the unicorns prepared to slay me, you grew pale."

"You are a demon," he said. "I will not deny you any more. Bring your kindred."

"I am not of demon-kind," said Simmu, "but this jewel at my neck may bring some who were with me once. Perhaps. And they are demon-kind."

Then she went to him and kissed him.

On the shore the unicorns were joining, one by one, and their heads rose against the moon, and sank, as they swam across each other's backs.

The man and the woman swam deep in the rock's deep shadow, gazing each into the other's face as they swam, till each saw how the other was blinded and grew blind in turn.

Later, the moon fell. And Zhirem's wide eyes were darkened as the light ran from the sky.

The holy men of the desert had positively taught him to fear himself and his own joy; the holy priests of the temple had inadvertently taught him to scorn the gods. Humanity instructed him in its faithlessness. Left with nothing, only Simmu had tendered him love. Zhirem could not bring himself to say, in that moment, or to think: Love is not enough.

To all demons wandering on the earth, the perfume of a spell, the peculiar fragrance of human witchcraft, was compelling. As they could not keep out of mankind's affairs, so they could not resist this lure. Generally they came to pry, never to participate, rarely to aid; though the Drin—and their lesser cousins, the foolish bestial Drindra—might sometimes join a human magician at some foul work, for sport.

The Eshva women who had nurtured Simmu for almost two years, they had forgotten this baby, as they had known they would. Short memories had the Eshva. And no other denizen of Underearth had chanced on Simmu afterward, which was strange, for the smell of sorcery went with the boy he had been from the first. Now, however, at large in a lawless country, making Eshva glamour, clad in an Eshva gift, a jewel polished and inscribed by Drin, and in himself physically altered from male to female, Simmu shone like a beacon for demons, which instinctively she knew.

She had no call on them, not really. It was because of Zhirem she hoped that her adoptive kin would seek her. Like a child which grows up in a pit of snakes, comforted by their skin and inured to their venom, Simmu had no conception of the danger of demon-kind. As intuitively as she enacted the impossible, her own sexual metamorphosis, thus she studied her gem, whispered and breathed over it, danced on the lake shore, and waited, without fear, hopefully, for strangers.

It was the second night in that spot. The unicorns had vanished and not come back; even the moon approached in a different form. All day, out of the harsh sun which blistered up the salt lake, Zhirem and Simmu—he knew her true name now—had slept in the wood's erratic shade. Their night had been unsleeping, a night of sensuality and pain, but this night Zhirem had gone away alone, walking with his head bowed, meditating on his shame and the sweetness of it. He was restless with a wretched pleasure in defilement. When the moon sank a little, he would return to Simmu with eagerness and despair.

Now, alone, Simmu glanced up from her witching, and found another.

It was a demon, an Eshva, drawn by Eshva things, and any who had met demons would not have taken Zhirem for one, despite his hair and his handsomeness. The Eshva was masculine. His hair was ebony, his eyes sable and his flesh of a starry pallor. Everything about him exuded subtlety, marvel and a pure unworldly beauty of design.

A thrill went irresistibly over Simmu, for beings of this

tribe had been the delight of her earliest years. Unplanned, she half leaned toward him, but the demon leaned away, playful and malignant. His eyes held this for Simmu to read: *You know our customs, some of them, but you are not one of us. You live also in the rude sunlight. Your flesh is clay, it will weaken and crumble. What you do with our spells and charms is well enough for a mortal, but among us it would be counted poor. Your silent footfall is a thunderclap, we are the air.*

Simmu felt the hurt of this, but did not cherish the hurt. Only she was driven to speech, which was a sort of defiance.

"You come because of this green jewel and its aura. That brings you. What brings the Master of Night, Azhrarn the Beautiful, your Prince, one of the Lords of Darkness?" She used many of his titles from respect and the inchoate, second-hand adoration that had rubbed off on her from the demonesses of her infancy. Still, the Eshva shrank away.

His eyes said merely: *Repent.*

Simmu laughed, aloud.

"Azhrarn," she said, "Azhrarn, Prince of Demons. Is there no way to call him?"

Again the Eshva shrank. A picture sprang from his mind to the receptive mind of Simmu. A silver pipe, fashioned for Azhrarn, might call Azhrarn—sometimes. But if he came, beware. And now the Eshva laughed with his eyes, and terror in the backs of them.

Simmu felt, perhaps, an instant of pride and that pride's cheat. Zhirem expected wonders of her, expected her powers to equal those of the lower demons.

"Listen, beloved," said Simmu to the Eshva, "seek Azhrarn for me. Tell him one waits kneeling. Beg him."

The Eshva smiled. The smile said:

I am not your slave, mortal.

Simmu stroked the gem at her throat. She spoke now without words.

The Drin made this. The Drin will make bargains. I will entice the Drin. The Drin will creep to Azhrarn on their bellies. Conceivably, Azhrarn will chide you that you told him nothing of Zhirem who would kneel to him.

The Eshva lowered his eyes. He shivered and folded himself into the night without replying.

When Zhirem came from the same night, Simmu said:

"It is possible he will be seen here."

"Who?" Zhirem asked, but he went white, even his beautiful eyes whitened. All was confusion to him, the unreal mixed with the actual, fire with water. He drew the woman to him, and took refuge in her body, though that also was a thing of miracle and perversity. There was no reason left in the world.

After the love-dance, they lay together, waiting.

The night and the night wind moved on the shore. The lake licked its margins. The hard metal fruit of the trees clanked. Nothing more, and the dark began to pass. So they shifted, the lovers, moaned and clung together and drowned themselves briefly, and rose to the surface of that depth, alert, unslackened, waiting yet.

A second day, a third night. Purple berries hung on a bush; they ate them. The evening was cold; they lit a fire which burned green from the wild wood they fed to it. There was a spring of water; they drank there like thirsty deer. They could not long keep from each other, for lust was new to them, and it was all they had. They began to lose purpose and fear and love and logic; they became two part-starved animals which endlessly coupled, which had been forever on the shore, forever would be, awaiting an advent which they had invented, something which would never occur.

In the fourth night, Simmu, more easily lost than Zhirem and more easily found, already two-thirds elemental and at home with strangeness, drew herself from his arms and went to the weird fire. She rocked herself above its cat's-eye flames and she cast into it the Eshva gem. No item made in Underearth was destroyed overhead without some notice taken by the demons. Simmu grinned like the she-wolf as the green jewel turned black in the green fire.

In the morning, however, the fire was black and the jewel was green again.

Zhirem sat beside the lake. He watched its salty shining. He did not turn to Simmu. He tried to see fish at the lake's bottom where none could be. He was empty, deadly amused by his dejection. Demons did not exist, or did not have commerce with men. He had been thrown into a black pit which contained Nothing.

The sun sank. A solitary bird soared over, jagged winged in the afterglow. The lake glazed and began to gleam like pink mirror.

Simmu as she crouched by the fire, Zhirem seated by the lake, both heard a soft crunching of the charcoal sand. Both rose and faced about with the hair shifting on their necks. From the western gloaming a shape seemed to weave itself, but it was not any shape they watched for.

109

A bent old man picked his slow way along the shore. His garments of formless black flapped about him, his hair hung down in iron ropes.

He came to Zhirem first, this old one. He lifted up at Zhirem a face like a fire-scarred arid rock, and out of this devastated face two eyes burned with a light Zhirem took for senility and madness.

"The black land crabs," hissed the old man, in a voice which was oddly powerful and arresting. "I look for the black crabs which crawl upon the land to mate."

Zhirem, half stupefied with a terror and an anticipation which had borne no fruit, said nothing.

The old man made an erratic gesture with his hand, graceful, uncanny. "How would you name me? Crazy, would it be?"

Zhirem stared. He said:

"Nothing lives in the salt lake."

"Crazy you would name me," repeated the old man. His voice rose and fell like a dire and improbable music. "Not so crazy as those who come here meaning to call up the Master of Night."

Zhirem caught the old man by the shoulder. But when he touched, a lightning seemed to ignite under his hand.

"You are a magician then," Zhirem said.

"Even a magician trembles at the name of Azhrarn."

Zhirem looked away. He looked into the air itself, searching. The old man turned from him, and made his arch-backed course along the sand to where the green fire burned, and where Simmu, clad now in her peasant rags, stood and gazed at him. As the old man got closer, Simmu raised her arms. It was as if she opened a gate to let him in.

When he reached the fire, the old man spat suddenly into the flames. A blue tongue flashed where he had spat, and Simmu dropped to her knees, without understanding why she did so. Her eyes swam as she met the mad burning of the old man's eyes. But, to her, the burning was not madness. It was a profundity of sight too awesome to withstand.

"You danced naked," said the magician. "I beheld your dance. I have noticed other things. To the north, a plump priest has expired. Beyash, fleeing a black talking bird, fell down a stairway to his death. Which does not gladden you, my little one, seeing you hate Death, and would not even give your enemies into his care."

Simmu shivered. She did not see the magician look over

his shoulder, and how Zhirem also turned as if at a shout, and came back over the shore to the fire.

"If you are a magician," said Zhirem, "teach me how to summon the Prince of Demons."

"Summon?" asked the old man, and never did such a soft murmur carry so great a menace. "Him you do not summon. Neither call to him, if you are wise. And for what should you wish to risk yourself in his presence? Maybe someone has told you the tale that those who call him may ask of him a single boon. The tale is not necessarily accurate."

"I would serve him."

"Serve him? Has he need then, do you suppose, of human servants? Has he not his own people for that? Men have misled you, Zhirem. You were not meant for the dark."

Zhirem's face grew like white steel.

"Never say that now," he said, "I have travelled too far."

"Listen," said the old man, and his voice sang and was a spell. "Listen," he said, and the whole ear of night obeyed. The trees listened, and the earth, and the water of the lake, and Zhirem sank down by the fire and listened also. Then the old man told Zhirem the story of Zhirem's own beginning. Everything was there, as if the old man had witnessed all of it, the muttering among the tents, the alarm of Zhirem's mother, the slinking in of the witch-woman. The night he spoke of when the cloud bore the child and his mother to the garden of green sand. He spoke of the well of fire and Zhirem plunged into it. He spoke of the price of this unique and total armoring, which left no loophole for hurt. For in burning off mortal weakness, mortal luck and happiness were also burned. It was some antique law of the gods, older than time. Men could not have too much. Ecstasy and vulnerability belonged in the same dish. A fear the cup would be snatched away was what gave the wine its savor, and as Zhirem's cup was sure, so was his joylessness. It was a price even demons, the magician said, would not pay to make safe a human they valued. It was the fire's light had harmed Zhirem, not the darkness.

Sweat ran on Zhirem's face, his eyes blazed drily, and he said: "What then?"

"What indeed," said the magician.

"I believe no word of yours," said Zhirem.

"Do you not? Go, and prove I am mistaken."

Zhirem met his glance with hatred and pleading. Then, like a dog which has been whipped from the hall, Zhirem got up and walked straight into the blackness of night, and the blackness parted to receive him and shut at his back.

Simmu, about to spring up and go after, discovered the hand of the magician had alighted on her wrist. And the hand seemed to bind her with a chain that was unbreakable, yet she loved the chain.

"For you, this," said the magician. "Your mother was a queen who ruled in a distant land. The kingdom is called Merh, and now it is yours. Do you want it?"

Simmu, enchanted by the touch of the magician, closed her eyes. Kingdoms meant nothing. She thought of Zhirem lost in the blackness and wished only to comfort him, but the chain bound her and she loved the chain. She laid her head against the old man's shoulder, and she sighed.

And presently she found it was the hard ground she lay on, and her hair was wound about her wrist, and the fire had died.

Zhirem entered a valley in the lawless lands, in the moonless abject hour before dawn.

The valley was ugly, and it had a pitiless aroma. All about lay shards and flints like razors; the gaunt trees had clawed the wind till even the wind was afraid to stay there. It was a place to meet death in, and Zhirem recognized it.

He picked up the razor shards as he walked, and let them go. He reached the valley's center where a chasm had been wrenched out by some huge meteorite's plummeting, a valley in the valley, and on its floor a black stream flowing with veins of red poison in it. A place of death for certain, and with many forms of death in it. It might have been put there as part of Zhirem's fate.

Zhirem halted on the chasm's brink.

He said, to the valley, and to the dregs of the night, and to any who might hear him: "All that is left of me is here. If any claim me, they must do it now."

The valley, where no wind blew, was silent. Yet in the silence was answer enough.

Now Zhirem had been told he might not die. Events had told him, and also an old man by a lake. To die is a fear, but to live is a fear also. Zhirem stepped off from the edge into space, and what he truly wanted is not simple to divine, nor did he find it simple, whether an end or the curse of not ending. If the rocks had speared through him with agony and death, maybe he would have cried out in remorse. But the rocks left him be, and how he fell was as if through gauze

112

into velvet, not a scratch on him, not a bruise. And when he dragged himself to his feet and gazed up the wall of the chasm and saw the length of his fall and knew himself alive and unharmed, then his cry of remorse and anguish was at life, and he had no room left in him to understand it might have been different.

Zhirem seized the flint daggers from the rocky floor. He drove them at his heart, his neck, the veins of his arms—and none pierced him. He sprawled beside the poison stream and lapped there. He lay with his face in water and his hair floating, and he felt the scald of the toxicant alter to blandness in his throat and belly; worse than bane, it did him good.

He could not support the horror of uniqueness. He could not persist with loneliness and without a goal. He crawled upright once again and, untying the priest's belt from his waist, he made a noose. He looped the bough of one of the fearsome trees and hanged himself from it. But as the cord tighetned, he seemed to hear the tree whispering spitefully: "Zhirem is too beautiful to die," and the bough snapped.

Stretched on the rock, Zhirem made no effort now to rise. A chill rain dashed itself into his open eyes, and mingled with rain, a shadow.

Through his daze and through the water, Zhirem made out a man, tall against the paling raining sky. Black the man was, blacker than the night had been, and the rain did not moisten his white hair and his white garments, whiter than the day would be.

"You cried for me," said the man, who was no man, but Death. "You cried for me but I may not come to you. Not for long years and long centuries. Only this can I give you," and he leaned down and laid his fingers on the brow of Zhirem so his senses and the whole world left him, and even dreams had no place in that dungeon of unconsciousness.

After Death had gone, another came.

Simmu leaned over the chasm's brink and perceived Zhirem on the floor of it, stone still in the rain with the cord about his neck and the broken bough nearby. And Simmu knew that Death had been in the chasm as a leaf knows winter has brushed it.

Neither had Simmu properly understood the magic story the magician had recounted. Maybe it had been meant only for Zhirem and no other. The well of fire remained a mystery to Simmu, and thus she saw Zhirem dead on the chasm's floor. And she saw her life dead there with him.

Her womanhood left her as she stared. Simmu became again a man, a youth, kneeling upon the brink, then jumping up and flying from the place, his old fear on him.

And, as Simmu fled, he wept, but the whole sky was weeping for Zhirem.

PART FOUR

She Who Lingers

1

In Merh, which meant nothing to Simmu, Jornadesh ruled.

Jornadesh, the commander of the armies of Narasen, he who had had her slain with a blue drink, who had made himself a king and shut up the true king in his mother's tomb, alive—all the sixteen years of Simmu's life, Jornadesh had been lord of Merh. At the same moment Simmu wandered weeping through the lawless lands, Jornadesh lay on a cushion of silk in the palace of Merh, lording it.

He had grown corpulent, had the handsome commander. The only exercise he took was at the table or in the bodies of his women. Luxury was everywhere; he battened on the land, but the land did well enough, in spite of him. It was rich and prosperous, Narasen had left it so. And for Narasen, what? Nothing. No rites, no honors at her mausoleum, no mark of mourning, however spurious, not a single spire of gold erected to her remembrance. Now this, for the dead, would be a small matter. Souls did not usually remain to spy or to brood. But for the soul trapped by Death's bargain in the Innerearth, bound to its flesh another thousand years, for that soul, the acts of the world had interest.

Jornadesh, leaving the cushions of silk for a bed of silver and the silken body of a girl, lapsed at length into sleep and had a dream, the substance of which was this: In the palm of Jornadesh lay a blue jewel, at which he peered greedily, admiring its lustre. But, even as he peered, the jewel began to change. It became a blue spider which crawled across his skin. And swift on this vision ran another: A blue flower bloomed in an urn, but when Jornadesh bent to sample its fragrance, the flower became a hand which gripped his throat. Last, the sight of a blue hill, but the blue hill split and spewed out a vast legion of scorpions, termites, venomous snakes and beetles, and these things, all of them blue, swarmed over Jornadesh, devouring him as they progressed, so he woke yelling.

Jornadesh did not like his equanimity disturbed. Even asleep, he wanted charm and peace about him. When he slumbered again and had the self-same dream again, he rushed heavily from his bed, calling for lights and for sorcerers.

"Does someone work evil against me?" asked Jornadesh. "Reverse the influence upon him, and let him perish in his own snare."

But the sorcerers could find no evidence of an ill-sending.

Jornadesh was not satisfied, though he retired to bed. Near dawn he had the dream a third time, and now he roused the whole palace with his cries.

The sorcerers were brought, and reminded of various instruments of torture secreted here and there in the byways of the royal establishment.

The sorcerers conferred. One said:

"Majesty, we are able to discover nothing. Indeed, who should wish you harm, seeing you are both just and virtuous. But if you are troubled, we have heard of a certain sage who lives on the plains beyond the city. He is said to have powers of divination. If you desire, we will summon him."

They hoped thereby to divert the wrath of Jornadesh upon this fellow, who was reputedly eccentric. Jornadesh, to their relief, agreed to consult the sage, and he was sent for.

He was a wild man. He lived on fruits and raw meat and dressed in the skin of a leopard. His beard grew to his knees but his head was shaved. When they led him into the presence of the king, he seemed unimpressed, and when they informed him that Jornadesh wished him to divine a dream, he only asked what it was. When he had been told, he sprawled down full length on the mosaic floor. He breathed deeply and his eyes rolled up and presently he began to writhe and groan. And after he had writhed and groaned quite a while, he roared out in an awful tone:

"Beware! Jornadesh and Merh, beware. She does not forget that you have not remembered. Beware of water, and beware of the unlocked gate, and beware the footstep in the street at night when no dog barks. Beware of she who lingers."

Then the sage was quiet, and he opened his eyes and arose serenely.

"Now what does this mean?" ranted the king.

"How should I know?" asked the sage scornfully. "I understand nothing of the power which possesses me. I only speak as I am given to speak."

"Take him and have him whipped!" shouted Jornadesh.

"I have been whipped before," said the sage.

And when the soldiers tied him and beat him, the sage made no noise and appeared in fact not to notice, though blood ran down his back. And finally the two whipmen began to howl, for they declared that every time the lash struck the sage he clearly felt no pain, though he was wounded, and they—with no wound—felt every blow. So they left off beating him and untied him and cursed him from the yard, and crawled whimpering to their beds, while the sage strode, bloody yet blithe, from the city.

Jornadesh meanwhile was in a frenzy.

"Who is it that lingers—who can it be?"

The sorcerers slunk to him.

"Perhaps, merciful lord, it is an unquiet ghost. Perhaps, generous lord, it is the ghost of Narasen, after whose unquestionably natural and inevitable death you wisely saved Merh from anarchy, and ornamented the city with the jewel of your magnificent reign."

"Narasen," whispered Jornadesh, and he went pale.

Before the sun had accomplished the zenith, Jornadesh had given Merh notice of a month of mourning for Narasen.

"Who is Narasen?" asked the children, born after her demise.

"Some dead bitch-lady," mocked the older ones, who just recalled her.

"A harlot," said the old women.

"A man-hater," said the old men.

Memory had not dealt kindly with Narasen. Her strengths and her acts of preservation had dissolved in an acid of fault-finding and malevolence. Besides, it had not necessarily been polite to speak well of her once Jornadesh ruled in her stead.

Now, however, incense was burned to the gods on behalf of Narasen, till all the temples reeked of it. Hymns in praise of Narasen were sung, and processions went up and down the streets, sounding gongs and entreating the people to reverence her name.

Jornadesh put on a coarse gray robe, and traveled northward along the river to Narasen's tomb. Outside, on the marble platform, the rites for the dead were declaimed freshly at great length and with much show—as they had not been on the first occasion, sixteen years before. When that had been seen to, Jornadesh addressed the tomb itself, assuring Narasen that she should be honored henceforth. Then he ordered the tomb opened, for he had brought caskets of treasure to adorn the burial chamber and her remnants—or at least, with which others should adorn them. But when they came to the door, they found it already accessible, and venturing in, though many bones lolled about the place, the bier of Narasen was vacant. Not a scrap of cloth or a wisp of hair remained, and the dust rested thick and showed no mark either of flesh or skeleton.

None who witnessed this thing experienced delight, but Jornadesh was overcome by misgiving. He fled back to Merh and shut himself in the palace. Here, guarded by his soldiers without, and by his strongest slaves within, he twisted in his bed, rattling with fright. Till, at last, he fell asleep and had the dream again.

2

Dead Narasen stood on a bank of gray shingles, before her a wide unflowing channel of chalky water, reflecting the chalky sky and three distant gray hills of Death's country, and Narasen herself, as now she was. And Narasen was gaudy in the monochromatic landscape, her skin blue as the hyacinth, the whites of her eyes nearly as blue but yellow in their centers as the topazes that depended from her ears. Her magenta hair, unstirred by the boisterous ineffectual wind of Innerearth, grew longer than it had in life and her nails were also very long, indigo in color. Narasen gazed at her reflection with no compassion. She loathed the world and the unworld alike, the gods, humanity and demons and even Lord Death, and she had not exempted herself from the catalog. But then, raising her eyes, for half a moment she was tempted, tempted to a dream of nostalgia. The farther bank of the river dissolved, became a golden plain, burnt with dark gold shadow, and there, between the pillars of tall trees, a golden leopard flickered. . . .

But Narasen caught herself, dispelled the dream, and the vision smoked away. She had sworn she would not indulge in reveries of the lost earth, neither to please herself nor to titillate her gloomy master, (Death was her master, she could hardly deny it). But Narasen, unlike the other mortal inhabitants of Innerearth, had kept her oath and fantasized not at

118

all. Amidst the splendors and joys of human illusion, she cut her path like a knife. She despised those who abandoned themselves to such hallucinations, and her frown was disliked and avoided. Indeed, Narasen was in some fashion dreaded more greatly than Uhlume, Lord Death. For Death did not frown upon his slaves. He indulged them. He was a sad, ghostly and terrifying father. The mortals who had bargained with him, and now lasted out their thousand years in his domain, vied with each other, actually, to try to warm his melancholy with what their dreamings created. But not Narasen. She had sworn and she had kept her oath. When she entered, the stone palace turned dull and dank, the music faded and the patternings sank in the floor. The human populace of the Innerearth chid her, reviled her, begged her to join them, to be merry and relent. Narasen had no word for them. She ignored them, she brushed them aside. She was yet a queen, and yet a cruel one. When Uhlume, observing the beauty and the song massacred in his halls, set his pale eyes on her, she bowed to him mockingly.

"I told you you should have pleasure in me," said Narasen. "Have pleasure then. For your thousand years of Narasen, this is all the pleasure you shall get."

But generally, she did not spend her timeless time in the palace of Death among the human slaves, she walked over the ghastly lands of the Innerearth, and grimly and without hope, she searched them for some variety, for a moss that had almost a color between the pebbles, for the intimation of a sun's rising or a night's descent, or a single star. She found none of these, of course, nor did she believe she would. *For this I sold my soul,* she thought. *For this I whored, and lay with a corpse and bore a child from my unloving womb. For* this! And then she would stare about, and her hate and her gall were enough to crack the hills, but they did not crack them. Though sometimes, presently she would look up from her anger, and notice the Lord Uhlume standing a small way off, on a hillside or in a valley, watching her. And she would go to him and say: "Do I grate on you, my lord?"

But the carving of his raven-black face told her nothing, and his bottomless empty eyes told less than nothing.

However, at this particular hour, Narasen, as she stood by the unlovely river, became aware that Death was away. It was impossible not to know these moments of his absence. A kind of vague lightening of the atmosphere of Innerearth occurred, and simultaneously, and paradoxically, its only interest flagged.

Now Narasen had recently been planning something for herself.

In the apartments of the Lord Uhlume there was said to be a certain spyglass. It would show the world and any place in the world that it was required to show. Narasen had heard as much from the chatterings of her fellow slaves, and for years that had been only minutes and for minutes that had really been years, she had toyed with the hot thought of visiting the private rooms of Death and finding out the spy glass and using it—a thing no other of the human population of Innerearth would dare.

Curious, Narasen's attitude to Uhlume. She feared him—no longer a mortal fear, but still a fear, for what was he but a sort of Terror made accessible? Even so, she treated with him as carelessly as ever, and more carelessly. Fear, besides, was to Narasen something to be fought with.

Thus, undaunted by scrutiny, Narasen returned to the dismal palace of Death, sought his apartments, and went in. There was neither lock nor guardian to bar her way. Generally, no one trespassed there.

The rooms were many and dark, and all of them apparently unfurnished. Maybe the furniture with which Death surrounded himself was so unlikely, so alien to the human eye or reason, that it was present but simply unrecognizable, and Narasen saw but did not assimilate what she saw. Or maybe Death, specter that he was, actually dwelt among nothing, blown out like a lamp when no one was looking at him. Whatever the reason, Narasen discovered not a chair nor a table nor a chest, and she began to suppose the spyglass to be stupid tale. Yet, in the very instant she supposed this, there the spyglass was in front of her, a crystal mounted in gold, lying in a corner. Which might tempt one to believe the spyglass was like the furniture—either in some other form which the beholder could translate if he wished, or else not there at all until wrenched into being by the determination of Narasen—for Uhlume long ago had told her, souls in unlive bodies were magicians.

Narasen, needless to say, did not bother with such theory. She took up the spyglass, rubbed off the damp and the dirt, and held it to one eye. At first she discerned only untidy gushings like smoke. Shortly though the glass grew clear and she peered straight out of Innerearth into the world and into Merh. At a carriage of silks and metals and at King Jornadesh in it with a bevy of his women, and the people of Merh tossing flowers in his way.

She had perhaps often considered things might be as they were in her city, but to have proof boiled and gurned in her.

"Ah!" spat Narasen, flinging down the glass, which of course did not shatter. "If I could curse as Issak cursed me, Jornadesh should be cursed for my murder, and not Jornadesh alone."

Just then, the quality of the air became different, more depressive yet more pleasing, which meant Uhlume was coming back.

Sure enough, not a second later, the door—there was a door, though not consistently—shot open and Uhlume came through it.

"Behold," snapped Narasen. "A robber is in your chamber. What shall I steal, my lord? The fabulous gems? The costly carpets?"

Uhlume said nothing and did nothing. Nothing really surprised him. At least, nothing had done so yet.

"I ask a boon," said Narasen.

"Name it," said Uhlume.

"I heard you have a spyglass which shows the world. I also heard you will permit your subjects a brief visit to the lands of earth. I hear that they rise aloft in their own dead bodies, and the flesh does not mortify, for you counteract decay with some clever magic. Well then, let me visit the earth. A night and some hours of day are all I ask."

"Some who pine to glimpse the world again, I will let go," said Uhlume. "As a rule, it makes them the more wretched. And there is a price."

"Death is a merchant," said Narasen. "What price?"

"The price you will not pay," said Uhlume. "All you see and all you do you must recount to me, must demonstrate to me in illusion, on your return."

Narasen smiled.

"This once I will do it. You shall feast on my adventures, you poor man-formed devil."

"No other speaks to me as you," said Uhlume.

"Then you are due for it."

The exit from Death's kingdom was simple but obscure. Death placed on the third finger of Narasen's left hand—the hand from which the top joint was gone—a gold ring containing a bit of sacrum, the sorcerous bone of the pelvis.

Once this ring was on, Narasen had only to step off from the leaden cliff where Uhlume had taken her, to find herself in a dark void, rushing upward. This passage of dark led into the River of Sleep, that river where dreaming souls strayed and mewed in panic, and it led beyond the river, through a thick smoulder of indecipherable dreams themselves. Narasen had come this way three times before, twice living and once dead. Now she beat on with no interest in the sights, hungry for what waited above, while by concentration of her will, she selected her point of emergence. Her head broke the surface of a sea of smoke, the shot straight upward, and everything was different. She was in the world again.

That difference. Another would have wept. But Narasen was Narasen. If she felt anything, it was her anger. She had been cheated of this.

It was the last hour of the afternoon. The sun hung low in a golden sky, and a dusky haze of gold washed over everything. The broad dark river was like beer, the plains were dappled leopard skin. The walls of a city seemed built of biscuit baked in saffron. There came the lazy noises of herds and the dim cries of men, all softened in the honey light. It was Merh and the city was Merh. The very scent of Merh it had, familiar to the native as the scents of her own body when she had lived. Merh, all gold, all sweetness. Merh not missing her, Merh not mourning her, Merh which had belonged to Narasen and which she had saved for this unremembering luscious indifference.

Narasen looked about her. She stood, as she had meant to, in the felons' graveyard outside the city wall.

Issak, the magician, had been cast here after she had killed him. Here, in an unmarked plot, his body had decayed, while his curse took hold of Narasen and her kingdom. Vividly, and with good reason, his words had stayed with her throughout her sojourn underground.

Barren as the womb of Narasen shall Merh become. Merh shall be Narasen. When Narasen ceases to be arid, so shall the land become lubricious. When Narasen is fruitful, then shall the land bear fruit. Merh shall be Narasen.

Narasen held out her blue hands to the markerless graves. Once before she had found the chink in the curse of Issak. This second chink had taken her years, but she had found it. Patrolling the vile Innerearth, it had come to her, the last sting in the scorpion's tail, which would make her, rather than Issak, rather than Jornadesh, the scorpion.

Narasen walked about the lonely piece of soil, testing with some sense new to her what couched there. Sometimes she would pause and stamp. And, from deep in their cavities, old bones seemed to shift, turning over in sleep, bidding her leave

122

them be, it was not they she wanted. At length she sensed a certain area beneath her, and she stopped and considered it. It appeared to her she saw right through the earth into the pit, at a skeleton, with a bit of the haft of a rusty spear yet jammed between its ribs. The skull grimaced up at her. The flesh was all gone, and the soul was gone—free, as her soul was not. But the bones of men in those days were imbued with the deeds and with the memories of the deeds of those who had owned them, as wax takes the imprint of a seal.

"Issak," said Narasen, though her voice was not a voice in the world. "The dead speaks to the dead. Recollect your curse on me and on my city."

Now when she said this, something moved in the skull, not any part of Issak, but a black worm. The worm came between the jaws of the skull, and first it lifted its head, and next it bowed to her.

"You acknowledge me then? Good. The curse was this, that Merh should be Narasen. And indeed it was. For when I was barren, Merh was barren, and when I bore fruit, so did Merh. But I am dead now, I was poisoned and I died and my skin is blue. Give me back the curse, bones of Issak, for you recall it well. Let Merh still be as Narasen. I paid a high fee to keep what was mine, and did not keep it. Others, who paid nothing, took Merh from me. Let Merh be Narasen still."

She was just and she was cruel. As if it accepted as much, the black worm nodded or bowed again. Then it detached itself from the bones of Issak. It pierced up through the grave till it emerged on the earth under the sky, and it wrapped itself three times about the ankle of Narasen. Narasen felt it like a coil of burning wire, and the heat of it rose through her whole body till she was filled and brimming. Then the worm shrivelled to a husk and slipped from her, and Narasen grinned her fine teeth which were now like lapis lazuli, and she looked toward the gates of Merh.

The gold air caught fire and the land flamed up to meet it, until the flame guttered out and night sank into Merh, deep as her deepest stones, and deeper. But in the night, a thousand lamp-lit windows had imprisoned the sunset in them, yellow, gold and red.

The gates were closing when a shadow came from the twilight road.

"Look, what is that?" one sentry asked another.

"Nothing, or nothing's brother."

But the first felt something brush by him, lighter than a

123

cobweb. He put out his hand to seize, and felt a woman's hair pass through his fingers. Yet very lank the hair was, disenchanting, cold, like weeds in a rank garden. The other sentry, less aware, discerned no touch, though something had actually touched him. A while after, a third man, blundering from the guard house, drunk, discovered a woman's handprint in the dust of the wall, and inside the outline of the handprint three or four moths alighted and then quivered, one by one, from the stone like burnt papers.

Two women had come tardily to a well, and were gossiping there. Nearby the child of the elder of them played.

The child glanced up. Out of the gloom floated a fearsome azure face, two gleaming eyes, a smile that was no smile. A hand drifted lightly over the child's head. The child, about to shriek, was dumb.

"Now, my son," called the elder woman across the darkness, "come here, for we must be going. Who is this," she added to her companion. "I have not seen such a woman here before." She could make out only a silhouette, it was true, and the glint of jewels at ears and waist and the shine of metal at throat and wrists. "Someone's rich maidservant, no doubt. Or some whore out for business."

In the dark, laughter that was not quite a laugh. The elder woman, misliking it, bade the other a swift farewell and hastened to gather up her ewer and her child and get home. The younger woman, delayed by the business of filling her jar, uneasily perceived the stranger bend over the well, trail her hand in the pitcher, then let it down into the water below. Then, as the young woman was moving off, a chill hand stroked her neck, and the woman took to her heels—too late.

Many were to endure that astringent petting.

Outside a tavern in the red light there, they saw a shape go by they took for a woman. One called and thrust his hand over her shoulder into her dress, but something in the texture of the stony breast his hand encountered drove him off. Another, snoring under a tree, his pot of drink beside him, never noticed a woman take up the crock and sample it and put it back.

The bakers, working till dawn at the cheerful hell of their ovens, shivered but did not turn. Hours later, mice crept from the vaults of flour and covered the alley with their bodies.

Some heard ropes creak down into the wells, and no one to be seen. A night bird flew to sip at a wet footprint by one of these wells, and ended its songs.

124

A girl lying in a garden with her lover, started and said: "How cold is your kissing."

"No colder than yours."

In the yards, the dogs did not bark. They whined, and stifled.

The whore in the archway said: "This is my place, be off."

The beggar, squatting on the temple stair, said: "Give me a coin."

A cloth vendor, staggering around a corner with too much wine in him, came face to face with a nightmare, prostrated himself on his belly and swore never to drink again, and, as her icy foot slid over his neck, his oath was made sure.

On its incline, the palace of Merh glowed in a perpetual rosy daytime of lights. Before the bronze doors, soldiers with crossed spears were watching, without much alarm or anticipation, to see if they could spot the lingering thing which worried their lord. Ever since the wild man's prophecy, Jornadesh had cowered in his rooms. So much for wild men and prophecies. So much for wise and majestic King Jornadesh.

Yet the palace gate stood open, and through the gate one came.

"No farther!" shouted the soldiers. "State your errand."

But this person who approached them did not check. Up the marble steps this person came, and by the glare of the torches the soldiery beheld a woman in a black garment belted with rubies, and gold at her neck and on her arms. But her hair was no color they had seen on a woman's head before, neither her skin.

"Now what prank is this? No tricks. We will have an answer."

But they received no answer, and the woman came on, and something in the hearts of these men shrank. Presently the youngest flung his spear. It struck the woman in her side, but there was no blood and the woman did not fall, but rather she pulled the spear from her and tossed it down, and her face was frightful with a furious derision. And she called out to them in a voice which was unlike any voice they had ever heard: "Get from my road!"

And at the sound of this weird cry, all the birds that massed on the palace roof, catapulted themselves into the sky with a brazen flash of wings, and flew from the city as if it were on fire.

The soldiers were finally appalled, and they removed themselves from the path of the woman, all but the youngest who had thrown his spear, and he was too afraid to stir. And the

125

woman pressed her palm to his face as she walked by him, and then walked on into the palace.

It is to be supposed that Narasen, whose house this had been, knew the byways of the palace well. Silently and mostly unwitnessed, she moved through them, and now and then some article she handled. At the doors of Jornadesh's apartments—formerly her own—the king's strong guard of slaves were dicing. But when they set eyes on Narasen, the dice were scattered and the slaves were scattered, and shortly Narasn stood unhindered at the entrance. And in she went, unbidden and undesired, as once Issak the magician had come in, unbidden and undesired by Narasen herself.

Jornadesh reclined in the innermost chamber, drinking much wine. His back, clothed in scarlet, was to the door, and hearing a soft footstep, he peevishly moaned: "Know this, girl, I summoned you to soothe me under the unjust threat of these foul dreams, which continually disturb my rest. Therefore soothe me, or you shall be slain, I promise you. If I am not to count my life safe, I am persuaded that you shall not. Hasten now, disrobe and pleasure me."

But Narasen trod noiselessly over the rugs, and going up to Jornadesh from behind, she raked his back with her corpselong nails, which rent his robe and his flesh under it, so he screamed. And screaming, he rotated himself ponderously about, and thus he learned the exact meaning and the exact instant of the prophecy.

Jornadesh's mood at this encounter with Nemesis was quite indescribable, and no description has survived it. Most probably he grovelled on the floor, shed tears and evinced other symptoms of utter terror, such as are common to all men, then and now.

But, "Hush," whispered Narasen. "This is no show with which to welcome your queen and prince, the ruler of Merh. Get up, put on your jewels and tokens of office. Tonight I will sit with you in the great hall of the palace. Tonight I will be your guest, and you shall give over to me the royal chair you stole from me. You shall bring poets to extol me, and women to rejoice me, all those women you have nauseated by your flabby hams. Now. Do as I say, or must I convince you further of my rights?"

And Jornadesh, insane with horror, obeyed her in everything. Although, when they went down into the hall, no one remained, for word of the supernatural had sped there before Narasen. The whole palace indeed was empty. Only a distant

126

wailing and a confusion of many lights indicated the direction the general flight had taken.

So Narasen sat companionless in that great hall where she had sat in the days of her living kingship. And she gazed about her at the alabaster lamps and the silver tableware, and at the bowls of wine and the plates of bread and meat which could no longer nourish her. On the wall hung leopard skins, the coats of beasts she had hunted, and above the royal chair hung a banner of silk which her father had captured from a mighty prince in war, and at her feet was a footstool with pearls crusted over it, the gift of another mighty prince whom Narasen had once spared by her sword.

As she gazed, the eyes of Narasen grew heavy with grief and venom. And soon she chanced to see, with those dreadful eyes of hers, the distortion of a random shadow which happened to have formed beside the chair, and the appearance of this shadow was like a child, a baby, and when the candles shimmered in the lamps, the baby seemed to kick and wave its limbs.

"And you—" muttered Narasen in her unwholesome reverie—" can it be that you are breathing yet while I am dead? You, you brat, without whose assistance no murderer should have bested me. I remember your mewling in the tomb, but I believe you are free of tombs now, and in the world where I cannot stay. Ah, would you were but here with me, beloved son, I should repay your kindness, and with interest."

Hearing her whispering there, her eyes unfixed, Jornadesh crawled away, and she did not detain him. He tottered to his stable and hauled himself upon a scrawny little horse—the first which would be docile with him—and he rode from Merh with his life. But he did not get far with it.

3

For a day, Simmu had wandered through the lawless lands about the lake of salt, weeping with the sky for Zhirem. It was another legacy the Eshva had left Simmu, their flawless vats of emotion—which they could afford, since their memories were short and their lives unending. Yet Simmu, wandering blind with tears and mindless with unhappiness and loss, would perhaps have gone on in this hopeless limbo for months—or till his strength failed and life with it.

When the light began again to ebb, more by chance than

127

plan, he entered a cave, fringed by the black plants of the region. And here he slept exhaustedly, though even in sleep his dreams were of Zhirem, and the tears poured from Simmu's eyes without waking him.

Then something happened in the cave. What thing? A sheaf of smoke with no flame, and yet somehow a sort of fire in it. And out of this—smoke, fire—stepped a man. The cave was too shadowy to see him, should any have been awake to stare. But he was dark, darker than the darkness, and cloaked almost it seemed with jet black wings. The radiance of his eyes came and went, catching some gleam that did not exist in the cave, and his black hair caught the same nonexistent gleam, so that his invisible face seemed rayed about with sheens and stars.

A short while he stood above Simmu as he slept and cried in his sleep. And then the man who had come from the darkness stretched out his hand. A net—stars, sheens, smokes and fireless-fire—appeared to weave from his hand over Simmu. And Simmu's eyes grew dry.

Then the man kneeled, and he ran the same sorcerous hand lightly over Simmu's body. And the body of Simmu, still in sleep, briefly responded to this tracery of touch, beginning to rearrange itself, to flower into breasts, to withdraw the blade of its maleness, while the young beard deserted the jaw, and the jaw assumed in moments the smooth-pored narrowness of a female chin.

The Demon—it was he, it was Azhrarn, and who else but?—laughed softly, for the Vazdru had vocal organs as the Eshva did not, or appeared not to have. He stroked back the hair of Simmu, and he sang in Simmu's ear in the way of Demonkind. The song may not be transposed. But somehow the song, or the fingers, conveyed the idea of languour and of forgetfulness, that Zhirem should disappear from Simmu's brain, that Merh might evolve there, and the consideration that the western roads to Merh would be entertaining.

Outside, a nightingale began its own music. Its notes were laced with a nervous brilliance, for it guessed who was near.

But Azhrarn, the Prince of Demons, for once went as harmlessly away as he had arrived, into the dark.

Simmu, the caress fading from her skin, returned to masculinity.

He roused at sunrise, partly because the nightingale, unbalanced by its experience, was continuing dementedly to sing.

Simmu rose, and moved out from the cave, and gazed into the sky. It was as if he had lain down the night before in agony with some wound or illness, and woken mended. He cast about him, trying—a human habit he had picked up—to recover what had hurt him. Someone had gone away, one he had valued—perhaps that was it. Yet now it did not matter, this absence of old stale love. And westward—westward lay a city that somehow, inexplicably, he knew belonged to him. A sudden elation blazed up in Simmu's mind. Merh—Merh, which was his. True, he did not covet a kingdom, did not grasp the notion of temporal power, rule and riches. He could not really have explained to himself what attracted him in the notion of Merh. . . . Azhrarn, who had induced the mirage, had clad it in his own rare glamour, and that was what drew Simmu, without his realizing it.

Soon, freed from pain, Zhirem extinguished from his thoughts, mesmerized by the tug of a goal, Simmu took his Eshva-wandering westward.

And even the black bizarre lands took on beauty that day. The sun gilded them and gilded their peculiar waters, and flowers were found in the thickets, and unusual fruits. Creatures jumped into the sunlight, sometimes running after Simmu, attracted by his demon-aura, confused at its presence the wrong side of night. Westward, too, the lawless wilderness began to melt. Tracts of green showed some miles farther on where the country descended. And the sun itself walked behind Simmu, and then overhead and eventually before him, indicating courteously the way he must go, till at last it dropped from sight beyond the green places.

The dusk was cold, but Simmu, always at ease with the whims of night and without Zhirem's human reminder, made no fire. He settled to slumber in the hollow ribs of a rock, swathed only in the herdsman's shapeless raiment which now did for either sex of his, and blanketed by hair.

About midnight, Simmu opened his eyes on a slim black dog which was seated before the rock. The dog regarded him with clear and luminous eyes, then it got up and padded away, and Simmu was irresistibly motivated to follow.

The dog, (Azhrarn was capable of many forms, even that of elderly gray-headed men who might haunt the shores of salt lakes,) bounded along in a glib and elegant way till it vanished into some trees. Pushing through these trees, Simmu emerged on an ancient earthen road. The road ran westward, folding itself downward with the land, while overhead burned countless stars, and everywhere around drifted the mysterious ambience of night. Simmu accepted the road and the night,

129

and started to move along with them. The dog did not come back, but presently Simmu detected another who walked behind him.

Simmu turned, with no unease, but with a marvelous slow, swirling excitement.

To say Azhrarn was handsome is a foolishness, for this mortal expression of a round world lies like a pebble at the gateway of what Azhrarn really was. Advisedly, however, did they name him The Beautiful, and that, too, was not enough, indeed as inadequate as to say: The sea is wet. His hair was blue-black, it was like no other hair, like the hair of some fabulous beast or a piece of starred night sky, transmuted through silk and water. His eyes, which had seen centuries snuffed out almost in a blink, were impossibilities—two things made of light which was black, two searing flames the shade of unmitigated darkness. He wore black too, yet somehow the black seemed full of all types and nuances of color. The eagle-winged cloak appeared to glare and shine with jewels or with conflagrations or with something preposterous and wonderful, yet it did not; or maybe, it did. He walked in a man's form, but the wolf, the panther, the bird of prey, these also were there. And so subtly he walked, so light, even the earth could not hear him, and Simmu only heard because he had been permitted to hear. And certainly Simmu, who knew him instantly, and still did not know him, (for such was the spell the demons could construct about themselves), Simmu certainly did not question why a thing which was more or less simple wickedness should manifest itself as a god.

"A fine night for journeying," said Azhrarn. Believe, his voice matched the rest of him, "But any night is preferable to any day."

Simmu was hesitating, inclined to drop down and worship. But Azhrarn, who liked to be admired, in the way of demons, somehow informed Simmu without speech exactly what response he required. And it was only pliancy. Thus Simmu, pliant, stood and waited, silent as any Eshva while a Vazdru Lord talked to him.

"You will have thought this a dull journey, however," said Azhrarn. "Should you like to travel more quickly?"

Simmu (pliant) gazed at him. Azhrarn snapped his fingers and a piece of the night tore open and out of it dashed two demon horses. They were naturally of a very definite blackness, accoutred in brass and silver, with manes like steam or smoke. Simmu had ridden on the backs of lynxes and leopards for fun in his childhood, and once an earth

130

horse had carried him, but the demon horse, when he mounted it, had no likeness to any earth thing.

Exhilarated, Simmu let the horse bear him as it would. It leapt forward after the mount Azhrarn had chosen. Immediately both seemed to be flying, and possibly they were. For sure, such horses could run over water, erupt in and out of Underearth at the whistle of their masters, and for speed, they would outrace any mortal thing, save tide or sun, over which demons had no influence.

The ride was wild and thrilling. The night had changed to a racing fluid thing, the stars going at a great rate, or suggesting that they did, dashing over and around the horses like silver streamers or a kind of storm of cosmic rain. And out of this racing stuff, objects burst and slid away. Simmu beheld features of the landscape, such as bell-shaped hills or indigo valleys, diluted with mist, pointing forests and slender mountains, and between these came other phenomena, white-walled palaces and chiselled ceramic towers pencilled up the sky, and the ugly towns of men all flung down the slopes like broken bricks.

After many hours that had seemed seconds, the horses ended their career on a wooded height.

"It will soon be dawn," said Azhrarn, "and that feverish lady and I share nothing. Stay in this wood. Tomorrow night I will take you nearly to the gates of Merh, child of the leopardess. Did you know your father died before he got you on her?" Azhrarn inquired. The youth had finally knelt to him, and Azhrarn caressed his hair. And Simmu listened only to the music of Azhrarn's voice, not hearing the words, while the caress made delicious nonsense of any logic.

Azhrarn observed him, idly and pitilessly, but with some pleasure. The macabre conception of Simmu, and his sexual duality, fascinated the Prince, and the beauty of Simmu appealed to him. Simmu's entreaty beside the lake of salt had been relayed to Azhrarn, but if Azhrarn had answered it and found nothing to intrigue him, it would have gone far worse with Zhirem and with Simmu than it had. Far, far worse.

In Zhirem, Azhrarn had felt no interest.

Where humanity foresaw only evil for him, Azhrarn foresaw only a propensity for despair. Demons liked mortals as they liked their horses—slaves to be ridden. Zhirem had none of that. Strength lurked within him, and good, or a struggling wish for goodness. The only hope of wickedness in Zhirem would come from the rejection not acceptance of Azhrarn, and Azhrarn understood as much, and thus turned him away into the night.

But Simmu. Simmu was to Azhrarn like a new instrument, one he had never played before. He was not sure what melody the strings and the soundbox would produce, but some melody there would be. And the first hand which would pluck the strings would be Merh, which meant kingship and the recurrent disruption of a battle or a murder. Azhrarn had often been a maker and deposer of kings. It was a childish exercise he contemptuously enjoyed on occasion.

But now a pale writing was in the sky between the trees.

Azhrarn laid one finger on the Drin gem at Simmu's neck.

"Simmu," said Azhrarn, "Twice Fair; you are well named. Think of Merh."

"Only of you," said Simmu, startlingly aloud and in a girl's voice. Azhrarn smiled, delighted by these initial notes from the new instrument. Then he and his horses were gone, and the dusky wood began surreptitiously to lighten.

That day Simmu slept—left to wait and to dream by a demon, as in babyhood. And, true to his word, his dreams were of Azhrarn. The second night, Azhrarn came back like the rising of a dark star. And that second night was like the first for marvel, for the wild ride and the dazzling past of things, and the sensual quality all and everything came to possess.

Accordingly, Azhrarn brought Simmu to Merh in two nights, a journey of many thousand miles and many many days.

Where the thick-boled columnar trees grew close about the river, there Azhrarn left the young man in the moments before the second dawn.

Now Azhrarn had troubled to know nothing of Merh, only of its part in this business of Simmu. However, this second night they had ridden through, fast as flying meteors, had been the exact night of Narasen's visitation. As the walled palaces and the daggered mountains had whirled by Simmu, Narasen had shuffled like a malignant paper about the streets of Merh. And when Simmu came to earth within sight of the city, the grip of her curse had already seized the place.

Knowing none of this, yet Azhrarn, whose senses were keener than razor's edge, laid his hand on Simmu's shoulder, and said: "Wait again for me till the sun descends. Do not enter the city till I am with you."

Simmu was content enough to be obedient. He climbed into a tree and stretched himself there and slept, with the variegation of sun and leaves on his skin. But Simmu had his own form of sensibility, and shortly, though asleep, he came to suspect, through his skin and his hair, that all was not well in Merh.

It was the tree itself. This tree so broad and vital, a pillar of enduring amber, which had begun, insidiously, to wither. And high above, a flock of birds had come to rest in the amber tree, but not one sang, and when the wind blew, some of these birds cascaded from the branches like blossoms. . . . In the river also, as the day went on, blossoms floated, and the perfume of these flowers was not precisely sweet.

Simmu dreamed of a man hanged from a dead bough, and Simmu woke shivering in the afternoon. Then he saw the traffic in the river and, craning about, he noticed other things.

Toward Merh, the plains had acquired a strange azure burnish; even the walls of the city had it, under a sky which seemed to have set the fashion with its scalding blue. Nor did any sound come from the city, as no sound came from anywhere about. No animal made noise, no bird and no man.

The afternoon intensified and wearied and started to fail.

Eventually Simmu leapt down from the tree, which had such a reverberation of death to it he could no longer bear it.

Curiosity, the entertainment of demons, the bane of men, curiosity which consisted chiefly of dread, now began to push Simmu in the direction of the city. And at the same minute as he was called, he was repelled, for the scent of his enemy—that enemy he always fled—was everywhere around him.

In the end, Simmu ventured into the fields that spread out before Merh. So he came on a richly dressed fat man in a scarlet robe, lying over the back of a horse. Both mount and rider had expired; both mount and rider, like the fields, had taken on a bluish tinge. At that moment, another of the bird blossoms plummeted down from the air, and that also was blue.

Simmu did not know where to run to, since death had encompassed him. The sun was slipping now over the western incline of heaven, but the sunset too promised a horrible purple blueness. And then, along the road from Merh's gate, came an animate walking figure, yet with more blue terror in it than anything else.

Narasen had remained in Merh for a longer time than she had bought from Lord Death. She had brooded there in the daylight, going up and down the streets to gloat on what she had accomplished. Revenge had neither soothed nor

133

distressed her, it was like a sort of makeshift meal when she was starved—something to staunch her hunger, but not enough. Now she took this route, searching for the corpse of Jornadesh. And, because she had done too much lingering and the protection of Innerearth was wearing thin, decay had begun to approach her body. She was more gaunt, bruised looking, altogether more dreadful, and her hair was like a wind clotted with rags.

Simmu froze at the sight of her. The last occasion he had seen this lady she had been dead in her tomb, and sliding into the earth with Death himself. Simmu remembered, and a ghastly fascination, like that of the rabbit before the snake, struck him down. Thus he waited in sick dazedness for Narasen to reach him.

She noted Jornadesh firstly, that colorful blot between the stalks of young (now poisoned) grain. Having noted him, she raised her frightful eyes and noted Simmu.

She had given the idea of Simmu a deal of thought. Though he had altered even more than she since last they met, she knew him.

Neither spoke, neither had need of words. Yet each was, in his own way, articulate. Then, cat-like, Simmu began to shrink, inch by inch, backwards and away from her. And she, cat-like, inch by inch, crept forward pursuing him, while, as a background to this, the light thickened, the garish mulberry sun lowering on the edge of the land, and six or seven more birds fell from the air among the blasted grain.

At the perimeter of the field was a narrow track. One less sure-footed than Simmu would have stumbled here, but he half twisted to stare at the track, and tensed himself as if after all to sprint away.

Then she did speak, in that un-voice of hers.

"Beloved. Stay, beloved. It is only Narasen, Narasen who bore you. I would only embrace you, my darling. Only that."

The voice, and the calculating false words it used, brought Simmu to a final extreme of fear, and he in turn screamed out. He screamed for Zhirem, without recollecting who Zhirem had been. And Narasen sprang forward, the leopardess yet, with all her claws in readiness.

But the sun had fallen, and the rending death-laden hands of the blue woman met—not the flesh of Simmu—but a dark lightning bolt which suddenly shot upward in her path.

"No, madam," said Azhrarn, soft as could be, "you do not harm what is mine."

Narasen let down her claws. She became as expressionless

134

as Death himself, and she took in Azhrarn coolly. She assumed the Prince of Demons could not hurt her as she was now, though she could not get by him.

"Oh lover of the earth," said she, "can it be that you, Lord of all wickedness, are protecting the innocent from the evil I would offer him?"

"Return to the country of your kind," said Azhrarn. ".You have overstayed your welcome in the world."

"Give me what belongs to me."

"There is nothing here of yours."

"Black cat," said Narasen, "go back and prowl in your crockery city, black cat. You and your cousin Uhlume, you two Lords of Darkness, I spit on both of you." And then, in her fury, Narasen smote Azhrarn across the mouth.

"Daughter," said Azhrarn, in the kindest of tones, "you have not been wise."

And indeed, she had not been. For from her right hand with which she had smote him, the flesh scattered like blue petals, leaving only the bare skeleton behind.

"Take that with you to Innerearth," said Azhrarn. "Tell the one you call my cousin, who is no kin to me, that he should keep his people in at night. Now go, daughter of bitches, go and play knucklebones."

And Azhrarn gestured at the ground, which parted and dragged Narasen snarling into itself.

Presently Azhrarn looked about at Simmu.

"And who is this Zhirem you call out to?" inquired Azhrarn. "I thought you were to think only of me."

"Only of you," said Simmu, and sank down at Azhrarn's feet. "But I am no longer as I was. I have seen death too often and too near."

"Demons do not meditate on death," said Azhrarn. "Remember the Eshva women and what they taught you."

"Death has taught me I am mortal."

And in fact, it seemed that Simmu was not quite as he had been. Some glittering garment had sloughed from him, some new grayer garment had been put on.

"Do not disappoint me," said Azhrarn. "There are ways to circumvent even death."

"Teach me them," Simmu cried.

"Perhaps," said Azhrarn. "For one, I will tell you this. To touch any part of this place is fatal, the woman has so polluted it with her venom. But that round your neck, that given jewel of Underearth, has protected you."

"You mentioned my father to me once," said Simmu

slowly, "but I do not recall what you said, save that it had to do also with death."

Then Azhrarn beheld for sure that a form of humanness had got hold of Simmu. Men, not demonkind, mused on their fathers. And yet, within Azhrarn, a flickering of malicious light came and went. It appeared to him that Simmu had abruptly arrived upon the threshold of his fate, and that his fate held all the seeds of upheaval and wildness that a demon could yearn after. And so Azhrarn, who had informed himself of all of it, lessoned Simmu in his surprising beginning. He made a story of the beautiful man-queen and of the curse of Issak. He told of her visit to the witch in the House of the Blue Dog, and the bargain struck with Uhlume, Lord Death. He made a dream of her liaison with the blond fair youth who walked from his tomb to meet her, whiter than marble and twice as cold. Simmu sat at Azhrarn's feet in the poisoned land of Merh and listened. And the grayness gathered about his eyes, and his mouth became the mouth of a bitter anguished man.

Later, still scenting destiny and mischief, alert for it, Azhrarn conducted Simmu through the very streets of the murdered city. Azhrarn's companionship was itself a talisman against Simmu's terror, and familiarity worked its own dreary healing.

The dead were all about. They lay in heaps. Birds and beasts, men and women and their children. The flowers had died, the trees; the wells were inky. The houses and the very stones of the roadways had a look of death. Everything she had laid her hands on, everything her foot or her hair or her robe had brushed had perished.

And those who had afterwards touched these things, or other men she had previously touched, had been contaminated; a swift and thorough plague. The city was dyed with it. Merh was a tomb, and the whole land of Merh, infected to its borders, and none spared—or almost none.

Simmu could not see all this and retain an actual shock at death. No, his emotion was transferred. It became a violent hatred.

Somewhere in the deep of the night, walking with Azhrarn over the slopes where the birds had rained from the sky, Simmu said aloud:

"You have cured me, my Lord, of my cowardice." He cried it as a mortal man, no longer in the unhuman fashion of before. "Now I will not hide or retreat. I will be the en-

136

emy of Death. I will seek his destruction. And I believe in my soul, O Lord of Lords, that you will help me."

"Simmu," murmured Azhrarn, "only men remember they have souls."

PART FIVE

Pomegranate

1

Simmu woke this time, not recollecting when he had slept or when Azhrarn had left him. The sun was glaring down on the corpse of Merh. Simmu had within himself a similar raw glaring which he could not evade. He had learned a great amount in the darkness. He had learned he was mortal. He seemed to himself very changed, almost unbearably so. The innocent elemental qualities which had enabled him to work Eshva magic, the pure ruthlessness and singleness of purpose and oblique sweetness that had made him unhuman before, all these seemed gone. Even physically, he experienced his clay. He felt heavy and leaden. He saw himself in retrospect as he had been—saw himself with amazed and uneasy wonder, as others had seen him. But he was not, in reality, so very altered. The metamorphosis was in his spirit, and his flesh did not positively reflect it. To another, still, he had that glaze of the marvellous and the strange. But to himself, he was less.

Presently he got to his feet, and with head hanging, trudged about the plain, purposeless as only a human thing can think itself to be.

Suddenly, out of the soundless, lifeless expanse, a voice called. Simmu spun to face it—only he or a lynx could have moved so limber and so swift, but he did not credit himself. And there, on the left hand, some thirty feet away, stood a weird figure, a shaven-headed bearded man clothed in a leopard's skin. Over his shoulders were the healing marks of whip stripes, and his skin was *blue*. Simmu looked at the skin and Narasen leapt to his mind's eye.

"Never be alarmed," said the sage, whom Jornadesh had had ineffectually whipped. "The poison is already fading from my system and has done me no harm. Besides, I see you also know a trick or two and have survived here. But everything else has died."

138

"Part of me has died," said Simmu.

"Then yield it to death."

"No, I grudge him the least portion," said Simmu, dismally recalling his pledge of the previous night, and how it appeared Azhrarn had grown bored with him and left him quickly after it, with no promise of return.

"To speak of death as if he were a man is to create a man to be death," said the sage. "Wickedness has also assumed a shape, and you travel by night in company I should not like to share."

Simmu saw a dead serpent before him in the dead grass. He kneeled and lifted the serpent and stared at it.

Proclaimed the sage: "I must warn you, the power which uses me—or I it, I have never been sure—is about to possess me."

"Is such a thing agreeable to you?" asked Simmu dully.

"I do not believe it is," said the sage, "but since I noticed you, I have been aware of a gathering in me, and that I shall be made to gibber out some nonsense or other. Which you will then be obliged to interpret for yourself."

Simmu trembled, not knowing why. The sage abruptly crashed headlong, flinging himself about and grunting as if in a fit. Then, from his frenzy, he called sternly and distinctly:

"Consider the blueness of Merh's poison and the blue face of the dead. Find the pomegranate drinker of bones. Shout of poison among the poison trees."

This delivered, the sage rolled over and arose with great dignity and calm.

"I do not understand—" faltered Simmu.

"I told you you would not," replied the sage.

"A drinker of bones—blueness—poison among poison trees—"

"Now do you think, pretty youth, I am going to interpret my own riddles to you? I will say only this. If you are seeking a particular thing and can put together the words I have uttered and use them, then the thing is as good as found."

"What do I seek?" Simmu shut his eyes. He let the dead snake fall. "I am Death's Enemy," he whispered, "so I am seeking the destruction of Death." Then he opened his eyes, and beheld the wild man some paces away. "Wait!" cried Simmu.

"No," said the sage. "You are too fair, and I am sworn to celibacy, and I do not mean to grow a third leg I may not journey on."

And he would say no more, nor glance behind him, and soon he was gone from view.

Simmu's hopeless goalless walking took him in a circular mode about the spot where he had woken. He did not mean to stray too far, and when the sun westered, a frantic eagerness welled in him that with the coming of night, another also would come.

The sun at length went down.

The silence, which was absolute, seemed to become impossibly more silent. Even the wind held its breath.

Huge and mercilessly cold were the stars above dead Merh. Next a moon ascended, a sickle blade cleaving the shadows.

Simmu could not fail to see, with all this glow, no one had come to join him on the plain.

And it occurred to Simmu, oddly, that he had known a desertion and a cooling of love before. And then, as he lay on the untender ground with the stars driving their spines into his eyes, a vague dream washed over him like a wave on a beach. Unicorns were dancing on a charcoal shore and he dancing with them.

And still half in the dream, Simmu rose and threw the peasant's robe from him. The moon burned him with her white fires and some of the new enamel of mortality unhardened from his soul. He thought of Azhrarn, and the body of Simmu shivered and rippled to the deepest cores of itself, and with satisfying lithe twists and tremors of delicious pain, it rearranged itself. And Simmu the maiden lifted her arms against the narrow moon and began to dance.

And as she danced, still her brain was more human than before, and with a woman's small deceitfulness she thought: *I am beautiful now, and he will return and I will pretend I have forgotten him, even he, the Lord of all Lords.*

But when he did come, (perhaps he had been delayed by another sport, perhaps he had been only awaiting just such a proof that the demon element in Simmu persisted,) there was no pretense. Dancing, a black smoke enveloped her, an incense smoke that drugged her and sent her reeling, not downward, but up into air. And looking through this smoke with unfocused eyes, she saw swimming there the moon and the stars, but more beautiful than stars, the two eyes of Azhrarn.

So she appeared to herself to be lying in nothing in the sky's vault with the arms of the Demon about her, but he gently said to her:

"You have been talking with a bald bearded leopard, and what did he say to you?"

"That I endangered his celibacy," said Simmu the maiden, and she wound her arms about the neck of Azhrarn. And as she touched him the exquisite sensation she derived merely from this contact caused her softly to cry out. But, as gently as he had questioned her, Azhrarn disengaged himself from her, and he said: "The time is mine to choose, and is not now."

Then Simmu turned her face from him and discovered it was not the sky she lay in but a black forest of feathers, an eagle's breast blacker and broader than a midnight. Or so it seemed. The eagle flew eastward, and the beat of its wings was thunder.

The thunder told her this: "In your brain I have seen the image of sage who mentioned bones and blueness and poison. I know the riddle, and will take you to the House of the Blue Dog, where it shall be answered."

A feather on the breast of an eagle, Simmu's transitory girlhood left him, and the world fled by beneath.

2

She was sleeping on a couch, the witch in the House of the Blue Dog, Lylas. She was dreaming of the Lord Uhlume. He strode over the world and she trod demurely at his heels and she knew herself valued, and she heard mankind exclaim: "It is Death's chosen sister."

She slept naked, did Lylas, all but her girdle of finger bones and her fabulous malt-brown hair that made a silken cover in which she moaned and softly writhed, dreaming of Uhlume's footsteps passing before her and the edge of his cloak which occasionally billowed over her skin.

Outside the mansion, the wild pomegranate trees whispered to each other nastily, and dropped their malignant fruit on the ground for their witch mistress to tread on in the morning. If the trees remembered Narasen, they did not say. But they discussed the moon and wished they could drag it down in their branches, for, being slaves trapped in soil, they resented the freedom of others.

Uhlume, in the dream, was striding beneath a gallows and as she followed, the rope rasped over the witch's breast. She opened her eyes and found the enormous dog of blue enamel licking her lasciviously. But seeing her awake, it barked:

"Something is coming."

"What, dolt?"

"There was a rushing of wings," said the dog. "Part of the sky dropped in the meadow and I hurried away. Then I glanced back and a man came who was not a man and with him a youth who was not a youth."

"Will you play word games with *me*?" hissed the witch.

"Delectable mistress, never," fawned the dog. "But as I am your servant, this is what I saw."

That moment, the brazen door of the witch's mansion was struck one ringing blow. Lylas frowned, for those who sought her aid did not normally make so vehement a signal. But she lashed the dog with her hair.

"Hasten. See who is knocking."

"I am afraid," grovelled the dog, but it bounded off just the same.

And when the brazen door gaped wide, there it stood, seven hands high and barking at the callers:

"Who are you?"

"I am Azhrarn, the Prince of Demons," said the tall dark man on the threshold, "and this youth you will conclude to be my son. Now, go tell your lady of the pomegranates."

The dog rushed to obey, with a loud clanking of its ceramic teeth, and its pottery tail between its legs and grinding horribly on the floor.

The visitors advanced more leisurely. They climbed the stairway the dog had galloped up and entered a room of many blue lamps with pink fires in them. Then a piece of drapery blew aside and the witch ran in. Her face was white and she cast herself down at the feet of Azhrarn so the rugs were awash with her hair.

"Lord of Lords," cried the witch, "be more welcome than my own person in my house, and have mercy on your hand-maiden."

"Suppose me merciful," said Azhrarn, "and get up."

The witch arose. She put back some of her hair so a flower-bud breast appeared through its veiling, but she kept her bone girdle hidden. Her eyes darted, making sure of her guests in a single swift glare, before she lowered her lids modestly. One guest was as naked—more naked—than she, and so was dismissed as only an uncommonly beautiful young man. But she had seen sufficient, being learned, to know the other was no other than he said.

142

"May I," entreated Lylas, "summon anything for my Lord? A chair of silver hung with rare velvet for him to be seated in? A wine of smoke made from the breath of a summer lotus? Shall music be played? Shall incense be burned? I ask no more than to serve you."

"Rest assured you shall," said Ahzrarn, and Lylas shivered. Then he laid his hand lightly on the shoulder of the young man beside him. The young man's extraordinary eyes flickered—Azhrarn had communicated some cue or information to him. And now the young man spoke in a quiet but clear hard voice that sounded as if it seldom liked to be used.

"My mother was Narasen, the queen of Merh. Do you recollect her?"

"I?" said Lylas smoothly. "Many enter my house."

The young man tensed. The witch, not even looking at him, started at a sudden danger in his person apart from the borrowed danger of Azhrarn.

"You wore my mother's finger bone at your waist," the young man said. "She made a pact with the personage you reverence, whose agent you are. When she was dead, you ground up the bone, as is your custom, and drank it in wine and thus renewed your youth, as constantly you do."

"Well," said Lylas, "it is true. I do recall the lady. But I am under the protection of my master, and I have done nothing that was not agreed on."

"Yes you have. One thing."

"What thing?" demanded Lylas, raising her head to gaze at the youth, and she did not care now for his lynx's eyes or the way he stared back at her with them.

"The poison from which Narasen died—you made it to that purpose."

"I?" said Lylas again, but she took a step away from him.

It was a fact. Lylas had not taken to Narasen, disliking Narasen's hauteur with Lord Death—the worse that he had not checked it. Lylas had grown envious, for she was jealous by nature. She had plucked a red pomegranate and dug out its curiously blue toxic seeds, and from this she had made a lethal liquor and had stored it in a little phial. And day by day, and night by night, she had smilingly played with this phial, thinking what might be done with it. At length she sent a spy to Merh—she had governance over certain of the lower orders, various worms and lizards. Her emissary took many months to reach the city and get back again, but it brought her news, and finally the witch put on a disguise (she had several) and she went herself. Here she sought the house of a

143

likely physician, a man who was currupt and avaricious and served greedy Jornadesh into the bargain. And, entering the house in an abnormal fashion and arriving unexpectedly in the physician's laboratory, she offered to sell him the phial.

"Now why should I have an interest in such muck?" demanded the physician, trying to conceal his alarm at her supernatural entry.

"Is there not someone in this city who is ambitious, someone who dreams of the throne of Merh?"

The physician coughed. "Merh has already a queen."

"Yes, and she will soon be in her bed in travail with a child. And when the child is born and she is weak from her labor, she may call for drink."

The physician said: "Your chat is treason."

But after further discussion he said: "Why should this poison be superior to any I could mix myself?"

"Because," said Lylas, "it is possible to adapt the dose in order that death occur at the most convenient moment. More, the draught is painless, yet renders the victim both powerless to resist or to cry for help. And it will show no trace until some hours after the corpse is cold."

"I have only your word for that."

"You have my leave to experiment."

So a poor urchin was bundled into the house, forced to sample the brew and presently expired at the predicted instant, painlessly, silently and in despair, and without turning immediately blue.

In exchange for the phial, Lylas received three pieces of gold. These she did not spend, having small need of coin, but kept them in a jar in her house. And sometimes, during the sixteen years since Narasen's demise, Lylas would take out these three gold pieces and play with them, smiling.

Now, however, she did not smile.

"It is a lie," she said. "Who told you such a falsehood?"

"It is no lie," said Simmu. "Be thankful vengeful Narasen did not hear it. Just now she came up from the Innerearth and slew all Merh in pique."

"Be thankful too," said Azhrarn, "if your master does not hear. Uhlume loves to make bargains with mankind, and who will bargain with him any more if they learn he is not to be trusted, that no sooner is a soul promised him than he permits his agents to slay the flesh and send the soul below before its time?"

Then Lylas went paler than ever. She had been very stupid, in the way only someone purely clever and sly could be

144

stupid, and now she perceived her stupidity. She fell on her face again and seized the feet of Simmu.

"Beautiful youth, I will do penance, I will do whatever you wish. Set me a task—I will perform it. Chastise me, I will suffer it. But pray do not betray my foolishness to the Lord of Darkness, Uhlume."

Simmu glanced at Azhrarn for guidance, and into the brain of Simmu there flashed a last bit of knowledge casually tossed to him by the Prince of Demons. And Simmu said to the Witch: "I will inform Uhlume of nothing, providing you will answer me a question."

"Anything," said the witch. Her second stupidity.

"Tell me what it was that you told Death, that he first agreed to make a bargain with *you*."

Simmu uttered this without thinking, at Azhrarn's unspoken direction. But no sooner had the words left his mouth than his eyes widened, for he sensed their impact. The eyes of the witch also grew wide.

"Ask me another thing," said she, "for that may not be told."

"No other thing. I will have this."

"Lord of Lords—" began Lylas, turning to Azhrarn.

But Azhrarn merely regarded her, and by his beneficent expression he somehow reminded her of the proximity of Uhlume's kingdom to his own, and of how simple a matter it would be for one Lord of Darkness to communicate tidings to another.

Lylas cursed aloud then. She cursed the pomegranate trees in the wild orchard for tempting her with their poison screaming to be utilized. She cursed the little phial, she cursed the physician and she cursed Jornadesh. She did not curse her own error, nor Simmu, seeing he had such a mighty guardian with him.

It had taken the devious intellect of Azhrarn to guess that, despite her current role of Death's servent, in the beginning, without some bargaining strength, she would not have approached the Lord Uhlume, nor would Uhlume have listened. It was plain, this witch had once discovered a weak point in the unbreakable armor of Lord Death. Weak enough that she had profited by it to become Death's handmaiden, two hundred years old, and older, yet gifted by him with a method forever to extend her youth.

Simmu, now fully aware of this, caught the witch about her elderly, fifteen year old throat.

"Since you love Death so well, I will send you to him."

145

"No," squealed Lylas, "I am not ready for that. I will answer." But, as Simmu let her go, a canny glint went through her eyes; she meant to lie.

However, Azhrarn said, "She has no need to answer. I have seen it." For he had read the picture as easily in her mind when she thought of it, as if he had glanced into an open book.

It has been mentioned before that at fourteen years of age Lylas, returning over the hills in the hour before dawn, had met Death beneath a gallows where three men dangled. It has also been mentioned that she and he talked there some while, but not the substance of their conversation. Here then, as follows.

"Master," said Lylas, "I kneel before you, for who does not understand you are greater than any king of the earth, greater even than the gods, and my heart quakes with dread."

Uhlume said, "Do you seek me?"

"No," said Lylas, "for I am young and vital. Yet I will adore you for your beauty and your awesome majesty, and I will tremble since, standing before you, my life hangs by a thread."

"All lives hang so," said Uhlume, Lord of Death.

"Today they do," said Lylas, "but one day, maybe, there will be found an antidote to dying. Alas then, incredible Lord, for your stern law is necessary and good. If mankind could live for ever, and laugh—you will pardon me, it is not my hope—laugh at death—ah then, what a monster should humanity become. And you, King of Kings, what would become of you?"

Perhaps the gods had made Death. Perhaps men had made him, the shadow of their terror thrown on a wall, a name that had taken on a shape. How long had he existed? Long enough to come, in however strange and opaque a manner, to an awareness of himself. Or to an awareness of what himself must be. And, as he was capable of dispassionte tears, as he was capable of emotionless grief, now he unfeelingly felt the pangs of a hollow disquiet. Not at the notion of life, for life was susceptible to him . . . but at the notion of a life which was no longer susceptible, life which could negate death. For even Death did not wish to die.

This, or enough of this, Lylas understood.

She went on in a low and husky voice, full of her fear, her admiration and her cunning.

"The wise and the wicked have tutored me, and I have heard tell of many things. Perhaps I have been misled and

146

you will correct me. They say that in the land of the gods, in Upperearth, there is a well in which is stored the water of Immortality. No mortal can reach the spot, and if he should, this well is moreover excellently guarded. However, or so my tutors told me, (and possibly they were wrong), there is a legend of another well, a well which lies somewhere on the earth itself. And the position of this second well corresponds exactly to the position of the Well of Immortality in the country of the gods, one being situated directly beneath the other. Now, my Lord, no human knows the location of either well, neither the well of Upperearth nor its sister on the earth. Indeed, this earth well holds only water. Yet my tutors said this: The one well lying below the other is no accident. That maybe it is a game of the gods, the someday the shaft of the Well of Immortality will crack—for it is reputedly constructed of glass—and then a few drops of the elixir of Everlasting Life will fall from Upperearth to earth and straight into this lower well, which has been placed so precisely to receive them. What a calamity, my Lord, if at that hour some human stumbled on the earth well, and learned its secret. For this one has no guardian. Or so they say."

Death gave no outward sign he was affected. But he said:

"Any why do you impart this story to me?"

"Because, my master, being a Lord of Darkness, you will know the site of the well of Upperearth—and thus can discover the site of the second well below it in the earth. And this being as it is, you should post your own guardians at the second well, against the day when the drops of Immortality may fall. Or, if that is irksome, make me your laborer, and I will see to it. Though I am small and young, yet I am intelligent. All my art shall be at your disposal."

"And you," said Uhlume, "being entrusted with this secret, will you not use it in the service of men?"

The witch, for all her sharpness and her rough life, was yet fourteen. Men had used her, and she them. But here was one who was more than man, more beautiful and more awful than any man could ever be. She had a need for an ideal, and this dark and terrifying ideal appealed to her youth and her unnaturalness. So she lay down on the path before Death and told him she would serve him without question and in despite of mankind, and the honesty of her murky passion shone from her brain and her heart and Death saw it, and was sure of her. (Though he made her his hireling in other things besides, thus binding her, and gave her her own form of everlasting life that came from drinking ground bones in

147

her wine—that she should not have a use for a draught of Immortality herself, if ever it did descend.) Maybe he was not that sure.

As for the mysterious lower well, Death found the place, as he could find all places. Though he had never entered Upperearth, for in those days the gods did not die, yet he knew the area of the sacred well. Accordingly, the situation of the mortal one was not taxing to discover. Lylas he took there, furled in the white leaf of his cloak. She did not see the way, but the destination she beheld in detail, for he set her down there to do her work, and left her to do it. His person was too abstract and too alarming to go randomly among men and give them covenants; he needed an intermediary. Besides, such trade would not have been to his liking. Instead, he loaned his agent extra powers and permitted her familiarity with his name. Most of her subsequent reputation was begun in that land, so that after, wherever she chanced to dwell, word would get about—It is she who has converse with Death.

She put on airs, the wtich, but she arranged things. By spells and various conjurings, she subdued the people of the region, who were ignorant at the time and primitive. She left an order and a myth behind her, and she left the guardians she had suggested. It was a great palaver over a tiny slimy mossy hole in the ground, which was all the second well had turned out to be.

Now, however, cowering with fright before Azhrarn in the House of the Blue Dog, conscious that the Demon had scooped the whole tale from her mind, (none could ever have got it from her mouth), Lylas commenced wishing she had not hired herself to Lord Death beneath the gallows that far-off morning two hundred and eighteen years before.

"Glamorous and magical Lord," she wailed, "do not use this knowledge. I would have fared better if I had confessed my other fault to my master—how I helped poison Narasen. If he learned that, he would punish me. But to learn I have betrayed the definite existence of the second well—Oh, pity me!"

But Azhrarn had somehow gone away between one of her panting breaths and another, and he had taken the youth with him.

Lylas screamed, and beat her fists on the floor.

Then at length she left off, got up and went to a table and opened an ebony box which stood there. Inside the box was a miniscule drum but not the drum of bone with which she called to Uhlume. This drum was of old red wood and the drum skin was the stretched hide of some red unidentified creature.

The witch seated herself and, biting her lip in her terror, she began to beat and tap on this drum with her seven-fingered hands.

Azhrarn could locate the secret second well quite without trouble, for he too comprehended the position of the first. But he did not take Simmu any farther than a hilltop, and here, under the white rain of the stars, Azhrarn told him what was necessary, and then bade the youth farewell.

Simmu smiled, a human smile with no pleasure in it.

"Now I am absolutely a mortal, you will leave me. But what am I to be to myself if I am nothing in your sight?"

"A hero," said Azhrarn, "the creator of confusion and upheaval."

"Yes," said Simmu. For an instant his green eyes glittered and the Eshva gleam of black mischief was in them. "And Deaths' death I will bring to him. Even though, my Lord, I do not see the way, unless the cistern of Upperearth should crack, and how is that to be?"

With scornful affection, Azhrarn said:

"Mortals possess destinies. You will find a way, for it is your destiny to do so."

Simmu gazed at him. His eyes once more were bleak.

"You have the look of another," said Azhrarn.

"Who?"

"One named Zhirem."

"Who is that?"

Azhrarn drew through his fingers the long hair of Simmu, and he said, "You called to him when you were afraid."

"No," said Simmu, "or if I did, I do not remember it, or him."

"Like demonkind, you forget," said Azhrarn.

"And I shall be forgotten," said Simmu in the plaintive voice of a woman, for under the caressive touch of Azhrarn, she had changed herself. "One day I shall call your name, O Lord of my life, and you will never hear me, or care to."

"I will hear," said Azhrarn, "and if you burn this green jewel at your throat once more in a fire, I will answer. Let that be a token between us."

Then Azhrarn kissed her on the mouth, and from that kiss everything that was Simmu, soul or flesh, seemed to catch

149

alight. But in that same moment of ecstatic fire, the Demon vanished.

Simmu—maiden, Eshva, anguished human man—was alone with his comfortless heroic task, on that starlit hillside of the world.

BOOK TWO

PART ONE

The Garden of Golden Daughters

1

It is not recounted, the exact situation of that second well. But doubtless it lay somewhere toward the earth's center, though far from the black and fiery volcanoes of that innermost region. The land of the well was neither fair nor prosperous, it was a desert through which one river took its way to a distant sea. And the life of the people of the land took place only along the two banks of this river. Here they farmed and fished and hunted the creatures of the river swamps. Out in the desert itself they did not often go, for they feared it, and wisely. There was no water to be had beyond the river, not for a thousand miles, or so they believed. No water, save in one spot. A day's journey from the river a solitary group of mountains rose from the dunes. They were nine in number, and they formed a rough circle, inside which was a valley, as barren and dusty as the rest of the desert except at its middle. Here a sort of mossy pit opened, small mouthed but deep, and far down in it, barely visible, lurked a muddly glaucous water. This was the secret second well.

Two hundred and eighteen years before Simmu's arrival at the House of the Blue Dog. Uhlume had deposited his self-elected handmaiden in the land of the well. She was fourteen; she was intoxicated with her own wit and her success. She was accordingly extravagant.

Lylas went among the people of the river in the guise of a priestess, and she performed miracles and left them in no doubt she was to be reckoned with. She told them she had come on behalf of a god, but she did not name him. Some aura Uhlume had lent her, however, gave what she said a sinister weight. Child-woman, whore and sorceress, clad in his invisible mantle of power, she gave her directions and they were obeyed.

The ring of nine mountains was sacred, she said. The valley in its midst was sacred. Most of all, the unimpressive pit

153

of slime was sacred. Therefore, each of these things must be guarded, and the people of the river should count themselves blessed that they had been chosen by the ominous unnamed god to protect what was his. The people murmured uneasily that they did. Then, said the witch, they would not grudge a certain portion of their young men, the strongest and best, to form an elite army to patrol the desert. The people murmured, less easily than before, that of course the god was most welcome. Another item, said the witch. Watch towers must be built to reveal any strangers who approached. They must be challenged and turned away, and slain if they would not turn. Quite so, murmured the people, shifting their feet. But, they added, would such measures be enough? No, said the witch, but they need not be alarmed. She herself would set guardians about the mountains, beings of a non-human nature, which should not inconvenience their mortal comrades but be fatal to any intruder. (The people sweated with fear and politely blamed it on the weather.) Lastly, said the witch, a wall was to be built about the mountain valley, so high no one could get over it, not even the honest sentries outside. And within this wall, the ultimate guardians of the well, were to be put nine virgin girls, each thirteen years of age, and they must not leave the valley until they had served there nine years, after which another nine must replace them—and this regime would continue until time itself stopped. Nine virgin girls? the people asked, surprised. Quite so, said the witch, and indeed, no man must ever enter the valley, and if one attempted to, he must be killed. But how would the girls survive? inquired the people. There was neither food nor wholesome water—begging the god's pardon, his well was undrinkable—in the valley.

"No matter," said the witch, "when I have finished with the valley, it will be more marvelous than any garden of the world. Your daughters will beg to serve there and when the hour of their departure comes, they will weep. In fact, you had better make certain that the nine maidens who are selected are as lovely as nine young moons, for I will not have ugly wenches in my garden, and the god must be honored."

She was fourteen, Lylas, and she was extravagant.

Out of her fourteen-year-old mind burst fourteen-year-old fantasies and she made them real. The nonhuman guardians—what monsters they were. Horned and hoofed and many-fanged, with bundles of snakes for tails and the heads of tigers and sometimes wings. Some breathed fire, some cried aloud in awful voices. They hid in caves in the rocky lower terraces of the mountains, or else they dug holes at the mountains' feet in the sand, but they would pop out and rage at whosoever went by, so the days and the nights of the desert grew clamorous, pyrotechnic and altogether less sweet than they had been before. Whole tribes of these beings the witch invented, not knowing when enough is enough. They did the river men no harm, it was true, but now and then some traveler strayed among them alone, and they tore him to pieces with their claws of adamant.

Meantime the people dutifully erected the high wall about the valley. No doubt they had sorcerous aid, for the wall was the height of nine tall men standing on each others shoulders, and built in only a month, it was said. A narrow door gave admittance, a door which would open just once a day, at the setting of the sun. And this door, needless to report, possessed a guard more frightful than those previously mentioned. Moreover the wall burned whoever touched it, and lightning shot from the top of it, in case anyone should forget where it was in order to avoid it. Even the elected and elite army of young men who patrolled the desert, manned the watch towers and the mountains' outer slopes, kept well clear of the wall.

At last, Lylas went alone into the barren valley with the well in it. She took a stone, one of three Uhlume had given her, and she threw it down. And where she threw the stone, a fountain gushed up from the very depth of the earth, cool and white from some subterranean cave. And presently she threw the second and third stones, and the valley became musical with the sound of waters. Then Lylas, by her own skill which was not inconsiderable, made the promised garden blossom. Some of it was illusion and some was real and some, nourished by the sudden influx of water, came naturally to be in the course of years. But it was an area of unrivalled beauty, and to the people of the desert, who had thought the surly river and its swamps the height of horticultural delight, the garden in the valley was like the dream of a paradise which they had never ever been lucky enough to dream. And for sure, the witch showed it to them. They sighed with yearning and the little girls of eleven or twelve or thirteen made round their eyes, and they began to ask, "May I please go and guard the sacred well of the god?" In this much, Lylas had judged cleverly. However, it was perhaps her mistake, setting maidens within the wall, though she thought all the while it was her masterstroke. She had had sufficient of men and of roving, this witch, and possibly it

155

really was her own dream she had focused in the valley—serenity in a green shade and nine virgins who, for nine years, would not have to put up with the goat games of men—games the witch had over-sampled and grown very weary of. Maybe, too, it was her own lost virginity she sought to contain pristine in the garden, she who had sold herself at an early age for coin and magic lessons. Nevertheless, to herself it seemed that this vanguard of innocent girls would prove the safest defense of all. Like many women who are themselves active, venturesome and crafty and see about them only women who are gentle, passive and home-loving, Lylas supposed herself unique among her sex and that no one was like her. The nine girls in the garden would be content, she believed, as no man could have been. They would play and wander and attend to their female affairs and never think to investigate the well or strive beyond it, while no man, (all men being potential heroes), could have kept from doing both.

Two hundred and one years after, meeting Narasen, the complaisance of Lylas was shaken. But by then she had dissociated herself from the guardianship of the second well, thinking her work there was completed.

The witch had Uhlume's help to keep herself ever youthful by drinking ground bone, and physically she did not change at all. Mentally there was also little change. At fourteen she had been in some ways remarkably worldly, but really, for two hundred and thirty-two, the age at which Simmu met her, she was rather immature.

Other than the witch, generally the earth was prone to alteration. And the Land of Well was no exception. Actually, the static traditions that the witch had introduced there were the very things which brought change about.

Firstly, the primitive people of the river became rather arrogant. After all, they had been chosen by a god to guard his sanctum. The immediate result of arrogance was courage and a spirit of exploration, which they had never felt before. The desert was uninviting, but now they looked at the river and began to make boats. In a matter of ten years of so, they were sailing down it, and finding other settlements and eventually the sea and a city or two, and it gave them ideas. One thing they noticed, no other settlement had been specially picked out by a god, and though a few claimed to have been, they had no proof. The arrogance begat more arrogance, and the river men became fighters and reavers, and they stole the best from everywhere they could and bore it home to the swamps, howling that it was for the temple of their god. Twice ten more years and they were doing nicely on their plunder, so constructing better ships and weapons to go with them and sailing forth to plunder more thoroughly. Fifty years, and there was a city on both the river banks, a fairly fine city of white walls, hanging trees and gilded steps. And when you came into this city, whose name was Veshum, meaning the Blessed One, you would see a statue on the western bank of black obsidian, depicting a grisly black god. Sometime the witch must have let slip a detail or two regarding the appearance of Uhlume, but the statue had neither Uhlume's beauty nor his remoteness. Rather it resembled the horrors that bounded and squawked about the slopes of the nine mountains, breathing fire and flapping their wings and rending the odd traveler who naively persisted in coming their way.

Now it is quite probably that no one would ever have troubled to come up river to Veshum as it had been, more probable still that no one would ever have bothered to trek over the arid mountain slopes just to see a slimy hole in a barren valley. But what with all the piracy and the riches the piracy accumulated, what with all the boasting of Veshum about its god, what with all the monsters guarding the mountain slopes and clawing travelers, and the young men patrolling the desert and shut up in the watch towers, and what with the story of nine virgins in an enchanted garden serving the god's shrine, word got about, and no wonder. Then men began to come to Veshum and worship the black god and lay jewels on his altar. And they beheld, too, the ceremonious choosing of the virgins, how they must be without blemish and radiant, how they were hung with gold, how they were conducted up the mountain and went through a narrow door which magically appeared at sunset in a great wall, from the top of which shot lightning. And when nine new ones had gone in, nine older ones came out, and they came out weeping as the witch predicted, cast from paradise to face a world they had barely known and did not understand how to cope with. A few threw themselves off the mountain side to their death instantly; the rest stamped resentfully to Veshum and took up the posts of priestesses in the obsidian temple with a very bad grace. Some got married—they were sought after, being compulsorily chaste and always beautiful, as had been stipulated. None of them were ever content. They pined for the garden, and sometimes slew their husbands or their subsequent children, and were of course forgiven, being holy. Once in a while, one of these women, heavily veiled and crying copiously, would go back across the desert, up the mountain slopes, between the forests of sentries and monsters, and sit down by the hot high wall. When sunset came, she would rush to the door, be growled at by the guardian, driven aside and burn her hands. Then she would stab herself, or something of the kind.

"But what is in their charge?" inquired the pilgrims who had come to Veshum.

"A shrine of gold," said the rich reavers (who had stopped reaving and now lived quite adequately off the gifts of visitors), "and the golden well beneath." For the witch, last fantasy, had covered the muddy hole with a delicate temple, apparently of gold and with an apparently golden cupola.

Then the travelers, or those who had not got too close to the monsters, went home, and said: "The men of Veshum set their bravest sons to protect the honor of their god. His sacred mountains seethe with devils and frights. In a garden too beautiful to speak of, nine virgin daughters of the city, lovelier than nine golden stars, tend a well of gold."

So the valley came to be called the Garden of the Golden Daughters, and Veshum became famous in that quarter of the earth. And two hundred and thirty years passed.

"There is no doubt in my mind," said the rich man, "that our daughter, Kassafeh will be chosen."

"Indeed yes," said the rich man's wife, but she kept her eyes on her embroidery.

"Our daughter, Kassafeh," repeated the rich man, smiling with satisfaction. His trade was importing rare silks up river from the cities on the coast, and sometimes his ships brought pilgrims to the altar of the black god and the pilgrims paid well. (The rich man's grandfather had been a cutthroat pirate, but that was all forgotten now.) "Yes, for sure, Kassafeh will be chosen. She is exquisite. She will be one of the holy nine, and we shall be proud, and how much handier then it will be to get the other four girls wed."

"Quite so," said his wife, not looking at him.

"Our daughter," cried the rich man in joyous possessiveness. "Yours and mine."

The wife pricked her finger, but she had blushed nearly as red as the blood.

Kassafeh was beautiful, as the rich man said, and more beautiful than he said. Her skin was pale and water clear, she

158

was slender as the pale new moon, her hair was the pale and pastel gold of a young sunrise. Her eyes—well, it was hard to describe her eyes. Yet, she was beautiful and all the rich man said, all he said but one thing, for she was not exactly his child.

It had been this way. The rich man's wife was not a woman of the river people but of the down river shore folk. While her spouse was rich, she was aristocratic, and born in a fine house she had been, high in the hills that stood above the sea. Now, when she was eleven years old, Kassafeh's mother had been told by her nurse: "You may go here and you may go there about the hills, provided I or your maidservant are with you. But whatever you do, you must not climb that tallest hill over there, the hill with a summit of bare rock." "And why must I not?" demanded Kassafeh's mother. "Because," said the nurse, "it is sacred to the gods. It is their High Place, and no one must profane it." Kassafeh's mother, as can be imagined, concluded immediately that of all the ground in the world she wished to tread, the tallest hilltop was the most urgent. So one morning, evading her attendants, Kassafeh's mother set out, and being agile and healthy, she raced the sun to the hill's summit and arrived there first.

It was a gorgeous spot. Far below spread the static seethe of the soft green hills, while the base of this one was scarlet in a tide of poppies. Far below, the sea was gleaming like a piece of silk, and here was a pinnacle of lovely pearly rock on which rested a wide blue sky. A marble altar stood to the gods at the very peak of the rock, but no one had dared tend it for centuries. Somehow they had got the idea that the gods came down personally from time to time and walked about on the peak, though the gods did not. However, belief is a strange thing, and could, particularly in those days, make other strange things happen.

Kassafeh's mother sat on the altar—she was an irreverent, careless girl—and gazed with love at the sky and the earth and the silken sea. It seemed to her after, that the hours slipped by when she was not looking, and the heavy gold of the afternoon sank down on the bare hilltop and she drowsed. Then, when she opened her eyes, Kassafeh's mother noticed she was not alone.

An unusual young man was there with her. At least, she took him to be a young man initially, although presently she began to wonder. His hair was a cobwebby gold and his eyes were most peculiar, like prisms which held all colors and none. In his flawless white skin were violet traceries of veins,

159

not ugly as they would have been in another, but quite beautiful. He was naked, save for a sort of bright blue cloak that fluttered from one shoulder—it really did flutter though there was no wind to lift it, and it seemed additionally to grow out of his shoulder rather than being tied around him. Because he was naked, Kassafeh's mother could see clearly that he had no male genitals; neither, however, did he look necessarily feminine. Indeed he was positively epicene, neuter even, and yet somehow extremely seductive.

It is a god, thought Kassafeh's mother. And she courteously got down from the altar and obeised herself. She was not afraid, for she would have found it hard to be afraid of anything so appetizing. She was of that specialized age and temperament which makes men rough and heavy things, fascinating but obnoxious, and here was a compromise.

The "god" did not move or speak, so Kassafeh's mother raised her head and next herself. She had the true aristocrat's lack of reserve, and put one arm about the "god" and kissed him, by way of experiment, on the lips. She felt very little, rather than sensual pleasure of caressing something delightful but unreal, a statue of polished onyx for example. As for the "god," he gave a kind of vague smile, and his golden lashes shivered.

Now, he was not a god, this personage, the gods stayed in Upperearth. Yet there were certain elementals of that region, or near it, a race of sky creatures or beings of the ether. They wandered among clouds and stars, bathed in the red incense of sunsets, twanged tunes off the elongated silver chords of the rain. They were rarely seen and rarely did they have contact with the men and women of earth, who, to them, were singularly gross. Rather they preferred to haunt the fringes of Upperearth, admiring the gods through cloudy windows. And they resembled the gods somewhat, though not enough really to be confused with them. It is possible that it was these wandering elementals of Upperearth, or more accurately *basement*-Upperearth, who had visited the hill top, been sighted and taken for deities. Why they visited is not known, nor the reason why this one came when Kassafeh's mother was sitting there. Perhaps he was curious to spy a human figure on the normally deserted peak.

But now, after Kassafeh's mother had kissed him and he had shivered his lashes, the elemental spoke in a faint harp-string voice.

"Kiss me not again," he said, "for my kiss may quicken you."

"Indeed," said Kassafeh's mother, with some skepticism, for she knew the facts of reproduction perfectly.

"My people can instil new life by a kiss, though, as you are mortal, it would also take the seed of a mortal man to form a child in you."

"If you are a god, I should receive honor in bearing your off-spring," supposed Kassafeh's mother. And she kissed the elemental once again. The elemental shivered all over on this occasion, and suddenly a delicious taste as of fruit and wine filled the mouth of Kassafeh's mother. She swallowed, and the elemental shut his violet gold-fringed eyelids.

"I warned you, but you paid no heed. It will take five children, I believe, before the seed of a man and the life I had implanted in you may commingle. Yes, your sixth child will be mine." And the elemental paled and giving a sigh of satisfaction, enervation and guilt, he let his impatient cloak haul him upwards, and soon he dissolved into the blue sky.

Kassafeh's mother went home after that with a certain perplexity, and told some lies to her nurse as to where she had been. Luckily no perceptible result followed, and by the time that she was married, several years later, to the rich grandson of the pirate, and sent to live in faraway, white-walled Veshum, Kassafeh's mother had almost erased the incident, which she ascribed to a dream or fantasy of her pubescent youth.

She bore four daughters and one son to the rich man. All five were comely enough, and the rich man had no complaints. Then one night he lay with his wife, and when he let loose his seed in her, such pangs of rapture overtook the mother of Kassafeh, that she shrieked with pleasure—a thing she was not given to, for she had found men, (that is, her husband) after all, rather a disappointment.

The rich man congratulated himself on his prowess, and when he learned his wife had conceived once more, he congratulated himself on his fertility.

The child was born after the allotted span with very small difficulty, and from the beginning Kassafeh's mother watched her daughter with interest and misgiving. And, as Kassafeh grew, so the interest and the misgiving grew. Although decidedly a mortal child, with no uncanny additions or subtractions of the flesh, and with something even of her father's shrewdness and all her mother's looks and more, yet there was an essence to Kassafeh none of the other children had. Her hair was such a wild ethereal powdered gold, and her eyes—for the eyes of Kassafeh would change color, not predictably or reasonably, but in the fashion of no mortal eyes. This precocity was studiously overlooked and ignored. It was put down to tricks of light or shade, to the facial expressions of the girl herself. But it was none of these things. It was obviously the inheritance of a part-fathering by something which had eyes like prisms, all colors and none. . . .

Thus, when the rich man spoke of his parenthood in respect of Kassafeh, Kassafeh's mother blushed. And he, recalling her solitary shriek of ecstasy, thought she too recalled it and foolishly blushed for that, since she had never cried similarly again.

Meantime, Kassafeh herself, very much her mother's daughter if not all her earthly father's, was listening at the door. And her eyes were shifting like pools from darkest green to palest, maddest gray as she angrily heard mention of the nine virgins and her likelihood of being chosen to become one of them.

I will not consent, she vowed, *to exist walled up in a garden for nine years. Besides, what good has it ever done any of them? They die like flies when they are released.* Then she bethought herself of how the nine virgins must be without blemish, and her eyes went to indigo and she to find a sharp disfiguring knife.

But when she had the knife ready, she glared at its point and at her water-lily skin, and she put the knife away again.

The great day of the choosing was the very day after that one. And Kassafeh must go, with the other eligible virgin girls of thirteen, to the square before the temple of Veshum. During the early years of this cult, the virgins had been taken from any walk of life, but, as Veshum got more opulent, so the virgins had had to be. Only the daughters of the rich and influential were recently considered for the honor of serving the god.

They were conducted up the temple stair into a hall, and from thence, singly into a cubicle, where the embittered, garden-exile priestesses examined them with cruel avid eyes "Not good enough," shrilled these priestesses. "Note these ugly splay feet, note this vast black mole. No, no, they will not do." Many of the poor girls ran out sobbing with humiliation. Yet there were always at least nine pretty ones with no blemish, and then the priestesses would probe further. "Now, what is this? Only thirteen and broken into! Pah, for shame, you little harlot."

When Kassafeh entered the cubicle, the priestesses turned more wizened than ever, for they could tell at a glance that here was perfection combined with utter chastity. This brat was going to dwell in the heavenly garden which they could never re-enter. How they hated her. But Kassafeh removed her garments and the priestesses smiled at her with love. "Ah," they congratulated Kassafeh, "what a nasty rash of boils."

"Indeed yes," said Kassafeh, who had made the boils from paste and silk dye the night before. "And I am never free of them. Always I have at least ten or twelve. The phyiscian can do nothing."

However, one of the priests was looking through a secret hole in the wall and, quivering with emotion though he was from all the nakedness he had been gloating on, this close he was sharp enough to know a fake boil from a real one. Accordingly he put his mouth to the hole and shouted in a dreadful voice: "The god chooses this maiden and will cure her. Fetch water and wash her body and the boils shall fall from her and she shall be whole."

Kassafeh scowled and the priestesses grumbled, but they did as they were told in case the voice might be of divine origin. Sure enough, all the paste boils abandoned Kassafeh in the water, leaving her wholesome and lovely.

"I will not go," growled Kassafeh.

The priestesses scourged her with velvet whips that left no lasting mark, and Kassafeh wept rebelliously. Soon after, the names of the nine virgins were proclaimed, and Kassafeh's was the ninth.

She had never reverenced the black image. She thought him vile, for, as a statue, he was surely unaesthetic. The gods, Kassafeh assumed, would be fair. Though she had not been initiated in the truth of her own conception, Kassafeh's mother had told her many stories of the airy deities of the shore people, and these were the gods Kassafeh was inclined to worship. Now she cursed the idol of Veshum and, as he did not strike her down, she became convinced he was an ineffectual as she had always supposed.

Kassafeh pondered flight, but it was not to be. She was locked in her chamber by scolding distraught parents, and dragged thence only on the morning when the nine virgins went up the slope of the nine mountain ring.

The other eight virgins were smirking and joyful. "How favored we are," they babbled to each other, as the priests hung gold ornaments on them. "How happy we shall be." "Baaa," bleated Kassafeh scornfully at them, "baa-baaa!" And when the priest stroked her breast as he set the gold necklace over it, pale-yellow-eyed, Kassafeh bit him.

Across the desert the procession from Veshum went, chariots with fringed canopies of vermilion, priests and priestesses shaking bells and beating drums and gongs, wild beasts on jeweled leashes for show, and a host of people who had come to stare. All day they journeyed, pausing now and then to drink cool wine and eat fruit and sweetmeats, till they reached the dunescape from which the nine mountain ring might be seen.

Here the patrolling army rode up and saluted them, several hundred stalwart young men, and from the watch towers smoke signals rose and horns were sounded.

The sun was westering, the sky altering to a deep blue-gold.

From their burrows and caves the monsters were peering and yapping gusts of mild fire at the procession. Some of the virgins, waxing afraid at the monsters, screamed and fainted. Kassafeh was not one of these. She looked at the captain of the patrol army, a handsome youth, with regret. But the captain knew his vocation and did not look at her at all.

From here, as the light thickened, you could see very clearly the electric flashes dazzling off from the top of the mountains where the hot wall was. The procession started up the mountain side. Bells and cymbals clinked and clattered, and the monsters licked their lips at the foreign travelers, warning them not to fall behind the people of Veshum. Just before sunset, the crowd rolled and scrambled over the last height, and stood before the awful wall.

It had a shimmering haze on it, the wall, like molten steaming metal. In one part, a thicket of black trees seemed to mask some living presence—the unseen ghastly guardian of the door? Then, as the sky grew brazen, a slit appeared through the thicket in the incandescent brickwork.

"Come forth, O holy daughters of the golden well!" cried the priests, "Come forth from the garden, your term of service is done."

And presently out trooped nine wretched snivelling maidens, rending their garments and their hair. They did not dare to disobey the ritual summons, but their hearts were breaking.

Kassafeh could not contain herself.

"Rejoice!" she cried loudly. "Be glad that you are no longer slaves—I would change places with any one of you."

But the priests quickly banged their drums and clanged

their gongs and drowned her out. Simultaneously, oblivious, some of the nine ex-guardian virgins were, as usual, throwing themselves off the mountain. The others wailed and shed tears. Kassafeh, cobalt-eyed with fury, shut her mouth.

And, in a tidal surge of musical crashings and chantings, prayers, blessings and the dim howls of the exiled virgins, Kassafeh and her eight companions went forward. Heat burned on either side like powerful furnaces, and from this heat a nightmarish something grimaced approval at them as they fled by it, which really was the door-guardian for certain. Kassafeh, as she ran, poked out her tongue at it.

And then the heat was gone, and the door behind them was gone, and all the commonplace world went with them.

The golden daughters had arrived in paradise.

2

On the inside, the wall was quite different, as was everything else. Here it was a lustrous palisade of jade and sea-blue ceramic over which rogue vines and climbing plants had spun a glossy web beaded with tiny fruits and flowers. The doorway opened high above the bowl of the valley; entering, the selected virgins always saw a panorama.

The inner slopes of the nine mountains were also unlike their outer surfaces. Lawns green as emerald cascaded downwards and were lost among a maze of trees, all of a hundred other greens, and nearer to the valley floor this wild green blended into turquoise and far off into a gentle liquid blueness, such as was never seen in the desert or along the dry burnt banks of Veshum's river. The whole valley was redolent of water, sounded with it, basked in it, and the fresh odor of sweet soil and abundant growing things was a concentrated perfume on the air never before scented by the nine maidens of the river people.

Now the sun was going out and the valley subtly turned itself from greens and blues, through goldenness, into lucid purples and ambers. Here and there a waterfall shone warm silver in the dusk and luminous stars appeared overhead. A roseate moon lit the garden in an unworldly way.

Before the entrance, a flight of wide translucent marble steps led down into the valley between the verdant mountain slopes. In the strange and rosy moon-illumination—which

165

seemed all part of the garden's magic, as indeed it was—the nine virgins espied something approaching up the stair.

A creamy lioness.

The nine virgins were stricken with misgiving and some clutched each other, as the nine virgins always did at this point, seeing a predatory animal advance on them through the twilight. But the lioness drew near and displayed not a sign of dislike or hunger. In fact, she rubbed her head against their legs, and she had no smell of the carnivore but rather of flowers. To many a young girl, no dream could be more endearing than this of the savage beast grown tame and fawning on her. All responded swiftly, petted the lioness, received the velvet kiss of her unthreatening, oddly fragrant mouth, and were willing to go after her when she moved to lead them down into the valley.

Beyond the steps, a mossy carpet unrolled over descending terraces. Through velure woods the nine maidens passed, led by the lioness. And how fearless were the woods to them, even their shadows genial, touched by the rose moonlight. Nightingales sang, and soft dark rabbits darted playfully between the paws of the big cat, who never glanced at them.

On the other side of the woods lay a small natural lake, fed by the waterfalls. And there was a ship at the lake's edge on to which the nine virgins, with nervous charmed cries, allowed themselves to be persuaded.

The ship was not like the serviceable masculine ships of the river people. It was a thing of delicate arching prow and swooping fishtail stern. It glittered and gleamed and from its slender mast transparent spangled sails opened their wings. It sped lightly across the water without help of wind or of oar. And the nine maidens stared about them amazed.

How many prodigies are necessary to prove you are in a land of prodigies? The pomegranate witch, extravagant fourteen, had put into the garden a wondrous excess of them. Some were toys for the children the nine virgins had lately been, some were mirages to trap the hearts of the women they must become.

On the far shore of the lake, orchards and groves of fruit trees added the resonance of citron and plum to the air; date palms rising in ribbed columns, fanned the face of the sky. On a hill clad in wine-red roses and inky hyacinth, stood a palace of white marble with open doors.

Miniature birds came flying in a cloud from the palace. They twittered to the vine virgins as if to welcome them.

In a hall where fountains played, a banquet had been laid

166

for the girls, as it would every evening be laid for them, though they never knew by whom or by what. They sat on cushions of silk and ate rare dishes, things even their father's tables had not provided them, and they drank wines and sherberts in crystal goblets and the flagons were never empty.

Above, in the marble dolls'-house palace were scented baths and beds of silk, from whose canopies pearls hung like water drops, as if it had been raining pearls in every sleeping chamber.

Something in the wine, or the pale smoke which drifted from the perfumed lamps, had made the nine virgins highly susceptible, as it always did. They sank to sleep on their couches and had visions of their own exhilarated content, and of the sacred golden temple which glinted to the west beyond the palace. They dreamed of the holy well they would guard and of the lions they would sport with and of the marvels as yet undiscovered in this country of marvels.

Only Kassafeh had a knot in her belly from the rich though quite illusory food, which had really been only roots and bread and similar life-supporting dull stuff, tempered by sorcery. Only Kassafeh turned and twisted angrily on her pearl-dripped hallucination of a bed. She trusted none of what she had seen, for such beauty did not belong with the graceless black god of Veshum. And when she slept, she dreamed of the handsome young patrol captain and she cried to him: "Take me from this place and back to the real world!" But he changed into a rabbit and hopped hurriedly away from her.

It was a garden of delights, the delights of girl children and of girl women. All the worldly pomegranate witch had missed?

Some of the fountains played delicious drinks, some scent, some had jewels swirling through them which could be plucked out; some fountains changed color like rainbows. There were a myriad rooms in the palace. And in the myriad rooms were a myriad things. Strange fascinating games, magical mirrors which showed other wonderlands, dolls so beautifully painted and dressed they seemed real, and which could be made, by the turning of a key, to move about, sing, dance and converse. Besides, there were great chests of garments, raiment more lustrous than any gown the nine virgins had seen in the world—or would ever see, for illusion is always superior. And near the fabulous clothes chests were caskets of gems and ornaments. Here and there would be found a musical instrument, which one of the maidens had only to pick up

167

to find she could play it and produce from it scintilating ravishing sounds. In another spot might be located a loom, somehow very easy to master, which could spill off, in response to the haphazard weaving of the maiden, incredible fabrics with glowing pictures in them which appeared almost alive. There were a few exquisite books whose pictures actually *did* come alive.

Beyond the palace, roses and other flowers filled the atmosphere with perfume. Fruit hung from vines and boughs, always ripe, always at its most eatable moment. On certain trees sweetmeats clustered, child's enticement, while in some of the arbors, ivory swings depended. Sit in one of these, and it would rock you as violently or as gently as you asked it to.

The garden itself had its own endless variety, for no part of it was ever quite the same, as if it constantly shifted itself a little, changing the shade of a blossoming tree, the angle of a distant slope. It seemed limitless, although its boundaries— the green upsloping inner walls of the mountains—held it safe as a loving hand. And from recesses in the foliage of this safeness came all manner of animals in a curious and soothing harmony. Downy white kids at play with the cubs of a panther, equally ready to include a maiden in the fun; tigresses who would invite a girl on to their backs and carry her, laughing and crazy, with flowers in her hair, for miles, and then lie down and accept her head on the gold-streaked flank which smelled applicably of cinnamon and oranges. Astounding numbers of birds in plumage of green and scarlet, would lift one lightly by her sleeves and fly her up into a tree and sing to her. Talking monkeys with rope tails and wise solemn eyes would tell stories of an elder world. Lionesses swam in the lake and other pools and streams of the garden, and should the maidens wish to venture there, the lionesses would bear them through the water, or else great blue smiling fish-beasts would rise and offer the handholds of their fanlike fins.

There were always young things in the garden, mysteriously so, for never did any male animals show themselves. Birds' eggs like lapis lazuli or green onyx would abruptly arrive in nests and hatch into glamourous birds, or else a new crop of baby tigers would come gambolling over the lawns— but there was no hint of congress or fertilization.

The sexual stirrings of young women were not encouraged. Blissful ignorance and a preponderance of all things else were intended to stifle them—as in most it did. But a girl grown suddenly disturbed and discontented without knowing why, would come on a bubbling crystal with a stem and mouth-

168

piece of jade. And being moved to smoke from this, the girl would sink back and in climactic inchoate dreamings her sensuality would be appeased in a form she would never entirely recall. The result of this being that she never afterward quested for a man to assuage her yearning and never missed one, but went instead to find the bubbling crystal.

As for the holy shrine, the golden temple and the sacred well, the duty of the nine virgins was self-imposed but enduring.

At first they examined the temple with awe. Next, timidly, they stole inside. The walls and roof were gold, the wide window embrasures were gold, even the shadows through the golden fretwork window lattices were gold. In the center of the floor, which was paved with bone, stood a golden basin. Going to the basin, lifting out a stopper of ivory, the nine maidens might gaze downward in the stupefied respect at a dim muddy glint, and they might smell the noxious mildewy odor of it. Truly, the sacred well was the only unlovely item in the whole garden.

Still, since the witch had reasoned that even the most scatter-brained of humanity required some purpose, and she had envisaged the maidens as totally scatter-brained, the well and the temple had a feel to them which instilled in the nine virgins a sense of importance and religious elevation. As a result, each group of nine virgins had always evolved some form of ceremony to do with the well. Generally, it would occur at sunset—associated with their arrival and the opening of the magic door. Generally, it was expressed in some species of dance and a bringing in of fruit and flowers to scatter about the gold basin, and these offerings, without fail, gratifyingly vanished before the next visit. Then the nine virgins would re-affirm their loyalty to the god, perhaps kiss the stopper in the basin, and whisper such words as: "Mighty father, behold your daughter and your slave." But later, some pride, (or unconscious resentment) always made the virgins re-avow their virginity at the well, in this sort of way: "Behold I am sealed, even as the sacred well is sealed, and by my purity I will keep pure the holy place of the god, and may I perish before I break faith with him."

The weight of all this, its significance, for it could not but acquire weight and significance from the force of belief each group of nine virgins wrought continuously in the valley, were by this time very great. How then could rebellious Kassafeh be immune to them? For immune she was.

The delights of the garden she was suspicious of. She

thought them traps, masks hiding the horrible face of the black god. Though she was tempted by comradely panthers, magic books and instruments, dolphins and sweetmeats, she viewed her very temptation with distrust, and denied it everything.

And somehow, the very marvels of the garden, seeming to grow aware of her denial, came gradually to ignore her. No tigress offered to bear Kassafeh through the groves, no dove flew to sit on her shoulder. Even the fruits of the garden did not taste so sweet to Kassafeh, even the roses were not so red to her eyes. And slowly, as a year went by, Kassafeh noticed other weird changes. For sometimes, walking restlessly about the park, she would, for a second or two, sight an area of barrenness, a blade of rock, a tract of grassless dust. Or she would hear raucous and unmelodic noises from a palace room, and going in find a maiden with one of the instruments, and two or three others sitting near, obviously hearing thrilling music of unqualified virtuosity. *Now I see behind the mask,* though Kassafeh vindictively, but she was frightened too. *Or maybe he is punishing me. Let me be punished then.* As for the rituals at the well, Kassafeh eschewed them. When she went there, she went alone, and lifting out the ivory stopper she sniffed the muddy stink. "That is more like you," she said to the god.

Doubtness it was the strain of elemental in her, her part-fathering by the sky-person, himself part-kindred of Upperearth, that made her unsusceptible to this paradise and its snares.

One year passed and a second year began. It seemed to Kassafeh the other eight virgins had become more sheeplike and silly than ever. Kassafeh wept often and secretly. She dreamed again of the young and handsome captain, and now he bore her away with him on an eagle's back, but when she woke up, she found a silly sheeplike virgin bleating in her ear.

"I too have been troubled in this fashion, Kassafeh. But I have smoked dreams from a bubbling crystal, and I was healed of all distress. And look, here is just such a crystal by your couch."

Kassafeh looked, and saw a murky glass with some murky fluid restive in it.

"Come," urged her fellow virgin, giving her the jade mouthpiece—which to Kassafeh was of dirty chipped enamel. However, disturbed as she was, Kassafeh accepted the drug and lay back with it.

Presently her head swam. Out of a darkening haze, something pounced on her. It was not a man, rather some caricature of a man, created by a fourteen year old witch-whore who had only contempt for the antics of the men to whom she had sold herself. He was at once comic, ridiculous and terrifying. Kassafeh's aloofness from the garden had negated the sensual and erotic aspect of the bubbling crystal; all vagueness and pleasure were taken from it, leaving only a crude comment of the witch's mind upon union with the male.

A hairy, stenchful and mannerless giant grappled Kassafeh. His teeth were pylons and his arms were iron chains.

A phallus, larger than a tower, rushed between her limbs and stove to pierce her. Kassafeh, not surprisingly, screamed.

When she awoke, bathed in sweat, she tottered to a window and vomited on the patchwork valley, which to her was now half green and half desert.

In later months, she took to climbing the inner slopes of the mountains. She would ascent to the very wall. She tried to discover the magic door, (the stair had, of course, moved itself to another place,) but from *within* you could never, in any case, see an opening, let alone get through it, save on that one day when the term of service was done. For all the illusions in the valley, the safeguards were concrete. Every monster was real, the heated wall, its trick door and the fiend who watched it.

The second year passed and a third year began.

By that time for sure, though there were nine virgins in the Garden of the Golden Daughters, only eight of them were guardians. The ninth was an enemy, trapped within the gate.

3

Simmu, alone, walked for a year across the earth to reach the land of the Well and its garden. Azhrarn had gifted him with three things, each in its way a pledge: the burning kiss, the token of the Eshva jewel, the location of the source of his goal. But Azhrarn, that conjurer of confusions, had left Simmu to seek the goal unaided, and Simmu—unaided—was to find the road a long one.

He knew himself, however, from the first, a hero—that is, one with a destiny to fulfil which should shake the world a

171

bit, at its corners. And this knowledge both uplifted and appalled him.

It was told that he had many adventures on his journey, for heroes then as now, were obliged to have adventures. Yet the adventures were of the sort to be expected when traveling through untamed lands abounding in ferocious animals, not all of them natural, where at every bridge and cross-path there might stand some local robber-king demanding toll.

Simmu, who had come to reckon himself mere human clay, was far from that, and, piece by piece, he began to rediscover it. Confronted by a pack of slavering starving dogs, he froze in alarm, his mortal wits deserted him—and let the Eshva magery seep back in its stead. Before he grasped what he was at, Simmu had commenced working glamour on the dogs. Soon they slumped panting and slit-eyed, and wagged their tails in tranced approbation. Tears ran down the cheeks of Simmu, refinding so definitely what he had thought forever gone from him, his demon upbringing. Necessity had been the key. Later, still half afraid, he had deliberately worked his way down into a gully where lions were basking in the sun. They scented man, and swaggered up snarling, but Simmu felt the Eshva magic rise ready to his hand, and clothed himself in it, and soon his fear and their snarling stopped. These lions did not smell of flowers but of lions, rank uncompromising smell of life, nor were they gentle, but prepared at all other times to rend and kill and eat what currently pleased and enchanted them, and their quiescence was therefore breathtaking.

Simmu's sensation of a heroic fate was cemented by these and similar deeds, which occasionally were witnessed, and earned him panic-stricken accolades from the peoples round about. However, he *was* changed, for he thought of his powers as a facet of himself rather than himself as a facet of his powers.

He kept himself also as a man. The impetus for his feminine metamorphosis—Zhirem, afterwards, Azhrarn—was gone. And indeed, Simmu the man grew hard and lean as the lions he courted, a bronze-sword blade in himself with the sunburst hair above it like a mane. Bearded, too, he was, a beard trimmed close by use of a knife, and dressed he was in garments which he had, as ever, stolen as he went by, but no longer an amorphous peasant robe which did for either sex, but the masculine dress of a wanderer who needs limbs and hands free for fighting. For of course, he had been fighting also. As with the dogs, faced with the initial fight, Simmu had

172

been unnerved. No one had ever taught him this art. He had never even scrapped with the other children in the temple courts—they had been too in awe of him for that. Thus, meeting brigands at a ford, he wondered what would become of him, and if, after all, he must fall in Death's net.

"Ho, stripling," bawled the brigands, "ho, pretty apricot-plumed youth. Ho, small fawn, tiny amber cat. This ford is our ford, and either you must pay us, or you must fight Ugly Pig, here."

And then Ugly Pig came forward.

Ugly Pig had been suitably named, though no pig, ugly or not, was as ugly as this one.

"By my missing ear and my seven missing teeth," compounded Ugly Pig, "I'm ready. By my ten warts I am," he added.

Ugly Pig had slain many. He fought with his knife and his strangle-strong fingers and his remaining yellow teeth and his groin-trampling feet. Simmu was of average height, neither short nor tall for a young man, and Ugly Pig was larger, both up and sideways.

For such an entity, the demons would have experienced vast contempt. The Vazdru and the Eshva, who took care to be beautiful in their human guise, abhorred ugliness more than goodness. And something of this aristocratic loathing influenced Simmu, and he made an involuntary gesture with his hand which showed it plainly. But Ugly Pig presumed Simmu was going for the knife in his belt, and rampaged forward.

And before he knew what he was doing, Simmu had darted aside and Ugly Pig had made lavish connection with a tree.

What none of them had foreseen was Simmu's feral swiftness and his senses sharper than a man's, all of which acted independently of his mortal brain.

Ugly Pig roared and shook himself, and whirled out his knife and came in again. And Simmu flashed by him and past him, and leaped upon his back as a young leopard would have done. And there he drew his knife and cut the vital neck vein of Ugly Pig. And when his opponent crashed down, Simmu flew aside, landing lightly on the grass, snarling and for a moment entirely bestial, with the unpredictable malice of a beast. It was the first occasion he had killed in person, given a man, as it were, to his enemy Death. But Simmu, fighting for his life, did not care.

The brigands hesitated. They were not used to such shocks.

Then five of them flung themselves on Simmu, and if Simmu had been only the human youth he considered himself, he would have perished that minute.

But Simmu was Simmu. He spun and swivelled and struck in deadly glancing slashes aimed for the vital points the tiger and the leopard understood so well. And try though they did to fell him and to slaughter him, the brigands could no more have felled and slaughtered a creature one third cat and one third wolf and a final third snake, and sorcerous to boot.

In the end, four more lay dead and the rest took to their heels, yelling it was a devil sent by the gods to pay them out.

Simmu also ran from the plane, for corpses made him tremble yet. But, leaning on a tree, shaking and wide-eyed, he nevertheless knew he could out-fight the murdering flotsam of the wilderness, not from proficiency but from sheer instinct—the training of his babyhood. And he laughed in his throat and cleaned his knife and went on. And thereafter whoever challenged him got short shrift. And some were not mere brigands but cunning in arms, and still he beat them and slew them, their skills no match for his lightning. Though once or twice they cut him, and a scar rose on his left shoulder like a white half moon, and one like a thunderbolt on his right thigh—like the very lightning he became beneath the blades of others.

Hence, a reputation ran before him, and often one stab of his lynx eyes was enough to send enemies away, no need for brawling.

But there was to be another adversary, far worse than beasts or men.

He was halfway to Veshum, halfway along his year-long road, with hero deeds behind him, and the bright mad spark of his heroic goal leading him on. He had already begun to hear garbled reports of the river city, its god and its garden, reports insubstantial as noises carried on the wind.

It was late afternoon in a country of hills and little villages. Simmu walked with a long effortless stride, his eyes low-lidded against the sun, playing a pipe he had recently fashioned as he journeyed. And in his mind, the dream was of another dusty walk, and one (who had it been?) who had walked with him and afterwards gone away, and the pipe made a song of the melancholy of his dream and the birds answered it from the thickets and from the sky.

And then the birds flew away, and the path along the tawny hill grew peculiarly silent and no breeze moved the thickets. And yet there came a kind of rustling, like a breeze through dust or leaves, at Simmu's back.

Simmu stopped playing. He stopped striding. He turned round.

Sometimes, drawn by the abnormal quality that clung about him, animals might follow Simmu, but there was no animal to be seen. The track was vacant. Yet, turning his back to it again, Simmu hesitated. For it seemed that something followed even so.

Simmu went on, and the awareness of another behind him went on as well. A man would have doubted himself, but Simmu's awareness was too fine to mislead him. The track wound round the hill's crest, and here Simmu paused to wait. But none came, and he moved on, and then, and only then, on came the thing which followed.

To be pursued is strange, disconcerting, but not inevitably menacing. Simmu knew as much, and thus the overt menace which his pursuer brought with it was the more sinister.

Simmu had grown to analyze his emotions and to title them—another human failing he had been without in his earliest youth. Now he knew himself afraid, with a unique and specialized fear. However, to turn revealed nothing, and to walk on seemed to invite nothing. He walked, and the sun started to sink and to redden the hills. And then Simmu became conscious of an extra redness in the sky over his shoulder.

This time, when Simmu turned, he did see—something.

It was like the after image of some fiery object, as if he had stared at the sun and then away and seen this shadow-printing on the air. It had no form, was not really present. And yet it *was*.

Below, off the track from the hill, one of the numerous modest villages squatted. As a rule Simmu did not bother to seek the settlements of men. He preferred the lonely dark which summoned the Eshva memory. But this sunset he felt himself driven by his fear to take refuge in the village.

He ran down the slope. The sun ran a fraction faster.

Just as Simmu came into the street of beaten earth, the day winked out into dusk and for the last, he glanced back. The track, the hill, the sky were empty. Yet somehow, superimposed upon the gathering veils of night was a filmy mark, black-red.

A peasant boy-child, eight years old, opened the door and

goggled up at the man who stood there: "Come see!" the child cried, overwhelmed at finding a new species.

Then the whole family came, two agreeable wives, (one holding a ladle) a husband, three adolescent sons and a shy girl of six.

They gazed at the vision with entertainment, for he was utterly unlike them. Lean tempered bronze, with a silver half moon on his bare broad young shoulder, and a handsome face that seemed to gaze straight back at them from the jungle, tongues of flame for hair and green flames for eyes.

"Be glad to enter," murmured one of the wives, and they all drew him inside.

By a fire-pit in the overcrowded earthen room, they gave him food and beer and they sat round him and looked at him as though he were a wonderful gem they had brought home from the hills. And when they wanted more than looking, the children approached, the girl to gather handfuls of his hair and the boys to examine the notched murderous knife with its stained handle. The man spoke of journeys and the two women flirted with their eyes in a nice undemanding way.

Simmu spoke hardly ever, but their company, which was itself like that of a cozy form of animal warren, lulled his nerves. The childish clambering did not trouble him, foxes and cats had clambered all about him and over him in his own childhood. Presently he showed them the wooden pipe, and when they made O's of their eyes, he played it for them.

The fire crackled and the watch dog was stretched at the threshold. It seemed nothing unwelcome could get in.

They lay to sleep together, trustingly, on the piled rugs. The fire guttered and slept too.

The dog did not wake, but Simmy woke. He woke to a red man kneeling on his breasts, (a man of nothing but redness, a vile red like old blood, hairless, featureless save for eyes like wet blood in the dry-blood countenance), a man, if man he was, who squeezed and squeezed at Simmu's throat.

Unable to get breath or to cry aloud, Simmu, being blinded and drowned in a quagmire of this bloodiness, lost his humanity and became that other he was. And the other summoned a resistance from within himself no man could just then have summoned.

With his left hand he seized the thing's own throat—which was substantial enough, though clammy and not like flesh. With his right hand Simmu chose his knife from among the fingers of the sleeping sons, and he stabbed up into the neck

176

he had seized which, now sightless, he could not glimpse but only feel.

The neck convulsed. A scalding fluid splashed on Simmu's chest. He thrust again, and then he could breathe and sight flickered back into his eyes. As he lay gasping, he partially saw the apparition, clutching at its wounds from which brackish ichor was spilling, begin to dissolve on the dark. And in a few instants nothing remained of it save a ring of pain about the throat of Simmu and his bruised windpipe inside it.

When he was more sensible, he roused the fire. No human in the house had woken, nor the dog. It was as if the visitation, meant only for one man, could be experienced only by him. Simmu turned his knife before the fire—the blade was coated with a substance which dropped from it in flakes leaving the metal burnished clean.

Simmu did not sleep again. He crouched by the hearth till sunrise. But no second thing came to hunt him.

In the morning, the girl child said she had dreamed a red bull had got into the house and ran thorough the fire, and the women laughed at her, as they plaited her hair, one plait each.

They did not try to stay Simmu when he left but they watched him go, and the girl child stepped solemnly after him a short distance up the street.

That day Simmu traveled with unease on his left hand and feverish alertness on his right. Nothing came near, however, until noon was past. As before, he was on a lonely track, as before the world seemed to muffle its noises about him. He turned his head and perceived no one, yet guessed the presence at his back. He had known, without reason, that the force which had attacked him was not done with the battle. Simmu shuddered but he kept on. Reaching a village, he made a detour. This night he should meet his foe in the open, and awake.

The sun sank. Simmu sat down on the crest of a sheer-sided hill, his spine against the rocky comb. He ate the meal of edible stems he had gathered as he walked, and laid his knife ready.

The sky's roof became indigo and the wind danced through the caves and gullies of the hills, but sometimes there would come a curious patch of ruddy darkness, between Simmu and the sky, the land, the after-image of a light where no light was.

The night turned its starry wheel. Sleep the fisher crept to

Simmu and kissed his eyelids, but he sent her away, though, being shameless, she returned later and tried to kiss him again.

But then sleep fled, for that which Simmu had been awaiting began to happen.

From an uncertain, half-seen thing, the ectoplasmic patch surged into mass and into shape, a ghost assuming flesh. Like a round of heavy dough with the leaven working violently in it, the entity heaved and toiled toward existence. Firstly the stars shone through it, then the stars were eclipsed and hidden by the solidifying bulk. A dough man rose from the mix, yeasty and foully red, and in the blank of face the two wet wounds of the eyes fixed on Simmu. Of the wounds in its throat there was no trace. It had been remade whole in whatever un-world it had returned to the previous night.

It moved uphill to Simmu with a very fast deliberate bounding terrifying to behold. Its hands were already outstretched to grip the windpipe it had been cheated of. But Simmu had risen, and as suddenly he raced to meet it.

The thing groped to seize him. As it did so, Simmu plunged his knife into the area of the heart—if heart it had, and, immediately extricating the blade, stabbed again into the awful neck. The thing made no sound, nor had it before. Additionally ominous, where the knife had struck on this occasion no ichor poured forth. And clutching Simmu, rather that its hurts, the entity hugged him and squeezed him, this time both about the throat and the ribs.

Simmu's eyes blackened. He could not breathe, his left arm was gripped, yet he strove to wield the knife with the other. The proximity of the creature was almost too horrible to bear—a slimy, wet-clay, swamp-like sticking of its body to his. He thrust the knife, as he thought, into its eye but again no hot life-fluid flowed down over him. Besides, the thing seemed stronger than it had been. It writhed at his attack, but its clutch did not weaken. Instead, lover-like, it pressed his head into its revolting unflesh as it choked him.

Simmu cut it once more in the back, but it was a feeble cut. His strength was failing, if the creature's was not. The world was rushing from Simmu and he thrashed limply in the helpless spasms of the asphyxiated.

And then the creature stumbled on the uneven hill slope, its grip slackened and Simmu, in a convulsive kicking motion, launched himself aside, and no sooner aside than forward again at the lower limbs of his adversary. One last floundering blow he delivered to those limbs, a blow that sent the red shape rolling off from the steep hillside and into the air.

Simmu lay on the ground and watched it fall, soundless, on to the neck of the hill below. At the impact the being seemed to shatter, burst apart, though quite noiselessly. And then, as before, it melted into the dark, leaving no atom of itself behind.

Simmu lay a long while face down on the slope.

His own physical frame was wrung and battered. Probably he could not survive many more such supernatural duels.

For he knew there would be others, though almost certainly no others tonight. Tonight the visitation would be mended in whatever region sheltered it. But tomorrow it would be galvanized once more to pursue Simmu and to fight with him. And tomorrow it would be stronger still. And the next night, supposing Simmu could withstand till the next, it would be stronger again. For clearly the thing was sorcerous and sorcerously sent, and he had no chance against it. Destroy it as often as he liked, it would come back to him the following night, always it would come back, till Simmu was slain.

4

Who had sent the red pursuer? Who but the one who had beaten on a red drum after she betrayed her darkest secret to Azhrarn and to Simmu?

In panic had Lylas turned to that drum with its unidentified red drum skin, for not carelessly was such an item turned to. And then the handmaiden of Uhlume, Lord Death, had tapped and coaxed and conjured, and what she had conjured she had set to track Simmu and to kill him. A long while it had taken, for Simmu's inherited Eshva quality had clouded the trail, his spoor was not quite human. But eventually the repellent conjuring had found him out, and, obeying the witch's geas, had begun its murderer-task.

Now this being, this conjuration, was evolved from a place neither on the earth nor in the nether regions of the earth, and yet accessible, a kind of black magician's psychic cupboard full of afreets. To open the cupboard required particular procedures, most of all a particular sort of intellect and intention. No one stumbled accidentally on such a sphere.

From the depth the fiend arose, and into the depth the

179

fiend would remove itself when its errand was run. Here too it was drawn after its battles with Simmu, that its injuries might be knit together by the unthinking but huge power of the psychic cupboard. It could never be completely overcome, as Simmu had divined, merely warded off for a space. It had, too, this quality, that each time it was defeated and so renewed, its endurance doubled. It had another quality, in some ways more dreadful. It could not be demolished more than once with any single weapon. Thus, the knife which had despatched it on the first night was useless on the second. (There was a direful tale concerning a king who had had one of these things activated against him, and maybe Simmu had even heard the tale and remembered it. On the first night, the king slew the sending with a sword, on the second with an axe, on the third night by strangulation with a cord. Being invisible and impalpable to all but the intended victim, the monster was impervious to the blows of any other, and so the king must sleep by day and rise to fight at sunset when the apparition manifested. On the fourth night a spear was used, on the fifth a bow, on the sixth a bowl of acid, on the seventh a mallet of stone. There followed seventy further grisly nights, for each of which the kind devised a fresh weapon and used it. Meantime the kingdom fell into ruin, invaders massed on the borders and the monarch's courtiers abandoned him. Finally, on the seventy-eighth night, exhausted by his hopeless and never-ending ordeal, the king drank poison. And reputedly the horror, when it returned that sunset, found only the king's ghost, bitterly chuckling on the threshold, which declared: "You are too late." But he was mistaken, for the sending, unable to find a body to mutilate, and being itself unearthly, ripped instead at the spirit of the king, so only a portion of his soul escaped the world entire.)

Simmu had no wish to strive inadequately seventy-seven nights, even could hs sustain his life that length under the onslaught. To be sure, his mind had already gone to Azhrarn's parting words: "Burn this green jewel at your throat once more in fire, I will answer."

Simmu guessed none but the Demonfolk could help him—if they would. But he had not wanted to call to Azhrarn. As a child desires to prove itself unaided in the world, so Simmu did. And he feared to lose the little of Azhrarn's love he might have earned, by imploring him too soon or too often.

Simmu's reluctance and the sluggishness of his beaten body delayed him. The night washed away and the sun came up, and no demon would answer by daylight.

Accordingly, Simmu sat on the hillside, partly angry and partly despairing, and filled by a sick yearning for Azhrarn who would—or would he?—reply to the token.

Not long after the sun had passed through the zenith there began again that eerie evil promise of impending arrival, that shadow patch on the air.

Simmu glared at it, trembling with fury and fear. Then he got up and gathered dry roots and branches from a downhill thicket, and laid a fire ready.

As soon as the western sun started its decline, Simmu lit the fire, and as one red light sank, the smaller flared up and he dropped into it the Eshva jewel from his neck. And then he bowed his head and prayed, as he had never prayed in earnest to the gods, to Azhrarn the Prince of Demons.

The night settled on the landscape. The red fire spat and danced, all else was blackness, and on the blackness, the patch.

Simmu waited. He waited for the advent of love or death.

Love appeared.

There on the hillside suddenly, a dark dove, which changed into an Eshva man, not to be mistaken, but not Azhrarn.

The eyes of the Eshva coolly levelled on Simmu. The eyes said: *Do not ask where he is, for he has sent me to you.*

Simmu began aloud, "I am haunted—" but the Eshva man silenced Simmu with an upheld hand, and gazing about, the Eshva conveyed this: *I know you are haunted now, and by what. Be patient.* And then the Eshva was gone as abruptly as he had come.

Startled, Simmu could only continue his vigil, his existence in the balance.

Presently the fire went out and Simmu took from it the burned jewel—which tomorrow would be restored to its greenness. He wondered if he would live to see it. An hour was sliced from the night, and another.

All at once, the simmer on the air began to come to the boil.

He, who had styled himself Death's Enemy, was about to die.

And then the most astonishing thing, more astonishing than death, happened to Simmu. With awful agony he felt himself convulsed, squashed, compressed. He would have cried out, but could not speak, could barely see. Or at least he saw, but from a different vantage. Everything had swelled five or six times its normal size, everything was of an unreal pallor—whitish hills against a whitish sky with black stars . . . or no,

a greenish sky and stars like—black sapphires—or. . . .
Simmu moved. All of him moved. He was roped, limblessly, in a night forest of ferns, gazing two ways at once from the sides of his head. A gentle hand took hold of him and he wound himself in a number of loops about the wrist of the hand.

Simmu had been transformed into a serpent, one of the silver serpents that adorned the hair of the Eshva. As he was realizing this, he made out with his weird Underearth-snake's eyes, a muddy clay-man on the hillside. But the clay-man conjuring had halted where it stood. Its outstretched arms grappled at nothing.

And Simmu was conscious that flowing from the Eshva—there were three Eshva, all told, on the hill—was a charismatic aura that hid his own presence as securely as his form was hidden, bewildering and stultifying the fiend.

The Eshva laughed with their eyes. They laughed at the fiend, able to perceive it but inviolate to and disdainful of it. And the fiend prowled round them, powerless to approach or to damage; powerless to find Simmu.

Now it was a fact that a conjuring of this type, once called, must find its prey on each successive night. And the conjuring could not, though it perfectly recognized that Simmu should be there, must be there, for he was nowhere else in the world, above or below it. And the conjured fiend began to seethe like a yeasty drink, and with no warning it foamed into fragments, and the night seemed to suck it down and curl it away into nowhere.

But there was in actuality somewhere that the conjuring went to.

The Eshva strolled on over the hills some way. They kept Simmu a snake apparently out of affectionate vague maleficence. His mind, crushed into the brain-box of the metallic serpent, was in a silly chaotic state; he scarcely grasped any more where he was or how he came to be there or why. He partly forgot his own identity, though some worry nagged at him, and even that he did not recall. Yet it was beautiful to be among the Eshva, the dream-burned ones, the wandering children of shade.

When he came to himself it was with another blast of pain, and some hours after. He was a young man again, the world was its proper size and color. The Eshva were leaving him.

He recollected everything in a frantic rush. He tried to question the Eshva. The Eshva intimated to Simmu that he was safe from the peril which had stalked him. But how could this be, seeing the peril must have its prey? Prey the peril had had.

Simmu watched them. Their eyes were soft with their dreams, innocently and dreamily wicked, telling no more.

But it was true, he was safe, his very blood and heart and hair could feel safety. Azhrarn had swept death aside. Once more Simmu's quest of the garden was freely before him.

Though he wished, with the leisure now to regret, that Azhrarn had come to him in person.

5

Near two hundred and thirty-three years old Lylas was and she looked fifteen, and she sat in the chamber where the blue lamps burned pink fire in the House of the Blue Dog.

She was playing a bone game, was the pomegranate witch. Not with the clean white finger bones from about her waist, but with chips and shards of stained and yellowish bone filched from upturned graves. She was Death's Handmaiden and liked his emblems round her. Tonight she was proud and spiteful, thinking she had made Uhlume's secret secure again, thinking of her youth and the endless years before her. But the bones she threw down, which were intended to form patterns that should show luck and prosperity ahead, showed only confused things, a future not as she had anticipated.

"Stupid bones," said the witch, "I will grind you under my heel for you are liars."

And she pictured the handsome youth with the cat's gaze, baulked of the garden and the well, and dying somewhere in a red swirling, and she giggled. Till the red swirling came up in the midst of the rugs.

Lylas stared.

"Out!" she cried, "out, you fool! Did I call you to be idle? Go finish your business."

But the conjuring did not go, it solidified and its bloody eyes expanded on her with an incredible message in them.

"He cannot have cheated you—return and search again!"

But the conjuring could never return. Generally it did not need to. Illogical yet activated, all it wanted now was prey. If not the prey it had been instructed to take, then the prey which had instructed it. And so much Lylas beheld, and slowly she rose and retreated before it.

Many and several were the powders and the dusts, the

183

symbols and the tricks which she cast in its path to stay it. Many and several were the chants and incantations she uttered to facilitate its exit from the world. But such a creation, once unleashed, was uncheckable, the double-bladed sword.

At last the wall was at her back and she could go no farther. She screamed a spell to transport herself, and transported she was, but the thing came after. Again and yet again she flung herself from one plot of the earth's ground to another. Finally, in a forest somewhere, empty of anything save the trees themselves, the apparition, weary of the chase, seized Lylas by her hair, and with two tremendous grinding snaps, he broke her in half like a doll.

All the bones of her girdle were scattered, as the other bones had scattered so inauspiciously when she played with them. Appeased, the conjuring dissolved into the night leaving her quite dead under the trees. Lylas could have been eternal, but she had never been invulnerable.

Later, one blacker than the forest would come for her, for she too had made the thousand year bargain with Uhlume, not thinking to keep it for millennia.

In the blue mansion, the blue enamel dog was already rifling her chests.

6

Simmu came to Veshum. He was seventeen and of rare appearance. His looks made both men and women turn to gape in the streets, not mere beauty but that shine of light inside, the flaring torch of purpose and defiance. Seeing himself so conspicuous gave him pause. But then he thought: *They will all know at the last why I have come.* He realized heroes must have witnesses. Besides, nobody ever questioned Simmu as to why he had journeyed here. They assumed that he, as with all the others, had come to marvel at their god.

Inside the Garden of the Golden Daughters, the nine virgins were each sixteen, having served three years there. This, the people of Veshum told Simmu without being asked. They were altogether flamboyant with their sanctity. The god by now had a golden garland on his coal-black head, golden anklets and a robe of scarlet velvet. Every ninth sunfall a black cow was sacrificed to him. Simmu saw the rite and did not care for it. And among the shops of Veshum, among the vendors of fine silk and exquisite jewelry, of gorgeous sweet-

184

meats and erotic incenses, one could buy small statuettes of the god which mimicked the larger one—they were considered lucky.

In the courts of inns, on the terraces of palm trees which descended to the river, Simmu, with hardly any prompting, was taken aside and informed of all he might need to know. Of the nine-year term of the virgins, of the golden shrine that housed the well, of the hot high wall and the patrolling army and its watch towers, of the ferocious monsters who dwelt on the mountain slopes. And one morning, as Simmu was conversing with a stonemason on a terrace, a heavily veiled woman of tragic appearance approached, and the stone mason said: "Take notice, stranger, for there passes one of the holy virgins of the Garden. Three years since, her term of service ended. She walked from the garden weeping, as they always do. And now she has stabbed her husband."

The woman, who naturally had not been detained for the murder—as the sacrosanct persons of the Daughters of the Garden were never detained for any crime, however heinous—now passed by, and Simmu could observe her closely. She was tall and slender, but bare-footed as one who mourned, and her head and face were thickly muffled in her veiling. Though he could not spy her features, Simmu heard her groans and lamentations, and her tears ran down her veil across her breast.

"Is she then sorry that she stabbed him?" inquired Simmu innocently.

"Indeed no," declared the man with some smugness. "It is a common event for the virgins to assassinate their families. They pine only for the Garden they may never return to and the wondrous presence there of the god. No doubt," he added in a low and portentous tone, "she will soon attempt to regain admission, which also is common." And he told Simmu in poetic detail how frequently the veiled and weeping exiled virgins would go out alone across the desert, ascend the mountain slopes, and sit down by the hot wall to await the sunset opening of the narrow door.

"But do none challenge them?" asked Simmu.

"Challenge a holy Daughter? Why should they be challenged? They are quite recognizable with their feminine attire, their veils and crying. Only foreigners are turned from the area. Additionally, the monsters on the slopes, set there by the god for the protection of his garden, can easily differentiate between one of the river people and an outlander, and all outlanders they tear in shreds."

185

"And when the virgins reach the door and it opens, what then?"

"There is a final monster, worse than the rest, which guards the door, and it will let none in save the virgins of thirteen whey they first come there in accordance with the god's decree. It wards off the unfortunate maiden, and presently she slays herself. It is always the same."

"Suppose one were to enter the garden?"

"Impossible!"

"True, it seems so. But let us say, for argument's sake—"

"No, no, I will not blaspheme, even for the sake of argument. None are ever in the garden save the nine fair young girls, chaste as lilies and sweetly ignorant, (as all women should be but seldom remain, alas.) And the playmates of these naive and lovely creatures are reputedly female beasts, gentle as lambs. For no male of any kind is permitted in the garden. Saving, of course, the suitable masculine penumbra of the god."

At this moment, the veiled and doleful figure of the murderess-virgin, having moved up the steps to the city street, slunk into the crowds. Simmu bade the stone mason farewell, and by a circuitous route went after her.

She was no trouble to keep track of. The crowd parted respectfully to let her through, and she wept and groaned continuously. It shortly became obvious that she was already on her way to seek the nine mountain ring and the door in the wall. Soon she, with Simmu a discreet distance behind, left the city by an unfrequented gate and began her trek across the dunes.

It was a barren, mostly shadeless region, but the resolute maiden walked on over it until noon blistered the sky. Then, coming to a solitary gaunt rock, over whose ledges the sand blew and the sun poured, she sat down to rest in a drop of shadow at its foot. Simmu, less noisy than the sand itself, approached her.

Among the demons, it was the Vazdru who sang in the ears of men to wake or to trance them, but the Eshva might have done as much if they had had voices. Simmu crept like the lynx to the woman's shoulder, and in her ear, demon fashion, he sang. No doubt, to a demon, it would have been a poor copy—what had the Eshva conveyed so scornfully by the lake of salt? *Your silent footfall is a thunderclap, we are the air*. Nevertheless, this poor copy was mesmeric enough to a mortal.

Deliriously lulled, the woman's tears stopped; she sank

against the rock and sighed. Simmu lifted her veil. Though her eyes were red and her mouth grown shrewish, yet she was most beautiful. Simmu kissed her face, and her shrewish mouth slackened; smiling somewhat, in the rock's shadow, she slept her first quiet sleep for three years. Meanwhile Simmu thieved her clothes, leaving her only his cloak to shield her from the desert heat—though this was more than any demon would have left her in a similar case. He still did not make needless presents to Death.

Then Simmu stripped himself of his own garments, and next of his male gender.

A year had elapsed. For a year he had been a man, and only that, welded in an incontrovertible mould. And the mould had become rigid, more rigid than it had been that adolescent time among the wild olives, when jealousy, love and fear had refound the change Simmu could effect in himself. Simmu was more a man now than he had been then. Metamorphosis was harder. It was not so much a rending and stretching he felt, but a wrongness. His mind was less elastic even than his unusual body. What had been a satisfying sweet pleasure of pain was now an act of self-denial or hate. He loathed it but he willed it to happen, for he must reach the garden, and this was the way.

And then, instantaneously it seemed, the struggle melted. He shivered and was no longer hero but heroine.

There had been greater changes to effect to achieve this reversal of the coin. Simmu the man, broad of shoulder, lean of hip. . . . Simmu the woman was as tall as he, tall for a woman, yet not uncouthly, so for Simmu was no giant; but the bones and muscles of the pelvis, the arms, the legs, the waist, the breast had all subtly disowned their maleness. The woman was slender yet curvaceous, high-breasted, smooth of skin, depilated ambiently of beard and body hair together—beautiful. More beautiful than the maiden who slept in the rock's shade. And as much a woman now as she had been man before.

Simmu, without inward comment, put on the stolen clothing, muffled face and tresses in the veil. Her feet, bare and delicate though not necessarily over-small, were unmistakably female. The dress, moistened by tears and dried by the desert's heat, had taken on the contours of two rounded breasts which once more were undeniably filled.

The sun had moved one hour nearer to the west when she went on, unaccompanied, the lovely lamenting exiled Daughter, now Simmu, making for the nine mountain ring.

Late in the afternoon, they saw her from the watch towers. The sentinels pointed and hushed their voices, somewhat awestruck as they always were at this macabre recurring pilgrimage. Also, let it be said, somewhat irritated, somewhat put out. It was they, or their comrades, who would have to climb through the bedlam of slope-lurking monsters after this girl and inevitably take up and return her self-slain corpse to the city.

They muttered together, the sentries; down below, various portions of the patrolling army, having spotted the advancing virgin, were muttering in similar vein.

And then, as the patrols and the sentries stood surveying her in pious, unfriendly resignation, a great activity began on the mountain sides.

Up from their holes and burrows, their caves and cubbies, surged a few hundred monstrosities, all grunting, roaring, yelping and howling. Fire snapped from their mouths and the air blackened with smoke. They flapped their wings, those that had wings, so vigorously that brass feathers clattered to the ground. They lashed their tails, and the tails (snakes) hissed. They showed their tiger teeth and pawed the mountain slope and the sand with their hoofs, and their horns rattled loudly as they struck rock and boulder and neighboring horns.

The soldiers of the patrol were astounded. Such a thing had never happened before, at least, not at the arrival of a virgin. Was this some omen? Or had the awful guardian frights of the god finally run amok? Nervously the army regarded its bows and swords, and asked itself how effective they would be, and if it might be blasphemy to resist. Concurrently, the hordes of frights were rushing down the mountain sides and over the sand, resembling an unlikely out-spewing of lava or water. The army and the watch towers were ignored. Straight for the lone figure of the virgin the monsters made. In horrified bewilderment, the army lost view of her in a cloud of wings, horns, scales, tails, dust, fire and smoke.

The guardians, naturally, were merely responding as ever to the advent of an unaccompanied alien near the mountain ring. Simmu was not of the river people, therefore she was a foreign trespasser. Therefore they would tear her in pieces. Why every single monster flew out to see to this bit of business is not sure. Possibly they sensed in Simmu less of a simple straggler, more of a true and definite threat—however, Simmu was no slower than they to react.

Before the cavalcade of guardians had quite reached her, Simmu had cast off her clothing, all but the veil which hid hair and face, and she had begun sinuously to dance.

Simmu had power, through this magic of dance, this evocative, provocative Eshva spell-weaving, to tame the wildest of earth's beasts. A touch of the hand was enough, sometimes less, a whisper of thought, Eshva-caressive, to ensorcel serpent, bird, fox or dog—her dancing had bound the savage unicorn, the man-eating cat. But these monsters the witch had left on the mountains, they were not earth beasts, but beasts of sorcery themselves, *her* beasts, a patchwork which she had invented. Yet, when Simmu danced, their fanged jaws dropped, their terrible horns were lifted meekly aloft, their wings closed, their tails slept. How could this be?

There was, for one, the demon jewel at Simmu's throat, the thing which had largely protected him, hero-heroine, in poisoned Merh. And now, perhaps, the jewel heightened the ability of Simmu's spell. But it would have needed a little more than that.

One unrecognized event had taken place. Simmu did not know of it, certainly no one in Veshum knew. Even the monster guardians did not. And while the guardians did not know, still the event had cast its dim shadow on them, changing them, weakening them, sucking the marrow from their vicious function.

The witch, she who had created them two hundred and nineteen years before, was dead.

Much the witch had done had been of that order of sorcery which was sympathetic or emulative. It was her installing of her own fantasies and cruelties into the enterprise which had ensured the strength of those safeguards of the garden. And though in the forefront of her mind she had set this task aside, in the back rooms of her brain she often recalled it with glee. It had been her masterpiece, her love-gift to Lord Death. And all that had to do with the garden had basked in her far-off subconscious delight in it, had drawn unending fuel therefrom. But now there was no fuel, no source, no distant key to stir the clockwork and get it running smoothly. The remembering brain of the pomegranate witch was trapped in the Innerearth, and few impulses rose from that domain. And thus the guardians rushed to Simmu, apparently eager as ever to prevent and to rend. But, leaderless at last, a dying flame, it took only a reasonably phenomenal magic to swing them from their duty, to harness and erase two hundred and nineteen years of pitiless intent.

189

Soon, the monsters fawned on Simmu.

They rubbed their tigery faces on her sides, and licked her with odd cloven tongues. The Eshva spell was sweet and they enjoyed it. Their lives had been long and mechanical. Even a monster, supposedly, can grow weary of unmitigated rending.

"Now, what is this?" queried the patrols as they watched the virgin start to move up the nearest mountain slope, escorted by gambolling, slobbering monsters. "Her head is veiled but she is naked," commented one of the sentries from his high vantage point. The others averted their eyes, not wishing to be irreligiously aroused. "I think," said one, "she is dancing." He had caught a glimpse and the spell had partly claimed him. Swimming-eyed, he wandered from his lookout post, an unheard of lapse.

"Do we follow the maiden?" demanded the men about the slope.

They had always followed in the past, but now, having received an order to that effect, they kept a gap between themselves and the monsters, who were no longer behaving as Veshum's famous guardians should. And because of this gap and the monsters themselves, they could no longer see Simmu-the-maiden at all.

It was now almost sunset. Shadows stained the desert from beneath mountains, watch towers, standing men. The sky was sponged with gold, the western plateau was powdered with red dusts as the caravan of the sun rode toward the brink of the land.

Concealed, Simmu climbed toward the hot high wall. From its summit the corona of lightning slashed, growing brighter as the sky deepened.

Simmu reached the place of the door.

She threw off her last veil as the sinking sun threw off the last veil of the day. Both veils shone and dropped among the rocks. Simmu murmured, from her mouth and from her mind, and the monsters sprawled languidly, lazily wagging their snake-tails, their indolently stirring wings like the sound of many brazen fans rising and falling. Simmu went toward the magic door which just now was forming among the thickets, precisely where the people of Veshum had explained it would. Already the heat of the wall was scorching, already the door was opening.

And then, between Simmu and the door, out of the thickets, came the last guardian, the sentry at the garden gate.

It could alter its size, this creature. Among the thickets it was tiny as a snail, its burrow no bigger than the circumference of a girl's bracelet. But, turning sentinel, it swelled, shot out arms, teeth, boney appendages. It became a snake, armored with lusterless scales, a snake with several muscular human arms, also scaled, furnished with claws of bluish steel. Its face, which was a face of nightmare, was somewhat similar to the head of a man who had lost both hair and wits. It was mad and grinning, composed of a square maw bladed with pointed fangs and two bulging insane eyes in color most unalluring orange, (the color of the witch's toxic pomegranates?) The palms of its many hands were also orange, but its tongue, which now and then spilled between its lips and teeth, was black. Horns sprouted from its wrists, its cheeks, its temples.

Simmu skipped back a pace and considered it. The air was full of the Eshva glamouring, but this final monster clearly did not respond to it. Simmu tried an arrow of thought: Let me by. The guardian of the door bubbled up a gross din, laugh or oath or phlegm, and spat in the air a gob of flaming matter. And then it prepared itself to seize Simmu, a lengthy preparation, full of savoring noises and a sharpening of claws on the ground. While behind it, the narrow door stood fully open on the garden of the secret well, though not for much longer.

Simmu spun to the monsters who had fawned on her. She extended her arms, she crooned to them and commanded them with her eyes. She thrust violent fancies in their receptive skulls, she stroked their backs until they frisked and rose up, their jaws once more clashing, their tails awake, their wings spread for battle. Simmu used her sorcery in a way she had never done before. Next moment, the hundreds of monsters lost their passivity and aimed themselves in one horrifying, concentrated body—at the guardian of the door.

Well practiced they, in their one art, that art they had perfected, the art of rending. The guardian had never rent, never had occasion to, for what trespassing stranger ever could have reached so far as the wall? As for the returning virgins, it had only growled at those, and they had fled and killed themselves. It was not ready, this final and worst guardian, not ready for any of what happened. And very quickly, despite its variety of defenses, its tough armor and grasping claws, the monster multitude of teeth and horns and hooves had dismantled it and blood-bathed tiger faces smiled from its vitals and brazen wings flapped over its scattered scales.

And across this gruesome scene dashed Simmu, swifter

191

than the red light which just then left the sky. And Simmu ran straight into the forbidden garden through the impenetrable door a second before it vanished.

7

No marble stairway descended from the door on this particular evening. Instead, a silken lawn tumbled there, gracefully down among the groves and woods of the valley, and all was serene in the delicate rose-water afterglow of the garden.

Simmu remained for some time on the slope, half unbelieving of her feat, yet exhilarated too by half believing in it. She gazed at the garden with a contemplative gaze, for she was wiser now in all modes of mage-craft, and she could smell magic and illusion as strong as the fragrance of the flowers and the scent of the water. Her own female condition she had had to struggle with on first arriving. Even as she cast herself joyfully down on the grass, a masculine pride had beset her, and her physique, held as a man for so great a while, strove to reverse itself. But she resisted her maleness, for the garden was a feminine thing and stocked with females—this fragrance also she could detect. She feared to betray herself—or himself—should she rove about here in a man's shape.

After a little, Simmu got to her feet, and she scanned the valley for the golden temple which housed the secret well.

The rosy garden moon had risen. Simmu's eyes, aided by the moon and less hampered by illusion than most eyes which had looked about in that valley, quickly caught a glint of gold—or the semblance of gold. Westward, the temple. And Simmu could no more have kept from immediately seeking it than could a thirsty man keep from drinking.

Simmu ran toward the temple lighter and faster than the illusory deer of the garden—some of which she saw. But they paid no heed to her, being unreal themselves, while her femininity disturbed nothing of the valley's womanly atmosphere. In fact the whole garden truly had the feel of being a woman or a feminine environment. Everywhere was the softness, the voluptuousness, the feline innocence which eternally had symbolized woman. Nothing decisive, harsh or independent showed itself, or, where it did, illusion glossed it over. Even the trees had fluid, curving postures. Even the hills were round as breasts. And into this, Simmu had thrust, fortunately in woman's form. It had not yet become a matter of rape.

Simmu came to the temple. Gold it looked, gold it was not, but a couple of centuries had imbued it (like the garden) with its own particular resonance. On the threshold, despite herself, Simmu was moved to an inner holding of the breath. She stole in, catfooted, her eyes gleaming on the gold basin and the stopper of bone which marked, with no doubt, the well. And then she heard a high wild singing behind her, out in a dusky garden. Eight girl voices raised in a song or a hymn.

Generally the virgins came to the temple at sunset to make their ceremony and their vows before the god, to strew their fruit and flowers. Tonight, as sometimes occurred as the years went by and the initial ardor slackened, they were a fraction later than sunset.

Simmu, hearing sixteen girl-feet on the path to the temple door, sprang into the nearest shelter, the wide embrasure of a window. And here she lowered herself to her belly, leopardess-like, and watched through glinting slits.

A kind of new golden dusk entered the temple.

Partly it was due to a golden lamp burning with an incense smell, which the first maiden set on a hook in the wall. Partly the temple itself, glowing in the lamp's light. Partly the shimmering golden raiment and ornaments with which the virgins were hung. Partly their loveliness, which seemed a golden thing.

They were all sixteen now, these eight girls, (Simmu puzzled for a minute why there were only eight, not nine, the prescribed number,) sixteen, and ripened in the garden to a passionate flowering without appeasement. And they had been chosen in the beginning for their unblemished beauty.

And now, in the gold dusk, they began goldenly to dance.

They had black grapes and green, scarlet poppies, sheaves of white lilies, hyacinths and roses, peaches and palm fronds, for everything bloomed continuously and at once in the garden. And these things they laid against the central basin as they passed, but first they would press the fruit to their lips, trickle the flowers across their bodies and through their hair. And as the dance, which seemed to have started a sort of soundless music playing in accompaniment, grew frenzied—for frenzied it did grow—they used the fronds to lash themselves. And then their garments began to loosen and were unwound and trailed aside. The garments seemed all layers of gold, now opaque, now less opaque. And under those layers

193

which showed the white hint of flesh, the dark bud of a breast's tip, the arch of a foot, a limb, were layers which clad the bodies of the sight maidens only as smoke clothes fire.

This dancing was lascivious, but meant only for the god. Eight virgins, who were denied the sight of men, danced to fantasies of the brain. And their eyes were burning but heavy-lidded, and their red mouths had opened enough to show the white teeth and the warm cave behond the palisade of the teeth. And they unveiled themselves to the ultimate smoky veiling, and offered, with naive abandon, their velvet bodies to the basin of the stoppered well. Till eventually they flung themselves upon it and rubbed themselves against the metal and each panted and sobbed and moaned through her flying hair as she clutched the bone stopper: "Behold, I am sealed even as the sacred well is sealed, and by my purity I will keep pure the holy place of the god, and may I *perish*— oh, perish, perish!—before I break faith with him."

Simmu, hidden in the window, was meantime experiencing some difficulty. Triggered by the stimulus of the eight virgins and their dance, Simmu's masculinity almost instantly attempted to assert itself in vehement spasms. Try as she— he—would to combat the onslaught, it was impossible. And even when, though not wishing to look away from the maidens' antics, Simmu had in desperation done so, the gasps and whispers and small groans were still enough to discompose her and presently him. And so, at length, irresistibly, Simmu the man lay upon the window ledge in the most definite state of masculine readiness possible. And with blazing eyes and gritted teeth and a hammering pulse, and some grim amusement at his own plight, he saw the dance out, and next how the exhausted virgins gathered their veiling and themselves from the floor, forgot their lamp, and stumbled into the night to become little girls again—or else to seek the erotic thing in the bubbling crystal.

After that, Simmu kept quiet on the ledge, preparing, by stringent discipline, to reverse his sex yet again. But as he was stretched out thus, a ninth virgin entered the temple, alone.

Now, the voices of the others had died away, and Simmu, setting discipline on the side, could hardly help but think to himself that here was a unique opportunity.

But then his intellect dispelled his senses, for he realized that this maiden was not like the others. For one thing, she was more beautiful, if such could be possible. For another, she was far less beautifully garbed, in plain and rather ragged

194

dress, as if the opulent illusions of the garden somehow had no effect on her. For the third thing, she shouted into the temple in a fierce parody of the former chant: "Behold, oh god, I too am sealed. And would I were not, the your accursed well were not!" And then she bolted into the darkness.

Astonished, in the window embrasure, Simmu came to see he had been given the answer to that vital heroic problem of his. Now he knew exactly how to crack the cistern of Upperearth and let the water of Immortality into the second well beneath.

8

Eight of the nine virgins were at their evening feast in their palace of marble. They reclined on embroidered cushions in the scented candle glow, toying with roasted meats, crystallized lotus shoots, candied figs and like stuff. Bright birds, perching on plinths, sang in endless harmonies, a black panther or two, a lioness, a cheetah, lay with their sculptured masks in jeweled laps, petted by jeweled fingers.

The virgins chattered and mused, rested after their religious frenzy in the temple. True to the witch's prediction, they spoke quite an amount of nonsense, but there was no one to disagree, and consequently they imagined themselves wise.

"I have a theory," remarked one, "that the moon is really a flower, whose petals are shed throughout the month till nothing is left. Then the new moon buds from the black soil of the night sky."

"How original," said one of the other virgins. They were not envious of each other's genius, having nothing to compete for.

"Yes, I have thought about it a great deal," said the original virgin, "and now I begin to wonder if the sun is not a burning fire which each sunset is quenched in wine. . . ."

"Or possibly it is a hole in the fabric of the ether, revealing the flaming world of the Upperearth." said a third virgin daringly, "the world of our god and master."

"How foolish is Kassafeh," said a fourth virgin, "to avoid us. What she would learn in our company!"

In this much, human taste had been inadvertently catered for; an enemy stood ready to hand: the ninth virgin.

195

"Now what is that I hear at the window?" asked the fifth virgin, who had very sharp ears decorated with pearls.

"At the window? Nothing."

"Yes. I thought I heard a laugh. Can it have been Kassafeh, spying on us?"

"Perhaps," said the original virgin, lapsing once more in thought, "it is starlight falling, and breaking on the ground."

"There," cried the sixth virgin, "I hear it too, at this window now. I shall go and see," and she ran to the window, and stared out and noted a slender female figure among the shadows. "For shame, sister," said the sixth virgin.

"Alas," murmured the figure mournfully, "I am regretful of my sins, and my heart is weighted with lead."

"It is Kassafeh for sure," shouted the sixth virgin to her fellows. "She says she is regretful of her sins, and her heart is weighted with lead." But when the sixth virgin looked out again, Kassafeh had vanished. "I do not entirely understand it," admitted the sixth virgin. "She has never repented of anything before. Besides, it seemed to me she had somehow grown taller, and her hair was not as pale as it usually is. And her voice, though she talked very low, still, it was not quite Kassafeh's voice. . . ."

"Yet it can have been no one but Kassafeh, for none save we nine are here." And the eight virgins omnipotently agreed on this.

The first virgin, she of the flower-moon, lay dreaming on her couch of swinging on an ivory swing suspended from this same flowering moon. Up in the starry sky she sailed, back and forth—and then the petals fell from the moon and the swing fell and the virgin fell and she was about to shriek when someone caught her.

She opened her eyes in pitch dark. The lamp was out and the draperies pulled over the window. Then she felt a soft movement at her side. She thought a lioness lay there, but a woman's hand caught hers.

A whisper: "It is I, Kassafeh."

"You do not—sound like Kassafeh," replied the flower-moon virgin vaguely.

"Oh, but I am. Who could it be but I? Oh, do not send me away. You are so sagacious and philosophical. You must advise me how I must expiate my sacrilege in ignoring the god."

Faced with the challenge of this, the feather-headed first virgin lost herself in contemplation. While she did so, Kassafeh—or was it Kassafeh?—slid nearer.

"Your very proximity is an inspiration," whispered Kassafeh—it was *not* Kassafeh.

Now the first virgin was certain her unexpected bed-mate was a woman. A girl's breast had brushed her arm, a smooth cheek had been presented to hers. And yet, suddenly, the first virgin began to tremble with an unspecified alarm.

"Do not fear me, blasphemous wretch that I am," mourned 'Kassafeh' in a still stranger voice, as if floods of tears—or gales of laughter—were being repressed. And then the first virgin's bed-mate set a gentle two or three fingers on her neck. Light as grasses were these two or three fingers. Light as grasses they fluttered over the hollow of her throat, the slope of her breast. And on the breast of the first virgin, the light grasses changed into a rhythmic cupping circling thing, a thing which discovered a piercing sweetness at its center, or the center of the breast of the first virgin, like a note of music. And the music leapt, or something like a fish leapt in the loins of the first virgin, surprising her no end. And even as she twisted, or her body twisted of its own will, to follow the leaping of this fish, (and the other fish, scores of them, which leapt after it) a mouth came down on hers, and the kisses of this mouth were like no other kisses she had ever known.

"Ah, but Kassafeh—" feebly protested the first virgin hoarse with a curious hoarseness, into this wonderful kissing mouth. But Kassafeh did not answer. And when the arms of the first virgin rose of their own accord to cling to and to explore the exquisite pressure of flesh which now lay over her, positively it did not have the feel of Kassafeh. A burnished singular feel had this body, hard, though flexibly muscled— the body of a lioness? But the first virgin, for all her brilliant philosophy, could not really fathom any of it. She was like a door, opening inch by inch, to let in a divine revelation. Perhaps the god was sending her, through this peculiar ritual, some mystery.

Simmu, especially cunning with women since he could also be one, was adept with this yielding girl. By deft touches, lingerings, mouldings, strokings, by use of mouth and teeth and tongue, of hand, fingers, the nails of the fingers, even by most skilful and intuitive use of other parts of himself, he transmuted this flower-moon child into a being of yearning and violent desire, who thrashed beneath him, urging him mutely on his path, without actually guessing where the path would lead. And when he had grown to his utmost and she to her most welcoming, he held her firmly and entered this second

197

garden door to that most intimate and pleasing of gardens. And though the gate was broken, as at the first even in the lushest and most eager garden it must be, and though the maiden—virgin no longer—gave a cry of pain, and another cry of greater pain, soon her cries were different.

Outside in the valley, not a sound. Not a sound to mark the double rape, rape of the garden by the entry of a man, rape of the first virgin, more willing than the garden.

"Oh, Kassafeh, did I dream this thing—"

But Simmu, demon lover, sang in her ear, and she sank asleep. He stole out into the night-washed palace and, man-shape quickly resuming woman-shape, stalked the marble corridors where only illusory female beast foot and slender real girl foot had trodden for two centuries and longer. And shortly another drapery folded aside, another lamp doused, another girl waking to find repentant Kassafeh beside her. Kassafeh who quickly changed into a dream of lust, better than the bubbling crystal, better, far better. And here too, a cry of pain, a cry of joy. And here too, demon song. And here a stealing out. And later still, in the black hour which is close kin to dawn, another chamber, another Kassafeh, another breaking and entering, cry and cry, song, and stealing out.

Three that night. Three virgins robbed of their sacred seals in the soot black. And the garden silent, making no sign, threatening no punishment. And the sky clear. Not even a rain drop, not even a crashing star.

But the weave of the witch's magic all coming undone. Her *sympathetic* magic. Simmu had picked up the key to it. And now he turned the key in thorough fast turnings. Heroes did not wait.

In the morning, six intact virgins, three deflowered virgins; Simmu over the hill, hidden in a tall and blossoming tree. Simmu, lazy and sleeping, resting for a second night's labor. And the magic of the garden coming undone, and, as it did, undoing an older magic, all the way up in the air.

Too clever, the witch had been, setting virgins to guard the lower well, directly beneath the Well of Upperearth. Virgins who must stay virgins, and who went to the lower well and vowed there: *I am sealed as the well is sealed and as I stay pure so will I keep pure the only place of the god.* Sympathetic magic. By vowing it they had made it so; two centuries and thirty-three years had helped. As they had endowed with resonance the temple, so they had endowed with life the well.

And as with the lower well, thus with the heavenly well above. Even Upperearth could not be quite impervious to such powerful and persistent sorcery immediately under, and, as the witch had once observed, the cistern in the sky was only made of glass.

Kassafeh, with her obstinate defiance—*Would that both I and the well were unsealed*—Kassafeh had given Simmu the answer.

Crack open the well-shafts of the nine virgin guardians and the well-shaft aloft would spring a complementary crack. Sympathetic magic at its most forthright and effective.

And if there had not been set nine virgins to guard the lower well, perhaps there never might have been found a way to release the fluid of Immortality.

Kassafeh, the ninth virgin, had her own ceremonies. Here she was at one of them in the early sunlight. Long since she had set up a stone beside a small pool, and plastered the stone with black loam from the bank, and named it "god." And frequently she would come here and make insulting gestures at the stone. She constantly reviled the god, hoping for some reprisal which would at least prove his existence. Even death seemed preferable to six further years imprisoned in the garden in the service of nothing, but that was only because she had never properly examined death.

And here she was, seated before the stone, her pastel hair like palest golden rain streaming over her shoulders, her eyes of an iron shade.

"Come then," she was saying, "strike me. How I hate you, or I would if you were actual. But you are not." And she threw some more mud at it.

Then, slipping from behind a tree, came the first virgin, all timid and blushing, and she hurried to Kassafeh and whispered: "Was last night a dream, dearest Kassafah? Or can it really have been you?"

"I?" asked Kassafeh, greatly amazed at being visited.

"You, dearest Kassafeh, you who blew out my lamp, who begged my help. Oh, I will help you, indeed I will. But I do not understand what took place between us—could you but tell me—or—perhaps demonstrate a second time?" And she slid her arm lovingly about Kassafeh's waist. Kassafeh seemed not as friendly as she had in the night, and certainly she did not feel the same at all in a tactile sense. "Oh Kassafeh, do not think I minded that you wounded me, the little red rose of blood upon the silk—it was blood offered to the

199

god, no doubt—" and the first virgin kissed Kassafeh upon the lips in a way Kassafeh did not take to.

"Leave me be!" cried Kassafeh, and jumping up, she fled. But just across the next stretch of lawn, who should she meet but the second virgin.

"Ah, Kassafeh," said the second virgin, giving her a brazen look, "what can you have been thinking of last night?" Sneaking into my chamber with your tales and lying with me in such a wicked fashion! I believe you have damaged me with your impetuosity for I found a red poppy in the bed. But," she added, running up and seizing Kassafeh eagerly, "no matter. None shall know."

Kassafeh struggled. "I have done nothing."

"Nothing, is it," mocked the second virgin, nuzzling Kassafeh's ear. "Something you did, and you shall do it again, I promise you. I never guessed you so artful, darkening the room and murmuring your tale of needing my solace—only to practice naughty games." And the second virgin laughed, grasping Kassafeh resolutely by the buttocks. Kassafeh bit the second virgin and once more fled.

But, no sooner was she from the lawn and into the woodland, than she almost toppled over the third virgin who lay sprawled upon the turf weeping.

"What's the matter?" faltered Kassafah nervously.

At that, the third virgin flung about and locked her hands around Kassafeh's ankle.

"You! Oh, you wicked one! How could you work such an evil upon me in the night!"

"Not I," cried Kassafeh.

"You and none other. I shall never forget your lies to me in that pitch black room, how you laid upon me your body, nor the delicious—dreadful—movements you forced me to embark upon; and how you hurt me and when I screamed for you to continue—that is, I mean, to cease—you laughed in a strange deep voice—oh, Kassafeh, never shall I forgive you for the red ruby I found beneath me. I cannot stop thinking of the delight—or rather, the horror—I suffered at your hands."

Kassafeh looked at her ankle in the stone lock of the third virgin.

"Pray let me free," said Kassafeh, "and I will lie down beside you and comfort you."

"Oh yes, by which, of course, I refuse you," postulated the third virgin, and let go.

Kassafeh fled.

There was an area of the valley where few things flourished and the desert remained. Only Kassafeh saw this place accurately, for by now none of the illusions in the garden could consistently deceive her. To the others, like the rest of their paradise, this was a spot of green lawns, fruit trees, mossy verges. Because of that, they had never observed the tiny square cave into which Kassafeh now edged herself. Nor was she discovered in it when the three fervent girls came wandering by, one after the other, bleating her name. None of the other five passed. Kassafeh concluded they had no reason to.

Kassafeh lay in her cave all day, angry, cramped, and deep in meditation.

Though Veshum deliberately kept its daughters unworldly, Kassafeh had learned enough to recognize defloration. And hugely puzzled she was, as well she might be, hearing of three deflorations in one night, supposedly due to her. But of this crime, Kassafeh knew herself perfectly guiltless. Thus, someone—or something—masquerading as herself, had done the deed. And it seemed to her it must be Thing rather than human, for how would a human ever get into the garden. This idea, rather than disturbing her, intrigued Kassafeh, for she was bored and not incapable of bravado.

Certain elements were consistent in the three stories—the lamp blown out and the chamber darkened so none should see what really came there—some foul devil-shape?—and then a piteous demand for comfort, and then other demands, apparently granted willingly by all three virgins. But there were six further virgins in the valley, and could it be the Thing intended to sample each of them?

Kassafeh, as was her wont, kept clear of the virgins at their evening feast. In the past two years she had come to prefer the roots and berries and plain water of the valley to illusory banquets. At the feast, five of the virgins chattered on in their normal idiot vogue. Three sat silent, with fever in their eyes and cheeks, and glances of scared jealousy at each other—for each suspected not she alone had had a night caller. They had not danced so well this dusk before the god.

The virgins repaired to bed. Five fell languidly asleep. Three twisted and wriggled, gasping whenever the night breeze stirred the draperies. But no one entered, and near midnight, all three succumbed to exhausted slumber with a dim notion they had heard someone singing or humming just before they did so.

But Kassafeh, not quite mortal enough to be influenced by

Eshva magic, was alert. Her own lamp she had already extinguished, and she crouched in a corner, eyes and ears wide. About midnight, vigilance was rewarded, for she heard a distant cry, thin as the cry of a night bird, but not a night bird.

With stealth, Kassafeh crept to the doorway and peered out. A minute after, from another doorway, a figure emerged.

Three years with her fellow virgins had taught familiarity. Kassafeh perceived at once that this was none of them.

Yet it was not the shape of a devil of monster. Rather the shape of a tall and slender—no, not a man, for a beam of starlight showed the outline of a high firm breast. . . . Maybe, a *demon*?

More adjacent to truth than she realized, Kassafeh prowled lightly after the soundless figure. Soon it stepped aside into another chamber—that of the fifth virgin, and Kassafeh set her eye to an aperture in the curtain.

Yes! A woman. A woman leant above the lamp, hair the color of apricots hiding the face, skin tawny from the sun, gold-tipped breasts in the lamp's light, which light was abruptly blown into gloom. And then a woman-shadow at the windows drawing draperies over the stars. Blackness.

And from the blackness a murmur, and next a question:

"Who is there?"

And a second murmur:

"It is I, Kassafeh."

And then the murmur relating its need for comfort, so Kassafeh smiled furiously, entertained despite herself.

And presently a gasp in the blackness, and a sound like silk sinking to the ground, and, following, a sound like a sure hand traveling over a domed hill, across a plain of vellum, into a valley of warm woods. And maybe Kassafeh did hear as much, for she was attending earnestly.

Now a sigh, now a breathless breathing, now a broken moan. Now words with no logic, now muffled surgings, twinings. Now the velvet rasp of skin on skin. And now a sharp, though not vociferous, cry, with, as its suffix, a deeper cry. A succession of cries and groans and great laborings for breath, as if a glorious murder were being slowly perpetrated in the bed.

Kassafeh, with a racing heart, lurked at the curtain, wilting with desire and bewilderment. And then she heard a voice, a voice she had never heard in all her life, say: "My thanks, beloved." The voice of a *man*. After which came another aspect of the voice, a kind of new murmuring, song-like, which set Kassafeh retreating, aware of sorcery, her fingers in her ears. But the demon song did not overwhelm her, not half so much as she had been overwhelmed by the voice of a man.

She ran back to her room, and there she waited, wishing she had a knife to slay him, or a phial of her mother's scent to entice him—and she was not sure which.

But the intruder, woman, man or demon, did not enter Kassafeh's chamber. It was another third virgin he sought that night. Almost as if, deliberately, he was leaving Kassafeh, whose name he used for a concealment, till the very last.

And possibly he instinctively did as much. For there was a fitness in so leaving her, she the most beautiful, she who had given him his plan.

There was also another facet, and possibly he sensed it, or possibly he did not.

If it had needed an extra focus to associate the supernatural Well of Upperearth with the puny well in the valley, Kassafeh must certainly have provided that focus. She, semi-daughter of a denizen of the sky, an elemental of Upperearth's lower caste, now a Daughter of the Garden. Thus destiny, or accident, or some obscure, unrecollected, prehistoric whim of the gods had brought each feature together to make the whole. And events ripened.

In the morning, Kassafeh had decided.

She had no use for Veshum's god, and a pact with demons might be preferable. Whatever else, this demon was systematically destroying the purity of the guardians, and thus must be bent on destroying the hated prison of the garden. Kassafeh had his ally in spirit, and much quickened in her flesh.

When the fourth virgin slunk up to her with urgent squeaks, Kassafeh was canny.

"We must not speak of it by day," said Kassafeh. "It shall be our mystery dedicated to the god. Tell no other. It is solely yours and mine."

The fourth virgin, pausing only to deliver a loving embrace, went away happily. So did the fifth and sixth virgins, whom Kassafeh harangued in similar vein. However, when the first, second and third virgins individually approached— they who had not been visited on the second night—Kassafeh humbly said this:

"Alas, after our quarrel I feared to come to you, but tonight I will come. Say nothing to the others. I believe what we do is a holy thing, and we are the favored of the god."

These lies she delivered, knowing the demon would quell

all who kept awake with his murmuring songs. Only Kassafeh could resist, and she would be ready.

That night, Kassafeh went to the feast. She put on a fresh robe, one which would look like riches to the virgins, six of whom no longer merited the title. And this night two virgins only chattered inconsequently while the other six gazed adoringly at Kassafeh, and surreptitiously pressed her hand when passing her the wine.

But when she had gone up to her chamber, Kassafeh sorted what she had put there ready. She bathed in the perfumed bath, which was only a fount of natural water. She put blue flowers in her hair, and crushed their juice to stain her eyelids, and her eyes simulated their romantic blueness. Until she doused the lamp, when her ever-changing eyes turned feral with excitement and unease, and blazed like the cat's, now amber, now gold, now iridescent pallid red.

While in the dark she took up and proceeded to hone a piece of sharp flint on a rock, both of which she had searched out in the garden. And even as she struck sparks from this tool of slaughter, she dreamed of love. And even as she dreamed of love, her foot toyed with the rope she had plaited of tough pliant stems, which she might bind him with, if she could at all be bound.

Additionally, she listened. And once she heard a distant muted cry, and she started. Later, a second cry, and she started somewhat more. For this night, the third cry must be hers.

9

The rose moon had sunk, the redder rose of sunrise was an hour away.

The night pressed itself to the earth in a last black coupling.

Simmu entered, with a lynx tread, a chamber equally black. No lamp burned; the windows were muffled. Kassafeh, the ninth virgin, slept in tomb-darkness, so it seemed. The way was already prepared.

As with the others, Simmu insinuated her female shape on to the couch. Unlike the others, the ninth virgin stirred immediately, and announced in a drowsy tone: "I have said before, I will not share my bed with panthers or other beasts." And she reached out her hand and placed it directly on

Simmu's maiden breast. "Now, who is that?" inquired Kassafeh.

Simmu could hardly reply "I, Kassafeh," on this occasion. Besides, the neatly placed and now gently exploring feminine hand was already playing havoc with Simmu's womanhood. So Simmu moved slightly aside from his companion, and let the male urge overtake him.

"Oh, sister," whispered Kassafeh, "you do not seem precisely as I remember."

"It is a bad dream I have had," whispered back a coaxing mellifluous voice, no longer quite a girl's.

"Poor sister. You must tell me everything," Kassafeh urged. "Only let me throw off these heavy covers, for the night is hot."

And saying it, she did it, and as she did it she grasped the lighted lamp she had muffled under their folds beneath the couch, and with a shout of triumph she sprang to kneel over Simmu, lamp in one hand, the raised honed flint in the other.

She had not seen a man for three years. Doubtful it was if she had ever seen a man like this man, one so handsome, so leoninely strong and so finely made, like new-minted bronze in her bed, looking up at her with unnerved, unnerving lime-green eyes.

"Well," said he, "will you kill me then?"

Obviously he knew she would not. It was surprise he showed, never alarm.

"Maybe I will slay myself," said Kassafeh, "rather than succumb to your lust, which lust is surely plain enough."

"Your eyes were molten, but they are now the color of a young night. From this I judge you will be gentle with me."

"What do you want in the Garden of Daughters—other than to lie with us, for probably there are women in plenty outside the wall."

"No woman like you," said Simmu. "And now your eyes are dark as hyacinths."

Kassafeh smiled and she laid the knife aside, and the lamp on the floor next to it. And, as she did so, he circled her waist with his hands, which almost met since she was slender, and thus he held her, and her lovely hair showered over them both.

"Are you of demon-kind? asked Kassafeh.

"I have walked with some that are," said Simmu, "and with one who is the Lord of Demons, Night's Master."

"And do you mean to inconvenience Veshum's doltish god?"

"All gods, but mostly Death."

"Tell me why you are here," Kassafeh said. "I will lie with you willingly, but tell me first."

"Then I will tell you," said he ,"but only one time."

And he told her of the two wells and how the breaching of the glass cistern had been mathematically reduced to the breaching of nine maiden-heads, and that Immortality would descend as a result and he should steal it.

"Why, you are a hero," said Kassafeh with wonder. And lowered herself into his arms with such amorous hunger that fires seemed kindled between them.

But Kassafeh yielded her citadel without a cry, or with a cry so soft only Simmu heard it.

It was the night which shrieked, the night and the violated valley.

First, a clap of thunder. The land cowered, the stars seemed shaken from their sockets and wheeled about. Then a thunderbolt, a terrible lightning tearing one section of the darkness from another, dismembering the sky, and flinging hither and yon a debris of scorched air. But the bolt struck; within the garden it struck. It smashed the gold dome of the temple, and the dome burst apart like eggshell, gilded pieces erupting far and wide. And down through the aperture the lightning bolt progressed, to uproot with a fearsome concussion the metallic basin with its stopper of bone. And this ultimate stroke laid naked the small round slimy well which had been contained beneath the hallucination of gold and ivory.

To these upheavals the lovers, knotted about each other in convulsions of pleasure, paid slight heed. The night had resorted to mimicry. Many a house has seemed to quake at such a moment.

But soon, lying spent, they heard the march of fate across the heaven. And over these onerous drum-beat footfalls, a silence poured. And in the silence came a sound to make the sinews melt and the hair rise and the heart stop: One single glacial *crack*.

It began to rain in the Garden of the Golden Daughters. To rain only in one place. The rain, a narrow cascade, dropped from some invisible but quite stationary origin, through the broken edifice of the temple, straight down the throat of the second well. The rain had a thick and syrupy appearance. It did not glint or glimmer. It was the color of lead.

The shower lasted a few seconds, or less. By then, the

source of the flow had been sealed up again, or had mended itself. No matter. The water of Immortality had been spilled and was now accessible.

Overhead, the thunders filed away. But clouds drifted like nets among the shoals of stars, and a cold wind raged through the garden. And when the cold wind had departed, a sense of some strange and altered thing possessed the valley.

The magic the witch had built there had crumbled, leaving fragments and rags. An illusory tiger, transparent as an orange ghost; a lightning-smitten ruin, no longer gold. The hot wall had lost its heat. Its crackling corona was extinguished. Here and there, stretches had collapsed in powdery rubble. Outside, the monsters mewed aimlessly at the stars, or scratched themselves. Below, the patrols—who had yet been intermittently searching for the suiciding maiden (Simmu) —had dropped on their faces in terror when the lightning struck, and now pointed abjectly at the quiescent nullity of the wall. A bizarre paradox: after two hundred and thirty-three years, there really was something to be guarded at last, positive Immortality in the second well, and no proper safeguard remained to keep it.

In the desert, adding a dismal background, wild dogs howled—why is not to be imagined. It was none of their business.

10

Woken by thunder, eight girls, only recently virgins, clustered on the lawn beneath the palace. The palace did not look as marvelous as it had, an edifice of plaster and posts and hung with sacking. On the slopes, no roses bloomed, no hyacinths. Wild flowers and weeds burgeoned there.

"It is a sin we have committed!" screamed the un-virgins to the wind. "Kassafeh made us sin."

A ghostly deer swirled through the woodland and the un-virgins wailed.

The wind abandoned the valley, the sun lit its eastern horizons, and unkindly revealed more raw facts. A raven flapped over, cawing scornfully. Yesterday it would have had the guise of a dove.

Kassafeh ran down the lawn to the gibbering eight un-virgins.

"Be glad," said she, harsh as the raven. "There is some-

207

thing truly precious now in the noxious well of the god. Come and see."

The eight girls glared at her with hate. If they had been brought up in a rougher clime they would have attacked and savaged her, but now only their glares had weapons, and their tongues.

"You are vile. You will be damned!"

"Jackals will eat you!"

"You have demoniac eyes—jackals will eat *those*!"

"The god wil turn you into a grasshopper!"

"Your name will be forever cursed!"

"Baaa," said Kassafeh, as once before, "baa-baaa!"

And then Simmu the young man strode down the slope. He carried a clay vessel (yesterday silver), bound with the rope of stems Kassafeh had woven to bind him.

The eight un-virgins shrank. Their eyes expanded, their mouths opened wide on huge screechings, and they pelted from the locality. Poor things, they really did not deserve their bad luck, nor the shame which they would insist on experiencing for the rest of their lives.

Simmu and Kassafeh went toward the wrecked temple, unspeaking, pale and drunken with the magnitude of events.

Bits of broken tin (gold) and stained and aged bone—the fabulous stopper—rattled under their feet. Cracks bisected the floor; the window lattices had shattered.

Trembling, Kassafeh and Simmu stared into the minute and slimy well.

"No longer does it stink," said Kassafeh. "The new wine has purified the old."

"Gray, leaden water," Simmu said. "Such a draught I had always believed would be golden."

"Oh, I beg you to draw it up. Let us see."

Simmu lowered the vessel by its binding down the shaft of the well. In awed fascination they waited rigidly till he raised the vessel again, and then both peered into it with starting eyes.

Leaden it was, that water. Sluggish, sullen.

"A small vessel," Kassafeh breathed, "and the well seems empty. Is this the sum of the draught?"

"One drop would be enough," he answered. "One drop, and a man may live forever, spurning Death from his door."

"One drop."

"Only one."

"Then drink, and grow immortal, Simmu."

"Be my sister," said he, "be as my wife, and drink before me."

"I? I cannot drink before you, whose hero-deed this is."

"I will drink," he said. "But not quite yet."

"Nor I," said she, "quite yet."

Accordingly, on the brink of everlasting life, they hesitated, as if one muttered at their shoulders: "Life is only life. There is also joy."

And presently, without either drinking, Simmu stoppered the vessel and roped it to his belt.

"Thus," said Simmu, "let us be going."

But Kassafeh lowered her eyes, now dark green as myrtle leaves, and she said: "I must remain, for here are my family and my home."

"Neither of which you love. Love me and live with me and I will wed you."

"Today you say so, but tomorrow it will be different."

But she smiled and she went with him.

Now, although the garden was destroyed, although the wall was innocuous and even here and there in rubble, and although the monsters of the mountain slopes had lost all incentive to rend and rip anyone, let alone one who could work Eshva glamour on them and was besides accompanied by a holy maiden of Veshum—despite this, still the patroling army remained. And the army, appalled at the collapse of centuries of tradition, was however in a mood to take captives.

Firstly, beholding over the broken wall eight frantic girls scrambling about and screaming in the valley, the soldiers had not dared go to their aid, for no one but female virgins were allowed inside. At length, though, common sense prevailed, the soldiers navigated the brickwork and attempted to rescue the screamers. Interesting then to decide who was the more afraid, the eight former virgins of this influx of men, or the men of touching the sacred persons of the virgins. After much debate, awkwardness, confusion (and screaming) the virgins were persuaded to speak.

And what a story gushed forth.

A demon man in the valley who had defiled all of them, defiled the god's shrine, and stole something occult from the divine well.

Recovered from their religious shock, the soldiers manfully concluded that the demon man was not a demon, for he had been seen in daylight. It was, therefore, some extraordinarily clever and evil magician. Honor demanded that they seek and mutilate him, ignoring his sorcery. The god would protect his army. And the army would protect itself if the god was engaged elsewhere. They were really very straightforward and insensitive men, geared as their days had been from twelve upwards to the endless desert camps, cheerless dry vigils and military bravura. So now, having elected vengeance as their main goal, they rampaged through the valley on horseback, dispelling any last vestiges of pastoral femininity or illusion, the ultimate rape. After all, the garden was already despoiled; their god wanted a head on a pike and a phallus on another pike. Their god was not such a mooning fool as everyone supposed.

Even the monsters dashed from their path—some had got into the garden and were investigating it with interest. Through the waterfalls plunged the riders, past the plaster palace, whooping with blood-lust, over the green places that had been the lawns of a paradise.

Simmu and Kassafeh heard them. They had been wandering slowly across the garden, unaware of an impending chase. Kassafeh thought they would die—odd reverie with the Immortal draught right next to her in Simmu's belt. Simmu led her to a tree, and they climbed it and hid themselves in the upper foliage.

Thereafter began a vast cantering back and forth beneath, much dust and many vows of torture on the defiler-magician. And they were indeed impervious to Simmu's magic, being so many and so incensed.

Simmu did not invite Kassafeh to leave him and add her tale of helpless rape to the rest. Nor did Kassafeh suggest such a course. Like two snakes they coiled themselves round the boughs and each other, and clung together in mutual mistrust of the remainder of the world.

Then came a man alone, riding his horse. And under the tree he paused and squinted up.

In another second, Simmu had unwound himself from Kassafeh, had sprung and landed upon the mounted soldier, bearing him to the earth. And when Simmu arose, the soldier did not.

Simmu laid his hand on the startled horse. It quieted to a statue.

But in a minute Simmu and Kassafeh and the horse, set going as once formerly a horse had been set going by a demon-touch-charm, were speeding from the valley.

Not toward Veshum, hardly that way. Toward the outer

environs of the desert. The unrelenting waterless desert the people of the river avoided.

"To take this road is death," said Kassafeh, "or they say it is."

"Death we are done with," Simmu replied, and they leapt the wall and raced down the mountain side beyond, among the dunes.

None followed. Or, if they followed, not for many miles. The desert, age-old enemy, drove the river men off, and their imaginary god had to go without his piked retribution.

Simmu and Kassafeh ran on, borne by the ensorcelled horse.

The desert, like every landscape, had its own persona. It was a situation of white glare by day, white glare glimmering from the sands up into the atmosphere. Beneath, faintly showed the contours of the dunes as if through mist or water. Above, a flat coppery sky rested on the framework of the glare. Sometimes a formation of rock came swimming out of the glare like a great thorn-backed fish; items at a distance were of a tindery brittle blueness unlike the fluid blueness of a watered country.

The heat of the desert was not like a heat, but like a whittling away. There seemed a sound in the desert, a high-pitched whistling, but there was no sound save the furnace wind raising the sand like smoke from the ridges, as if the dunes actually burned.

The word of the desert was this: I am made from all the dusts of the bones of men who have perished here, and my rocks are monuments to mountains I have ground away.

There were no green places, no springs. To this desert, such as these were wounds which it had healed with aridity. What it could not eradicate, it buried.

By night the sand chilled. Frost scaled its surfaces so it shone with a pure black shining. It was beautiful as only such a spot could be beautiful—because it had warped the natural laws, and here it told you the hideous was fair. And was believed.

Simmu and Kassafeh entered this domain, and soon any lightness of heart or determination left them, for the desert fed on such emotions. They had not been prepared either with provisions for their bodily needs or provisions of the spirit, for the World-Shattering Deed was accomplished. What must evolve in the deed's wake was yet uncertain and unformed.

They would not return to Veshum, nor to any bank of the river, for all its banks, to the very sea, were the dominion of the river people, got in their days of reaving. For the desert itself, none had ever charted it. Only at its extreme borders was it traveled by the caravans of men. "A thousand miles, it is said, without water," Kassafeh ventured, a prophetess of doom and despondency.

But, since there was no returning, they went on, the horse plodding now, its feet sinking in the deeper sands, its head hung low, and shortly Simmu dismounted and led it, with Kassafeh alone on its back.

They struck eastward, so gradually the sun fell behind them.

They began to yearn for drink with a desperate yearning. The desert became the color of thirst and the wind the voice of thirst. Not only their throats cried out for liquid, but their bodies, their minds. And they began to picture to themselves basins of water and pools of water and fountains and even Veshum's dull river. But neither spoke of this to the other. And two thirds of the day burned to ash.

Then the horse dropped to its knees, and in slow sighings, it died. It lay spilled on the desert which would soon cover it and add the dust of it to the dunes. Kassafeh wept, but her tears were very nearly dry.

Close by, a rock, tall as a tree, offered blue shade, and into this Simmu led Kassafeh, and they sat down there and stared at each other's faces.

"We have drink," said Simmu. "This." And he unbound the clay vessel from his belt, and set it on the ground between them.

After that utterance and that gesture, a lengthy silence and immobility. Kassafeh's gaze, bleached transparent gray in the glare of the dunes, absorbed an opaque tint, almost purple.

"But will Immortality quench our thirst? Feed us? Protect us from the fury of the sun, the cold of night?"

"Whatever else, we will not die here."

And Simmu took up the vessel, unstoppered it, raised it, and in one continuous motion—drank.

This done, white-lipped, great-eyed, he sat there as if shackled to the rock itself, while Kassafeh, just as pale and deranged, seemed poised in the attitude of one about to fly from him.

Again a pause, after which he said:

"Kassafeh, do not let me go alone on my journey."

And suddenly resolute, Kassafeh put back her hair and grasped the clay vessel, and she also drank.

And now they both were shackled, though their eyes wildly searched the other for some sign.

An hour or more they were so. And then gradually it was borne in on them that though they were thirsty and hungry, they felt no longer any debilitation, nor any threat of death. Presently they rose as one, and deserted the shade of the rock. And despite the sun, which rained its scalding western light on them, they felt themselves abruptly remade in some original material able to resist such blows. Disconcerted they might be, these two, scourged, burned, robbed of moisture and of very skin—but not of existence. All the dangers of earth had become to them a field of fronds which lashed at their bodies as they passed, but from which they would emerge now, and always, scathed but intact. And as every man might foretaste his own death, so they tasted life in their mouths.

And they did not hear the impalpable one who muttered: 'Life is only life.' For here too, at this hour, was joy.

PART TWO

Death's Enemies

1

For how many days—or months—Simmu and Kassafeh, first of the earth's immortals, wandered in the desert is not remembered. Maybe not so very great a while. Maybe a very great while. The desert was all one, and time in the desert all one with that specific oneness. Certainly, none but immortals could have survived. Though there were certain well-kept secrets of survival in that place, which it would yield only to such as Simmu and Kassafeh, who had outlasted its rigors. The desert no doubt was astounded, finding them still alive on its bosom far in excess of the expected span. Well then, the desert perhaps promised itself, they will be dead tomorrow. But tomorrow they had not died, nor any tomorrow. Eventually, the desert, its arrogance shaken, revealed inadvertently such items as these: some inner regions of the rock stacks where obdurate thorny plants stuck up, whose stems contained a drop or two of moisture, a deeply hidden stream bed in a cave where a trickle of water ran, a fossilizing bush trapped among boulders, branches like broken sticks, but with three brown living shoots.

So they wandered, subsisting and imperishable, these two children for, despite everything, they were very young, with the sort of youth that has nothing to do either with years or immaturity.

And they grew thin, beautifully thin, for they were beautiful and thus it must be. And they were rather silent, partly because the desert imposed quiet. Yet Kassafeh was not inclined to chatter. She had been mentally alone three years, and could in any case communicate much by flamboyant gesture and expression, not to mention her chameleon-changing eyes. Simmu she stared at and watched constantly, the way the woman stares at and watches the man she loves, endlessly enthralled by him and her own reaction to him. She had come to love him almost in the moment the lamp shone upon him in the bed, but really she knew nothing of him. He had arrived as a stranger, charmed her as a stranger, taken her away with him as a stranger. And a stranger he remained. He did not speak of his past life, gave it no importance. He did not speak of future, though clearly there would have to be one of significance. In the present he was a hero, demon-kin, a young leopard, and her lover. That was enough for Kassafeh. As for Simmu himself, he had recaptured something more of his former self, his faunal self, intuitive, speechless, emphatic. And if he loved Kassafeh, and possibly it was not love he felt for her, it was because she too had something of his animalness, and certainly the beauty of an animal. He would return from some foray and find her sleeping in the noon heat, half in shade, half in sun at some rock where he had left her. Tanned, limpid-limbed in slumber, her hair a polish of sunlight raying from her exquisite, not-quite-human face, and he would see in her the gazelle, the lynx, the serpent—his own psychic menagerie. More sister than wife. But he was always eager to couple with her. And indeed the acts of desire were their only recreation in the desert, the rest being the endless search for sustenance and destination.

All the while, their being together in this way bound them one to another with insuperable ties. Their being together, and the vessel Simmu carried at his belt.

At last—when should it be? A month, a year later?—they crossed over a high range of dunes, he walking a space ahead, and they saw below an alleviation of the land. Not that it was green or flowering, but it was less of an ochre, less netted in by the gauzy glare of the sun.

And when they came down on to this plain, they found an abundance of the thorny plants that contained water, and here and there passed a stunted tree, which had usually died for lack of it.

In the next day or two they discovered and utilised a derelict road which in many spots was lost in blown sand. Near sunfall they would make a halt. (Simmu, who had frequently been a night traveler, now complied with the request of Kassafeh: night was a better time for love.) At the third day's halt, by the rock which they elected their camp, they beheld a small snake dancing either to the sun or the desert or some dust-devil which had teased it. Simmu drew the snake to him in the old manner, and it wound itself about his arm, sizzling quietly. Kassafeh's eyes, a dazzling blue, asked plainly: *Teach me also to do this.* So Simmu began to teach her, and she was fast to comprehend the unhuman lesson and diligent in practice. She would become an adept inferior only to Simmu himself.

When the cold night gathered, frosting the plain with rimy tufts, they knit themselves together for warmth. Yet here, the night was not so fierce, and they had evolved a fire from the litter of stems and dead wood.

Kassafeh gazed at the flames, and she said aloud:

"I see in them a city, and the city is yours."

"There was a city, but no longer."

"You will be a king," said Kassafeh, unaware of her own obstinacy in the matter. The yet unproven approach of civilization had reawakened the instinct of a merchant's daughter; she was only proportionately a child of the ether.

Simmu glanced at her without understanding, but her physical attraction set his faint irritation aside. In his arms, she was all and only elemental innocence, sky and fire and feline. He had been fascinated by her cunning, (the lamp under the bed), but best had been what came after.

Though even a word is sometimes enough. Or two words. City. King.

2

Yolsippa the rogue came staggering over the plain in the dawn. He had accidentally unearthed, or rather unsanded, the road an hour previously. Now he ploughed on, going in the wrong direction—yet deeper into the barren area of the desert—instead of away from it. He was of this fashion: in his middle years (which years had taught him little save villainy, and what is more, inefficient villainy), gaudy, gross, a luckless but predacious gambler at the world's game. In his left ear was a simulated ruby, in his right nostril a ring of debased gold. His clothes were a patchwork of every hue, texture, pattern and fabric, periodically gemmed with glass jewelry and currently somewhat rent and soiled, as indeed all of him seemed to be. In his belt stuck a ferocious knife, with which perpetually he had tried to rid himself of a diversity of unfriends, creditors and the law. But this knife had never tasted life-blood, due entirely to the clumsiness, unpreparedness, lack of skill and weak stomach of its wielder. Not that he pitied any, save in the most philosophical and nebulous form—he would weep at executions and clap on the shoulder beggars, ignoring their begging bowls—but it took not much to reduce Yolsippa to a wobbling-kneed coward. Bizarre then that this person should have selected the career of pickpocket, cutpurse, thief and, most consistently, charlatan. Not two days and ten miles back, Yolsippa had been practicing this latter art of his at a small town on the desert's edge. Yolsippa had bottles of green unguent to remove unsightly blemishes, bottles of red unguent to heal sores; amulets to protect against demons, resins to incite lust, powders to incite greater lust, and tinctures to drive lust away. And he had, too, heroic tales told in garish pictures, and tales of an erotic nature of similar ilk. The people in the town were amenable folk, and willing to buy Yolsippa's crackpot wares more for the interest of something new than out of belief in them. Trade was going well, and then disaster struck.

Generally Yolsippa was not a sensual man, but there was one thing and one thing alone which could stir him instantaneously and irrepressibly to amorous frenzy. This singular thing was a member of either sex who happened to be cross-eyed. Now the reason for this is a matter of conjecture. Possibly Yolsippa, in his tender years, had been nursed by a woman with just such a feature, who had toyed indelicately with him, so that ever after, the erection of his weapon became associated with the strabismus of his nurse. Now and again Yolsippa had taken himself into a brothel and there lain down with straight-gazing harlots, in an effort to be rid of the ridiculous taint. But it was no use, the perversion remained, indeed, many afflicted by the squint had been most grateful for it. However, the cross-eyed being that Yolsippa had suddenly caught sight of in the desert border town was none other than the local prize-fighter, a man near seven feet high with a prodigious girth, the belly of a boar and the thews of an ox.

Yolsippa completely comprehended the unwisdom of his passion, but no sooner had the two bloodshot, squinting eyes been fixed on him, than he began shuddering in a seizure of profound desire. Nor was it any use to seek his own medicine for dispelling such emotion, since it was made of water, spirit and mule's urine.

Thus, shutting up his wares in his cart, Yolsippa stole down the street to the tavern, whence the prize-fighter had retired. Sidling along the bench, Yolsippa sat intimately beside the object of his amor and murmured in shaking tones:

"Awesome sir, I am wondering if you could suggest to me any place in which I might repose tonight?"

"Attempt the doss house," grunted the prize-fighter.

"I was wondering," whispered Yolsippa, "whether I might share your own chamber—I will remunerate you, naturally, but lodging is scarce hereabouts."

"How much?" demanded the prize-fighter, who did not consider his bed sacrosanct and had not had a well-paid fight for a month. Yolsippa, quivering from heel to pate, named a figure. The prize-fighter named another. Yolsippa, sacrificing avarice to love, complied.

Never was bridegroom so impatient. At length it grew dark, and Yolsippa directed his steps to the room of the prize-fighter—to find him not yet home. Which was all to the good, seeing he would return muzzy with drink.

A few heartbeats after midnight, the prize-fighter came blundering up the stairs, barged drunkenly in, and crashed upon the bed. Yolsippa, however, dared not permit those seductive eyes to close. He playfully reached out a hand and caressed the prize-fighter intimately, and when the prize-fighter merely grunted bleary encouragements, Yolsippa presently crawled aloft his bulk and with moans of urgency made ready to effect an entry.

The prize-fighter had been thinking all this while that it was one of the tavern wenches, and now learned that it was not. With a gruesome roar, sloughing at once covers, a degree of drunkenness and Yolsippa from him, he arose.

Despite prayers and protestations of respect, Yolsippa was seized by the scruff of his patchwork robe, also by hair and beard, and whirled up in the prize-fighter's far-from-yielding grasp.

Then, indecision overtook the prize-fighter. Growling, he strode about the chamber with Yolsippa tucked beneath one arm. First the prize-fighter thought to castrate his assailant, and seized a hooked blade from a rafter in which it had been sticking, to accompanying cries from his victim. But the pleasure of this notion palled, and the prize-fighter now considered garrotting and began to loosen his belt. But no sooner was it off than the satisfaction of this intent also faded. Then he sought the narrow window and tried to cram Yolsippa through it, meaning to throw him into the open sewer two or three floors below, but Yolsippa was too stout to achieve the free air, and presently the prize-fighter hauled him back and with a bellow of wrath, charged from the room with Yolsippa yet beneath his arm.

Down the stairs they thudded, Yolsippa screaming for help and the prize-fighter trumpeting oaths, amid entreaties for silence from the adjoining apartments.

Reaching the street, the prize-fighter betook himself and his burden to the door of a stable, and knocking assertively, the prize-fighter yelled that the mad horse be brought out. At which Yolsippa, demolished by abbreviated lust and terror, swooned.

He recovered himself about a mile from the town and into the outer plains of the desert. On all sides thorny plants stabbed upward and quite a few into the hide of Yolsippa. At first it was the land which seemed in heady unheaval, but after a moment, Yolsippa ascertained that it was not the land but himself being pulled over the land by a piece of thick rope extravagantly in motion. And from this deduction, Yolsippa next arrived at the understanding that the rope was tied to the tail of a galloping horse. Whether it had been mad in the beginning was not certain, but for sure it was highly incommoded now, and striving to vent its spleen on what had been attached to it. Yolsippa shrieked for mercy, and the horse responded by galloping with increased energy. Definitely Yolsippa would have perished in a few minutes more had not the kinder face of luck been briefly turned toward him. The prize-fighter, in his incompletely sobered drunkenness, had not thought to search out or remove the large knife in Yolsippa's belt, and this knife Yolsippa abruptly recalled. Then, rolling and painfully dragged through all types of hard floral obstacle, Yolsippa hacked and sawed with the knife till the rope parted, and flung him sprawling into a dead bush. The horse, fortunately not whirling about to kick or chew him, dashed on and was soon lost to view. Yolsippa lay in the bush, crying from minor injury and despised passion, and whining in the coldness of the night.

Absolutely, Yolsippa had not the vaguest idea in which direction the town lay. All around yawned the unlovely outskirts of the desert, and here Yolsippa shortly began to stagger, now this way, now another way.

At first he felt relief when the sun came up, but not for long. In an hour or less, the heat sent him crawling into the shelter of a rock, and there he spent the whole day, growing parched and desperate. And when the sun sank, he felt again a momentary respite at the cool, which inevitably turned to misery as the frost formed.

"And what have I done," Yolsippa interrogated the gods, "to deserve death in such a place? It is you who cursed me with my sexual foible, and here I am because of it. It is not just."

The night thickened and then started to retreat. Yolsippa, having dozed wretchedly, stumbled up and resumed his abstract wanderings.

"I reiterate," he hoarsely ranted, as the sky began to prize up the eastern lid of its vault to let out again the fierce lion sun to maul him, "I reiterate, it is not just to let me die here. What sin have I committed, beyond a simple indiscretion—you should have smitten me when I robbed the judge's house, or when I stabbed the tax collector in the buttock—but not now, not merely for a thing I may not help!"

And perhaps the gods, for once, heard the accusation of a man.

Mostly on his hands and knees, Yolsippa pulled himself on to the derelict road, pawed off sand, and with a feeble shout stood up. Thinking the road led somewhere, he negotiated it in a series of the swerving floundering dance steps a man executes just before he drops senseless. Actually the road did lead somewhere.

Yolsippa came on the sleeping couple, girl and young man, below the rock and beside the ashes of a fire. Yolsippa, untroubled by squints, was able to ignore their sensual posture. No food or drink was visible, and Yolsippa, dehydrated to the edge of insanity, groaned in despair. Then noticed the vessel set on the ground a pace from the sleeping couple.

Very ordinary the vessel appeared, small and made of clay, and with a bit of plaited stuff bound about it, no doubt for carrying purposes. But it might contain a drink of some sort, in fact, it must.

Yolsippa, with demented caution, crept forward, gripped the vessel, yanked at the stopper, caught a glint of liquid and, with a sigh of ecstasy, raised the pot to his lips to drain it.

Two seconds later, Yolsippa felt the vessel seized from his hands with a violent unexpectedness that sent him sprawling on his back. And as he lay there gasping, he stared up to see the very wide-awake young man crouched over him, oddly reminiscent of cat or hunting dog, and with the most terrible enigmatic sort of dangerousness burning from his eyes.

"I did not mean—" attempted Yolsippa.

"Did you drink?" asked the young man, and it was like the hiss of a snake.

"I? Drink? Never. I am not thirsty."

"You drank," said the young man. He stoppered the vessel.

"It was but a drop."

"One drop is enough," said Simmu.

It was.

Thus Yolsippa the rogue became the third of the earth's immortals.

3

"Pray do not walk so fast," shouted Yolsippa. "If you do, how am I to keep pace with you?"

"Perhaps," called back Kassafeh, "we do not mean you to keep pace with us."

"But only attend one instant," croaked Yolsippa, catching up to Simmu and Kassafeh as they paused to rest in the shade of a gaunt but living tree at noon. "I am like an orphan among men. You, by your carelessness—if what you tell me is fact—have made me an outcast and pariah. What kin do I possess save you? Immortal—am I so?"

"Yes, and be off," said Kassafeh, tossing her head.

"No, you misread me," panted Yolsippa as they clambered over rocks in the afternoon—Simmu in the lead, Kassafeh a stride or two behind, Yolsippa trailing valiantly in the rear.

"Listen," said Yolsippa, kneeling by Kassafeh as she split open one of the thorny plants for moisture, and presently—inaccurately—copying her, "I may be useful."

In the dusk, still on the plain but in a greener, milder stretch, Simmu went foraging, and Yolsippa stole up on Kassafeh as she combed with her fingers her pastel hair beside the fire.

"What is a hero?" demanded Yolsippa, striking a fancy shyster's attitude.

"*He* is a hero," asserted the maiden.

"Indubitably. And, as a hero, he has a duty to the earth of behaving in a heroic manner, of acting out heroic acts. What does a hero do? Does your young man know? He must be a fiery example for all men, but is he conscious of this?"

Kassafeh narrowed her chameleon eyes, and in them, somewhere, Yolsippa glimpsed a merchant's daughter evaluating his words.

"A hero," elaborated Yolsippa. "Ah, did I but have with me the fabulous antique books of legend, illustrated in extinct dyes and set about with jewels, which belonged in my stores. But alas, my stores were stolen in a town of thieves and deceivers. . . . But do I know enough of heroes, steeped as I am in arcane lore, to instruct your young man in his

221

part? What, for example, is he doing idling here? He should be engaged in the slaughter of monsters, the foundation of a great and magnificent city, the redemption of the world."

Simmu returned as the stars returned. Simmu had an armful of roots and some figs from a tree he had found growing.

"What, no meat?" Yolsippa demanded.

"I do not eat dead flesh," said Simmu.

"Pah," said Yolsippa, who was losing his awe of Simmu fast, "but he eats dead figs, murderously torn from the branch. Champ, champ, and the fig perhaps yet half alive and screaming in its unheard fig-voice."

"I do not eat men, who walk. Neither beasts, who walk. I never yet saw a fig tree walking."

"They may learn," said Yolsippa. "They may learn to run away from *you*."

"I see you are a visionary," said Simmu. "But understand me. It is not from pity I spare the beast and the man. I would give nothing to Death. Consider this killed fig; only scatter a seed from it upon the ground and a new fig tree may spring therefrom. But scatter the bones of the eaten deer, and does a new deer spring from them? Or does a child bud from the bones of a dead man? I willingly give to the black lord nothing that may not be replaced."

Yolsippa gnawed upon a root.

"I note it is truly a hero, after all. Fight Death then? Yes, most heroic. But you must have a citadel, a fortress wherein Death may not creep."

"Men shall become the fortress. Immortal men."

"Ah, but how will you portion out the drops of Immortality? Come," said Yolsippa, "would you have chosen me, if you had had a choice, to be a part of your brotherhood? No. You must be discriminating. Only the best must live forever. Who desires a hierarchy of riff-raff?"

Simmu, his meager supper done with, had produced the slim wooden pipe and began playing it. The sound was a strange and almost eerie thread in that place, more color than noise, woven through the red sheen of the fire, the dark vault of the night with its relentless staring lights—lights that made Yolsippa recall an old tale that not only did men study stars to read their fates, but that the stars studied the earth to read their own fates from the movements of men.

Kassafeh gazed at Simmu, drowning herself in him.

Yolsippa, reluctant to let go this one absurd good turn luck had done him, began to recite to the tempo of the pipe, as any showman must be able to do, a vision of Simmu's citadel.

Tall towers, tall as aspiration, gates of gold through which only he elected few might pass, roofs to touch the sky, to tempt the high-stepping gods to tread them, or else to mock the gods. And all in an elevated place, a region of rarity, a country where eagles came rather than doves. Indeed, a kingdom of heaven on earth. And before getting into it some test, some proving, some ordeal must be undergone. Only the best for Simmu's High City. "Learn by me," said Yolsippa with low cunning, "I am a mistake. But by our mistakes are we educated." (He had never learnt by a mistake; he was aware how useful it would have been if he had.)

But Simmu's eyes were blind to him. Were the ears deaf? Yolsippa could not tell if his counsel took hold. Indeed, this unusual youth had the slightest look of one who feels chains tightening on his limbs, a millstone being fastened on his neck.

"It is no use," chid Yolsippa, when the pipe stopped and the fire sank and the stars stared yet more unblinkingly, "no use stealing Immortality and then shirking the responsibility of what you have done. Or maybe it is only muddy water in that pot."

For an instant, Simmu's eyes spoke to Yolsippa.

The eyes seemed almost to whisper, traitors to the brain behind them: *Would it were.*

Near midnight, Yolsippa awoke, grumbling with chill. The fire was out, and of Simmu and Kassafeh there was no sigh—they had gone elsewhere to enjoy their love. Yolsippa wondered if they had then gone farther and abandoned him, and sitting up with a grunt of unease, he beheld a thin black dog standing on the other side of the cold fire.

Yolsippa had an aversion to dogs. Frequently, dogs had seen him off various premises. Yolsippa took up a stone and prepared to fling it.

But something in the demeanor of the dog checked Yolsippa. Somehow, he did not quite desire to throw a stone at it. Slowly but undeniably, the hair rose on Yolsippa's neck.

And then, from behind him, came a little stirring, and Yolsippa whirled about in alarm. And there he saw a woman particularly to his taste; large of breast and hip, narrow of waist, and clad only in a revealing transparency, above which beamed a smiling, welcoming mouth, and a pair of astoundingly, and completely crossed eyes.

Yolsippa, in a tumult of unnerved lust, lumbered to his

223

feet and advanced on this, to him, most seductive of females. And the woman beckoned with great urgency, and Yolsippa began to run with his lust somewhat ahead of him—and collided suddenly with a dead tree.

"What is this?" cried Yolsippa, much aggrieved, for the woman had vanished—or become the tree, or been the tree from the first. A moment after, Yolsippa ascertained that the sinister black dog had also vanished, and by the cold fire there now stood a tall cloaked man. Very black of hair was this man, and clothed in a sort of electric blackness, and his face was somehow in shadow, even though the stars shone bright.

Now Yolsippa knew enough to guess who was standing on the other side of the fire. So Yolsippa prudently kneeled down, and rubbed his face in the dirt and uttered certain pleas for leniency, as it seemed wise to do, adding: "Not far off you will find a beautiful youth and a beautiful maiden, doubtless more pleasing to your lordly eyes than my graceless self."

"Be at ease," said the dark man. "It is you I require."

Which, rather than easing Yolsippa, prostrated him yet further into a burrowing posture.

But the dark man appeared not to notice, and seating himself casually by the ashes, he snapped his fingers and there srpang up a garish though warming blaze.

"You and I," said the dark man, "are of like mind."

"Oh, my Lord," moaned the abject Yolsippa, "never compare my dross to the black, many-faceted diamond of your incomparable brain."

The dark man laughed a dark laughter. The sound thrilled Yolsippa even as it convulsed him with fright.

"This theory of a High City," said the man, "the chosen within, the unchosen clamoring without. . . . Such a scheme is interesting. Men as gods, mortal men grown jealous, kingdoms set on their ears."

Yolsippa, heaving a musing tone, ventured to peer up. Still he could not quite see a face. He was sorry and relieved not to see it. He edged nearer the fire, and lifted himself, though ready to obeise himself instantly if the occasion warranted.

He would never have dared voice his thought, would Yolsippa, which thought could be any event have been read by the entity across the fire, had he been desirous of reading it. Yolsippa's thought was this: The Prince of Demons has only one terror: boredom. He will risk chaos for mankind to alleviate his ennui. Yolsippa was a shrewd fool.

"If I may serve you, Prince of Princes," offered Yolsippa aloud.

"You shall build a city to rival my own of Druhim Vanashta," said Azhrarn, the Prince of Demons.

"I? Oh, my Lord, do I have the skill? But naturally I am willing. Brick by brick, if you will have it so."

Then he caught a glimpse of a pair of black eyes, friendly and terrifying, which seemed to be glancing right in at his soul and leaving some knowledge there. Yolsippa understood he would not have to build the city personally. Others would do that. Yolsippa understood he was to be an overseer, (he, slit-purse, night-prowler, seller of ineffectual potions). And he was going to oversee the creation of one of the most remarkable and most strange citadels erected since time's beginning. A city of gods on earth.

Yolsippa was alarmed at his promotion; simultaneously he swelled with vainglory. And then a smoke billowed and in the smoke came a lightning bolt, and the plain was empty of Yolsippa and of the Prince of Demons, and the fire went out for a second time, in ashes.

At sun-up, Kassafeh did not precisely search for Yolsippa, but momentarily, as she clawed out her hair, straightened her rags, she kept an eye for him to come blundering up, vociferous with advice and protest. Simmu did not appear to notice the man's absence. Was he glad to be relieved of such a reminder of his heroic role?

Later, when the two moved on, following the green of the plain into the east, Kassafeh began looking over her shoulder. Finally she spoke.

"Can the fat man have left us? Or is he lost? Suppose a wild beast attacked him?"

"He cannot perish any more than we can," Simmu said tersely, reluctant, as ever, with his first words of the day.

"But if a jackal tore him open—" exclaimed Kassafeh luridly.

"I imagine he must heal. For he could not die."

"But," said Kassafeh, "he was most concerned with your welfare. That men recognize your fabulous deed."

"Woman," said Simmu very sharply, "he spoke of a city, and you listened. A city for you is a courtyard decked with roses and awash with scented baths. You say hero to me, and see me a king, and Simmu as king means Kassafeh as queen, with pearls in your hair and silk on your body. But I have seen a city with only dead in it. Cities are cages. Why do you wish me to rule in a cage?"

225

"I wish nothing," said Kassafeh haughtily. "You are the hero, not I. You said you would wed me, but I do not clamor to be wed. Did I not gladly fly just such a scented silliness as you describe? As soon as we reach a habitable area, I will leave you, and you may do as you please."

Thus they walked all day in silence. But at night he wooed her back to him under the moon. Much of the time they were at one. But not at every time.

And still she looked over her shoulder. And now and then she pictured a city of gold where she ruled as a queen, not from power-lust or greed, but as a child plays in her mother's garments. And besides, this man she honored she would wish others to honor. Armies bowing before him, women weeping with desire.

They passed, in a few days more, through a couple of towns, poor enough places, but Kassafeh was conscious of her rags, for she had been the daughter of a rich merchant. In the garden she had been proud to be scruffy, it was her protest. But now she wanted golden armor for Simmu and silver satin for herself. On a white elephant decked with rubies they should travel, flowers strewn before them; trumpets blowing and incense going up in fogs. Instead, an urchin threw a pebble after them. It was not good enough.

It was said to have been this way. A man would seek his bed, would fall asleep, would experience a curious and exotic dream. Would wake, as he believed, next morning—to find his household in an uproar, screaming and wailing that he had been gone ten days or more. Some of these men were carpenters by trade, and some were masons, and one or two were architects who waited upon the whims of lords.

Now there was one such of these, an architect and scholar of no mean reputation, and in high favor with the king of his land. One morning he regained his senses and called for his servants, but no one came near him. Then he left his bedchamber and walked out into his house, and found it full of the king's soldiers, who, when they saw him, shouted in fear and amazement.

Upon inquiring what the matter was, the architect was informed that he had returned from a feast at the palace of the king, and gone to bed with his young wife, and in the midst of the night, the young wife had been disturbed and woke to discover herself alone in bed and the casement windows open wide. She accordingly got up and searched for her husband and presently ordered up the servants to search also. But there was no trace of the architect beyond one of his soft house shoes lying in the upper branches of a magnolia tree beneath the window. Next the wife, in her dismay, sought audience with the king and he, supposing the architect to have been murdered, cast all the servants into prison, and the wife into another prison for good measure. Then the king, who had been very fond of the architect, put on deep mourning and fasted and cried and became a shadow of grief.

"But how long have I been gone?" demanded the architect in horror, "surely but one night?"

"Indeed not," said the soldiers, "it is three months since you were seen in the kingdom."

The architect made haste to dress and hurry to the palace. Here the king fell on his neck with sobs of joy, and ordered the instant release of the innocent wife and servants.

"And now tell me," said the king, "why you deserted me just as you were about to design for me a summer pavilion? As you instructed, I had imported for the building a hundred slave gangs, their overseers and masters, besides quantities of food to victual them, not to mention bronze and silver and precious marble for the structure. . . . Where have you been, and doing what, that you abandoned the project in the middle of the night, leaving only a shoe behind you?"

"Well, my king," said the architect, "I will tell you everything and you must judge for yourself if it was a dream, as I reckoned it to be, or if I am mad, or if perhaps, such an adventure can happen to a man."

The architect had gone to bed, as was generally known, with his young wife. There they had sported till each was satisfied and thereafter slumbered.

But in an hour or so, the architect was roused by a marvelous noise in his ear, somewhere between singing and speech. Opening his eyes, he confronted a handsome young man with coal black hair and lordly demeanor, who said: "If you would win lasting fame, gather up the instruments of your trade and follow me."

"Follow you where?" asked the architect.

"You shall see."

"I shall not see if I do not follow. And who are you, bold sir?"

"A subject of the Prince of Princes, and one of the Vazdru."

Hearing the name of the upper echelon of the demons—whose existence he did not credit—the architect concluded he was dreaming and determined to enjoy the dream.

"I will follow," he declared, and stepped from the bed.

Gathering various items from the adjoining room, the architect was soon ready. He had not troubled to be quiet, since it was a dream, and certainly his wife did not stir. The Vazdru prince next conducted the architect to the window, which stood wide, and pointed to a bizarre carriage drawn by black dragons and balanced up in the air. Even more convinced by this that he was dreaming, the architect chuckled with approving pleasure and jumped into the carriage, which started with such a jolt that his left shoe fell off into the magnolia tree.

The dragons raced away into the night. High in the air they bounded with clattering wings which struck green sparks off the clouds. Below poured cities and forests and the shining broken glass of oceans. The architect peered at it all, grinning and nodding, enthralled at the breadth of his imaginative powers, which powers he had not before guessed he had. Meanwhile the Vazdru prince guided the dragons with an elegant hand on which dark rings flashed, a smile of tolerant amusement on his face.

After three or four hours of enormously swift flight, a gilded line appeared in the east.

At once the Vazdru sent the dragons diving earthwards. They touched the ground on the broad shore which divided a range of lofty mountains from the waves of a glimmering sea.

"The dawn is near," said the Vazdru, "and I must leave you. But there a road is marked which climbs the mountain side. Go only a short way, and you shall see one who will guide you."

The architect nodded, and when the dragon chariot and the young man together disappeared, he was vastly tickled.

"Now I am nothing if not a cunning dreamer," the architect congratulated himself. "A wonder, for I never recall any dreams of note before this one. No doubt I have been saving myself."

The sun was just now starting to lift on the left hand of the mountains, turning their eastward faces to rose and milk. The shore, meanwhile, took on a smooth crystalline sheen, and the limitless foldings of the sea swam inland to catch pink fire on their silver backs.

"Quite charming," said the architect. "At the same moment he was struck by a particular and not quite explicable oddness in the landscape. It was a sort of innocence coupled to a sort of menace, a sense of a primitive and unspoilt geography, where humanity had not yet encroached in sufficient numbers to leave its seal. Another thing, as the sun's face came above the mountains, it seemed both larger and more clear than usual. The architect was further entertained by this notion. That the earth, being flat and having four corners, must, near its edges, give way to remote, unsullied and infrequently-visited domains, and here, perhaps, was one such domain, close to an eastern perimeter, and far from the interior realms of man. "Not only is the dream imaginative," said the architect, "but also logical. Always supposing that the earth *is* flat," he added. For he had sometimes thought it might be round, which in those days was a grave error.

Shortly, he advanced up the shore and perceived a flight of steep steps carved in the side of the mountain. Obedient to the Vazdru's suggestion, he began to climb them, but before very long he found a black donkey tethered to a post, and on the saddlecloth of the donkey were embroidered the words: "I will guide you." Nothing loath, since it was a dream, the architect loosed the donkey and got on its back, whereupon the donkey began to carry him briskly up the mountain.

The air grew thin, but it was wonderfully sweet and exhilarating nevertheless. At length the stairway ceased upon a plateau.

Before, the peak of the mountain towered upwards, but in the heart of it was riven a tall wide gateway. The donkey trotted straight in this gateway, and on the other side the bemused architect saw a sight.

The inside flank of the mountain fell, and rose, and fell, and on all sides the flanks of other mountains did likewise. Some started up as if they meant to pierce the sky with their eager phalluses, others sank in natural terraces as if they would plumb the cellars of earth. And from these slants and staircases and thrusts and descents of stone, a most ethereal and beautiful jigsaw of half-formed buildings was arising. Here a portico, there three towers, a piece of delicately ascending wall, a balustrade, a bridge. The effect was of a cameo, for the mountains were of a gorgeous material, snow white to a certain depth, pink beneath that, strengthening into veins of rich red at the core, and the portions of buildings had been fashioned and coaxed from the actual stuff of the mountains.

"Why, now I have it," exclaimed the architect to the donkey. "This must be my dream. To construct a city from the living rock, from the lovely bones of the earth itself."

As the donkey bore the architect downwards and along

and upwards over the slopes of this emerging metropolis, he caught glimpses of the augmentation of silver and jade and burnished bronze and yellow brass, of porcelain cupolas and tiles of onyx. In parts the city was fully formed, a colonnade all finished and singular to behold, a paved street, a plantation of trees which made the atmosphere more refreshing, above, fantastic casements of leaded glass. . . . And now, too, the architect perceived men at work among the treasures—masons, carpenters, joiners, bricklayers, and gangs of slaves striving with a will not generally found among slaves unless the whip plied their backs, which now it did not. Indeed, the air rang with the work-a-day noise of pick and anvil, haulage and pulley, shouted order and clatter of cart.

At a certain spot, the donkey halted.

Down a walkway lined with lemon trees, came a gross man clad in a gaudy patchwork. One walked behind to keep a parasol in position over the man's head, another ran before and bowed to the architect.

"Welcome, Lord Architect," said this man. "Here is the Lord Overseer."

"What a dream this is!" cried the architect, enormously amused.

"So it is," agreed the bowing man. "I am a slave in a silver mine, but now that I sleep, I have only to serve this fat man, who treats me well enough, and every night I feast till I am round in the stomach. And then a girl comes to my couch and we play games together of a select nature. And she tells me, too, it is a fine dream."

"But the dream is mine, my good fellow," said the architect, something peeved, "not yours or your doxy's."

The fat man approached.

"You must know," said he, "we are engaged in building here a city to house a hero. You, as an architect, shall design the citadel and the palace of this city. You name is well known, and we expect much of you, the Prince of Demons, and I."

"Indeed," said the architect, "and, no doubt, as it is a dream, I shall not be paid."

"Fame shall be your reward," said the fat man.

The architect laughed heartily.

"I am a-fire to commence. Lead me to the site and thence to a chamber where I may work. We must be swift. I do not wish to wake before I am done."

"No fear of that," said the fat man.

Everything was arranged in accordance with the architect's

specifications. He lacked for nothing. If he required an instrument he had forgotten to bring with him, from somewhere the proper article was achieved and brought to him. Slaves of a most unusually eager and friendly disposition ran at his beck and call. All concurred with him that the dream was an enjoyable one, and appended that freedom awaited them in it, when their dream tasks were completed, and they prayed fervently not to rouse before this sublime event. When night fell, a feast occurred in a marble palace already standing. Intoxicating wines and succulent meats were set ready on the table, and luscious black-haired maidens danced with silver serpents, and though they would not lie with the men, there were women in plenty, many of great beauty and breeding. One, a princess with emeralds at her throat, toyed with the slaves and announced with pleasure that she had never before had such an opportunity to slake a passion she had for the lower strata of socety. While a comely peasant added she would certainly never have dared such sexual extravagance had she been awake.

The architect went celibate to bed, however, and for many hours lay awake, afraid that if he slipped into slumber in the dream he would stir alert in real life. Through lying awake, he came eventually to hear fresh activity about the city site. Going to the window of his chamber, he saw new work gangs had replaced those that operated during the day. These labored by lamplight, and by the light of small forges where they hammered mightily. All were of similar and remarkable appearance, a squadron of repulsively ugly dwarfs with jeweled loin-guards and luxuriant sable hair. "Ah, the demon Drin," said the architect smugly, recollecting the excellent metal work upon the buildings. Returning to his couch, he fell asleep despite himself. He woke with surprised delight still in the dream, and persevered with his creation of the citadel in elevated spirits.

A long while the arthitect continued his creation, all the time assured he was but passing a single night in his bed. Once he was interrupted by the fat overseer, who approached him and inquired concerning the state of the architect's own country, his king, the king's wealth, and the number of slaves kept to assist in the erection of buildings. The architect gave this interruption small thought.

One dusk the plans were completed. No sooner had the architect laid aside his scrolls and ink than a shadow fell across the table.

"I will come to supper presently," said the architect.

"Alas, you will not," said a voice, and turning, the architect found his original guide, the Prince of the Vazdru, at his shoulder.

"Ah, but you will not force me to leave before I see my plan in progress?" cried the architect.

"Three months have elapsed," said the Vazdru with a scornful look, "which to a mortal is a lengthy while. Besides, your king mourns, your wife and your household are in prison. You had best return."

"What nonsense," muttered the architect, "it is only a dream."

But the Vazdru was not easy to argue with, and the architect did not attempt further resistance.

Outside, the weird dragon chariot lurked against the deepening sky. The architect mounted it and was whirled up among the stars. Arriving, after a long journey through clouds and miles above the lands of earth, the architect was deposited in his bed, where, it is true, he did not notice his wife sleeping as when he left her, and dropped into profound unconsciousness.

"And when I came to myself," said the architect to the king, "all was as I had been warned."

Despite the sorcerous quality of the tale, the king was impressed, and heaped wealth on the architect, so glad was he to have him back. The architect, however, remained somewhat uneasy. Now, for sure, he knew there were such beings as demons making mischief in the world, and he had not forgotten (though he omitted to tell the king) of how he had been questioned about the king's slave gangs.

Sure enough, two or three nights later, the hundred gangs of slaves were somehow snatched from their pens, and along with them the food for their victualling, not to mention quantities of marble and precious metal the king had stored for his pavilion.

4

Something had guided Simmu and Kassafeh eastward from the beginning. In the desert, a stubborn facing out of the sun, followed by an equally stubborn turning of the back to it, had kept them in this direction. Later, much later, after their days or months in that arid zone, the pursuit of greenness had led them on into the east. East, the gate of sunrise, the phoenix corner of the world.

As with the site of the second well, the exact site of the mountain city is not perfectly to be expressed. But eastwards it lay and, as the architect related, somewhere near the world's edge. Though maybe to place it near the world's edge is simply metaphor. For how much nearer the edge could mankind get than to obtain Immortality?

Whatever else, the city was surely built, by men and by demons, all at a whim of Azhrarn's. Azhrarn, who had not even spoken to Simmu since that night they learned together from the blue witch the secret of the second well. Or had perhaps Azhrarn watched the young man without in turn being noted? Seen no longer a pliable Eshva youth or hermaphrodite maiden, but a hero, looking irrefutably masculine and of the earth? Once or twice, possibly, some demon mouth had whispered in the sleeping ear of Simmu: "Eastward still." But not the mouth of Azhrarn.

Not much befell the hero and heroine on their road east. For one thing, after the sojourn in the desert, they had a wild unique appearance, more animal than human, and so humanity put a distance between itself and them. Sometimes dogs were sent to chase them from a village. (Simmu would charm the dogs, or Kassafeh would, for she was clever now at this art.) Sometimes, thinking them of a nomadic religious order, men and women would bring offerings of bread and wine, and beg for healing or prophecy. Simmu would remember, on these occasions, the temple of his childhood, a journey among the villages, and some disaster would haunt him he could not properly recall, and the shadow of a companion he could not put a face to or even a name. But Simmu was no healer, then or now. And though he carried a cure-all at his belt, he hoarded it, gave not a drop away. Indeed, he saw men dying, flies thick on them and despair thicker, and not for a moment did he pause. The thought had taken hold: Only the best must survive, not a hierarchy of riff-raff. Gods, who had such power of life or death as he, most choose carefully. And one day he would have to choose: *Shall I immortalize this one, or this?* But not yet. Everything was very clear cut. He did not torment himself with such puzzles as: *Had I saved that beggar there in the gutter, would he have become some great philosopher or magician, using eternity to good advantage?* Nor did Simmu ask himself what would become of his own self. He was too young. His life had not yet begun to show its limits to him when he abolished them. He had been aware of

233

death simply as a violent act of murder perpetrated in the midst of living, what he had confronted in poisoned Merh. He had taken up arms against death, but really he did not fully know what he had done.

The lands they went through, Simmu and Kassafeh, began to have an emptiness, not merely of peoples and of beasts, but of all familiar things. Woods and forests grew there, it is true, flowers bloomed, rivers ran, but each with a kind of lifelessness. Wherever men have once walked, a type of mark is left, a footprint of intent. This footprint is the thing which other men interpret as life. A tree on which no human eye had ever fallen, a hill where no human voice had ever whispered, shouted or sung, they had, of course, their own animation and being, but not properly discernible to a man, who could not and cannot help but recognize things by their innate relation to himself.

It may be that they reached, at the very last, the wide shore in the dawn. It seems nearly always to have been dawn there, for the city was erected in dawn's actual gate, and had the colours of a dawn, alabaster, rose and red. Did they happen on it, or were they led the final miles by some sort of instinct, or even by a demon—most probably in animal shape, cat, fox, serpent or black dove? And when they got there, did they climb up the steep stairway at once, that stairway now ornamented by columns with capitals of gleaming silver, or did they linger by the ocean, ignoring the entrance to the city, or ignorant of it?

This much is positive. They had departed in every way from their own kind and they were ready, primed for a wonder. Even Simmu, who during Yolsippa's preaching of responsibility and heroism had flinched at his own chains, even Simmu was ready, was primed. The blood of kings was in him somewhere, after all, come down from Narasen, the only gift she gave him apart from his birth.

So they wandered up the steep stair, in at the gateway now hung with gates of brass, into a new winding, terraced country of stone and marble and metal. The city looked, in the morning colored like itself, as if it might, in a moment, take wing into the sky. That was the fundamental appearance of it, like something poised but not static: a bird about to fly. And as it lifted itself, pausing but ever on the brink of soaring from the roseate rock, it caught both their hearts, the youth's and the maiden's, for it was like a beautiful virgin, and they the first with their love. Connubial staleness would come later.

The streets, the thoroughfares, the squares and colonnades and parks, all seemed deserted. Nothing moved but the heads of trees, the clouds, the shadows of trees and clouds, and the sun up the sky.

"Who dwells here?" Kassafeh murmured. "Some great emperor that the world has forgotten?"

They went softly down and up and down. Windows shone with glass pictures, fountains crystallized, shattered, crystallized, the wind brought the sough of tree and cool air, but no noises, no scents of men. Kassafeh, strangely, was not reminded of the Garden of the Golden Daughters. The city at least was completely real, not an illusion.

They slipped through the avenues and along the walks, ran up staircases, across courts. They came to the citadel with its domes of mosaic, and before the huge doors reared an obelisk of green marble. Cut in the obelisk, in letters of silver, were these words as follows:

I AM THE CITY OF SIMMU, SIMMURAD,
AND HEREIN MEN SHALL LIVE THAT LIVE
FOREVER, BUT ELSEWHERE SHALL MEN
RISE AND BLOW AWAY AGAIN LIKE DUST.

"Who wrote these words?" asked Kassafeh.

But Simmu stared silently. He was like a bridegroom on his wedding day, longing to be bound, afraid to be bound, and no escape either from fear or longing. In the net.

And when Yolsippa materialized, suddenly, from the palace door, bowing absurdly, clad in real velvet with real metal in his ear and nostril, Simmu began to laugh. And as he laughed, his eyes were full of the tears of that utter panic-striken loneliness a man feels who knows he will never be alone again.

5

Lylas the witch had forgotten she was dead. She turned luxuriously in her slumber and stretched out a languid hand to seize the collar of her blue dog. Her hand closed on air. She opened her eyes.

She lay on leaden ground, and all about stone pylons rose, a-drip with stony moss. A tumultuous wind raged in gusts, but it was not chilly in that place. Neither cold nor heat ever came there.

The witch put her hand on her waist and felt, not the girdle of bones, but an awful jagged join in her own flesh. The witch opened wide her mouth and screwed tight her eyes, and clenched her fists and contemplated a wail of terror. She had now remembered everything.

After the devil-being had snapped her in two pieces, Lord Death himself, as was his wont, had come to fetch her down to the Innerearth. In the shocked condition of one recently slain, she scarcely noticed this, and sank into a coma, a common lapse of the newly dead. The coma lasted no time at all, or at least, no time in the Innerearth. Months passed in the world overhead, a year, more. (Simmu breached the Garden of the Well, broke the divine shaft of glass by sympathetic magic, stole the draught of Immortality, wandered the desert. The city of the eastern corner, rose-red Simmurad, was built by demons and abducted men, and Simmu entered it with Kassafeh and was greeted there by obsequious Yolsippa. . . . All this while the witch lay comatose on the floor of Death's country.) Maybe she willed it so. There were certain problems she would have to face on waking.

And now she had woken.

Presently, though, Lylas shut her mouth, relaxed her body, darted a glance or two about. The Innerearth's miserable aspect did not depress her, she was generally impervious to such influences as sight and sound. However, she noticed the landscape appeared empty, and it occurred to her that though she had probably remained here unaware some while, none had come to disturb her, a fact she found encouraging.

She was not sure who she feared the most, Lord Death, whose trust she had abused and whose secret she had inadvertently betrayed, or Narasen of Merh, whose murder she had abetted. For sure, both must be confronted. There was this added confusion that perhaps neither Lord Death nor the woman had yet discovered Lylas' deeds.

But Lylas' principal virtue was her opportunist and optimistic nature. It took only a little cogitation in this latter vein to return much of her confidence to her. Soon she rose to her feet, shook out her multitude of hair and smoothed her smooth cheeks with her palms. Then she wrought, from thin air, a golden girdle to hide the scar in her otherwise creamy perfection of a skin. These items attended to, she stepped from the shelter of the stone tree-pylons—and came face to face with the striding figure of Death.

No brave resolve was after all possible. Besides, there was something in the aspect of Death which was quite over-whelming should iron control once give way. The witch fell on her face. As he came nearer, she dissolved into shudderings and moans, but when the white cloak swept over her, she seized its edge convulsively.

"Your hand-maiden beseeches you," cried Lylas.

Uhlume, Lord Death, stopped and looked down at her. His face was such a beautiful clarity of nothing it took her breath away and left her panting. She could say no word and was glad, for it seemed to her she had been about to confess her fault to him, and maybe he did not know her fault.

"You recall that you have died?" Uhlume inquired.

The witch gasped and managed speech.

"I attempted a foolish spell, but somebody, a greater magician than I, reversed its effect upon me. Forgive my silliness, Lord of Lords."

It came to her then, quite unexpectedly as she lay at his feet, that Death, having made her his agent, should have made her also invulnerable to such a peril as had overtaken her. He had no agent now, on earth above. Or did he have one, one he favored and protected more efficiently than she? Lylas realized she had risked and lost her life in Uhlume's service, and he did not seem to care. She felt cheated, and a deal of her apprehension left her.

"I will assume, Lord of Lords," said she, "that, as your servant, I am still bound by your law, and may not return to live above."

"You may not return," said he. He did not speak cruelly but he was implacable.

"Shall I serve you here?"

"Your service is done."

"Give me leave then," said the witch, "to sit here awhile and resign myself."

"You are free to do as you choose," said Death. And, from standing over her, he was suddenly half a mile away.

The witch stared after him with startling rancour. Having passed into Death's country, she had curiously—or perhaps logically—lost some of her awe of him. And with her awe and fear went her adoration. She began to feel cunning and clever again. She began to think of Narasen and all she remembered of her. If Death had remained in ignorance, and plainly he had, of the witch's mistaken plots, Narasen certainly knew nothing.

A second time, the witch arose. From the illusory air she

formed a flagon of wine, and took a good swig of it. The illusion made her tipsy in a most satisfying and swift fashion, and thus fortified, Lylas selected a certain direction and began to walk in it. She had decided to seek Narasen out, and either by her arts or by the power of divination open to all in that nether region, she had located Narasen's position instantly.

After some hours or minutes of effortless walking, the witch came to the bank of a dull white river. Here, on a tall rock, sat a dark blue woman.

The witch had not anticipated Narasen in this form, all coloured with the poison, and the effect made worse by that extended sojourn of hers in Merh. Her skin was an indigo almost black, within the indigo face, indigo eyes with two bits of blazing gold inlay (irises) in them; Narasen's hair was purple and the nails of her left hand, which rested on her left knee, were purple too, and as long as the hand they grew from. The right hand, resting on the right knee, was pure white, a skeleton hand of bone—Azhrarn's doing.

The witch checked. Narasen presented an aspect so terrible and so exotic, even Lylas could not ignore it. Awhile Lylas stared, and Narasen paid her no heed. Narasen was brooding. She had a look of her brooding, like venom fermenting in a vat. Lylas crept close at last, affecting a fear she did not feel, and concealing the other fear she did.

She threw herself flat before Narasen and kissed her indigo foot.

Narasen raised her lids, looked at her.

Lylas whispered:

"Are you, awful majesty, the lady Narasen, queen of Merh?"

Narasen did not answer, but her black mouth curled a little at its edge, downwards.

"By your beauty and your state," Lylas moaned, "so I recognize you as she. But truly, how regal and fearsome you have become. I should name you Queen Death."

Narasen reached out her hand—the bone one—and lifted the witch's chin. Lylas shivered the length of herself. It was not all play-acting.

"I am Narasen," said Narasen. "What there is left of her."

The witch crawled on to her knees. She took the bone hand in hers and kissed that. Narasen laughed, unpleasantly. "You are ever the harlot you were," she said. "Go seek your master, and practice your wiles on him. Or do you love him less now you are his prisoner?"

238

"Death is Death," said Lylas. "Do not send me away. Tell me what troubles you, elder sister."

Narasen spat on the gray land. That was her answer.

Her fires were cold now. Not only her skin had darkened, not only her hand had gone to a bone. She had taken death to heart. She had sat here a mortal year, longer, musing on Azhrarn, musing on her son, who had destroyed her. Maybe she had even had a thought or two upon the matter of blueness and the blue witch and the poison in the cup, but that would seem a leaf in the wind now. It was Simmu who haunted her. All she could see was his brightness which mocked her dark. To be dead was a state which played odd tricks on dreams of vengeance.

"Oh my elder sister," whispered the witch, laying her head in the lap of Narasen, "why sit in this bleak country with no illusion to sustain you?"

"I have sworn," said Narasen.

The witch smiled, and hid her smile in a fold of Narasen's black dress. "I have not," said Lylas. Then she built about the two of them a palace very like the palace at Merh, or as the palace at Merh had been. Hot sunlight shafted between the pillars, the pelts of leopards lay under Narasen's feet. Narasen sneered, but her eyes were brighter.

"Given the means, I might erect a palace here, quarried from the foul stone of the place itself. The treasures of some king's tomb could ornament it." Such a thought had never occurred to her previously, but Lylas had touched off her dry powder. "However," Narasen added, "for now I will permit this make-believe, seeing no road to the other. But if Uhlume comes by, dismantle the picture. I would not have him think I weaken."

Lylas grinned in the black fold of the dress. She had heard a secret ambition, seen a secret vulnerability. Narasen and she were conspirators.

"My weakness, not yours, elder sister. The weakness of my longing to please you. Count me your handmaiden."

Narasen drew up a handful of the witch's hair in her fleshed fingers, let it pour away like water, drew up more.

Lylas suffered the game to go on and on.

6

Lylas began this thing, seeking only to be clever and to make soft the hard bed on which she found herself. But Lylas disliked men, and now resented Death. She pretended, in order to escape the wrath of Narasen, that she admired her; Lylas strove to please Narasen. She made the illusions which Narasen, under the yoke of her enduring oath, would not. Only one time had Narasen consented to make illusion, recounting her re-visiting of Merh to Uhlume, which had been part of that supernatural bargain. Only that one time, and she had not shown him everything, only how she had walked the streets of her city till no living thing drew breath there—Uhlume had watched, expressionless as ever. He had not been shown the confrontation between Narasen and Azhrarn, when Simmu had escaped her, when Azhrarn had punished her insolence, gentle in the way of the demons and terrible in their way. Lord Death received less than his due, but asked no more. He did not appear to notice the right hand of Narasen, all bone. Perhaps Death was unobservant. And after she had paid her reduced fee, Narasen had sat down to brood, and brooded till the long-haired witch came to her.

Narasen, seeing the witch fawn on her, even in pure knowledge of the reasons for and the falseness of Lylas' demonstration, was nevertheless succored by this food. Narasen sneered at Lylas, looking through her with those dreadful blue and yellow lizard eyes. Narasen appreciated the glints of genuine terror that showed themselves in Lylas' demeanor. Was not her whole act of fawning prompted by terror? Narasen the queen had once been accustomed to such abasement and, on occasion, such fear from her subjects. Accustomed too to those charms of surrounding that her pride had denied her in the Innerearth, which now Lylas fashioned extravagantly from the air to please her. With Lylas, taking no responsibility for it, Narasen could stroll once more the golden rooms of a palace, ride once more across the golden plains where the leopards shone in the shadows. And when the illusory night came down to fill the illusory windows with illusory stars, Lylas, a supple, sly and beauteous child of fifteen, slunk to Narasen's knee and laid her head, with its quantity of hair, thereon. Narasen would stroke the hair and,

240

at the touch of fleshly fingers, Lylas would smile and shut her eyes, and at the touch of the bone fingers, Lylas would shiver and shut her eyes more tightly. The truth of the matter was, some portion of Lylas delighted to be afraid, though only of one she felt she might, by subtle wiles, keep tame. And so she found joy in this fear with Narasen. And, from acting adoration, adoration stole over Lylas. And, from acting a seduction, she was seduced.

Others in the Innerearth, who ventured from Uhlume's granite palace to investigate the golden light of the new palace which now reared up, brilliantly real as were hallucinations in that country, were met at the door by phantom guards with swords. Next came a naked maiden, clothed in hair, who ordered them to prostrate themselves before her mistress. It was the old thing. What Lylas served must be greater than any. Maybe Lylas wondered if Death would get to hear of it, and what he would do. But the contempt and resentment which had struck her suddenly on her fall into this cellar, sustained her. Narasen did not fear Uhlume, never had, not in a perfect sense. And certainly, Death never came to chide them. As for Death's subjects, fascinated by this new arrogance of the awful blue woman who so plainly despised them, they paid her homage and crept away. And later, it was not only Lylas who took up that name: Queen Death.

Lylas crouched at the knees of Narasen and let her breasts bloom through her tresses till Narasen, unappeased long years, seized her delicious tormentor and made much, with hands and mouth, of what she found under the hair. Lylas proving agile, versatile and willing, they were soon most intensely knotted. Thereafter, stretched slackly in exhaustion, they were presently confidants and into knots of another kind.

Narasen poured out, one drop at a time, her gall. Lylas learned how Narasen yearned for Simmu's pain. Lylas clung to Narasen, whispering. She too confided, not entirely truthfully. She spoke of the awful secret which Uhlume had entrusted to her, the secret of the second well. (Narasen listened, as if bored.) Then Lylas spoke lyingly of a rumor she had heard. That Azhrarn favored Simmu and had sought knowledge of the second well, to give Simmu a hero-deed: the chance to wrest Immortality for mankind. "I am dead," Lylas whispered. "I cannot prevent such an act. But Uhlume will blame me. Advise me, wise mistress, what I should do."

"You liar," said Narasen, twisting the witch's hair. "Your own snares caught you, some game you were at. You betrayed the secret while you lived, did you not? Making eyes also, no doubt, at the Black Cat of Underearth, Azhrarn. Yes, you would sell anything."

Then the witch felt it wise to break like a brittle reed. She wept on Narasen's knee: "He came by night, Night's Master. Who can resist him? I was in terror and he read my brain. You know his cruelty, great lady, who faced him as I dared not—" And she kissed the bone hand copiously.

Narasen mused. At length: "And is Azhrarn, then, the lover of my son? Yes, I recall he loves him well. But Uhlume will not love Simmu, if Simmu has been clever. Has he?"

Lylas clung to the knees. "I fear he has. It is all my fear."

"There is a glass in Death's hovel, which shows the world. Let us see if you are right. If you are, we will then seek the black and white one himself. Can Uhlume, fear-maker, be afraid, I wonder?"

Lylas stared at Narasen's dark face (dark almost as Death's own).

"Death may turn his rage on me. I never meant betrayal—but will he reckon that? And if he spends his wrath on me, Simmu may escape him. And surely, my queen-king, you wish Simmu to suffer, not your handmaiden?"

"It has all led to this then, has it?" inquired Narasen, smiling. "You have made yourself useful, you think, to me, in order to protect you from White Cloak's wrath? But there is no wrath in Uhlume."

"I beg you—"

"Beg me then."

Lylas slid down the length of Narasen and embraced her feet. Lylas knew she had gambled.

Presently Narasen rose, and Lylas went after her.

They moved from the lamplit night of the illusion to the never-dying gray un-light of Innerearth, and crossed the bleak landscape.

Such tricks that realm perpetuated upon dreams of vengeance. Impulses were as abrupt and total as brooding was indefinite and long. Even the psychology of human things was out of joint and curious there. Passions unmatched, hopes ridiculous, cravings unreasonable. How, in such a place, could it be otherwise?

Uhlume came back, from some battlefield, some plague-ripped city, some solitary death-bed, and found Narasen in his apartments, among the dark shadows and the emptiness, as once before he had found her there. But the witch cowered

242

behind her, the witch kneeled to Uhlume and hid her face. Did Uhlume notice how the witch kept hold of Narasen's black dress, as if keeping hold of a talisman?

Narasen shook off this hold. She smiled at Uhlume.

"Welcome home, sir, to luxurious abode. How is the world? Where have you been in it? Did you take joy in your visit?"

Uhlume regarded her. The witch pressed her face to the floor. Narasen said:

"One place you did not go to, I believe. Would you care to see, in your magical glass, where I have been looking?"

Lord Death did not take the glass, but Narasen raised the glass so he could see in it. She raised it a good while, but her grip did not falter.

From the beginning, it seems Death had known her as some special thing, an omen or an enemy. He gazed into the glass, as ever expressionless, and she gazed at him. Death gazed upon a dawn, a city in the dawn, on Simmurad. He recognized instantly—or appeared to—what Simmurad portended. Nothing in him changed, yet somehow he was altered. (Lylas reacted to this alteration. She threw himself full length under her hair.)

Again, time had sneaked past in the Innerearth. The few days of Lylas' waking from coma, Narasen's seduction, their conspiracy; the few hours even of seeking the glass, showing the image in the glass to the Lord Uhlume—mortal years. Five years in Simmurad, they say.

The Image:

Rose marble, gilded towers, enamelled domes. Beneath, streets slimly peopled, and what moved there, the beautiful and the best. Lovely women, sorceresses, hair to their waists, jeweled eyes; men, handsome and strong, magicians, and wise.

The whisper of the Immortal City had spread.

Many set out upon a quest to seek it, died searching for life, slaughtered others on the way. Some found it ("Eastward, eastward it lies"). Many of these few were turned away. Yolsippa the rogue, the wretch who took the gift as a cheat and understood its worth the more, he it was who guarded the brazen gates of Simmurad. If and when a man came there, Yolsippa could cry the challenge from the high gate-tower.

"Who are you, and what? State your business, and your name, your virtues and your learning, your powers. What can you offer in exchange for the most precious gift, for the gift

243

all men covet? Tell me, bearing in mind that later you must prove all you say."

Some were angry, some afraid. Some lied, and perished, striving to prove what they could not. A minute quantity of men, a more minute quantity of women, were brave and well-tutored enough to breach rose-red Simmurad, to receive, in a thimble of black jade, one drop of muddy liquor, the Elixir of Eternal Life.

This, Death saw. He saw a kind of glow from the people of Simmurad, inner fires, unquenchable.—Did he see the pallor of their faces?

He beheld Simmu. Simmu in a library of great shelves, each shelf massed with gemmed and ornamented books. Simmu read as if he hungered and must be filled. He was alone. He had locked the doors. He read as he had never read in the temple, in his youth. His eyes burned as he scanned the pages. He did not look quite as he had, the thinly muscular bronzed youth, the hero entering the city, innocent, still feral, not yet fettered. Now Simmu, young and handsome though he was and would always be to time's cessation, now Simmu had a glaze of age, a hardening, a petrification.

She had it too, the slender fair-haired girl, lingering outside the doors. Kassafeh, the wife of Simmu, wed to him five years before, in a vast strange night ceremony in the citadel of Simmurad. Kassafeh, her eyes leaden, her hand on the door, unspeaking, not attempting to knock. In youth years pass slowly. These five years of eternal youth had passed like centuries. Kassafeh, also, was coming to a hardening of her ageless flesh.

Alabaster dolls, their clockwork stopped. Did Death see that? No, he saw life which did not die.

Narasen, who had seen before in the glass all she wished to observe at this moment of her son and his fortune, had not taken her eyes from Uhlume. How she watched. She made herself a student of his face, his stance, his gesture.

"Can the Fear-Maker be afraid?" she had asked. She believed it.

All men, no doubt, would believe Death must tremble at this threat. So, carried by their vote, he must.

The magic glass, held in Narasen's hand, suddenly shattered. It fell to pieces, and those pieces into pieces, till only fragments like sugar, lay on the ground.

"Are you angry, my Lord?" Narasen said. She stared as if she loved him. In a way she did; he gave her hate, her second food.

Uhlume's pale eyes were wide. They were dry and blindingly bright. Facially expressionless, it was his hands that spoke. From the tips of them, blood burst. The blood was oddly as red as the blood of a man. His brain—who could tell that? Perhaps he strove to make in himself this wild and static bleeding anger, beacause humanity expected it of him. Where the drops of blood fell, the ground cracked. The red speckled his white garments. His eyes were so wide now, his face was taking on an expression at last: madness.

"Azhrarn gave the city to Simmu, Azhrarn is the lover of Simmu," Narasen said. "But the Black Cat is nothing to the White Dog. Find a way, Death, find a way to murder Immortals."

Death lifted his bloody hands and covered his eyes. His cloak and his hair blew back, twisted, flared—there was no wind to stir them thus. Death turned and strode from the granite palace. He strode across the country of the Innerearth, his hands before his face. The blood stained the gravels underfoot. The blood sprang up in red flowers with black hearts, black stems, poppies, the flowers of death. The blood of Death dappled those white still waters of Innerearth. The waters caught alight and burned, and black smoke made clouds in the featureless sky.

In a cliff of iron was a backless chasm, and into it Death walked. The blood ran from the mouth of the chasm, ten rivulets. No sound no movement came from the chasm. Only the blood came. Only the blood of Uhlume, Lord Death, one of the Lords of Darkness.

7

The witch lay an age, importunate, at the feet of Narasen. She was yet in alarm that Lord Death would return to punish her for letting slip the secret which had permitted Immortality to mankind. But Death seemed to have forgotten this secret and her part in it. Death seemed to have lost sight of all things. He had accused no one, had said no word. At last Lylas embraced the knees of Narasen in her former way, and praised her intelligence and her manipulation of Death's mood. The fragmented sugar of the magic glass crunched under the women's feet as they left the apartments of Lord Death.

Outside, one of Uhlume's thousand-year slaves, heeding

Narasen and where she came from, bowed to the cindery ground, and Lylas smirked.

The Lord Uhlume sat upon the plateau of an eastern mountain.

Far below, the horizon was burnished by a sea; nearer, a stair cut in the mountain led to the plateau from the shore. The plateau itself ended against the mountain's final upthrust wall, and in this wall were set two gates of shining brass.

The Lord Uhlume sat with his back to the gates.

Death could go here and there through all the places of the earth, for on very inch of the earth some thing had died. Or very nearly. At the world's edges the sea, the mountains endured, and were young in their millennia. And within Simmurad nothing had ever expired. Only this far, therefore, to the head of this stairway, could Death ascend, because only this far had death ever ascended—some fish floating belly uppermost in the primaeval sea, some blade of grass withering upon the mountain flank, these had made his journey possible to the plateau. No farther.

Somehow, a chair had moulded itself from the pearly rock, offered itself, and Uhlume had seated himself in it. Somehow a black spreading shade tree had grown, or fantasized itself behind the chair, to dapple it in a parasol of shadow through the long, long dawns of Simmurad.

Death sat in the shade.

One hand rested beneath his chin, one on his knee, bloodless now. A white cowl covered his white hair, partly concealing that face like a carving of black polished wood. His black lids were lowered. The thick fringe of albino lashes lay upon his cheeks, but he did not sleep. Men in such a pose might look vulnerable. You could perceive how terrible he was thus for he did not look vulnerable, even with the lashes lowered on his cheek. Those shut lids are like the lids of boxes closed on a wisdom that pierces through lids.

And then he raised his lashes, and his eyes were open.

Four men rode up the stairway in the mountain and reined in their horses on the plateau about thirty feet from the shade tree, the chair and Death.

They were travelworn and they had a wild stare.

"What now?" one asked who carried a bow upon his back.

"There is the gate," said another.

"Even at this moment," said the third, "I do not properly believe what is told of this city, though we have sought five years to discover it."

246

The fourth rider turned his head.

"Who sits there, beneath the tree?" he asked.

"Which tree? I see none," said the third rider.

"I see the shadow of a rock," said the first.

"It is a man in a white robe and cowled in white," said the fourth rider.

The second rider cuffed him.

"He is trying to distract our purpose by mentioning phantoms. It has occurred to me," he went on, his wild face become wilder, "that only one of us will be chosen. Do they not say that in this city men must undergo ordeals of strength and sorcery before they are permitted the Drink of Life? Well, we are equals in all things, my brothers. And I doubt they will take all four." Then he drew his sword, and he sheared off the head of the fourth rider, who all this while had gazed at Death beneath his tree. Having done that, the second rider slashed his horse with his whip so it bolted, weary though it was, toward the brass gates.

The first rider instantly unslung his bow, set a shaft to it and loosed the string. The shaft took the second man between the shoulder blades. With one loud cry, he whirled from the horse and fell dead, just before the gateway. Suddenly then, the first dropped on his saddle—the third man had stabbed him. Now only the third man remained alive.

He dismounted slowly and walked across the plateau toward the gate, but his head hung. Near the gate, he turned and looked over his shoulder, but no one followed. He rapped on the gate.

Within and above, a voice called:

"State your business and name."

The third rider stood away from the gate. He began to weep. In the midst of weeping, he laughed, and roared: "Is that the fat thief they say is porter at the doorway of the Immortal City?"

Within and above, no one answered.

Then the third rider became aware of a figure on his left hand, just before the gate, and he stared, for the figure sat where the second rider had fallen to the arrow. But it was not he. It was one robed and cowled in white who sat in a chair of rock under a spreading tree, and his face was hidden in shadow—the dead man sprawled at his feet.

Uhlume was now able to approach the gate, as far as death had approached.

The third rider wiped his eyes.

"If I believed all the tales, I would believe ill of you," said

247

he trembling. He ran at the gate and rapped a second time. "Let me come in," he pleaded, "for my death is out here."

No answer. The fat thief, apparently, had taken exception to insult.

The third rider looked at the Lord Uhlume. The third rider sank on his knees.

"You have turned cutthroat now, my lord, have you? You rob the flesh before the allotted span is done? I heard another story. King Death is wed. He wed a woman whose skin is blue, whose hair is a storm cloud. She nags him so he is glad to get from home. They say she nags him, his wife, Queen Death, till he will give her anything. They say she asks for obscene presents. One night she went to a land and poisoned it; all she breathed on or touched she slew, and she came back to her husband and recounted her deeds to him, and numbered those she had slain, and King Death exulted." Then the third rider crawled to the gate once more and knocked, but his knock was feeble.

"The fat thief is at breakfast," came the cry from within.

The third rider crawled from the gate, the other way. He glanced up into the cowled countenance of the Lord Uhlume. Then the third rider stabbed himself and died at Death's feet, on the body of his comrade.

Above and within, Yolsippa belched, his breakfast concluded. He did not always attend the gates of Simmurad, but when he did, he reclined upon a couch, cushions under his head, and he ate and drank for diversion, for, being immortal, he had no need of food or drink to keep his health. The food itself was exotic and curious, summoned by sorcery, perhaps partly constructed of sorcery, but Yolsippa's rich robes were greasy with it. Now, having wiped fresh grease on these robes from his fingers, he opened a trick portal high in the wall of the mountain, and peered out.

The four horses had run from the plateau, down the stairway; they were gone. The dead men remained. Yolsippa clicked his tongue. Then he noticed the cowled figure seated by the gate, visible only through the branches of the shade tree.

"Pray enlighten me," cried Yolsippa, "if you are he who knocked at this gate of the Immortals?"

Death did not glance up, but he answered softly—though Yolsippa heard him—"I do not knock at any gate."

The voice struck cold, even on Yolsippa.

Yolsippa shouted down: "State your business and your name."

It has been suggested Death laughed at that, but Death did not laugh, it was not in his nature, even in his nature as now it was. "Fetch your king, I will speak with him," was what Death said.

"Ah now, The Lord Simmu, who is like a son to me, is not at the beck and call of all comers."

Death said no more; Yolsippa said a deal more. But somehow, it was borne in upon Yolsippa that Simmu must be brought, and so eventually Yolsippa left the gates and went to seek him.

Simmu had been reading. For almost five years he had done little else. He crammed himself with books to ease the hollowness inside him. Yet he felt crowded. Even the sparse crowd of the beautiful and the wise in Simmurad crowded him. He, who had once wandered freely, who, by his deed had become responsible for others.

Simmu had fallen asleep across a book. The candles had burned out in their sockets. Simmu's hair spilled across the pages. His eyelids moved with dreams.

Yolsippa, the rogue, finding the library doors locked, picked the locks and went in. He roused Simmu with no subtlety, shaking his shoulder. Simmu started awake. His eyes flashed.

"Why did you wake me?"

He could speak fluently and often as any man now. He could sound petulant too, as a child. Yolsippa had broken into more than the room, he had broken into Simmu's dream. And there had been weird sweetness to the dream, which concerned dusk in a grove, a companion with dark hair, both he and Simmu children. . . .

"At the gate is a strange apparition. Part of your destiny of heroism doubtless."

Simmu had risen. He paced the floor, lion in a cage.

The dawn light caught him. He was rare, but not as he had been.

"Yolsippa, I would I could make you vomit back that drop you stole in the desert, your immortality."

"Life is good," said Yolsippa, but he sighed. Dully, he missed something in his life, the sourness and the fear that had added paradoxical zest.

"Tell me again who is at the gate," said Simmu. "This time, make it clear."

"Not a demon," said Yolsippa, "yet curiously, he put me in mind of a certain great lord. . . . But this one is clad in white. Now here I will confess, I did not take to him. Indeed, he had the appearance of some personage I had met before, or rather, seen in the distance and avoided. And his hands were black—"

Simmu shouted, with no words. Flames seemed to leap in his hair and his flesh. He crackled with them.

"Five years," he said. "The old raven is slow. And did you not recognize him?"

Yolsippa grimaced and held up his palms wardingly.

"Never tell me," said he. "I am prudent, even in my persisting condition. I do not pull the tails of wolves."

"Here is the moment," said Simmu, turning from Yolsippa, forgetting him. "Now I shall learn if I have sold myself to bondage for nothing, or if my triumph will repay me. *Death*," he added, striking his open hand upon the open book, "stay for me."

Then he snatched up his outer robe from the chair where he had cast it, belted it on. It was patterned with silver, Kassafeh his wife had woven it with skills her mother had taught her in the silk merchant's house. Simmu did not remember it was of Kassafeh's weaving.

Somewhere a woman sang from a high tower in Simmurad. The song was melancholy. No other stirred in the city or crossed the path of Simmu as he went out into the morning.

Light-footed he still was. And on a green lawn of the citadel a leopard stalked a short space by his side, acknowledging vague kinship. But Simmu came alone from the marble streets to the gates of Simmurad, and worked their mechanism.

The heart of Simmu pounded and even his eyes were paler. He stepped out on to the mountain plateau.

The Lord Uhlume raised his head, and looked.

Once, in Narasen's chill tomb, he had spared this crying child.

Simmu looked back.

Once, in Narasen's chill tomb, Simmu had confronted this threat and felt the cold of its passing and its promise.

"Well, black man," said Simmu, "you have been some years in getting here. You would have been my terminus, but I am yours. I have been reading, about the world and all the wonders in it, all the lands there are for the taking, and the laws for the making. One day, (and I have endless days, you will agree, black man), one day I will lead an army from this stronghold, and we will conquer the world and set it free of you."

Did Uhlume recall the tone of Narasen?

Uhlume said: "You will live forever, but you will do nothing. Your youth has crystallised, and your ambition with it and your very soul. Now I see this, and I inform you of it. Will you dream of snaring all men in such a trap as you are in?"

Simmu relapsed in silence, the foundering inexpressive silence of a man. Then he collected himself.

"You teach me excellently. I will bear your lesson in mind. I admit, I have been idle too long. But answer me this, my lord. Do you fear what I have done?"

Tonelessly, Death replied:

"I fear it."

"And you will do battle with me?"

"I will do battle with you."

Simmu smiled.

He walked slowly nearer and more near to Death. When he came to the slain men, he glanced at them, without disgust or compassion. Simmu came to the exact vicinity of Death. Simmu put out his hand and touched the mouth of Death. Simmu shivered and his eyes flickered, but he mastered himself again.

"My fear is ended as yours begins," he said.

"Fear is not the greatest evil granted men."

Simmu spat on the hem of the cloak of Death.

"Now hurt me," Simmu whispered, "destroy me."

Something—expressionless, awesome, untranslatable—formed and vanished on the face of Death. A single scarlet drop of blood spilled from the corner of his mouth, but he raised his sleeve, and the blood was gone.

Simmu, fascinated, trembled. He struck Death across the cheek, and the blow seemed to shatter Simmu's spine, but yet he stood and breathed and was whole.

"Fight me now," Simmu murmured. "I am anxious to enjoy the fight."

Death put back his cowl. His ghastly beauty seemed to fill the mountain and to crack it. He laid his own hand upon Simmu's breast, and stained it with blood. His touch was gentle, terrible. His touch stopped the hearts of men, but not the heart of Simmu. Then there was a white swirling and Death was gone.

Simmu blazed with fury.

"Is that then all? Come back, black crow. Return and fight me."

Then it was that the dead man who had lain uppermost at the feet of Death, raised himself, and said to Simmu. "Be patient. He will return. Anticipate him." And crashed backwards, an empty corpse once more.

And with a grim joy, shaking and grinning, Simmu re-entered the city of Simmurad and searched for his wife, to lie with her. That night Simmu toasted Death in the rose-red wine. He hung about his neck the green Eshva gem he had not worn four years. You could see Narasen in his face, like flame through a lamp.

What Death did then was a ritual thing, like the steps of a dance. Indeed, he did what was expected of him. He called his minions, or rather, those beings which were not his minions but which were affiliated to him in the brains of men.

He called Plague from some hole in a yellow landscape of crippled trees and swamp, and sent her to Simmurad. She drifted in and out, and some fell sick, but the sickness fled from them. The human Immortals were not invulnerable, but half a day's fever left them laughing at the novelty.

Then Death called Famine. Famine was also laughed from the gates of Simmurad. Death called Dissent. Dissent crept by night into Simmurad. They fell to blows there, but Dissent was quick to notice, huddled in his greenish robe, that they fought gladly. Dissent also was a diversion. And when, duelling in the marble thoroughfares, a man's hand was shorn from his arm, a masterful surgeon, who had gained his bit of eternity in the city for his skills, sewed the hand to the arm with silver thread. And since each part was immortal, neither the hand nor the arm mortified, and presently worked in unison as before.

Death sent a snake of corruption through the walks of Simmurad, and they played with it, decked it with undying flowers and trinkets. It wound itself about a tree of fruit and sulked there in its dark enamels.

"Come, Lord of Bones," Simmu whispered, "you can do better."

Kassafeh sat at a loom of bronze—in memory of the demons, there was no golden thing in Summurad, gold being the unloved metal of the Underearth. Kassafeh's chameleon eyes, these days, were uniformly cloudy and obscure, the colors of deep dungeons or the floors of lakes. She was bored. Boredom was the tragedy of Simmurad. Simmu was the only star in her sky, but the star was distant. She no longer loved him, had not been able to retain her love in the face of his indifference. She had become at once more shallow and more supernal, the two parts of her dividing to her origin. She ate boxes of sweets ensorcelled from the harems of kings, she dressed herself in the clothes ensorcelled from empresses' backs. At other times she charmed birds from the air— though not often, for seldom did birds visit Simmurad. She would gaze at the clouds, dreaming. She did not understand Simmu's war with death, had never arrived at an understanding of Simmu. She brooded on her wedding, a whole temple of priests kidnapped by the demons to see to the business, as a joke. Even as her veil was lifted, she had been aware of demon amusement, and of some dark suggestion more interesting to Simmu than herself—Azhrarn, who never visibly entered Simmurad, or Death, who threatened it. Kassafeh yawned, left the loom, ate sweet gelatine, her somber eyes brimming with tears.

"I shall grow fat, and you will hate me," she said to Simmu.

She knew he did not care enough to hate her.

Simmu did not even hear her. He was looking for Death, who did not fight him.

The ritual was completed, useless.

Death roamed the world.

Men would come on him, seated upon a hillside, his white cloak flapping in the winds of earth, a white vulture. He was no longer merciful with that compassionless compassion of former days. Where he strode, sometimes the earth smoked, and little things crawled from their burrows and died. Where he passed, children slumped at their play. Phantoms, attracted to his wake like birds to the plough-riven furrows, swarmed at his back, the nightmares and symbols of human panic, given shape.

He was seeking, as a man scours an attic for some valuable relic he knows was there, whose features he cannot recall and cannot put his hand to. He walked the earth, and the long strides were years.

One night, when he stood on the bank of a shallow river, Uhlume beheld his own reflection, but negative and reversed, in the water. He looked up and saw Azhrarn on the farther bank, regarding him.

"What news, un-cousin?" asked Azhrarn. "Three places

now you cannot wander, Upperearth, Simmurad and Druhim Vanashta of the demons."

There was this between Lords of Darkness, these two, and any others that there were, a sort of allergic yet loving rivalry, a sort of unliking affection, a scornful unease, xenophobia and family feeling.

"Your game," said Uhlume.

"Truly, mine, un-cousin. But I have grown somewhat tired of it. Its significance eludes me. Humans are graceless and cannot sustain the artistry of the Vazdru. Did you admire the city of Simmurad?"

"I have not observed the inside," said Uhlume.

"You must try to. Indeed, un-cousin, you must."

They stood and watched each other, one pale as marble, black-haired, clad in black; one black as that black, white haired, clothed like a black tree in snow.

"Who would have thought," said Azhrarn, "Immortality grasped by mortals could become so static? Perhaps the war is between us, un-cousin, you and I. Though, if it were, I should decline it."

Azhrarn rasied his hand above the shallow river. Something fell from his fingers and burst there. A picture evolved.

Demons were the friends of men only for as long as men entertained them. Simmu had shrivelled in the remembrance of Azhrarn like an autumn leaf. Yet the Vazdru, who could un-remember anything, forgot nothing.

Uhlume beheld a man in the picture of the river's surface. He wore a scarlet robe fringed with gold, a scarab of inky jewels hung on his breast. His countenance was young and handsome, dark bearded, and his hair also dark. His eyes were lined and cruel, they showed him as he was. His eyes hurt and despised and mourned and sank back into a mind like a cauldron of snakes. His eyes were explicitly sane with a profound madness. Blue-green they were. Eyes to quench thirst.

In the picture, cool as stones, these eyes watched a man who died before them, writhing and slate-lipped from some intricate poison. As this unfortunate twitched to stillness, another was dragged forward. He screamed out. "Spare me, mighty Zhirek! I have done you no wrong." But to no avail. A cup was thrust against his mouth and he was forced to sip, and presently he died in a fit at the bare feet of the one he had named "Zhirek." This Zhirek leaned back in his chair, he took the cup of poison and drained it. He let the cup fall negligently. He sighed, half shut those eyes of his. The poison, which had dispatched so vehemently, did not harm him.

The picture winked out.

"Once he called to me," Azhrarn said, "but I found his companion more pleasing. Also, to you he called, un-cousin."

"I recollect," said Uhlume.

The moon rose over a hill.

Azhrarn was gone, only a black and wide-winged bird, flying.

Death turned, and vanished too.

A last nightmare, spilled from Death's spurious entourage, lowered itself to drink at the river, glimpsed itself, and fled screaming.

PART THREE

Zhirek, the Dark Magician

1

The magician, Zhirek, walked through the streets of a great city. His robe was the color of beetles' wings, his hands were ringed with gold, the scarab of black jewels hung on his breast, but he walked barefoot, which was his affectation.

He was well known by sight, and well feared. His dark hair, his handsomeness . . . Many a pale girl languished in a window at the look of him. Others turned pale for different reasons. Sometimes Zhirek went hunting. That is, he would go straight up to a man, stare in his eyes, and so bind him. The man would at once abandon whatever he was doing and follow Zhirek mindlessly. In this way, carpenters, masons, clerks, merchants and fishermen had left off gainful employment, deserted their scattered wares, unprotected and at the mercy of thieves, deserted also their wives and dependents. Even slaves had been taken from their masters. None of these men were seen again. A complaint had gone to the king of the city. He had trembled when he read it. "I will have no dealings with Zhirek," he croaked. Truth to tell, Zhirek had already had dealings with the king, arriving, unannounced, at the height of some celebration, and mocking him. The king would have had Zhirek seized and chained for his insolence. But Zhirek had done some curious work on the thoughts of the king. The king had, all at once, believed himself a dog. He had bounded into the kennels and champed on bones, and even, it was said, mounted a bitch hound and coupled with her heartily. Recovering his wits, the king had learned a lesson of avoidance. "No dealings with Zhirek," he repeated. "We must regard him as our trial, our curse. To pray to the gods for deliverance from him is all we may do, and that secretly."

Zhirek was altogether avoided, save by those who fell in love with his appearance, and even they were afraid of him somewhat, being not entirely fools. He had a house a short distance from the city. It was old and partly ruinous and overhung the sea beneath. Weird glows played through the roofs of the house by night, along the barnacle-crusted walls, the mossy stone beasts that leered from the stairway. When the magician was from home, the doors of the house were never locked, indeed, they stood wide. Only one robber was ever unwise enough to venture in the place, and he came forth a shambling dribbling idiot, never able to describe what he had met. Zhirek certainly kept no servants beyond those he ensorcelled to do his will. Now and then a fearful storm would blow up from the sea, and rage and smash against the green bastions of the old house. Then those who dared to be abroad, would perceive Zhirek on a high tower, regarding the sea, and sometimes he would throw something down from the tower into the waves below, as one might throw a scrap to a starving wild animal. No one doubted, Zhirek had some pact with the sea people, that folk whose numerous and diverse kingdoms spread under the ocean, to the interest and consternation of men.

The storm clouds were gathering in the sky over the city this day that Zhirek walked there. People shrank from him, bowing themselves to the ground. Women snatched their children and ran indoors with them.

Hard on the jeweled towers of the city pressed the blue-black storm clouds. Rain spotted the hot streets, but not the robe of Zhirek the magician. A gate opened from the courtyard of a rich man's house, and a white-faced girl stole out and kneeled down in Zhirek's path.

"Take me as your slave," said this girl. "See, I have put on flawless gems to bring you as my gift."

Zhirek did not hesitate, nor did he glance at her.

Yet when he passed by, she caught his ankle.

Zhirek stopped then, and looked at her. Her hair brushed the street, and behind the eyes of Zhirek many ghosts stirred. But he said quietly to her: "Am I to kill you?"

The girl raised her head.

"I will die without your love," she avowed. "But I think you serve Death himself, you send so many to him."

"Death," said Zhirek. "There is a joke in that you will never know."

Then his eyes smote hers, and she let go his foot and fell on her side. And thus she lay a considerable time in the rain, till her attendants dared go and bring her in.

In the market place of the city, they were hanging a murderer.

Zhirek paused to watch the procedure, and when the felon danced on the rope, Zhirek himself grew white, though none witnessed it, being too afraid to observe his face.

But, as he stood there, one spoke behind him, saying his name not exactly as it was. The magician turned swiftly, but no man was there, none who might have called *Zhirem*.

2

Years before—more than five years, less than ten—Zhirem had woken in the valley of death, beneath the broken-boughed tree, the cord still round his neck with which he had tried to hang himself when other means failed. The rain yet fell in that part, but it was some days and some nights, he did not grasp how many, since he had come there. Zhirem lay on his back in the rain, remembering dimly a shadow which had touched his brow, and brought him the relief of a sort of pseudo-death, all of death he might achieve for centuries; unconsciousness.

Zhirem had meant to die, but death was not to be had. Zhirem had meant to serve the Master of Night, Azhrarn, the Prince of Demons, but neither was his service accepted. Zhirem's nature, like a water of melancholy, washed him under. Everything now had been taken from him, his striving after goodness, his hopes, his pride, even that human revenge upon fate—to destroy his own life—for he was invulnerable. A terrible predicament he was in, to be utterly suicidal, and unable to perish.

At length he got up, quite aimless, and sat on a rock by the venomous river. Here eventually, he recollected a companion, Simmu, who had become for him a woman. He recalled how Simmu had followed, pursued him, how she had danced, binding the unicorns with her Eshva spell of sorcery and sex, and binding also Zhirem. She had augmented the shame of Zhirem and his sense of nullity and despair by the pleasure she gave him. Yet now he grew hungry, with that dismal itch to lie with her again.

But Simmu the maiden did not seek him. And when, after a long while, Zhirem crawled and dragged himself from the inner valley to its upper bowl, and from there shambled out again into the lawless black lands, and to the very salt lake where he and Simmu had dwelled with their green fire and their green and piercing lust, he did not find her nor any trace of her.

The urn of the rain ran dry, and the sky cleared. It was dusk by then, the lake of salt luminous and uncanny in the tween-light. Zhirem wandered back and forth there, thinking of the old man, the sorcerer, who had rejected Zhirem's service on Azhrarn's behalf, but who had drawn closer and ever closer to the shining-haired girl who was Simmu, while she seemed to dissolve to a femininity, sweeter, deeper, wilder than that which she had assumed for Zhirem.

The holy men of the desert of his childhood had taught Zhirem to fear himself and his own joy; the holy priests of the yellow temple had inadvertently taught him to scorn the gods. Humanity instructed him in its faithlessness. Azhrarn dismissed him, Death shunned him. Left with less than nothing, yet Simmu might have tendered him, once more, love. And at this season, for this hour, love might have been after all enough, at least enough to stop the bleeding of his soul. But Simmu was gone, youth or maiden, he or she had renounced Zhirem, or so it appeared. (How could Zhirem guess that day and night of all-encompassing weeping Eshva grief which had been Simmu's? Nor the darkness and Azhrarn stepping from the darkness to cast a demon spell of forgetting? Or that, in despite of that spell, Simmu still did half remember the image of a companion, a second self?)

For Zhirem, night spread its blackness like the blackness within him. He walked across the lawless lands, going in no particular direction, and his mind was like a mound of dust.

Months he journeyed, living off the country where he could, starving when he could not, both processes of equal indifference to him, so that he tore up and ate berries and roots from habit merely. Here and there a beast sought to slay him, and could not and slunk away. Here and there he met men, or women. In a village, a hundred miles from the lawless lands, he was mistaken for what he had once been, a priest. A group of women had come to him and one had an ailing baby, but he turned from them in loathing, and when the mother flew after him, he struck her. It was his first naked brush with the cruelty within himself. It made him feel, this cruelty, almost alive, as once compassion and gentleness toward the sick had made him feel.

Zhirem did not really notice how the landscape altered. Weather, day and night, uphill and down were all one point-less similarity. He might as well have sat on the ground in one

259

place and not moved, but the active nature of his youth was not yet to be sloughed, he walked as instinctively as Simmu would have wandered in the Eshva fashion. Then, one sunrise in a forest of huge and bladed leaves, Zhirem roused from the ferns on which he had dropped down haphazardly in weariness the midnight before, and beheld a man seated close by.

This man was soberly dressed in a mode that suggested a true and actual priest. His face was tucked into neat, nearly motionless lines, that implied calm, confidence and unquenchable complacence.

"Good day, my son," said he, from two controlled pink lips which widened just so far and felt no need to widen farther.

Zhirem sighed, and lay back on the turf, for he was exhausted.

Overhead, the cavernous arches of the forest, set with panes of early light, briefly soothed his eyes and heart. But the man continued talking.

"You are in a poor state, my son. Although it seems to me, from the remnants of your apparel, that it may once have been a sacred robe, and that you, therefore, may be as I am, a traveling priest. Now is this so?"

"Not so," murmured Zhirem, and tears formed between his lids, he could not have said why.

The placid priest took no note of this.

"I think, my son, that I shall accompany you, for I believe you might profit by company. But I had better apprise you of one item. I am a very pious man, indeed, I have dedicated my life to piety, both in worshipping the gods and in succoring mankind. And for this, many years ago, a certain beneficence was bestowed on me, at the gods' direction, or through some other powerful agency. The beneficence is this—that all harm, wherever possible, shall avoid me. The lightning shall not strike the place where I am situated, the sea shall not overwhelm the bark wherein I sail, the savage beast shall eschew eating me. Now is this not a fine thing?" Zhirem said nothing, and so the priest elaborated. "You may imagine," said he, "I am in demand wherever there is a feast. Frequently I am invited to the festivities of strangers, for they know that while I am present the house is safe, even in the roughest climate. For the same reason, ships clamor to carry me as their passenger, gratis, for whatever ship bears me may not sink. Unfortunately," added the priest, tucking his face a little closer together than before, "there is this proviso.

260

Should I be in the proximity of only one other, and if some danger should threaten us, it will choose him in my stead. But I pray you not to be daunted by this fact, for I am sure I can aid you in your search for your soul's true desires."

"No, you cannot," asserted Zhirem, rising and striding away.

The priest instantly also rose and hastened after him.

"I am not accustomed to this attitude," declared the priest. "There is much you may learn from me."

"Only learn this from me," said Zhirem, halting and staring in the priest's face. "No harm of any sort can come to me, and I wish for no companion."

"Come, come," cried the priest, "such arrogance is unbecoming of your youth. The gods—"

"The gods are dead, or sleeping."

"Heaven forgive you!" screamed the priest, the tucks of his face coming altogether undone. "But woe and alas, oh misguided man, I see heaven has not."

This last was a reference to a huge cat, a tiger of simmering eyes, which just then trotted out of the trees toward them.

"I will pray for you, my son," promised the priest, "while you endure your agony."

Now Zhirem had been some while without happiness, and nearly as long without impulse. His torpor left him suddenly in a burst of racking amusement, so he laughed aloud.

"You had better run instead, priest," said Zhirem.

Just then, the tiger tensed itself and sprang at him. A short space from his breast, something spun the tiger sideways, and it rolled, spitting and snarling in the fern.

The priest's jaw dropped.

The tiger collected itself, and began to pad about Zhirem, raking the air futilely, till finally it drew aside and contemplated instead the priest. Patently the tiger meant to devour one of the two men, and though the priest was protected by a beneficence of sky spirits, or whoever had extended it, no alternative flesh was to be had. This being the case, the tiger plainly decided to ignore the beneficence.

"I will accept my doom quietly," opined the priest as the tiger raced at him. Alas, it was not quite possible, and Zhirem stumbled away into the forest, stopping his ears against the shrieks. Later he sank down under a tree, shaking with horror and with a terrible madman's laughter that came to him in the stead of tears or pity.

Evening had fallen when he emerged from the forest at the

outskirts of a prosperous town. No sooner was he on the road than people hurried to welcome him with lamps and garlands.

"Come to our feast!" they shouted. "The wine merchant's daughter is wedded, but last year there was an earthquake here. Come and sit in the house and keep us safe."

Zhirem realized they had got rumors of the priest with the beneficence and mistook their man. He tried to undeceive the throng, and while they debated, another crowd surged up.

"Come to our feast!" they shouted. "The corn merchant's son is home from the sea, but there is the usual fear of earthquake and you will keep us safe."

Then the two groups began to quarrel with each other over who deserved the priest's protection, and next came to blows. Zhirem evaded them and went away into the town, and through the town into the night country beyond.

Near midnight he heard the sea, whose voice there is no mistaking, and he smelled the salt perfume of it. Coming to a headland, he gazed down and saw another town ablaze with lights, and a harbor where ships lay as if asleep under a thin blue moon. Beyond the harbor, the ocean stretched out, a folded restless dark.

To Zhirem, the beauty of the world was new, he had discovered it through pain and outlawed solitude, one consolation given when all other pleasure seemed past. Thus, he seated himself on the land's brink high above the town, to watch the sea, forever changing and unchanged. And a profound stillness overcame him so that when a man's hand fell roughly on his shoulder, Zhirem cried out and leapt to his feet, almost ready to kill what had shocked him.

"I meant no offense, Father," declared the man, rough as his hand had been, and backing away. "Were you communing with the gods? I beg pardon, I thought you dozed, and I said to myself, said I, this sacrosanct gentleman should not have to doze here on the cold night cliffs, when there is a fine lodging already prepared for him aboard our vessel."

Zhirem perceived he had been mistaken again for the lucky priest.

"I am not the one you seek," said Zhirem.

"Yes, but you are," asserted the man stubbornly. "I guess your reluctance. You have heard we are a band of pirates, but this is not just. Perhaps we are somewhat ready with our knives and here and there may have gained a bad reputation. We need your virtuous presence all the more."

"The fellow you hoped for," said Zhirem, "was devoured

262

by a tiger in the forest. This I can swear to, for I witnessed it."

"Now, Father," quoth the man, "it should be beneath you to tell lies. Perchance you have already bound yourself to another ship? Forget the rogues. We sail at dawn and you shall be with us."

Zhirem was about to turn aside, when six other mariners stepped up the slope, obviously prepared for violence, should Zhirem further resist. And, although they could not have injured him in the slightest, their intent and fevered desperation to take him—and he the wrong man—moved him once more to that bitter, part-insane humorousness which now haunted him. He therefore agreed to go with them, and was conducted with stealthy speed, through the back alleys of the town, to the quay and a disreputable ship.

"I will do your vessel no good," Zhirem assured the sailors, "and I hazard you merit no good to be done you, so it is well enough."

The sailors ushered him aboard and into the cabin, and went off muttering. Presently a drunken captain entered, who treated Zhirem most courteously, though bolting the door on him from the outside whenever he had occasion to go on deck. This man also consistently titled him "Father," though the captain possessed three times Zhirem's number of years.

Accordingly, the ship left dock at sunrise with Zhirem aboard.

Now the sailors, pirates or otherwise, had particular reasons for desiring whatever protection they could lay hold of. The sea beyond this coast was fair and calm, and not given to tempest save at the changing of the seasons. However, two or three days' journey eastwards of the land a belt of sharp rocks extruded from the water, and on these many ships had been wrecked. This, in itself, was mysterious, for the rocks were clearly to be observed and easily navigable, save in storm or fog. Yet survivors had returned from that spot with supernatural tales, of mists and gleams, freak lightning and unhuman voices, and of bells sounding deep in the hollow of the ocean.

The first day of the voyage, Zhirem sat, bolted in the cabin, while an inefficient bustle of activity went on outside, not to mention several brawls and a whipping. The first night, confident in the talisman of the priest, the sailors drank riotously, which was followed by further brawlings. The second day, discipline was excessively lax, and the second night, the riot resumed. On this night indeed, the captain, drunker than the rest of the crew, begged Zhirem, in his capacity of priest, to come and bless the assemblage.

"Oh, I decline," said Zhirem. "They are blessed enough in you."

The captain was flattered, and commenced toying with Zhirem's hair, but Zhirem struck his hand aside and the captain made elaborate apology.

"It is," explained the captain, "the singular darkness of your locks which intrigues me."

Zhirem cursed him for this, in memory of the old notion of dark hair and the demons which had dogged him in the mouths of men; which had, it currently seemed to him, set him on the road to hell. And to a hell, indeed, which had rejected him.

The captain accepted Zhirem's oaths, unsurprised apparently at a swearing priest. He slumped belchingly asleep, but Zhirem remained insomniac, though uninterested in the stale cabin, the rowdy deck or in anything much. The motion of the ship did not precisely nauseate him, but disorientated, and depressed his spirits beyond even their low ebb.

Dawn broke, and it was the third day.

At noon, the jagged rocks were sighted, and an hour later the ship began to pass between them. No sooner was she fairly in, however, than the sky grew strangely somber, not overcast with cloud, but rather as if a smoked glass had been set between heaven and earth. Then, as the light faded, a mist, in color lavender, began to rise as it seemed from the ocean itself. The sun swam in this mist like a huge silver ghost, the sea was veiled in the mist, and the tops of the masts; the rocks vanished alongside, before and behind. The captain gave the order to put down anchor till the fume should disperse. He had continued optimistic, seeing he carried the lucky priest. The sails hung heavy with not a breath of wind.

"Now what is that noise?" demanded one man of another.

"The anchor has caught on a rock."

"No, it is a fish, swimming about the chain."

Three went to look over the side, and in a minute, all three uttered a wild cry.

They fled back across the deck, and shouted at their fellows:

"There is a monster in the sea!"

"It is green, but has the shape of a woman!"

"Its hair is like the sea-wrack and its lips like malachite. It rattles the chain and grins at us."

264

"And in the water it thrashes with its lower half, which is that of a smooth gray whale."

The captain was called from his cabin. He entreated Zhirem, on this occasion, to come with him on deck, and took Zhirem's arm.

"See, nothing ill can befall us, the priest being aboard." The sailors clutched Zhirem's rags, kissed his feet.

Zhirem looked beyond them all, into the mist, unspeaking, awaiting their fate and his, pitiless of both.

The lavender mist shrouded the ship now from bow to stern. And through the mist began to pierce pale lights. Like phosphorous they were, but gliding here and there they took on the aspect of malignant life. Then came a dim booming from the depth of the sea.

"It is the bell," despaired the sailors.

"Whatever it is," said the captain, swigging mightily from a leather bottle, "no harm can come to us." Hard on his words, a lightning hit the yard, which splintered at its top into a wreath of fire. "No!" cried the captain, waving aloft at heaven, showing Zhirem to the invisible sky. "Behold, great gods, we are protected—you must not hurt us—"

The second lightning struck the captain himself, as if in answer. Zhirem, naturally, was uninjured.

The sailors screamed at this phenomenon. The bell tolled in the sea and the lights came and went vigorously.

"Save us!" entreated the ship's crew of Zhirem.

"Save yourselves," Zhirem replied. (His second naked brush with his own cruelty, his basic aversion to mankind.)

In a panic, the mariners next decided to weigh anchor and turn round, to procure an exit from the region, which was obviously accursed.

Zhirem stood at the starboard rail, silent, dark and emotionless as a symbol of fate itself.

The anchor was raised. The ship put about, or attempted to. Like creatures condemned, men and craft performed the actions which accomplished their doom. Presently, with a dreadful sound, the vessel speared herself upon a rock, and split.

The sea water rushed up, no longer unseen, foaming as if from some demoniac vat. With massive shudderings, the ship settled to her death. Her bracings opened, her timbers burst. Always the ocean was on hand to fill in the gaps left by wood and iron, to fill also the straining mouths of men.

The spine of the vessel gave suddenly with a frightful snap. The masts crashed inwards. The floor of the deck and the belly of the hold became a spiral of boiling foam which hungrily sucked and swallowed.

"And am I invulnerable also to you?" Zhirem asked softly of the erupting breakers as they combed his body. He was appalled yet quickened. The horror and hope of dying once more swamped him, and the sea clawed him into itself.

He was dashed downwards, with the rest.

Unspeakable nightmare—of asphyxia, of entrapment, of blindness.

The water lassoed him, spun him. Viridescent black, it scalded and bound his eyes, it roped his neck with his own long hair, tighter and more tight; it bound his limbs with his rags, with weeds and with the vortex itself. He strove to breathe and salt liquid entered into his throat and lungs. Yes, the sea, indifferent to the sorceries of earth, the sea would slay him after all.

Zhirem spun toward the ocean's floor, feeling no pain, his sight fading and a miserable pleasure in his heart, his thoughts gone to abstractions. Only vaguely did he comprehend how other men swirled past him, as if they all tumbled through a green air. Men who kicked and noiselessly shrieked, whose eyes started, whose faces were turning black as the ocean strangled them, while behind them the bubbles of each of those escaping last breaths jostled back toward the surface.

Zhirem tilted his head, lazily, the whirlpool slackening, to watch the gems of his own last breath rise up. But the water in his wake was empty of bubbles.

Still downwards he dropped, still aware. And now he saw that he alone dropped down a living man, for everywhere around him cascaded the dead sailors with huge ghastly pop eyes and bloated cheeks. For sure, the sea came and went in Zhirem's lungs, but from its fluid element was somehow distilled for him enough of gaseous breath that it sustained him. He breathed as a fish breathes, and as freely. Zhirem could not drown, not even that. He was proof even against ocean.

Then the old fear swept him and, coupled with it, the fear of where he was so helplessly going. And fearful was this area indeed to which he had been plunged, was yet plunging.

Like a stone flung into the abyss, thus he descended, but his momentum was gradually subdued rather than increased. It was more like a fall upwards, into space. But all was green, greener than greenness, though murky and full of inky insinuations, half-glimpsed shapes, and made startling by the abrupt flash of a million little bright fish, exploding across his

266

vision like sparks from a furnace or from his own staggering brain. . . .

Presently, however, the illumination of the sky was lost in the deepness of the water. After that, Zhirem fell through liquid pitch, and perceived only with his skin and nerves as glaucous denizens of that sphere bustled by, now and then with a fiery streak of eyes, seeing him but themselves unseen. Then again, this blackness was dissolved into a nebulous sight, lit by some source impossible to trace. It occurred to the falling man he had traveled a stupendous distance, and had entered another fabulous reach. Pillars of rock stretched up beyond him, and down where he must go. At first bald and scabbed with barnacles, they became lovelier in their lower terraces. Here they were forested with gigantic ferns, and spangled with minerals or obscure unprecious jewels. Among these towers and altars of drowned cliffs lay the remnants of the drowned cities of ancient lands, pylons and walls, where the black phantoms of enormous molluscs perched idly to preen each other, like vast crows upon the ruin.

Zhirem was cold beyond the numbing cold of the sea. The forests of the ocean caressed him with many-fingered hands as he slowly plunged between, but the fallen walls of men mocked him: they too had endured, as he now must, in this prison.

The ferns wrapped the dead sailors in their tendrils.

A silken scarf, with eyes of leaden flame, stole into the forest. It kissed the dead with its silver mouth, and sucked one, whole, within its belly.

Still Zhirem, a flung stone, slid downwards.

He passed the level of the ferns, the ruins and the great molluscs. He entered a level where the source of the faint luminescence which had been aiding his sight, became evident. Far, far below, as far from him as would the earth appear to a bird in flight, he beheld a shining solid of cool light caught among the tangled roots of the cliffs.

Softly the light diffused about Zhirem, changing the wicked dragon-blush of the sea, by melting stages, to the thinnest jade, while the light itself burned from coolness to warmth and a shade of color almost of rose, but a green rose.

A shell was set in the rock, a fan like ribbed porcelain, larger than a palace doorway, and this it was which glowed, as if a huge lamp stood the other side of it.

The lengthy fall of Zhirem was nearing its end. Amid the final strata of the rock he sank, toward the magical shell and its radiance. He marvelled, with an abject, dream-like wonder, at its beauty and its size. Nine times his own height was the last of his descent from the shell's apex to the floor of the sea. The sand, mercurial as powder, clouded up and furled him in.

And there he lay upon that floor of sand.

The whole of the ocean was above him, and seemed to press upon his very bones, as if it would crush him out against the rock. Zhirem's human senses rebelled suddenly and utterly, and, in a rush of terror, left him altogether.

Even after he had fainted, he continued to breathe the water, while to his quiescent body small creatures came and ate the remnants of his clothes, being unable to obtain his flesh.

3

He revived to an exquisite yet fearful sensation of being everywhere touched, stroked, teased, tickled, embraced, investigated. Unconscious, this attention had sensuously stirred him, but rousing, his instinct was to strike out wildly. Nevertheless, he remained passive, only opening his eyes, at which he heard a peculiar vibration in the water about him, almost a sound, not quite a sound.

He was frightened by what he saw, like drugged-dreams made real, amused also, that madman's amusement filling his brain till he laughed, the way he must now laugh beneath the sea, noiselessly and with pain.

A few of the tiny fish creatures yet lipped him with gentle toothless mouths. They had stripped him naked, quite defenseless, yet not defenseless, for his beauty had armored him in a way no clothing could have done. The beings who clustered around him, who had played with and fondled his body, were as capable of attempting to rend him and, on failing to rend, of hating him, which hatred might have damaged in more devious fashion than their claws and sharp teeth.

There were ten of them, and they were women, or at least, females. Shallow perfect breasts budded on their slender torsos, but the breasts were green and their tips a darker green, and their mouths so dark a green they were nearer black. Between these brackish lips showed the white dentition, unseparated, a single band of enamel. Their noses were almost flat, their nostrils wide; on either side of their delicately formed jaws were the petals of gills, continuously expanding and contracting. Their eyes were all one colour, like emeralds, the pupil a narrow horizontal slot. Their hair was the acid green of quinces. They had no lower limbs but the tails of sharks or whales, and mounted in them, like secret gray flowers, their vertical genitals. These maidens it was who had petted him, tongued him, if in lust or only inquisitiveness he could not decide. Their looks were innocent and merciless, yet they smiled.

His eye ranged beyond them, and made out others whose skin was amber and whose tails, slowly stirring the ocean's sand, were black. Breastless and male these others were. They carried long blades in their hands of honed metal, though the blades of their masculinity were sheathed and retracted in the manner of fish. Some of these males also held up lamps of translucent stuff burning with a waterproofed witch-fire. The light made a yellowish ring that spread from the great shell to encompass Zhirem and those who surrounded him.

He lifted one hand, quietly, to see what they would do.

Again he heard—or felt—the sonorous vibration in the water. He realized it was a form of speech, that his visitants were registering surprise. First, presumably, at his descent to their abode, secondly, that he lived and could move.

Then came a flurry, the sand gushed up, resettled. Another was beside him.

She kneeled by him, and she could kneel, for she had legs and feet. Neither was she naked, a whirling, sea-lifted garment clothed her, held at her waist with a broad belt of cold gems, while her arms were ringed with bangles of pale and phosphorescent electrum. Her skin was white, whiter than human skin but glowing and flawless, and if it had the faintest tinge of greenness in it, this vanished at her lips, which were rose-red, at the rose-pink edges of her rounded nails, on the rose-pink embossment of her two round breasts which gleamed through the fabric of her gown. For her eyes, they were human enough, oddly human considering the rest, large and blue and the lids gilded. Only her hair admitted the sea. That was a blue mixed with green. Strangely, the exact color of Zhirem's eyes.

Some time she gazed at him. He returned her gaze, unnerved, perplexed, actually not thinking her quite mortal. Then, with no modesty and no hestitation, she set her hand upon his loins, and stared at him without compunction, awaiting what he would do.

No sensuality remained in him at that moment, besides, her touch was like the touch of the sea itself, impersonal and alien.

He sat up and lifted her hand from him.

At once she nodded. She put her hand instead to her left ear, then showed to Zhirem a glimmering drop, a pearl. Before he could comprehend, she had reached forward and pressed this drop into the cavity of his own left ear. Immediately, her lips began to move, she spoke, and he heard her—not through the water, but softly inside his ear where the drop of nacre had lodged. What she said, however, conveyed nothing. It was language, but not any language of man he had ever heard.

Then she stopped speaking, leaned to him again and lightly tapped his mouth. He must speak, it seemed. He said:

"Your speech and mine, woman, will not mingle."

He heard his own voice, as he had heard hers, inside his head. She heard it too, and listened, and after that kneeled beside him silently, as if deep in thought. Then at last she spoke again, and he understood her, for she spoke his own tongue.

"Do not be discourteous to me," she said, "My father is a king here."

"I have been less discourteous to you, than you to me," he answered.

"If you mean that I set my hand upon your phallus, it was no discourtesy, but merely to ascertain if you were human. Generally, drowned men do not fall so far, and if they do, they are lifeless. Yet you live and seem a man. But since there are others in the sea who appear mortal and are rather less, I have tested you. For none are so prudent in the matter of their organs as humankind."

"That proved, how then do we hear and comprehend one another?"

"Through the magic of the pearl. For speech itself, there are many differing peoples who dwell beneath the sea. Of necessity we learn each other's languages, and also, for recreation, the tongues of men, for we are clever in such learning, and magicians."

"This I have been told."

"And this," said she, "you did not believe, till now you must."

"I ask only one thing," said Zhirem, "the means to regain the ocean's surface."

"What will you do there, that you are eager to return?"

Zhirem looked away from her. His heart became a stone. The sea-girl said to him: "The choice is not yours to make. You are in the kingdom of my father. He will decide your fate." And Zhirem was almost gladdened, in a wretched way, that he must dismiss hope of his escape to the nothing that waited him above. "How are you named?" she asked of him.

"Zhirem," he said.

"And I," she said, "the Princess Hhabaid, daughter of Hhabhezur the King of Sabhel."

Then she said she would not have him, a human, carried to her father's city naked as one of the shark-maidens or whale-men, who were beasts. A weird conveyance stood nearby that Zhirem had not noticed earlier, and from this was brought a robe—like velvet but not velvet—and Zhirem was clad in it.

"And why, princess, do you take such trouble with a human?" he inquired of her. "I am not of your tribe."

"The sea peoples come of human stock," Hhabaid replied. "In most particulars, you will observe, we are human. Though more cunning."

She instructed him to enter the conveyance, which was the image of a fish of dull green-gold. Hhabaid sat down in the mouth of it and he beside her. The whale-men lifted up a shadowy veil and revealed the team that were to draw the carriage, and which now started alert—a shoal of miniscule gilt-colored fry, each with a silken bit and caught in a silken net to bind them in the shafts of the golden fish. Hhabaid guided them by tweakings and twists of this net, but for motivation they required only the open-jawed golden monster at their backs, thinking it an enemy which pursued to eat them. Forever they were in flight from it and it forever behind them, till the safe veil was flung over the shoal, and it supposed itself in security and sank to feed and sleep—till the veil's next lifting, when again the awesome pursuit began. From this, more than anything else, Zhirem learned the people of the sea were cruel and callous, both with beasts, and as it must be, with men.

Indeed, Hhabaid now ordered the whale-men up into the higher waters to search for any bounty which had come down with the drowned ship. For this purpose they set their recurrent spell of mist and lightning to wreck vessels on the rocks above, and for this purpose, to search for treasure from the wreck, had this princess come from her city with her retinue, believing such activities sport. Instead she had found Zhirem. Better sport?

One of Hhabaid's attendants touched the shell with a

golden wand. Soundless, the shell folded together along all its ribs, a great fan for sure. When the way was clear through the rock, the gilded fry were permitted to dash forward.

4

The peoples of the sea were magicians. She had told him. It was a fact.

An artificial sun burned over the city of Sabhel, giving it warmth, illumination and color. It was a globe of sorcerous glass, vivid with the miraculous fires that blazed within it. Thirty silver chains secured it to the cliffs that walled in the city, and in the glare and smoulder of it the water was the sunny yellow-green of canaries.

Fish like rubies, opals and jades flocked through the sea-sky of Sabhel to bask in the radiance of the glass sun. Unusual plants resembling marine palms, giant tamarisks and cloud-haired cedars soared toward the heat and light of it, their stems wound with vines, sea weeds and yawning exotic flowers. Red orchids set flame to the sands and devoured the fish which came to perch on them.

The city of Sabhel was something like the cities of earth, but how bizarre. Its colossal towers, pagodas and domes of polished red coral were fifty stories high or more, and pierced like needles by a thousand gates and archways and apertures like windows, their frames set with turquoise. But there were no staircases in Sabhel, for none had need of them, who could swim up or down at will through the water-air.

The carriage of the Princess Hhabaid rushed through the water midway between the tower tops and the flower-grown floor, or street, of the city. At other levels, above or below them, similar conveyances raced behind their permanently terrified teams.

The palace of Hhabhezur was also of polished scarlet coral, but decorated with gold scales, smelted, so the story went, from the gold sunk with ten thousand ships. A rank of crystal pillars supported the porch of the palace, which was some seventy feet up from the "street." In each of these pillars were embedded the fossilized figments of the ocean, marvelous shells, sea dragons, surreal vegetation.

Hhabaid's carriage drove within the palace. Here she checked their career by use of the net and bits, and ordered her attendants by gesture to veil the team of fry and stable them. She then conducted Zhirem to a vast chamber without a ceiling. All about, gold pipes sent up into the water a constant stream of perfumed dye of several colors, which subtly patterned and scented the sea inside the room. Near the room's farther end was an enormous closed crystal tank mounted on four bronze turtles. In this tank Zhirem was amazed to see birds flying about among the flowers and foliage of dry land. A bubbling at the tank's four corners and a hissing in and out at the mouths of the bronze turtles, gave some idea of an apparatus for drawing air from water—even as his own lungs and the lungs of his hostess-captor were doing. He assumed the closed tank to be filled with the gases of earth, and that the birds flew there as, in a room in the world above, fish might swim in a pool.

The king entered, Hhabhezur. He was another proof that, though they preyed upon men, his people were humanly descended, for he showed signs of age, and his wickedness was drawn in lines about his mouth. For coloring he was not exactly of his daughter's shade but swarthier, and his hair blue-sable, and all of him weighted with his stolen gold and his robes thick with it. Courtiers followed him, blue-haired and blue-eyed they were, and two or three brought their hunting dogs with them, slim blue swordfish on leashes.

Hhabaid spoke to her father in the tongue of Sabhel. That she had sent word before her of the mysterious stranger was obvious.

"I have begged my father's clemency on your behalf," she said through the pearl in Zhirem's ear.

"That is kind of you, madam. What is my offense?"

"Why, coming here," she answered.

"Let me eradicate my offense by departing."

"Be still," she said. "I'll tell them you are a brother to us since, in our way, you can breathe beneath the sea. Otherwise they would slay you."

"Let them try to slay me."

She did not, as another would have, a human woman, dismiss this as a boast of strength or valor. She paid it heed, and turning swiftly to her father, clearly drew attention to Zhirem's challenge. The king replied to her, and at this, Hhabid drew from her gemmed belt a little dagger. She took Zhirem's arm, and attempted to drive the blade, with the sluggish motion of any violence under water, into Zhirem's arm—but the dagger broke in two pieces. For Zhirem, he felt, in an unexpected burst and for the first time, power and

273

an arrogant joy in the thing which protected him. He grinned at the aging king, and said to Hhabaid:

"Explain to your father, I am a magician too."

"He knows it."

The king spoke then, in Zhirem's own language, showing he had grasped all their interchange.

"Though you utter only the vocabulary of the land, yet I believe you are of a cousin country beneath the sea. Since you have persisted in pretending otherwise, we conclude it is some un-friend of ours. Nor may we kill you, it appears. But reckon on this, we shall not let you go."

"Then let him be my prisoner, father," said Hhabaid. "I took him and he is mine by right. Then let us send for ransom for him to our neighbours, and so discover his kindred. Meantime, he shall serve me."

The king laughed at her, a short laughter, for to laugh under the sea was a painful and stupid exercise only rarely indulged.

"Whatever you could have him labor at," said the king, in Zhirem's tongue so he might not miss nothing, "make him toil earnestly, whether upright or on his belly."

The courtiers laughed, either at the jest or to please the king with their discomfort. Hhabaid blushed, a blush like a rosy smoke that pushed through her cheeks and throat and so away. But she said coolly in spite of that: "I do not obey you in everything, my father."

She dwelt in apartments of turquoise. In the midst of them was a courtyard with a garden in it. Living hedges of tethered green fish milled sedately. Tall seaweeds offered shade from the sun, and when the sun grew dim, (to simulate "night"), to the pallor of a golden moon, then shell lamps were lit.

One of the green-haired fish girls was lighting these lamps as Hhabaid drew Zhirem into this garden. Harps stood on the sandy walks so the tides should strike them as they gushed through. An octopus in a cage of orichalc glared, but his ink sacs had been amputated, he could not show his absolute hatred.

"Keep no note of my father's jest," said Hhabaid. "You are my hostage, and I retain you for ransom. But you may take your pleasure with these slaves if you wish. I have heard men desire them very much, excited by their tails. But they are a degenerate race," she added, "dumb and witless. Our ancestors bred them for amusement, mating their own

274

women with the beasts of the sea, with sharks, whales, dolphins, serpents and the great fish of the deep."

"I do not want these half-women," said Zhirem. "But your technology confounds me. If I desire anything, it is to learn your magic."

"Will you teach me then, the trick of yours?" she demanded, "that knives may break on *my* flesh?"

"Surely I will," Zhirem said.

"You lie," she said.

"And so do you," said he, "but it shall rest for now."

She stared at him haughtily. Barred from much laughter, they were not a humorous folk, the people of the sea.

"There is a room here, adjoining the courtyard, where you may sleep," she said.

"Will you not cage me too?" he asked, glancing at the octopus.

"If I could, I should. But you cannot be bound, for no force can be used against you."

She went away, her slave attendants following.

All movement beneath the ocean was graceful, but hers exceptionally so. He was already accustomed to the element, its constant laving of his skin; his terror had left him and curiosity remained. Goalless, he had found a goal, and no small one: to gain the magic of Sabhel. Hhabaid would help him to that goal. He had seen into her eyes. Her eyes held what the eyes of Simmu had given freely. Thinking of her loveliness, scarcely concealed with the floating gown, tensed him to a desire that now warmed him, made him intoxicated and eager. Old guilts, old anguish had no place in this lower world. Zhirem had left himself behind among the split timbers of the broken ship. So it seemed to him. In a measure, so it was.

Some days passed, counted by the flaring and dimming of the glass sun. Zhirem walked about the garden courtyard, or through those by-ways of the princess's apartments that were not kept locked against him. The courtyard had a roof of crystal vanes, which presently were shut that he might not escape into the outer environs of the city.

Rich clothes were brought to Zhirem. Strange food was brought, weird in appearance, of weird taste and constructed weirdly, always upon skewers or in stoppered vessels that it might not float away. He became accustomed to drinking the peculiar wines of Sabhel through straws of fluted jade, and to the whizzing of roast fish-meats about the garden should he let go of them.

275

Sometimes a brazen bell would boom from a cupola of the city. He could not guess its function, other than to alarm shipping overhead. He did not question the tailed slaves who waited on him, for they appeared to have neither speech nor brain, and did only as their mistress instructed them. And her instructions to them seemed often to have been eccentric. They would bring him food less appetizing even than usual, or else poisons—he knew them for that, for their nature was obvious enough, though he drank them down and took no ill from them. Indeed he constantly must swallow the salt sea itself, nor did it harm him. On one occasion, some of the ocean-tailed slave men rushed in and attempted to seize him and could not. On another, the furious octopus was let loose from its cage, and finding Zhirem ineligible to attack, slew several of the hapless slaves, whose uneaten bodies were then left long hours to rot in Zhirem's vicinity, before the octopus was subdued and the grisly debris removed. Yet again, one sun-dim, or night, Zhirem awoke from the couch Hhabaid had provided, and to which, since any sudden rapid movement might dislodge him, he must secure himself by means of loose silken straps, to find three of the fish-maidens strapped in with him. These then commenced toying with him in such a fashion that his lust became unbearable and agonizing, for he could not bring himself to penetrate their foreign though mammalian orifices. From all these events, and others, Zhirem concluded he was being put to the test and constantly observed, probably only by his captrix.

One dawn, or sun-bright, he found a table of books laid out for him. The pages were of white shark skin, and not written on in the way of the books of dry land. The words were embroidered in black silk, and then each page lacquered with a clear glaze to protect it from the water. Of these interesting volumes, only two were in land tongues, which Zhirem recognized from his childhood tutoring in the yellow temple. These two he accordingly began to read. Both concerned legends of the ocean kingdoms, and he concluded both had been copied from human tomes and in the original languages, to titillate the multi-lingual sea people. Having nothing better to distract him, Zhirem was diverted by reading. Imagine then his irritation when, the following sun-bright, he discovered the two books had been removed, and only those left which he could not dicipher.

Later, a while after the sounding of the brazen bell, a figure entered, veiled in jet black to the ankles, for ankles she had, and two feet below them.

"The princess has sent me to teach you the tongue of Sabhel," declared the vision. Zhirem could tell nothing from the voice, for the magic pearls which enabled hearing under the sea, (the better, now one resided in each of his ears,) yet distorted all timbre and nuance. However, the edge of the veil was weighted with gold nuggets to prevent its floating up; the nails of the white feet were rosy and the toes ringed with jewels. From this he knew it was none other than Hhabaid herself, trusting to disguise.

She had been spying on him a huge time, through chinks in the walls and magnifying glasses in the overlooking towers. He had allowed her the game, and did not confront her now.

Thus, the language lesson began and, finding him swift to learn, she seemed inclined to prolong it, and so they continued till the next bell sounded. At that, he inquired what the bell might portend.

"It is the Prayer of Sabhel," answered the veiled Hhabaid.

"A call to prayer?"

"Indeed not. We do not demean ourselves by praying in person to the gods, who long since dismissed our people. But out of respect for the gods, if not love, the bell rings. The message of the bell is this: We do not forget heaven, though heaven forgets us."

"And how did the gods anger you?"

"I see you do not credit that the gods exist. This is unwise. Centuries ago, and centuries before that, my race lived on the land, and they forgot the gods were above them. The gods then grew peevish, and opened the enormous valves that hold back the rain. One year the rain fell to the earth. The rivers and the seas overflowed. The whole world was flooded to its four corners, and nearly all men perished—save for the magicians. A few survived in curious boats, but others discovered methods, through their spells and sorceries, of existing under water. And these were my people, who became eventually so prosperous and content in their submarine cities that they disdained to leave them, decades after when the great flood was drained. How idiotic then the gods must have looked. And we are the sea people, that landsmen fear. We rule the waters, and no sorcerer, however sagacious, has jurisdiction in our country. Even the Prince of Demons must be courteous with us."

"Must he so?" mused Zhirem somberly.

"So he must."

277

The veiled and "unknown" lady visited frequently after that. He never accused her of her identity, and she became easy in his company, teaching him intelligently and well, and now and then, taking small liberties, such as to stroke his hair or press his hand. Otherwise, the testing ceased. Soon he could converse with her in her native language most fluently, at which she brought him a variety of the books of her people, and only retrieved them when they had been read. Yet, though the works were fascinating, they gave up no sorcery to him.

"I see that your mind is hungry for knowledge," said the veiled Hhabaid one early sun-bright. "Indeed, I suppose it to have been starved. Now admit to me, Zhirem, are you not of my people? Your wits are as quick as ours and you can live in the sea. What extra proof is needed?"

"Perhaps," lied Zhirem cautiously, "I am some foundling of your race?" He had sensibly lost the habit of laughter here, or he would have laughed, thinking of the desert where he had been born, miles from any sea.

"This may be so. Then you are entitled to acquaintance with our customs."

"With your magic, too. I recall, I mentioned my wish to learn these arts. But, of course, I petitioned your mistress, Hhabaid."

"Oh, she will not remember," said the veiled Hhabaid, "for she is cloddishly stupid and has no memory."

Her coyness and the transparent trap she set by reviling herself as another, might have been infuriating in someone else, but in her it had a ridiculous half-acid charm, as if she mocked herself. As she elaborated, he believed that she did, and certain of the faults she stressed might be real ones which she owned she had.

"I did not form that opinion," murmured Zhirem.

"Did you not? I will speak frankly. She cares nothing save for her own pleasures."

"I believed she took some pleasures in me."

The veiled Hhabaid was not such a liar that she denied it.

"I think she does. But she is fickle, rash and intemperate. And there could be no sweetness for you in her attentions. She is so dull and plain."

"Then I confess my unwisdom, for I thought her beautiful."

A pause. Then: "Did you so? With her hair like rags, her round eyes, her shortness of stature—no, she is not worth looking at."

"I should find it hard to look at any other thing, were she with me. In fact, I yearn for the moment when I may see her again."

Hhabaid did not resist this potent cue.

"You may see her directly," she said, "for here she is!" And she lifted up the veil and tossed it aside to swirl about the garden and affright the fish hedges.

She appeared very lovely, vulnerable, proud and alluring. He had not the pedantry to undeceive her. Like many intellectually astute persons, she was in some respects a perfect fool, which struck him, in his desire and entertainment, as delightful.

"Why, madam," he gently said, "you amaze me. Was it just, to play such a trick on me?"

"No," said Hhabaid, "but neither am I just. The catalog of my faults, as I have said, is long."

Zhirem went to her and kissed her brow, her lips, her throat, and would have proceeded in this thrilling and descending mode, but she stayed him with both hands.

"The reward for your cleverness at lessons is not Hhabaid," she told him, though her eyes brimmed with surrender.

"What other recompense is worth anything?"

"To be instructed in the magic of the sea folk."

"Certainly, that is not worthless."

"Nor safe," said she. "The ancient laws of the cities of the sea forbid that any landsman be tutored in our sorcery. But with you I make exception, since I reckon you are obliquely kindred to us. Also because my father, who was disappointed that none paid your ransom, now turns impatient that you are kept as my guest here. He bids me make haste and be done with you. He will be rid of you."

"I cannot be taken or slain," said Zhirem, making a prisoner of her by her blue-green hair, that color of his own eyes, and kissing her once more.

"Oh, not slain perhaps, but Sabhel contains a million traps and snares, harmless in themselves yet unbreakable, which, unwittingly, you might be drawn into. Then he can keep you locked away in some black place forever, without food or joy of any sort, and I shall not dare to free you, for Hhabhezur is terrible in his wrath."

"It is not love you owe your father, then, but fear."

"My duty I owe him," Hhabaid replied, but Zhirem supposed it was as he had said. "Now, let me go, and I will take you to that dreadful spot where you shall learn the magecraft of Sabhel."

279

A hidden way beneath a hidden door in a secretive room of Hhabaid's apartments. Downwards, and into inky gloom, Hhabaid moving before him, the feet of neither touching any floor, swimming through the ink, and then toward a pallid glare. At length, a pair of gates of heavy gold, lit by lamps of witch-fire, burned dully out of the murk. No bolt to these gates, but roped about them, holding both their leaves together, a serpent black as oil with a great flat head, on which were enamelled, in the tongue of Sabhel, the words: *Who would pass me?*

Hhabaid instantly swam to the serpent and set her fingers between its serrated jaws. At her touch—or taste—it immediately slid from the gate, one side of which folded open.

"Go before me," Hhabaid told Zhirem, and he swam before her through the gate; at which she took her fingers from the creature's jaws and followed him. The gate swung shut of its own volition and the serpent coiled about it once more.

Beyond the gates of gold stretched an avenue of granite pillars, ringed with gold and with tall lamps hanging down from them, giving out an eerie cold light. Hhabaid led Zhirem between the pillars and they came into a vast hall, also coldly blazing with lamps, bright enough that everything might be seen.

It was a hall of death. A hundred kings were seated there on chairs of green bronze. Gold footstools supported their feet, and gold lay heavily on their shoulders and arms. The flesh had long deserted them but they had not gone to bones, for the sea and its organisms had changed them into statues of coral, red and pink and white.

"We are long lived, but at decease, our kings are brought to this hall. Each of the lords of Sabhel are seated here, and will be seated here," said Hhabaid, as she and Zhirem drifted between the chairs. "It is our most absolute custom, for then our kings may never totally die, but become one with the substance of the city. It is all they have of obsequies, for we possess small religion, having rejected the patronage of the gods."

At the end of the massive hall stood another obstruction, a massive door of stone. It had no visible guardian, but when Hhabaid approached it, it rumbled like distant thunder. Then

Hhabaid kissed the door, and it slowly opened, again into a blackness.

No sooner had they entered there, than the door ponderously closed, with a vibration that set the water humming.

"Whatever occurs now," said Hhabaid, "do not falter, but press on after me."

"So I will," said Zhirem.

A moment more, and they were in a jungle of heaving slippery giant weeds, which wrapped about them, painless but vehement to distract. And through these weeds, directly in their path, appeared a mighty glowing face, large as the door had been, which grimaced and snarled, and whose pointed teeth dripped with slime. Straight at this face Hhabaid launched herself, and vanished in the ghastly mouth. Zhirem following her fast, caught his breath at the stench of that aperture, which abruptly enveloped him, and threatened to render him unconscious. But Hhabaid darted ahead, and Zhirem kept pace with her.

They swam, it seemed, through the cavern of the monstrosity's obnoxious mouth, and presently, far worse, down its throat, a lightless stinking plunge toward a bubbling pit—the stomach—from which gases rose impossible to inhale. But just as Zhirem felt himself stifled, the effluvia dispersed and the whole horror disappeared. Hhabaid and Zhirem had thrust through into a silver cave of faint-shining water. Nothing was there save at its farthest back, where stood a man-size robed image of red metal, now almost entirely crystallized to the green rust of verdigris.

Hhabaid went to this image, and setting her hands on its shoulders, raised herself to the height of its mouth, into which she blew.

Instantly the image responded by drawing in a breath of its own, and bubbles rushed from its nostrils and ears. Its verdigris eyes swivelled to look this way and that, and then it spoke.

"Behold me, I am your mentor," the image said. "Who would learn of me, then enter me."

At which it split entirely in half, dividing exactly from the crown to the hem of its robe. Within, the case was yet the shape of a man, just roomy enough another man might enter and stand there.

"Have no fear," said Hhabaid. "Obey, and grow wise. Or, if you are a coward, we can return."

But Zhirem advanced to the image case and stepped into it,

281

no doubt with misgiving, but not to be deterred. Then the image closed again, confining him in the dark in that small man-size piece of sea.

For a moment or two, inside the man of verdigris, Zhirem had pause to wonder and be troubled. Then his mind was swept from him. For in the brain box of the image had been stored the art and science of a thousand magicians, maybe more, the genius of Sabhel.

A year became a second there. Yet, in some manner, still it was a year.

It seemed he saw a younger world whose mountains touched the sky. It seemed he saw the flood cast everything down, wash away mountains and sky, and mankind with them. Then came the dream of magic, in which it appeared to him he moved and lived in the bodies of others, felt their pain and glory, and knew their heartache and ambition.

Their cruelty and their pride etched deep channels into his own latent cruelty and his own dormant pride. His skull sang. He practiced thaumaturgy, necromancy, cast glamour, bane, fascination, uttered incantation, summoned elementals and sent them packing. His fingers cracked. He sewed upon parchments, in great books; chiselled in marble and in the sand itself runes of power and the mathematics of destiny. It came to him sure as a fire which melted and a mould which reformed, an alteration of his spirit and his heart, or perhaps only a finding. And what he found was his own wickedness, the dark of his soul, which all souls possess. And he clung to it, embraced it, like one upright pillar in a tumbled house, while the motives of the wicked who had preceded him filled him, and their skills. He was crammed with their knowledge, arcane and marvelous. The philtres mixed under his own hands, the stones leapt before his own will. A thousand or more had been before him and now gave up to him all they had.

The brain of some, in the chamber of the image, had burst, and they had come forth madmen, or slumped forth dead. But when the two halves of the verdigris cracked wide to let him go, Zhirem came forth a magician.

Hhabaid paled when she saw him, paler than she had been from watching in the cave. She had not expected the cabinet of the image to destroy Zhirem, but neither had she expected quite what she perceived in him now. Something behind his face, itself unseen, gave his expression new accents. She had hoped for his love. His appearance warned her from her hope, though she did not heed the warning.

"How you are changed," she said.

"How I am changed. Your people are clever to withhold such learning."

"Many hours have passed," said Hhabaid.

"You have betrayed your city," said Zhirem, "for I might take it now, if I wished."

"No," she said, "for you are not the only magician in Sabhel." But she turned and began to swim from the cave, and soon he followed her. He did not smile. His look was inward, brooding, cold and vital.

No illusory guardian stood up on this occasion, as they went from that place. The tall weeds shrank aside, the stone door gave smoothly. In the hall of dead kings, the corals sat impassive.

"I might shatter them, these relics of Sabhel which have such worth."

Hhabaid said nothing, but she swam more quickly.

They returned through the avenue of pillars to the gates of gold. There the serpent roped, this first and last sentry yet barring their exit.

"You watched me, and may now do the same as I to hold him," said Hhabaid.

But Zhirem went to the gates and tore the serpent from them. At once the creature swelled and enlarged, rearing up in the murky water with its razor jaws clashing and its eyes on fire. But Zhirem spoke one word of Sabhel-the-Sorcerous which had to do with these circumstances, and the serpent broke into fragments like round black coins, that exploded in all directions into the gloom beyond the lamps. Only its eyes remained intact, but presently went out in death.

The golden gates swung idly. Hhabaid said:

"By such a deed you have earned the hate of Sabhel. Why did you do it, when to pass without violence was so easy?"

"To know myself," Zhirem said, "as now I am."

"Sorcery is a strong wine, and you are drunk on it."

"Do not anticipate I shall sober."

Once through the dismal water, they re-entered Hhabaid's apartments via the hidden way.

Hhabaid left his side immediately, and he made no move to prevent her. Instead he sought the familiar annex of the courtyard, and lay down there as if to sleep, but sleep he

283

did not. The effect of his tutoring still splashed and glittered, dazzled and stormed through his thoughts.

The city darkened to sun-dim, the sun faded to a moon. Zhirem rose and drank the fish-colored wine of Sabhel. He went next to the princess's library and there took down various books and scanned their pages, discovering he could read more languages than formerly, not merely that of Sabhel. Some pages, even, he retained a dim memory of dictating himself—or rather of former magicians dictating them, whose recollections he had pilfered in the image-case. But such intimate associations were leaving him. Only their personal arrogance, the inspiration of his, remained, the cruel callousness of the sea people.

He knew Hhabaid awaited him, and that this time few locks could stay him. Indeed, when he tried her doors, she had not locked them against him, even those of the bedchamber, partly from love, partly from pride, knowing he could break in on her.

But she stared at him, and twisted nervously between her fingers a long veil of golden stuff.

As he came nearer, she said: "I loved you from the moment I set eyes on you. But I would not lie with you. You have the ability to get free of the city now. I advise you, Zhirem, to be gone."

"Another veil?" he asked her, plucking the golden gauze from her hands. "I knew you in the black one well enough. Your veiled words are as plain. Do you fear me?"

"You are like my father now," she said, "like all the lords who step out, magicians, from the image case. I did not think this change would be so in you, but in you it is yet stronger and more terrible. Yes, I fear you, but it is my love bids you fly Sabhel."

"Let your love bid me to other things," he said.

And he drew her against him, and wrapped the veil about her waist and his two or three times, and tied the gauze and so bound them together, that even the tides of the water should not separate them. Then with one arm and hand he bound her further, and with the other peeled from her breasts the gemmed bodice, and the cobwebbed silk that clouded her thighs he tore loose in handfuls.

She shut her eyes, but soon a wild passion overcame her, and fiercer even than he, she clawed the garments from his shoulders and clung to him and softly cried her love to him and sank her teeth in him at length, savage as if she would devour him, forgetting her fear and all things save his flesh.

284

So they turned, ceaselessly winding about each other, in the green ocean-air of the room, in slow whirling motions appearing almost aimless, till she seized with her hands the jewelled bed post above and roping Zhirem instead with her lower limbs, slid her narrow feet down the length of his back. He thrust home through the ring into the depths of her, and the light became a redness and the silence a sound. To laugh under the sea brought pain and a bursting in the lungs, to love under the sea, worse than all laughter, brought a noose which tightened at the throat of each, yet seemed, in some anomalous way, to increase pleasure.

The hearts of both thundered, galloped, their eyes blackened and silver stars cascaded through their vision as if galaxies were born of the action of their loins, which in curious sort so resembled the action of the pestle within the bowl, which can create fire. And as they mounted, through waves of heat and sensation, into an even more stifled blindness, an even more brilliant fire, death seemed to brush them, then to clutch them, grinding them out upon each other. The fire was struck suddenly. The woman flared up, her body became a whirlpool, her hands gouged the fragile minerals in the post. Zhirem shook from his eyes sufficient of the blood-darkness to glimpse her face, almost as beautiful, demented and terrible as a spell, as a wickedness, but not quite, before the blaze leapt from the tinder of her body into his. The ceiling seemed to crash upon them. Their fires were extinguished in a blackness resembling a faint. In the black, if he had needed to, he could recall another time when he had known that love was not enough, as now he knew it.

Dimly, through their separating emptied state, there came to them the vibration of doors thrown back, and the upheaval and rocking of the water which this caused.

King Hhabhezur's jest had been that his daughter should use Zhirem in her bed, and that he should be made to "toil earnestly." But in his perverse reason, either Hhabhezur had not reckoned she would—or else he had built upon the belief she might, for now he entered in wrath, making their coupling his excuse.

"That a king's daughter should play thus with vile flotsam not of our people, sub-stock of some damned and nameless race—"

Hhabaid, releasing Zhirem and released, drew round herself the gold veil which had bound them, hiding herself with anger and shame from the stare of the king, of his escort of shark-tailed soldiers and that of two or three courtiers poised in the rear.

"I did no more than I was told."

"Far in excess, rash minx. For this man——"

"For this man," said she, "beware. Not only is he invulnerable. He has arts to match your own."

The king's face became terrible, his evil nature rising to the surface of his skin like the blood.

"What have you done, sluttish daughter?"

"She took me visiting the man of verdigris," said Zhirem. "He has lessoned me."

At once the king raised his hand, and from it shot a spinning flax that braided itself about Zhirem, far enough from his body that his invulnerability did not interfere with it, near enough to secure him—but only for an instant. Zhirem, too, had raised his hand. The flax unravelled, melted, and out of it flew a bolt of steely radiance. The king shouted. A shield of brass appeared before him, deflecting the bolt, but on every side the shark-men sizzled, writhed in grotesque contortions, floated calmly—lifeless. (Beyond them, unharmed but appalled, the courtiers fled.)

And now the brass shield shivered, and was a brassy urn, tall as the figure of Hhabhezur the king, which abruptly it contained.

"You would have slain me if you could," said Zhirem. "Now your daughter shall rule in Sabhel." He spoke three words.

In the brass urn, Hhabhezur screamed. Bubbles gushed from the mouth of the urn, then a crimson fluid. Last, a spear rose up from the mouth of the urn, crimson all its length, but it vanished swiftly.

"You will not weep, Hhabaid," said Zhirem. "You owed him duty but no love."

"I will not weep," said she in a very little voice, her face turned from him, "because the sea people, whose eyes are ever full of the salt sea, have no tears of their own to shed. But kill you did not have to. Do you mean to be the king of Sabhel?"

"Your coral city is nothing to me," Zhirem said.

"And I am nothing to you, that you will leave me here."

"Our commerce is done," said Zhirem, "as much as either expected of it."

"Your commerce, perhaps, not mine."

They regarded each other unlikingly. She had stayed his

appetite, hers had been increased. Maybe the souring of romance would not have come this swiftly to them, if violence and shock had not forced the pace. Left to itself, love might have lingered a few hours more.

"I want no woman with me," Zhirem said, "but I thank you for investing me with a magician's powers, which I shall use in the world above."

"Expect no joy there. I curse you. And all Sabhel will lay its curse on you, for the murder of my father, the king."

"Oh, worse merely than murder," he said.

"What will you do?"

"He is my safe conduct through your city of traps. You advised me excellently, Hhabaid."

The brass urn had become instead a cage. Zhirem moved about it. He sealed it with magic. He ensured that none save he could take Hhabhezur from it. Zhirem pulled the ends of the king's hair through the mesh of the cage, and knotted them in his fist.

"This is his state. So I will carry him."

"We are not a tender people," she said, "but you make soft babies of us."

"I surprise myself," he said. "But I was promised to wickedness long ago. The dogs have caught me up at last, the hounds of the demons."

"Truly I will curse you, if you do this."

"Curse me then. I will, for my part, remember only your sweetness and your gifts."

He left her, dragging Hhabhezur in the cage of brass.

Hhabaid tore in pieces the veil, she who could not weep, next tore her hair, as if to complement her heart, which was torn already.

6

An ominous quiet lay over the city as Zhirem, hauling the cage by the king's hair, emerged between the upper towers of the palace into the rich canary-yellow water of late sunbright. A burnished red panoply, the roofs and domes and minarets, set amid their seaweed gardens, sank below. Neither citizen nor slave threaded between the fantastic arches, no carriages dashed along the thoroughfares. The stillness was that of a cat about to spring—Sabhel had been quickly alerted, as Zhirem had guessed it must be. Hhabaid's doing or that of the fleeing lords of Hhabhezur's court.

When he had risen higher yet, higher even than the high cupola where hung the disdainful prayer-bell of the city, a gushing up behind him, like a black smoke, caught his eye. It was some hundred of the shark-men soldiers, bringing nets to cast about him and spears tipped with the white stings of submarine creatures to aim uselessly at him. After these, the blue-haired lords were riding in gold contraptions strapped on the paved backs of bleak-eyed giant turtles.

Shouts and challenges blurred through the hearing-pearls inside the ears of Zhirem. The tailed slaves drew closer, flung their nets, jabbed with their spears—the spears shattered and the nets dissolved.

Zhirem paused. He showed the lords the trophy in the brass cage.

"Have you not yet learned I am invulnerable? And now I have your magic, what use are any of your tricks?"

The lords frowned. The turtles grinned on their golden bits, with no amusement.

"Then give us our king, whom you have slain."

"No. He is my final safeguard."

"We must have his body—he must sit in the stone hall, where the sea remakes men as coral. It is our only religion, our covenant with eternity."

And one, less arrogant than the rest, said quietly:

"You do not need Hhabhezur's flesh. We will give you safe conduct if we must. Besides, what have you to fear from us, self-protected as you are? I beg you, let go the cage."

But Zhirem, trusting them little, but mostly out of perverse humor in seeing their despair, paid no heed.

A great distance they pursued him, however. Beyond the city and among the groves of snakelike palms where the orchids bled upon the sands and sucked in the fishes alighting on their petals. But though the lords pursued, they were powerless, and they knew it.

They reached the huge shell gate that led from Sabhel.

Here, once more, Zhirem halted briefly. He joked with the lords of Sabhel, telling them the water beyond the gate was too cheerless to please them and that they should follow no more.

"I will make this pact with you," said Zhirem, "that when I am secure on dry land, I will send the body of Hhabhezur back to you. But if you trouble me further, I will destroy it.

To cement the bargain, I will accept Hhabhezur's ransom in advance."

Then he smiled at their grimness, and he asked them for their rings of gold, their jeweled collars, their armlets of orichalc and their electrum daggers set with emeralds in sheaths of indigo sharkskin. These items he slung in his cloak, and as he did, his memory stirred like the water, bringing old stale visions which suddenly pleased him with their irony—a young priest in a yellow garment, who healed the sick and refused their coins, who put the silver torque his temple gave him in the hands of a crippled farmer. A youth presently falsely accused of the theft of a silver cup to pay a harlot. . . .

Zhirem struck the shell, and uttered magic to it.

The shell folded back along its ribs. The icy darkness of ocean appeared, out of the range and glow of the glass sun.

Zhirem passed through with his heavy cloak and the heavy cage, and shut the shell gate behind him, and bound it with a seal of closure that it might take the lords of Sabhel some days to unravel.

In the pitch black then, three or four miles from the gate, Zhirem evolved a light, the witch-fire he had learned how to summon. And by its glare, he summoned other things.

The black molluscs came at his spell, and bore him upwards between the rocky piers, through the rubber-fingered forests, by the drowned citadels of men which he mocked in his turn: You must endure, but I ascend. On a pillar of crumbling marble, he sorcerously burnt his name, to leave his brand there in the sea, the things a boy would do, yet, when he did it, not quite that. And the letters of his name were altered; the last symbol become that which then the human magician took, so he was no longer Zhirem, but Zhirek.

Higher, where the sea turned the shade of a green shadow, he called the sharks to him, and they carried him and his burdens up onto the world of the sea's surface, and later, to the shores of the dry land.

7

He slept that night on the cold shore, but it was not cold to him. He could summon the earth's fires, too, and brought one to light and warm him. A tent he made, out of night air it

289

seemed, black velvet. Just within the door, Hhabhezur looked with his dead eyes, propped inside the brassy cage. Already, fish-king, he stank, or would have, if the arts of Zhirek the magician had not outlawed the stink with dark and fragrant gums burned in the fire. All these luxuries were to hand for a magician for, in those days, there was little the true magician could not compass.

Zhirek gazed at Hhabhezur.

"You have what I may not have," said Zhirek, "death. But I do not want death now."

Yet the congealed eyes of Hhabhezur were unanswerable, and they seemed to say: This door you cannot breach, this luxury you cannot summon. Death does not obey Zhirek. However weary Zhirek shall become of the desert of life, this cool drink may not be his, for centuries, or more.

"You are putrid, king," Zhirek told the dead.

The dead eyes glowed from the fire:

Your gaze must fall down before mine.

Zhirek stretched out to sleep on velvet. He would have disdained this couch in the days of his priesthood. He dreamed of women, all the forbidden women he had been denied and warned from enjoying. Golden and pale and cinnamon and amber. They lay with him, but at the summit of his ecstasy a whisper would say to him: *Love is not enough.* And when he turned restlessly, another whisper: *Nor life.* And, near dawn, the third: *Neither sorcery.* But, being now wise and educated, he forgot.

When he woke, the sun was high. The flesh fell from the body of the corpse like azure leaves. Zhirek, with a dagger from Sabhel, smote loose the left great toe of the king, which was now a bone.

Outside, the sea boiled on the beach, shot with translucent colors, stormy, though the sky was clear.

Zhirek waded out a short distance. He tossed the bone to the sea.

"I promised you his return," he murmured. "I did not stipulate the fashion in which he should come."

He walked some days, along the coast. This was not the land he had journeyed out from in the pirate's ship; another country. He walked it barefoot. He had never worn shoes since he was a child. (Soon it would be thought his affectation; since Zhirek was so powerful, surely he need not lack for shoes.) No longer did he drag the cage of brass with the

290

putrefying king in it. Zhirek had equipped the cage with legs. It, too, walked.

Three times, on the fifth day, Zhirek passed small villages on the sea's brink, where the narrow fishing boats were drawn up on the shore, for the sea was rough and uncertain, and the fish grown shy.

At the first place, the men who sat on the pebble-scaled beach got up and ran headlong from the walking dark one with the brass cage of death walking behind him. At the second village, a man entreated him: "You are clearly a mage. Tell us how long this weather will keep us from the sea, for our woman and our children starve—"

"I will bring you fish," said Zhirek. And he spoke to the sea and a wide comber rolled in on the beach and left there some twenty fish flopping and gasping. The fishermen were amazed, for no land magician they had ever heard of had power over the sea or its creatures. Yet Zhirek, who had learned so much of the sea lord's magic, mocked the fishermen, for when they lay hands on this unexpected catch to take it up, a second comber smashed on the shore, soaking the men, their nets and their craft, and plucking from the shale and from their fingers every one of the fish. Zhirek stood and watched it with a baleful expressionlessness.

The fishermen cursed him in fear and anger. A man, more angry than the rest, flung a stone, which of course shattered uselessly on the pebbles at Zhirek's feet. But Zhirek said words to the seething ocean, and then to the man he said: "When next you venture onto the sea, your boat will go down and you with it."

None answered, for they all believed him.

The third village was more prosperous. Evening was settling like a broad-winged bird upon the water. A tavern with yellow lights, and loud song coming from its doors, stood on the cliff path that led from the shore. Zhirek entered the tavern, the cage keeping pace, and silence fell and even the lamps fluttered as if they were afraid.

"Bring me wine and meat," said Zhirek, and when it was brought, he ate and drank in that old listless way of his. The horrid cage lurked in the shadow, but the odor of its corruption—faint now, for little remained of Hhabhezur's flesh—stole about the room and turned the revellers pale and sick.

"Surely, it is an enemy who has wronged him, and he a mighty sorcerer," they deduced, but they took their leave with some haste, and soon only Zhirek, the tavern owner and his family remained.

In the dim flare of the fish-oil lamps, Zhirek sat, chin on hand. Near midnight, the storm swelled and the sea crashed on the shore. Zhirek took the knife from the roast and smote off the clean bone of Hhabhezur's left forefinger, went outside, and flung the bone into the sea.

The tavern owner, peering after, thought he discerned vague glimmering shapes far out on the crested waves of the ocean, men with flying hair and strange chariots and the phosphorescent gleam of sharks' backs. There was a wailing in the wind like a woman's voice.

Zhirek returned to the tavern.

"Give me your bed to sleep in," he said to the tavern owner, "and the prettiest of your daughters to lie with me."

In terror, the man complied. The daughter, who went to Zhirek in loathing, presently began to moan with love, and in the morning, made bold by sentiment, would have detained him, to no avail. Then, stupidly convinced she could deal with him as a man since she had found him a man in bed, she shrilled and shouted after him till abruptly Zhirek spoke and her noise stopped. She remained dumb from that day onwards.

He came to a city by the sea. Its towers went up into the morning and its birds flew over the bleached-red disc of the sun. His weariness came to Zhirek, that weariness from which he could never properly be rested. He was even growing weary of spite and wickedness and injustice, even this quickly. But he did not acknowledge it. Meeting men on the high road that ran along the cliff beside the ocean, he had changed their faces to the colour of olives—so they beheld each other and began screaming—a childish viciousness. And farther on, passing a well, he had turned the water in it to the appearance and smell and taste of blood, one of the oldest and vilest of mage-tricks. Then, reaching the walled city, its towers, the birds, the market place in the great square, the tiered citadel, it seemed to him, though he had in fact regarded few cities, that he had seen a thousand. And, in his weariness of spirit, at last the urge came to him to be only in one spot, unmoving. The motive impulse of his youth was done with him, for in his soul he was no longer young.

He went by the city, however, searching its outskirts. Here and there he perpetrated some subtle unpleasantness—it acted as a fuel, to keep him going, otherwise, it occurred to him, he might simply stop in his tracks, turned to living stone.

(He had been glad to leave Sabhel, even that land had wearied him. Magic and love had come too easily. It had all been too easy, either that, or unobtainable.)

The cage walked after him. Hhabhezur, minus toe and finger, was all bone now, rattling.

A ruinous house loomed up in powdery greens and grays. Zhirek climbed the rotting stairway, through a decayed garden with the bare rock of the cliff showing through it. Doors creaked, teetering on their hinges. Inside, the mosaic floors had been picked clean by thieves. Through broken windows spray and raw weather blew, for again the storm, which had followed Zhirek up the coast, was gathering. Salt water flushed the cellars where part shattered jars now rooted seaweeds.

The melancholy and the wreck of the house had caught Zhirek's morbid fancy. Perhaps some phantom superimposed itself here of the ruined fortress in the desert, where the mad old priests had piously misused and foolishly caressed Zhirek when he was Zhirem and ten years old, extravagant in their attempts to ostracize his "devil." "Build no palace in the world. . . ." What irony if, having succumbed to all the traps they had warned him of, that hankering for their poverty had persisted.

Yet, by his craft and by use of men, taken mesmerized from the city or dragged thence by those already under Zhirek's spells, the house was somewhat put to rights. Thick rugs lay on the floor, merchandise stolen or procured by even more sinister means, draperies blew before the windows. Sometimes women came, wandering like sleepwalkers, along the shore road, up the stair where the stone beasts leered, across the noxious garden, through the house to the canopied black bed of Zhirek. That bed, which, with its posts and carvings and dark, resembled by unconscious accident or gloomy design, nothing so much as a tomb. At other hours, men died to amuse the magician—though he derived small amusement from their pleas, their pangs, their death. He was jealous of their death, or else he strove to drive himself to feeling anything—jealousy, pain, rage, for all emotion was smoldering out in him. Even cruelty became a habit.

Once the king's tax collectors ventured there, though the house was rife with sorcery. Zhirek dealt with these visitors, and then himself visited the king. That was the day when the king reckoned he was a dog, mounted a bitch, ate bones.

With his own store of bones Zhirek was miserly. He portioned Hhabhezur, waiting for the storm to rant over the ocean before he slung the morsel to them. And the storms came less often as the months went by and next, the years. As if the sea people of Sabhel had also grown tired of passion and dispute.

How prolonged the time, endless. Time without meaning, that which the mother of Zhirek had been warned of, when insistent, she had demanded for him the terrible fire of Invulnerability. "There is no benefit which has not a sister in misfortune." He pondered it himself, in the long quiet evenings when, the whole of the land and sky seeming colored by the glaze of the sea, that silver quiet entered even into Zhirek, briefly. How must it be that he, given so much, could only misuse and suffer from it? When, vulnerable and ignorant, he might have gleaned hapiness and comfort from his life, both for himself and others. He had been thrust toward evil, but evil had rejected him; Azhrarn, by proxy or in disguise, had rejected him. Why then had Zhirek not returned to his spoiled innocence, tried to mend the torn garment? Because he had never done good save through a fear of doing evil. Evil no longer a threat, paradoxically, evil was all he could set himself to practice.

One day Zhirek attempted an experiment. Going through the city, the doors as ever slamming, the crowds left on the street as ever bowing down and turning sallow, he came on an infant boy-child playing, overlooked, in a gutter. Something in the child almost touched Zhirek, the red-yellow shade of its hair, maybe, though its eyes were not green. Zhirek fashioned from nothing the semblance of a harmless sweetmeat, and offered it to the child, who took the gift unquestioning. Just then the mother came running. She grasped the child and lifted it and stared at Zhirek in shrinking fright. Zhirek said, with a desultory, still experimental gentleness: "Ask me for something."

"Then save my child, which you have poisoned," the woman shrieked at once.

"No, but I have not," Zhirek stated, and stretched out his hand.

At that the woman jerked back, and turning her foot against a stone, stumbled and lost her grip on the child, who fell. Its skull was smashed instantly on the rim of the gutter.

Though he knew the event sprang from what he had made of himself in the city, yet Zhirek accepted it as his portent that evil must continue to attend on him, as the crow circles the gibbet.

294

But some further years later, standing before an actual gibbet with the murderer dancing on it, one spoke behind Zhirek saying his name, not exactly as it was.

One spoke, and a soft though bitter cold spread over Zhirek. He realized that, for a moment, Lord Death had stood at his shoulder.

8

The sun set and night arose from the sea. By the light of an alabaster lamp, stolen from a kingly mausoleum by men in the magician's thrall, Zhirek sat reading from a black and silver parchment, stolen in like manner from the same location. The book contained certain lore and instruction regarding the most dangerous of magics, raising the dead and similar stratagems. Zhirek perused it idly, but a sound in the house caused him to put the parchment aside.

None entered now the dwelling of Zhirek, unless they were called by spells. It was well known that fearsome things guarded the place. Yet again, an odd sound, like metal striking on the echoing stone floor below—someone had come there, someone immune to Zhirek's safeguards, and apparently to fear itself.

Zhirek lit the way with weird glowing witch-fires, as he descended into the hall of the stone floor, and glanced about.

The drapes blew before the windows, and uncanny shades dipped and flitted. A huge candelabra blazed with a dull light amid a lace of yellow wax. A rat, which had been feeding on the wax, darted across the paving. On a stand of gold rested the last of Hhabhezur—only his skull, which Zhirek, in a final dreary malice, had retained. Just beyond the light, a tall chair of carved ebony had assumed a curious sheen. Zhirek approached and found a robed figure seated there, its head covered with a pallid cowl. In its white-gloved right hand it held a staff of iron ringed with gold, which it had used to strike upon the stone floor to attract attention.

There washed over Zhirek the kind of frightened exhilaration that a boy or a woman might feel, meeting unexpectedly a near-stranger with whom they had fallen in love. Zhirek trembled, and the tremor amazed him.

Very slowly, the cowled head was raised. Within the white frame of the cowl was only black, and two colorless burnings—eyes.

"Do not ask me who I am," said the figure to Zhirek. "You know me. We have met."

Zhirek remembered—like a dream remembered—a shadow which long ago had touched his brow, and delivered him, for a small space, from despair and frustration, by the gift of senselessness. Now the recollection turned him faint.

"You are Death," he said. "Am I to go with you?"

"No," said Death. "The fire put you beyond me, for centuries at least."

"But you are here," Zhirek said.

The left hand of Death rested on the arm of the ebony chair, itself as black, being ungloved. Zhirek half fell forward suddenly, and grasped this hand, the bare skin of Death.

To touch Death was literally that—to feel the touch of death. A release to some, a dread to most. But to Zhirek, who could not die till his enduring flesh had worn itself out, that touch was bliss and comfort. Like a drug, it overcame him, almost stunned him—Death's only possible gift, the half-death of unconsciousness, the promise of an ultimate rest from self-doubt and the pointless, roiling wickedness of man's existence. But the black hand was withdrawn, and semi-aware, Zhirek sank against the white-robed knees of Death. In a way, Zhirek really was in love with this stranger.

"Do not—" Zhirek faltered, "do not leave me. Let me serve you."

"Another you would have served," Death said.

"Others planned that service for me, but a demon refused it."

"I know it all," said Death. He did. He had studied the matter, Zhirek's life and the paths he had trodden.

"You," said Zhirek, "you I would serve."

"To the detriment of others, will you serve me?"

Zhirek smiled, his eyes fast shut, like a child nearly asleep.

"You have seen my love for others, Lord Death."

"One might stay you."

"None, but you."

"Simmu," said Death, "called in your childhood, Shell. Simmu a youth, or a maiden. Will you serve me in despite of Simmu?"

Behind the lids of Zhirek, the slightest movement.

"The demons reared Simmu, who presently betrayed and abandoned me. Simmu was the stair by which I made my way into hell. Simmu was the snake beneath the stone. But for Simmu, I might have lived well on the earth, a healer, a man without appetites, or else blind to them. And at the last, when nothing was left to me save Simmu, was Simmu to be found? See, I am alone, Lord of Lords."

"In this one thing, you are bitter."

"Oh, I am bitter in much. I curse the mother who set this fate on me. I curse Simmu who seduced me that I might see the worms crawling in my own soul. I curse Azhrarn, I being the only mortal, perhaps, who may do such with impunity. I curse the woman in the sea, Hhabaid, who led me to this meaningless power of sorcery that I can only misuse. I curse the whole world which fears me and yields to me, and will not fight me, and cannot destroy me as I should be destroyed, who am a cancer in it. Only you, Lord of Lords, bring the balm I require. Death is all I ask, and all I may not have."

"To die is not as you believe," Death said. But no more he said of that, for it did not suit his purpose. Instead, Uhlume, Lord Death, gave particular information and bizarre pledges to the man who rested against him, as if from pitiless labor. The bargain was not of the former sort, involving bones . . . but then, Uhlume was not as he had been, since Simmurad, a sore on his heel, had chafed him at every step.

Zhirek became the bond-servant of the Lord Uhlume.

In the morning, the old house was already empty, though it would be half a year before any dared explore its vacancy.

In the sea, the skull of Hhabhezur, thrown at last to the waves, bobbed slothfully, unclaimed. Hhabaid lay with some blue-haired lord, the new king of Sabhel, her husband, and Zhirek was only a scar upon her heart. Her father, (headless, haphazard coral in the hall of stone,) was even less.

Eventually, the skull progressed to the floor of a shallow reef. Fish lived in it, barnacles covered it. After many seasons, a trailing net entangled it and brought it into the boat of a fisherman, amidst the catch.

"Why," said he, "here is the head, or all that is left of it, of my poor father who was decapitated by pirates and cast overboard, thirty years ago at this very spot. Surely it has come to me for burial."

And, being a dutiful descendant, he bore the skull home, and went without food that he might have built for it an expensive tomb just beyond the village. The tomb was the wonder of the district, and pointed out by parents to their children as the deed of a good son.

Then, one morning, as chance would have it, the skull of

the real father was washed up in the cove below the village. But, not recognizing it and reckoning it unlucky, the fisher folk threw it down a dry well, and shovelled in dirt to obscure it, avoiding the area thenceforth.

PART FOUR

In Simmurad

1

Yolsippa the rogue, gate-keeper of Simmurad, woke from a dream of cross-eyed maidens, to the familiar yet comparatively infrequent sound of blows on the brass gates.

Yolsippa opened the trick portal and glared out, bleary-eyed.

"Who is that?" he shouted. For some while he had dispensed with the rest of the rigmarole.

Outside the gates, it was not quite dawn. The dark was surreptitiously slipping from the mountains, the sky heightening but not yet brightening.

"I say again, who is that?"

From below, out of the shadow, a voice called:

"One who would enter."

Yolsippa sighed, poured and drank a goblet of wine.

"All and sundry cannot enter here. This is Simmurad, City of the Immortals. What can you do? What are you good at? Do we need your skill that we should let you in?"

"I am the magician, Zhirek," said the voice, "and I can do this—" at which a lightning ripped the shadows, battered the gates, showing up a handsome black-haired, black-bearded man in a yellow robe, with gold rings on his hands and a black jewelled scarab on his breast. "Another such bolt," said he, "and your gates will crumble."

"Contain yourself," said Yolsippa. "You shall come in."

The mechanism of the gates was activated and Zhirek advanced through them. He was barefoot. Descending hurriedly to intercept him. Yolsippa beheld, however, that the magician's robe was heavy with gold and his forearms with bands of electrum and orichalc. A collar of gold set with sea-colored gems folded over his shoulders and his breast beneath the scarab.

"Alas, honoured magnificence," said Yolsippa, "the lord of Simmurad, Simmu (who is like a son to me), permits neither woman nor man to bring gold into the city, out of respect for a certain prince who might be expected to visit here, and does not care for the metal."

"Azhrarn must avoid me then," said the magician. "My gold enters with me."

Yolsippa deemed it prudent to remonstrate no further.

They had come together, the two of them, inside the inner court of the wall, where great trees grew, partly obscuring the city.

"Behold," said Yolsippa, directing Zhirek with pride and trepidation through the trees, so he might note Simmurad spread before him, the marmoreal rose red and milk white just now beginning to take color from the sky, though here and there lamps scorched in the towers and colonnades. "I will conduct you personally to the court of Simmu."

Beautiful Simmurad was. Beautiful, but strange. It moved Zhirek for a moment, as generally only natural things had come to have the power to move him. With Yolsippa at his elbow, in the pre-dawn glimmer, he walked up and down the levels of the city. And even Yolsippa, stumbling, belching, fat and gaudy in his greasy, jewel-encrusted garments, could not detract from the aura of Simmurad.

Many palaces there were, and all of them appeared empty, save here and there was the isolated wink of a colored window lit by a lamp. The lawns were smooth with grass that never died—and never seeded. The trees rang with leaves that never fell—or freshened. These eternal static manifestations were the work of magicians already in the city, or of the demons years back. Nature had been made to imitate the Immortal men.

The animals in the city were young, but were eternal too, each infected by a drop of the Drink of Life. The leopards sipping by the pool, had an oddly doll-like look; even in movement, they were somehow immovable. Yolsippa had something of this quality himself. And when they crossed a garden, brushed by the sun's first rays, there were men and women there, strolling under the trees, and they gave that exact impression of puppets or elegant waxworks. They stared after Zhirek and mocked Yolsippa, but their eyes might have been made of glass. It was as if, without knowing or being troubled by it, they were slowly calcifying, the calcification beginning with the topmost layer of the skin, creeping inward till it reached the organs and the mind.

The citadel ascended into the morning. Yolsippa paused at

the obelisque of green marble, that Zhirek might read the inscription.

I AM THE CITY OF SIMMU, SIMMURAD, AND HEREIN MEN SHALL LIVE THAT LIVE FOREVER . . .

"Is this place then, a prison for Immortals?" Zhirek inquired.

"It is a gift," said Yolsippa. "I was present at its inception. A marvellous prince—"

"Azhrarn."

"I should not presume—"

Zhirek was already striding away, approaching the doors of the palace, going through them.

Dawn began to brim over into the citadel, tinting everything through ranks of crystal windows.

"You will wait here, my lord. It is no less than custom," Yolsippa attempted. Zhirek, to Yolsippa's relief, complied.

They had entered a hall with a domed ceiling that soared upwards over their heads, and a floor set with silver discs. No guards, no servants stole about through the splendor, and no slaves, yet all was clean and tended—by the spells of the geniuses who had been permitted to exist here. Yet, so uninhabited it was, it might have been some ruin suddenly come on in the desert or the midst of the sea.

Zhirek seated himself. He appeared composed, actually terrible, should you get close enough to see the shapes of cruelty drawn about his eyes. Yet a turmoil had begun within him, something he observed analytically, almost with fascination. It was only the pulse and the belly stirred by a memory. The brain was cool. He waited for Simmu as if waiting to taste again a wine he had once been drunk on, which had made him sick, which now he meant only to taste and then to pour away, and afterwards, uproot and burn the vine.

An hour passed. The extended dawn still irradiated the hall. Then Simmu came, but not alone.

Like a king, for he was a king here, Simmu walked into the hall attended by his court, or a portion of it. The women, with their hair plaited with everlasting flowers, their exotic clothes in the modes of many lands; the men, warriors, sorcerers, sages, old and young, ageless now. Each was like the other, like those Zhirek had already witnessed—figures of wax.

And Simmu himself, he also had the taint. Yet it was Simmu, Simmu correct to the smallest detail, lynx-green of eye, amber haired, the narrow beard like parings of that amber; the nervous, cat-like, graceful demeanor—much of a girl there in him; however, a man. He seemed no older than in the past, indeed, he had not physically aged, or barely. His phase as hero had brought certain alterations, but these Zhirek bypassed. It was the other alteration which caught him. The thing which made this Simmu, though recognizable in all ways, quite unrecognizable—another. Zhirek was unsure how the revelation affected him, though he was undoubtedly affected by it. All his emotions, which had deserted him when he came from the sea, seemed to have gathered here in Simmurad to hammer on his lungs and heart. (Zhirek gave no sign of his reverie or its disturbance.)

At Simmu's side, one final discord, Zhirek paid heed to a sullen beautiful girl with glittering fair hair.

Yolsippa emerged. He bowed ridiculously to Simmu and to Zhirek.

Zhirek arose. He had perceived the face of Simmu also betrayed no sign of knowledge. Simmu gazed at Zhirek blankly.

'Does he feign, or has he forgotten? Where did the girl hide herself, who hung on me by the lake of salt? Simmu the maiden . . . Shell.' Then he noticed that Simmu frowned, almost foolishly, as if recollection had been jolted.

Now will he insult me further, Zhirek wondered, *by pretense that he can just now call me to mind?*

But Simmu did not speak. It was Yolsippa who blared out in his showman's yap:

"Zhirek, who claims himself a magician, of which I have seen evidence, presents himself as suppliant to Simmurad's lord."

How often has this scene, or its sisters, been enacted? As many times as Simmu had subjects in his kingdom. If any retained an interest in the ritual, it was not obvious. But they congregated in the hall to vet those who came begging for Immortality, as if the affair were important.

Simmu spoke then. Still frowning slightly, he spoke to Zhirek:

"You are a magician? We have magicians and to spare."

"Rejoice, then," Zhirek said. He found he could not quite bring himself to use the name "Simmu"—the name he had first learned from Simmu's female voice beside the lake of salt. "I do not mean to add myself to your folk. This loudmouth mistakes my purpose."

Simmu's court murmured, more interested than before.

"What, then, is your purpose?" Simmu asked.

"To see this township which mortal men refer to as the City of Living Dead."

The murmur swelled, extinguished itself.

"Your jest——" Simmu began.

"No jest, to live forever, your lives worthless, spent in goalless atrophy. The rat in the cage, running from one corner to another and back again, lives better."

Simmu had whitened, pallor under pallor.

"Now you mistake us, magician. We bide our time before our plans are put into force—and we have the time to bide."

One of the men, Simmu's courtier, cried: "Let this gentleman demonstrate his sorcery. I, for one, think him a simpleton."

Zhirek glanced at the man.

"You should be careful of me," he said, "for whatever I might choose to do to you, you must live with till time's ending."

"Beware of *me*," the other retorted. "I, too, am a magician." And he pointed at Zhirek and the pointing finger shot forth a tongue of fire. Zhirek ignored the fire which could not hurt him. He stood in the midst of it, and said: "Fire is a dangerous toy for you to play with." At once, the flames went out. Simmu's court whispered. The cunning surgeon who had gained his eternity in Simmurad on his physician's merit, stepped forward.

"You must not think, sir," he said, "that because we are vulnerable we can be destroyed. True, fire would disfigure, but it would not burn us quite away. I have made a silver foot for a lady who was burned—it masks her own damaged flesh, but she has no discomfort with it. Indeed, I will go further, since I convict you of attempts to undermine our fortitude. I have made a medical study of the phenomenon of Immortality. I will tell you this; even should you cut out the heart of a man in Simmurad, you could not kill him. He would be as if sleeping, and I should come at once and construct for him a heart of silver. This would proceed on a clockwork principle—for I have procured many occult skills from commerce with the dwarfs of the Underearth. And my clever silver heart would work as well for the man whose fleshly heart you had despoiled as his own, and better. Another item—I have actually removed and repaired a damaged eye, and re-attached it in the head of a man, where it immediately commenced its work as if no trouble had befallen it."

"And now inform me," said Zhirek, "how many children have been born in Simmurad."

The surgeon folded his hands.

"I have observed that procreation and birth are spontaneous extensions of the fear of death. A warrior, on the night prior to battle, may quicken the wombs of several women. In a famine usually many children will be born. Thus, having in Simmurad no terror of death, we are less responsive to the sensual urge, and perhaps, infertile. It is not necessarily a misfortune, since it leaves us the more space for other pursuits."

"The pursuit of what?" Zhirek inquired.

This time, Simmu answered.

"I have a modest plan to subdue the earth, choosing therefrom those of high value, and conferring on them Immortality."

"A scheme to intrigue your master, Azhrarn," said Zhirek, "war and savagery everywhere. But after the conquest, what? A sedentary world of clockwork immortals. I do not think he will favor that, your black jackal of Druhim Vanashta."

Simmu reddened, a curiously bloodless rush of blood to his face, the flush of the wax figure. But he came to Zhirek, raising his hand to strike the magician. Zhirek reached and caught his hand, and at the contact, both checked.

"I am invulnerable. Do not strike out at me, you will wound yourself," Zhirek said.

Simmu seemed bewildered. His eyes searched the countenance of Zhirek, seeking a clue to the sensation which had flooded him. But memory lay trapped under a slab of demon-sorcery, circumstance, and the years themselves. Nevertheless, the touch of Zhirek's fingers about his wrist was like a blow in itself, and a mortal one.

"Who are yóu?" Simmu said.

"You have my name."

"We have spoken previously. I do not remember the occasion."

Zhirek let go of Simmu. He recalled ironically the unvocal Eshva communicating of Shell. The magic of Simmu, vividly perceptible and attractive to all who met him for the first time in Simmurad, was wasted on Zhirek, who had been ensnared by the positive, un-human, total magic of Simmu's childhood and youth.

The court stirred uneasily. The girl with the fair hair stared at Simmu and at Zhirek with eyes that seemed to have changed color.

"No matter," Simmu said. "You do not understand us, Zhirek. Come, I will show you the treasures of this city. I will explain to you my plans so you may properly comprehend my ambition."

Simmu led Zhirek through the palace. Simmu, as if deliberately to contrast himself to what he had been, debated at length with all Zhirek had said. Sometimes, at the turn of a stairway or hesitating to indicate some ornament of metal or stone, sunlight or shadow lending originality, Simmu revealed himself as Shell. These visions, which came seldom enough, wrenched at Zhirek but, perched above his own tumult, aloof from it, Zhirek lost none of his equilibrium. Simmu, however, grew progressively more feverish and at a loss. He had dismissed his courtiers, Yolsippa, the staring girl who was his wife. His hands shook as he opened the doors of Simmurad. He began to take on the look of a beast in a snare.

They entered eventually a lofty chamber, whose whole central expanse was put to the use of a marble platform, and on the platform, a vast war-game of the sort an emperor might play with. The huge board counterfeited the earth, seas of blue glass scales, land masses cut from the polished wood of many trees, with mountains upraised and here and there pasted with crystal snows. Cities were modelled on the board too, miniature but marvelous, while ships the size of beetles sailed the glass oceans. And there were armies, the toy figures constructed from ivory and exquisitely painted, their swords splinters of steel, and their machinery of war running on miniscule oiled wheels. It was a bellicose toy, but a toy nevertheless.

"I have learned a lot in this room," Simmu said. "My library is well stocked with all manner of books—I read of conflict and here I practice it. When the army of Simmurad is formed, no legion of the earth shall be able to withstand it, so finely drilled and so excellently equipped it will be."

But, having said this, his face closed on itself.

Simmu leaned upon the board, scattering the ivory armies where his hands descended.

"But I have this stumbling block to overcome, Zhirek. I must fight this war, for as a hero I am bound to it—yet no one must be slain, for I would gift no one to Lord Death. How is it possible?"

Zhirek did not reply. He stood at Simmu's back, and the impulse stole over the magician to lay his hand upon the fiery hair of Simmu, to comfort, or to be comforted. Zhirek did not obey the impulse.

"Death," Simmu said then, further scattering the toy ar-

305

mies with deft malicious battings of his hand. "Death came to Simmurad. I confronted him—or did I dream it only, as I have dreamed it all, my life, the demons— No," he smiled, half turning, so Zhirek saw the green gem he had lifted from within the neck of his robe and twisted between his fingers. "No, each wonder is real. Yet, if Death were enraged against me, why does he not return? I offered myself to oppose him, but his retaliation was slight and childish. Surely by now he should have found some breach through which he might enter."

"He has," Zhirek said.

Then, for an instant—but completely—Simmu came alive. Only with his eyes did he ask the question, and waited, as a leopard waits to spring, to hear it answered.

"Yes," Zhirek affirmed, "I am the emissary of Lord Death."

Simmu laughed; Zhirek was familiar with the laugh, not from the lips of Simmu, but from his own, the insane peremptory noise that had its basis in disgust or confusion but never in mirth.

"That, then, is why I believed I had met with you before. I had met your master at my gates. What comes next? What has he sent you to do?"

"To fill your veins with misery, and your thoughts with dread. What else?"

Simmu leaned again on the platform of the game.

"Misery and dread are strangers to those who live forever Your master requires another method. Still, as emissary, I make you welcome. Why did he choose you for this work?"

"Because I understand your wretchedness, Simmu, the punishment that life lays on you in exchange for its retention."

"Simmurad is a place of delight, marvel and intellect. We are the gods of the earth's eastern corner."

Zhirek watched him. Zhirek had come to see that truly his remembrance had been wiped from Simmu's thoughts—either by pain, or by the demons who had so frequently attended Simmu's existence. Zhirek saw too the chains of responsibility hanging on Simmu, chains he had balked at but which now he scarcely noticed as he crawled beneath their weight. Simmu's eyes had become hollow. Mingled in them was hate and pleading. As Zhirek had once begged, in vain, a reason for his life drom the Prince of Demons, thus Simmu now begged from Zhirek, equally in vain.

The doors to the chamber of the war-game swung wide. The fair-haired wife of Simmu entered.

"My beloved," she said to him coldly, "am I to be excluded from everything of yours? I am Kassafeh," she said to Zhirek, "and if Simmu is the king of this city, then, as his wife, I am the queen of it. And you are Zhirek, the magician."

"Also, he is the servant of Lord Death," Simmu told her.

Kassafeh shrugged, and jewels flashed on her shoulders.

"I do not credit that death takes the form of a man," said Kassafeh, her voice coarsening, showing her merchant blood. "Nor am I positive we are irrevocably immortal. I think it is some trick of demonkind to make us suppose we are. Few knock on our gates in recent years," she said to Zhirek. "Why do so few wish to win eternity if it is real? Is it as you say, we are named 'Living Dead'?"

"In fact," Zhirek replied, "Simmurad is rarely called to mind in the world. It has passed already into myth. Only desperate men believe in it."

"I will take them war," Simmu whispered, "then they will believe."

"No," Kassafeh cried, "you will sleep here, my thin cat of a husband, sleep without strength and without love. You, a hero as I once thought you. I could forgive your faithfulness, your indifference, but not your apathy." She lied in this, but the words sprang to her lips, surprising her with their false vehemence. She had not often railed at Simmu. It was the presence of Zhirek which stirred her to anger and an awareness of herself. And abruptly she inquired within herself: *This handsome stranger—have I begun to love him in Simmu's place? If that is so, I shall wake havoc in myself. I have had no lover save only one.* Which was true enough. Brooding and weaving and the eating of sweet gelatine had sustained her for years, but were not sufficient, she who had saved her self-respect through fury and defiance in the Garden of the Golden Daughters, a prison less destructive even than the congealed paradise of Simmurad. *Yes, when I look at this dark man my heart lifts and my lungs hurt me. I feel my life, of whatever span it is. Zhirek I will love.*

2

They feasted in Simmurad. On dishes evolved by sorcery, or dishes brought by sorcery from the tables of kings, stored by sorcery, revitalized by sorcery and set piping hot, fragrant and instantaneous upon the board. In a park of rolling lawns and plumed forests at the center of Simmurad, they hunted lion and deer, which dropped with spears in their hearts, lay still a while, and then, the wound healed, leapt up and ran away. Trees, heavy with fruit, bowed almost to the ground. But the fruit had no taste, no perfume, unless a witch had walked by and created a scent for the tree from some spell. The leaves of the trees and the petals of the flowers which never withered, had all the same texture—like waxed paper.

Music was played by unseen fingers. Exercises were played with chessmen by the citizens of Simmurad, and exercises with checkers and with plaques of jade, and exercises of throwing or shooting at a mark. In the chamber of the War Game, Simmu and his court conquered the world three times in an afternoon.

Drugs were sorcerously procured from that world so far from the gates, and sampled. Wines and sweetmeats and clothes were similarly procured, rare and extraordinary books and peculiar plants and astonishing animals, and gems and weapons and cosmetics. Over the floral things magics were set to turn them into more waxed paper, the beasts were given a drop of gray liquid to make of them more toys. Simmu was prodigal with the fluid of eternity; somehow it had lasted, never evaporating, such a little going such a long way, as if the clay vessel in which it remained might never run dry, as the adder never runs dry of its poison.

Much they did in Simmurad to impress upon Zhirek the glory of their lives and the magnificence of their future. But he was like a shadow in their midst, and by the shadow of him, as if by a strong light, they were able to see their own boredom and futility staring at them. They might have done so much, but—always about to do it—it was never done. Security had eaten their marrow. Zhirek guessed, as he had conveyed, their plight. Though, as he assured them, he at least could hope, eventually, for human terminus and change.

At night, when the hunting and the exercises and the feasts and the debates were done, Kassafeh would lie alone in her fantastic bedchamber, going over all that Zhirek had said, and all he had done, every expression and gesture. Lamps lit the room throughout the night, not because she feared the dark, but for company and cheer. Once she and Simmu had shared a bed. More recently, she had thought to bring another man to this one, for there dwelt in Simmurad many handsome men. But her fires burned low, and their fires lower. The wise surgeon had the right of it. She had not taken lovers, but her virtue was the product of laziness and disinclination. Then Zhirek had appeared to galvanize inertia.

Many nights she lay awake beneath the yellow lamps, (to which moths were never attracted, for no insects and few birds came to Simmurad—as if they avoided a plague.) Many nights alone. Beyond the openwork shutters the vista of the city under the isolated scattered stars of the far, far east of the earth, two or three windows shining as hers did, the glacial noise of fountains, the leaves striking, heavy as lacquer fans. Finally, Kassafeh arose, took from chests the chains of rich jewels, the embroidered silks, caught herself evaluating them.

"I am the only merchant's daughter in a city of magicians," she admitted. She cast the finery back in the chests and left the room.

It was to the great library she went, stealing through the lightless corridors and up wide stairways, lit only by the stars. She moved secretively, like a felon, through the palace and, coming to the library doors, found them, as ever, locked against her. Simmu was within the library; the glow of a lamp seeped under the doors, she thought she heard him muttering to himself like an old man. She had guessed he would be here, for here he was to be found more often than anywhere.

She had seen Yolsippa pick the locks of a quantity of doors.

She took a silver pin from her dress and put the training to use.

Simmu lay asleep on a narrow couch, and all about him books and parchments littered the floor. The lamp was nearly out, but it showed Kassafeh as much as she desired; there was enough light to despise him by. She had come for that purpose, to despise in order to take courage for what came next. To Simmu's good looks she was not impervious, however, and without meaning to, she crept close and gazed at him, and so she heard how he moaned in his dream.

"Zhirem," said Simmu, "Death is everywhere. I saw you dead, under the dead tree, the cord about your neck and the rain falling in your eyes."

Kassafeh, arrested by the familiarity of the name "Zhirem," leaned yet closer.

At that moment, Simmu's body arched upwards from the couch, he went gray, and he cried out as if a knife had been thrust into him. Tears ran from the corners of his lids, sweat trickled after the tears, and the beard began to fray from his jaw. Kassafeh grew rigid with alarm; in this state she witnessed other things: The contours of Simmu's face and physique, altering, the very skin and scent of Simmu altering—the flowering within his shirt, unmistakable but impossible, even the flung-back head, somehow changed, the agonized features—female.

It was terrible, this transformation. It had been so long unpracticed, while Simmu adhered to the physical format of masculinity. And it was terrifying to observe the event, and the convulsions of pain and near-pleasure followed by deeper and more gruesome pain, that chased each other over the countenance of Simmu—now man, now woman.

Kassafeh had not forgotten what she had assumed to be the demon-aided illusion of femininity Simmu had put on in the Garden of the Golden Daughters. But she had never properly seen it, never properly understood—as she had never properly understood her husband at all. Now, as well as being frightened by this sight of the metamorphosis, she was also horribly insulted by it. For she perceived that Zhirek the magician had stimulated the dulled lusts of Simmu as she had failed to do. And could she miss that Simmu, a woman, was more vitally beautiful than Kassafeh? The unloving husband might become, additionally, the rival.

Kassafeh turned and fled, precipitately shutting the library doors after herself, yet with a stealthy frenzied quiet. Simmu was her enemy. She hated him. Hate happened very suddenly, for she was starved of drama as much as of love.

She darted up the silent stairways of the palace, toward the rooms Zhirek had been given. She was actually trying to outrace the woman who still lay unconscious on the couch below.

3

The apartments of Zhirek were splendid, an extra measure to impress him. By day, windows gave a view of that particular lawn where the snake of corruption Lord Death had sent coiled impotent and sullen about the fruit tree.

Kassafeh hesitated at this door, though she discovered it unlocked. Even in Simmurad, and so early, Zhirek's reputation was unreassuring. Yet love, or the form of love which motivated her, made nonsense of caution, and presently she slunk inside. Her strange eyes glowed in the lampless dark.

By starlight only, she observed the bedchamber, the bed with its draperies, and the man stretched there.

Zhirek lay, by contrast with her husband, still as a carving. Indeed, a remarkable stillness, the lids of the eyes down and unmoving, the hands loose at the sides, the mouth closed. The slightest breath did not appear to flex the nostrils. The rise and fall of the rib-cage was so negligible that Kassafeh, for a moment, believed Death's servant had actually died, despite his cold boast of invulnerability and longevity. But, having reassured herself he breathed, however shallowly, she went to him and embraced him.

He was cool as a stone and did not wake. She did not concede as yet it was some sorcery that held him. Fired by this second hand brush with Death, she trembled, discarded her garments, loosened Zhirek's and lay along him on the bed, caressing for a long time all of him she might come at, with her hands and her mouth. She burned, but he stayed cold-asleep. Nothing of him roused. At last, shuddering and exhausted by her disappointment, she shed tears. But even the proximity of unresponsive flesh had soothed her, and eventually she slept.

Dawn startled her alert. She opened her eyes and was startled again, for the open blue-green eyes of Zhirek met hers, nearer than the pillow.

"I came to you in the night," she said defiantly, "but you had no use for me. You think me brazen, but I have never known a man save my husband, who in the beginning, in any case, forced me." This lie appealed to her and she brightened. "I am chaste," she whispered, abandoning herself gladly to her passion, "but you I could not resist."

"I made no advance to you," he said.

"Do not shame me," she pleaded, partly in earnest, lowering her lids.

"I did not come to Simmurad to couple," he said.

"Perhaps you are impotent," said Kassafeh, "as the wise physician tells us immortal men become."

"I shall have a death," Zhirek said.

"Then that is answer enough, and I am parched for love."

And she began to kiss him and cling to him, and the thought came to him that, as a male, Simmu had lain with this woman, a thought which provoked an insidious lust in Zhirek greater than any Kassafeh could entice. There was, too, the uncanny sleep he had woken from, which Uhlume Lord Death himself had granted Zhirek. These slumbers were no less than replicate deaths, death as Zhirek supposed it. The

311

vital organs seemed to stop and the senses vanished between one indrawn breath and another. No dreams troubled the sleeper, or, if they did, went unremembered. Dreadful tomb-pits were these trances, but to Zhirek, so odd had become his turn of mind, they were a promise and a refreshment. And arousing, washed momentarily clean of the stigma of his in-vulnerability, Zhirek felt life quicken in him.

Thus, he rendered Kassafeh what she required of him, while the bed-chamber steeped itself in the carmine dawn.

Later, she asked him: "Will you destroy Simmurad as clev-erly as you destroyed my virtue?"

"Simmurad also is easily destroyed. Already the destruction has begun, and is not of my doing."

"And do you serve Death, or is that merely a story you tell to bemuse my husband, who believes he has made himself Death's enemy?"

"I serve Death."

"I will serve you," said Kassafeh. Apostasy fired her blood as love had done. "I will help you in whatever manner you suggest. I have no loyalty to Simmu, for he has no care for me, Indeed, none of us care anything for each other, it is dif-ficult even to hate, since we have grown immortal—if immor-tal we are. But I will hate Simmu for your sake. Besides, he is a fool. He took me from a place of lies, and I believed we should be famous in the world, he a hero-king and I his wife, but we have ended here, which I now think worse than the place of lies he took me from. And we are forgotten and no one speaks our names. Nothing is real, save only you, be-loved. Tell me how I may serve you."

Enigmatically he looked at her. He did not entirely need her service or her help in anything, but the symbol of her traitorousness had a magical value.

"Bring me," he said evenly, "the vessel in which the Draught of Immortality is kept."

"I do not know its exact location," she said, "but I will nevertheless find and bring it to you."

He saw cruelty flame in her eyes, the brief spark of living abrasive heat, warming her as he had been warmed those mo-ments by the cruelty within himself.

Simmu woke alone, his body racked with pain. He had be-come a woman in his sleep, altered once more to a man as the dawn returned with its reminders of the city. Simmu knew well enough what had befallen him, and its cause. He did not recall his earlier time with Zhirek, their childhood or

312

their pairing, he never would since Azhrarn had lifted the memory from his brain. Only vestiges, ghosts, shreds of emotion floating in his dreams were left to Simmu of that love affair, sufficient to disturb him, insufficient to explain the hold Zhirek seemed to possess over him, thought and flesh. And Simmu was suddenly no longer exhilarated but afraid of the arm of Death reaching out for him. Afraid, therefore, of Zhirek. Afraid of his own body which could become melting and female and betray him to Zhirek.

Simmu went from the library.

He sought his own apartment, passed through all its pleasing perspectives, unseeing, opened a silver chest, removed a silver box, gazed down at the stoppered clay vessel within.

It was no profound secret where the Draught of Immortality was kept. A short thorough search would have revealed it to any. Now it had occurred to Simmu that it must become a secret. With a slow but frantic activity, he searched the chambers for some new spot to hide the treasure. Like a miser attempting to conceal his hoard, this was how he searched. And Simmu, who was ageless and young, felt a weight of years begin to press on him, all the years that he had yet to live—eternity, even in the same instant that Death's shadow loomed across his future.

This paradox and his physical discomfort wore him out. At length, instead of hiding the clay vessel more cunningly, he set it down beneath a tall window, and leaned his forehead on the crystal. In that way, he saw Kassafeh and Zhirek poised together on the balcony of a tower, stretched into the morning as if expressly to be seen.

Simmu sensed what was between them, rather than beheld it, their conspiracy. A dislocated pang of anger or envy, dulled and remote, went through him and then away from him. Now he felt only sorrow and foreboding. How human he had become, with all the anguish and clumsy confusion of men.

He touched the green gem at his throat, the Eshva gift; he recalled the vow of Azhrarn, already honored once before, to heed the gem's burning in fire. But Simmu was aware Azhrarn had lost interest in him, Simmurad a test that Simmu had failed. To burn the jewel in fire would bring no one, not even those who had come on the last occasion, Azhrarn's servants.

On the balcony, Kassafeh embraced Zhirek, and he did not repulse her kisses.

Only Death and life remained to Simmu. And though

313

Zhirek, Death's agent, was in Simmurad, Death himself could not enter the gates, for nothing had ever died here, nor ever would.

Simmu took up the clay vessel in its silver box, and abruptly it came to him that his wife would be the instrument whereby the Draught could be taken from him. Wherever he should hide it, the woman would seek it out. And then Simmu dropped the box clattering on the floor and, lifting the clay vessel, pulled out its stopper. Once he had sampled this fluid with reluctance. Now he set his mouth at the brink, and tipping back his head, deliberately drained those last persistent drops of Eternal Life. Some while he waited, head back, vessel tilted, till he was sure he had had all of it, and no single element of moisture was unswallowed. And then he slung the vessel from him so it broke in empty shards against the wall.

Exactly then, Kassafeh stepped into the room.

Her eyes were the color of dusk, lover's eyes, but her foot ground on a piece of the smashed vessel, and looking down at it, her eyes changed to a sizzling yellow.

"What have you done?" she cried.

"There well be no more Immortals," Simmu said, "neither can you take a love-gift to Zhirek, save only Kassafeh."

Now the eyes of Kassafeh were the color of green iron.

"I saw you asleep," she said. "You were not yourself. It was a woman I discovered on your couch. You had better call your demon-people to rescue you."

"In any event," said Simmu, "you should not expect gentleness from Zhirek, whatever you take or tell him. Neither is he the hero you wish to be associated with."

Kassafeh flung up her head.

"Baaa!" she shouted at him. "You are a sheep like all the rest."

And she ran away with frightened fury in her breast.

4

The long dawn evaporated; day passed through Simmurad. Later, the sun set, a brief powdering of red on the walls, swift as sunrise never was. Twilight filled the gardens and the colonnades like a blue snow, and the strange eastern stars shone down.

The lamps were lit for the feast that was nightly held in

Simmurad. Since Zhirek constantly appeared at these feasts, few citizens would stay away, drawn to curse his somberness and display bursts of wild merry-making before him. Only Yolsippa was consistently absent. Unliking of Zhirek in the extreme, he grew very attentive to his position as gate-keeper, and kept to the gate, solacing himself there with fatty foods, red wines and orgiastic dreams, procured from a witch in Simmurad, of cross-eyed persons of a lascivious disposition.

In the bright hall of the feasting, fountains played and sorcerous clockwork birds trilled in silver cages. Zhirek came always behind the rest of the feasters, and when he entered, that shadow entered with him, to chill and stimulate the Immortals. Tonight, however, the shadow was deeper and more than usually chilling. Fate seemed to pad at the heels of Zhirek, robed in cold silence.

Zhirek wore black and a golden collar he had taken from the lords of Hhabhezur's court and over that, the scarab of ink-black gems which an emperor's tomb had rendered him. In one hand he carried a shard of clay pottery, and he walked to Simmu's silver chair, while Simmu sat motionless in it, watching him.

"You have saved me some work," Zhirek said, to Simmu, but all threre heard him. "I had pondered how to be rid of the Drink of Life, but you have solved my problem, drinking it down yourself. The vessel is broken and dry."

There was an outcry in the hall. Some shouted that Zhirek had lied, and asked for Simmu to deny it. Others, forgetting too easily they had accepted Simmu as their king, insulted him. Demands were made as to the purpose of their great scheme to conquer the world, if men were not now to profit by it.

Simmu rose. They fell quiet, anxious to hear his excuse or denial.

"There will be no more Immortals," he said, as he had said to Kassafeh. "We are the first, and last. It is true, the Elixir has been drunk to the ultimate drop." This time, no noise. Positive realization had subdued them all. Simmu confessed bitterly: "It is this man, this Zhirek, who has put such doubt, such horror in my heart that I could not any longer blind myself. Our lives are worthless. We are like birds that cannot fly, like roads that lead nowhere, save into some desert." None challenged him; he had clearly half reckoned that they would, maybe trusted that they would, that arguments could be advanced against his dismal declaration. Only the skilled surgeon was heard muttering that his life was far from worthless, that he had much study to perform that would benefit mankind. But his voice was scarcely audible and each sentence unfinished, as indeed, all his studies had been. "No," Simmu said. "It is irrevocable, this state we have come to. I do not comprehend why it should be that safety of life should rob us of our best qualities. But so it is. Zhirek has torn open my vision. I do not know what path to choose. I am afraid, but even my fear is sedentary and uninspiring."

Then debate did break out, as before it had broken out against the awful statements Zhirek had made.

"Who desires extinction?"

"To live only for mild pleasure is better than to lose life."

Simmu had seated himself, and did not answer, nor Zhirek, who stood dark as the gathering night itself before Simmu's chair. Kassafeh stared only at Zhirek, her eyes a curious complementary darkening purple. She had gilded her lids and put sapphires and flowers in her hair for Zhirek's sake, but he did not appear to notice her. When she had warned him that Simmu had drunk the last draughts of the Elixir, Zhirek had merely nodded. Now a personal alarm beset Kassafeh. She sensed, as each in that place suddenly seemed to, annihilation breathing on her neck—negation, if not death. And with her stare she entreated Zhirek: *Beloved, I will be your slave. Do not condemn me also.*

Then Zhirek spoke.

"None of you have anything to tremble at," he said, "for Death cannot enter Simmurad. Nothing has ever died here, nor can it die, all being immortal, even to the grass of your lawns and the lions in your hunting park. And Uhlume, Lord Death, can only walk where the condition of death has walked before him."

And he smiled about at them, and they shrank from him, even the magicians and the wise men shrank. Their faces took on the rictus which the faces of men had assumed in Zhirek's house when poison was offered to them. Somehow, there was not one present who did not guess what Zhirek meant to do and was yet unable to prevent him. It was a symbolic thing, but utterly destructive, as such sympathetic magic must always be.

He began.

He lifted the scarab from his breast and set it on the floor. He murmured the spell softly; in that room of enchanters, no doubt a few were schooled in it themselves. The jewels quivered—Zhirek spat on them—their glinting facets turned to a dull obsidian sheen and, with a clicking sound, began to run about the floor. The scarab had become a living creature.

"No," Zhirek said, "Death cannot enter Simmurad till something has died here—an excellent motive, I hazard, why none of you has left these walls. Though you say you have no need to avoid Death, yet you avoid him."

Zhirek paced slowly after the scuttling beetle. He let it circle between the legs of the tables, under the silken caves of draperies, but always he pursued it. At the center of the hall, the beetle paused to investigate a red flower fallen from some woman's fingers. As it did so, Zhirek brought down his bare hard foot on its back. So still the hall, the crack of the carapace was heard throughout. Zhirek removed his foot. They glimpsed, straining to see, the shattered beetle crushed on the petals of the flower, and a stifled moaning went up. The fact of death had breached Simmurad. Death himself might follow as he willed. A vast wind roared through the palace, unprecedented, seeming to announce him.

Zhirek's sorcery gripped all of them. At the second when panic strode among them bidding them fly, not one could shift himself. Even their eyes grew rigid, fixed on the miniature dead thing at the hall's center. Only Zhirek raised his head, looking at Simmu, as immobile as the rest, but not as expressionless. Simmu who had faced Death, struck him, challenged him, Simmu grinned with a terror worse than any other's. No delight in the battle now. Zhirek had stripped him naked and truth smote him like a sword.

The wind smashed in the windows of the citadel. It was alive, this gale. It stalked across the floor, it swirled and settled and formed itself, and Uhlume, Lord Death, stood in the core of Simmurad, city of the Immortals.

"Welcome, Lord of all Lords," Zhirek greeted him. "These people cannot bow to you, for they are prevented from doing anything. I have worked the method of their own spiritual atrophy against them. They resembled wax, now they are mesmerized to stone, unable to run from you or show you courtesy. They feel nothing, but they see and they hear. Pronounce sentence, my lord."

In this hour of his triumph, Uhlume was impervious. But he looked about him, gazed long at everything. His blank white eyes gave away a sort of hunger, even greed, as they dwelt on the face of each who had defied him.

After some minutes, Uhlume said: "Beasts are in the parks, but they may be spared. The debt is owed me by men,

317

who made this war in full knowledge of what they did. However, in this hall, one is missing."

Zhirek glanced aside. Kassafeh had vanished.

"She slipped the leash of my spell by some means unknown to me, but, even so, she will be trapped in Simmurad. For the beasts, I will send them out of the city, if you desire it."

"They shall live in the Innerearth," said Uhlume, "there is a woman there who may value them, to hunt perhaps."

"One request then, my lord," said Zhirek, "before I complete my service to you here."

"Name it."

"Simmu, who calls himself your enemy, owes me also a debt. I plan a separate destiny for him from these others. A worse destiny."

"Cruelty," said Death implacably, "is your food, not mine. Even now, not mine."

"Then you will grant it to me? Yes, my lord, I mean to commit an act of such savagery that it will rip and gnaw on me, soul and brain, for all the wretched centuries I must endure. It is the only thing which will keep me from madness—to rage, to suffer and to regret. While my heart beats, it must bleed, or I cannot bear what must be borne, that numbness in me that only pain can alleviate. Give me Simmu, my lord, with your other gifts."

"Take him," said Death. "And then, give me Simmurad completely."

Kassafeh ran through the night avenues and gardens of Simmurad. The shadows were generous to her, wrapping her close, hiding her from any supernatural and far-sighted eye. But the stars were merciless on the marble streets, and when the moon rose like an apple of green jasper, she approached despair. Then, for none apprehended her, her preservation seemed miraculous. She was not aware she was in a trap, that, run where she would, she could not get free of it.

She had abandoned the hall the instant the windows shattered. She had not planned what she did. Her rapid departure was instinctive. That she could break out of the cage of the mesmeric spell was another matter. Wise men and magicians alike, they had stood rooted and entranced. She, though she felt the weight of the spell, was able to elude it, given an impetus of insane fear. Of course, she was not only a merchant's daughter. Zhirek's sorcery had missed her for the same reason that the illusions of the Garden of the Second

318

Well had not ensnared her, nor the Eshva glamour Simmu had used there. The blood of her second father had immunized Kassafeh to earth-magic—the bluish ichor of the sky elemental that was mixed in her blood.

For Uhlume, she had not seen him. But it was enough to sense his advent. Like all Simmurad that night, though immortal, she cringed at Death.

It was the gates she made for, both to rush through them and to enlist the aid of Yolsippa, he being the only free man in the city, through his absence from the feast. Actually, it was his companionship she needed more than his dubious wits. She, too, had been betrayed. She had not yet had the leisure to grieve.

Near the gates, racing on her bangled feet, three spotted leopards dashed past her, going another way. The gold rings of their eyes unnerved her in an abstract fashion. She guessed they had found—or been granted—an exit she had not.

Then the road swept upward to the carven mountain where the brass gates reared, closed and gleaming in the moonlight.

She climbed swiftly up the stair that ascended the mountain wall, and went through the small doorway of the gatehouse.

"Yolsippa," she cried, "Simmurad is lost!"

But Yolsippa lay, burping and snoring intermittently, upon his couch.

Kassafeh seized the wine jug and up-ended it over Yolsippa's head—to no avail, for he had already drunk the jug empty. So she struck him repeatedly, and as she did this, she heard a far-off but ominous thunder, and the stone beneath her feet and above her head seemed somewhat to vibrate.

"Yolsippa, wake and be accursed! Simmurad is lost—come, open the gate for we must be gone."

Yolsippa woke, and prudently he asked her:

"Who has taken the city?"

"Death has taken it, with Zhirek's collusion. Some doom hangs over us—I have no notion of it, but I am afraid."

Yolsippa sweated and staggered to the levers which would activate the gates.

"And for Simmu, what? Does he not heroically battle Death?"

Kassafeh let out a scream that might have believed itself a laugh. She shed sudden tears, for whom she was uncertain, but she shrieked at Yolsippa to hasten.

Yolsippa, though, directed a suspicious look about him.

319

"The gods, who abhor me, have resumed their vigilance. The gates do not respond to the mechanism."

"Oh, this is more of Zhirek's doing," Kassafeh lamented.

Yolsippa toiled and Kassafeh added her strength. Her tears, his sweat dropped on the levers, but the gates refused to part.

"Shall we climb from the portal?" Kassafeh demanded.

"Too vast a distance and too sheer a wall, damned be the idiot who designed it."

However, impelled to look about for what threatened them, they opened the trick window and glared forth.

The green moon gave all its glow unstintingly.

At first, the night seemed innocent, sky above and mountain tops about them, and before and below the sheen of that huge horizon of the sea. But soon the thunder sounded once again, and the moon's light on that watery horizon crinkled and fragmented like a splintered mirror.

"The sea," Kassafeh groaned.

"Surely, it is unsettled," admitted Yolsippa.

"And much closer," Kassafeh reported, "than before."

Yolsippa craned and squinted, but did not wish his sight confirmed. For the ocean, gray and cold as if it had spilled up from some inner deep where colors were unknown and warmth unheard-of, gathered, seething and rocking, at the very foot of the mountains. And now and then an enormous wave would comb it up against the flanks of the rock, and all the while, it seemed to rise a little to fill the hollow basin of the night.

Zhirek, who had learnt inside a man-shaped case of Verdigris the lore and mage-craft of the sea folk, now summoned the waters of an icy, primaeval ocean and all that they contained.

Where they began, the breakers turned from their usual courses. Their tides expanded, evaded the calling moon, which, even in the days of the earth's flatness, had her say in the movement of salt waters, both green and red. From some submarine womb, a giant surge beat up. A valve slid open, or was shattered. From depths, from abysses, waves erupted, exploded. The sea drove inland, rising, drinking the eastern shore, its beaches and its marmoreal escarpments, but thirsty most of all for Simmurad.

Zhirek waited on a high, high roof, his prize—Simmu—stretched like a frozen thing at his feet. Zhirek coaxed the sea in the words of an ancient and untranslatable oceanic witchery. He felt nothing, or not much, only his unhuman power, a drunkenness already soured in his throat. Death was gone, his impulse for vengeance satisfied, if it had ever truly existed save by proxy, or if vengeance had ever truly been his aim. But the sea answered Zhirek.

It filled the lower valleys of Simmurad in a joyous gushing, tumbling over the high ramparts and pouring downward, so the noise of waterfalls and rain storms ornamented the thunder of tall combers drumming on the mountains.

Grandually, the gardens and the walks, the beautiful colonnades and courts and underpasses of the city succumbed. Up steps the sea glided, over the heads of trees.

The water slipped almost self-effacingly into the feast hall of the citadel. It had already half-quenched the green obelisque before the doors; it had reached the words I AM, and it mouthed them lovingly.

When the sea carpeted the floor of the hall, lapping the slender ankles of the immortal woman and the erudite ugly feet of the sages and the boots of the warriors, they did not stir. When the sea became bold, mounted their limbs, stroked and grew intimate with them, not even then. Held in the trap, hypnotized, they did not feel it, though they understood it all. And when the water brimmed up their chins, their mouths and over into their nostrils, throats and lungs, they did not choke or struggle, and their eyes were pebbles. Vulnerable, they drowned; immortal, they lived as they drowned, but living was no use to them.

Even in those seconds, infinitesimal creatures clustered on them, the architects of the ocean. The coral of this sea was white. Its palisades would be years in their building. But at Zhirek's bidding the coral-makers had come and would congregate, till every immortal of the city had been sealed in his own individual prison of spiny white carbonate.

What Zhirek had seen in the Simmurians, their petrification, he had brought to pass on them. They had been wax dolls. Now they were pillars of limestone. They would not die. But Death had triumphed.

Presently, the sea washed the roof of the hall, and the primitive fish that swam in it swished in and out of the windbroken windows.

But the sea had still some way to travel, till it had swamped the tallest towers of the city, and now its tumult had grown gentle and seductive. It kissed before it devoured.

That much Kassafeh heeded, for as the water crept

321

stealthily up the stair toward her, it would hush and croon, trying to soothe her into submission.

"We are lost," she dolefully decided.

"A riddle I cannot answer," Yolsippa heavily agreed, "for we cannot drown, yet we must. And though this city life is sometimes irksome, yet I do not wish to relinquish my senses. However, pray do not increase the level of the water with your tears."

"And pray do not instruct me," snapped Kassafeh. "You are too stupid to effect our retreat, and I have been trained to nothing useful and cannot do it either." Kassafeh stood by the door of the gate-house on the topmost stair, the water two or three steps below, and the indifferent sky of pitilessly watching stars and moon above. "Neither will you send me any help," she accused them.

And then she saw a pale-winged gull which was cruising between her and the stars.

The upheaval of this sea upon some distant shore had roused the gull. In an unnatural world of tidal rising and displacement, it too felt moved to unnaturalness and flew by night. That iridescent fish leaped in the sea had also attracted it, and perhaps too, the aura of oceanic sorcery. Now it felt a new force lure it.

Kassafeh stared at the gull, and by the Eshva charm Simmu had taught her, she drew the gull down to her. But having grasped its thickly feathered sides, she gazed at its wicked profile, and wondered—what now? Her speechless entreaty penetrated its skull, but where might she send it for aid, and who would understand a message of raucous beak and wings? The gull, regaining mastery of itself as Kassafeh faltered, slashed at her hand and shot upwards into the air. But her cry for rescue was blazoned on it as if in luminous dye, for any psychic or unearthly enough to read it.

Kassafeh did not know her heritage, the sky-being's kiss which had begun her in her mother's body. Neither did the angry gull know anything of it as it flung itself aloft. While for the wandering elementals of Lower Upperearth, mankind was a species of movable clay, which very rarely, and generally by accident, became interesting.

Certain of these sky persons were bathing in moonlight pools on some plain of the ether invisible to men, when the gull burst through the midst of them. Now on its sides they immediately noted, with dim, drowsy surprise, Kassafeh's plea most plainly marked. And though, with pale golden sighs, they might have dismissed it, a drop of blood from the ferocious beak of the gull fell on the transparent skin of a bather. He—for while sexless, they somehow yet resembled the male rather than the female—regarded the drop and said: "This vital fluid is that of one immortal. Besides, though crimson rather than violet, the ichor of our kind is mingled in it."

Then they were intrigued and, sinking in a spangled drift downwards, soon viewed the upheaval of a sea, and Kassafeh up to her knees now in the water, cursing the sky, while Yolsippa, in his turn, reprimanded the masters of Upperearth.

The elementals slipped closer. They leaned out from their blowing cloaks.

"Do not blaspheme," they admonished with limpid rancour, for they had always been sweet on the gods.

"Then save us!" Kassafeh cried, seizing a pair of fragile feet, demented and uncaring as to their race or nature.

The elementals saw her bloody fingers and her extreme beauty, and recognized her as a poor relation of themselves.

"Possibly we will save you," they said, caressing her long hair vaguely. "But we have no inclination to deal with the other."

The "other," Yolsippa, bowed low into the water.

"Even now coral forms about my knees," he said. "I am resigned to living death. I would simply presume to inform you that his maiden greatly relies on me, and would suffer at our parting."

And when Yolsippa said this, Kassafeh remembered all at once how she had parted from Simmu, and suddenly her slow tears flowed as fast as if she had become the sea itself, and so she realized she had wept for Simmu all this while without owning it.

"You notice," said Yolsippa modestly, "how the maiden is distressed at the mere mention of leaving me."

Two of the elementals dipped abruptly and lifted Kassafeh by the waist. Despite her banquets of sweetmeats, she was slim and light to carry, almost as if her bones had been hollow as those of her ethereal kinfolk. She rose in their delicate grip, and with their free hands, they brushed the drops from her cheeks.

"Do not weep. Your gross and revolting companion shall be saved."

But she thought of Simmu in the thrall of Uhlume, and did not cease weeping as they bore her away.

The water had encircled Yolsippa's large chest and fish were nibbling at him, and coral, obedient to Zhirek's summons, crusted, as Yolsippa had reported, on his feet and calves, a painful process.

The elementals flitted about his head, disdaining to touch him till the last moment. When the sea filled his complaining mouth, they dragged him up by portions of his clothing, hair and beard. They were far stronger than they appeared, though some ten or twelve of them were essential to his elevation. Thus, upside down, silly with shock and alarm, and alternately blessing and reviling them, Yolsippa also was conducted from Simmurad.

In this manner, Kassafeh and Yolsippa evaded the fate of the city. But whether they evaded Uhlume is another matter.

How Zhirek left Simmurad is unknown. Whether by way of air or sea, his pace was swift, and Simmu was borne with him. And Simmu, rigid in the mesmeric trance, was yet capable of sight, so that the final vision his unblinking eyes received of Simmurad was that of shining towers beneath no less shining water. If he was perversely glad or sorry, or if he had emotion to spare at all for the drowning of that place, is hard to say.

Dawn came, at their backs, and the conveyance Zhirek had used was grounded in a valley, far westwards of the flooded city. No trace of water was here in any sort. It was a bowl of rock, gilded by the sun, rouged by shadow and voiced by winds, and nothing but sun and shadow or the wind had ever entered it till then.

Zhirek touched the forehead of Simmu with a ring of electrum, and his lips with another of green stone.

Simmu's paralysis dissolved. He shut his eyes against the light.

Quietly, Zhirek said: "Because you have survived your court, you must not anticipate compassion from me. I mean to destroy you, and am bound to it. You have heard my words on the subject. Nothing is altered, or will ever be."

Simmu's face was white and his gestures enervated.

"If you mean to learn if I fear you," he said, "I do. Yet, coupled with the fear is this sense of familiarity in your company. Since you are my destiny, perhaps it is only that. How will you destroy me?"

"You will discover shortly."

"So I shall. But in Simmurad you claimed me for a debt I owed you."

To remind you of it serves no purpose. Rest assured, you will pay it."

"I might escape you."

"Never."

Zhirek left Simmu in the shade of the rock and went away about a hundred paces.

Simmu lay where he was, obedient through weakness and bewilderment, his instincts of self-preservation long gone. He looked at Zhirek, about whom a smoke quickly clouded up. Some enchantment was in progress. Zhirek kept no watch on his captive, yet Simmu judged an invisible tether of some kind kept him bound, or would do if he attempted flight.

The sun became a golden furnace above the valley. It wore Simmu into a sick and feverish doze.

He dreamed he sat on a hillside, playing a pipe made from a reed. The sweet thin notes of it brought all types of animals to his feet, but eventually a young man came, a young priest clad in a yellow robe, barefoot and dark of hair. It was Zhirem, recalled in the dream as he would be forgotten on waking. He seated himself beside Simmu on the hill, and, in the dream, Simmu found himself instantly and painlessly metamorphosed into a woman.

The physical body of the Simmu who dreamed this dream did not, however, change, or even attempt the change. Suddenly, there was no ability left in him to effect it. He had finally been deserted by that one bizarre sorcery of his own flesh, which, at this hour, might have proved his salvation. Perhaps Zhirek's mood itself had robbed Simmu, perhaps his returning anguish at Death. Whatever the thief, it had burgled him totally.

Sleeping, half-smiling at an unremembered love, Simmu did not know his loss.

PART FIVE

Burning

1

It was a garden of sorts. High stone walls showed nothing but the sky, which was darkened with starless black. Fine green sand lay underfoot and four brass lamps were lit at the garden's four corners, exaggerating the trees of black wood with orange fruit and the shrubs which gave off a strange scent, and highlighting too a well of stone in the garden's centre, but fire rather than water seemed to glow deep down in it.

Beneath one of the lamps was seated a woman. Her face was not beautiful, but it was young and smooth, and it had a pair of eyes amazingly lustrous and flawless teeth whiter than salt, while her head was crowned by long brown hair, which might have been a glory to her, had it not been matted and tangled with metal rings and pieces of bone. However, there were other oddities about this woman, for her hands were extremely thin and wrinkled and the shade of tanned leather, and her feet likewise, where they poked out from her garment that was made of filthy pelts. Moreover, she was milking the venom from a golden snake that lay upon her lap, and as the jar filled up, she cackled to herself, and her voice was that of a crone.

There was no apparent occurrence in the garden or in the black beyond, but suddenly the witch-woman raised her head and shot a glance about her.

"Who is at my door?" rasped she in her crone's voice.

"One who has used it in the past," came the answer out of the air. After which a smoky cloud appeared against the sand, unfurled and took the form of a man. He was dark of robe and hair, his arms were crossed on his breast which glinted with gold, and he watched her with the coldest eyes that this witch had ever met.

But: "Well, well," said she, staunchly sharp, "you must be the father of magicians to force an entrance to my garden, for there are such safeguards on the place no other has ever come in before, unless with my connivance. Yes, you must be wiser than the night is black, and your powers extraordinary."

"I do not deny it," said Zhirek the magician.

"What then does the mighty one desire of me?"

"To test the strength of the well, a second time."

"Ah!" exclaimed the witch, "now I remember a child of four or five years, shadow-haired and beautiful, and his eyes like cool water—which now resemble two splinters of ice from the winter of the world."

"I, too, remember," Zhirek said. "It was told me once, and has come back to me in some detail."

"Now," said the witch, "do not blame me for your discontent. I warned your mother when she entreated me to render you invulnerable, but she would have it so."

"And sold you her white teeth in payment," said Zhirek.

"Such things are always my fee. I have gained several advantages through the years—this hair from the head of a prince, no less, and the skin of one fair maiden and the features of another not so fair, but she was young. And if you were of a more friendly disposition, I could reveal to you a hidden item I have purchased from one who had renounced love, though she was well fashioned for it. That is how I keep myself immortal, by my patchwork dealings, and I pay no forfeit to the gods' law of balance. Though you are very wise, my lord, concerning that balance, maybe in that I am the wiser."

"You are a hag," he answered, but without vehemence. "Is the fire still hot in the well?"

"While the earth is flat, that fire will burn. It is an old fire, but enduring. Do you remember all of it? That only a child may survive these flames and be proofed by them, for they feed on wickedness and knowledge. Is there such an infant you would bathe therein?"

"First I would learn this," he said. "If one, already made invulnerable by the fire, were to throw himself again into the well, what then?"

"Ah," repeated the witch savouringly. Her face grew sly. "That is your theme, is it? The reply is swiftly given. Leap into the fire and you will return unscathed. Indeed, it will vomit you up in a moment without a hair singed. Even such destruction cannot harm you, who were once laved in it. Your span is armored on you, honored magician; you cannot slip the fetters." And she grinned a hag's grin with his own dead mother's teeth.

The face of Zhirek showed nothing.

"As I thought," he said. "And how many others have you lowered into hell this way?"

"Enough," she said, "but never one who came back to berate me. I will add that, if you are considering my murder, you may save your energy. The fire conveys various protections on those who are its guardians."

"Then you are invulnerable too?"

"Through my guardianship, I am. There are rules to survival, so as not to tip the scales of life and death, good and ill. I have the trick of it."

Zhirek turned from her. With his hands he made a sign of power and spoke words that had no sound. Another figure began to harden out of the air. The witch stared with her wide girl's stare. Presently, she saw a young man standing in the garden. He was slender and handsome, with curious hair, and eyes the green of the strange gem about his neck. He wore the robe of a king, but his face was colorless and his expression was of hopeless fear. He made no move, nor did he speak or fasten his attention either on Zhirek or the witch.

"Now mark me carefully," said the witch, "if this is he you would set within the fire, it will consume him utterly."

"That is conceivable," Zhirek said. "Yet maybe the fire cannot quite consume him, for he has partaken of a certain drink that makes men live forever."

The witch took a step back.

"You shall not do it," she said.

"I will do it," Zhirek said, "and in doing it, I will put a stop to this particular trade of yours. Till the end of time Simmu shall lie screaming in the Fire of Invulnerability, forever burning, but never quite burned away. And none will dare the fire then, old woman, not even at your urging."

"You must detest this gentleman very much," said the witch. "What vile crime did he commit against you to inspire such hate?"

"Not hatred," said Zhirek. "It is love. That is my predestination, to work kindness out of hate, evil out of love." Then Zhirek went to Simmu and kissed his forehead, but Simmu did not move, or speak, or fix his eyes on anything. "You are the only wound I am able to give myself," Zhirek said to Simmu. "Your terror and your agony will dwell with me through all the years which are to come. I shall run from this spot. I will seal my ears against the memory of your cries, I will writhe and sweat in horror at what I have done to you. So I shall live."

Having spoken, Zhirek laid his arm over the shoulders of Simmu, and gently guided him forward.

"Again I say—" began the witch.

"And again *I* say," Zhirek forestalled her, "that I will do this thing. Consider my powers. Respect them and be silent."

At that the witch crouched down in a corner of the garden. She doused the lamp there, and wound the gold snake about her waist. And she put her two hands over her mouth to remind herself she must not challenge Zhirek again, for she knew how terrible he was, as one who has often seen a certain house recognizes its shape even by night.

They reached the edge of the well, Zhirek and Simmu.

Far below its stony lip, a vast swell of light was coming and going. Here the child Zhirem had fallen, held only by the cord tied into his hair. Deep in the unimaginable holocaust he had swung, till all jeopardy and all delight were scalded from him.

Simmu turned then at last, and he looked into the eyes of Zhirek, Simmu had renounced or mislaid, once more, the facility of human speech. Nor, despite his terrified face, did his eyes question or plead or even deny what was about to happen. The eyes of Zhirek were equally unequivocal. It was their last communion together, and something actually seemed to pass between them, but it had no name, nor could they have named it.

To the crouching witch, they were a symbol, dark and light, the candle and the shadow, two aspects of one whole. Through her clamping palms she muttered her own magic to shield her from the sight of their baleful disintegration.

Zhirek now indicated that Simmu must step on to the well's lip and Simmu obeyed him. The glow deep in the well flared, as if primed. The well was not so high as Zhirek had thought—he had been, of course, a small child when he saw it formerly.

"Simmu," said Zhirek, "if ever you gain means, punish me for this and take your revenge on me."

Simmu shivered, and swayed above the fire as though he would cast himself into it.

At that, Zhirek struck him from behind.

The blow toppled Simmu instantly from the lip. He vanished into the well.

The flame-glare dazzled. The whole garden was caught in a

329

single tremendous brilliance, which then sank away. But there was no outcry from within.

"What is this?" Zhirek said as he stood by the well. "I recall my own voice howling in that pit, yet no voice comes from it now."

The witch ungagged her mouth.

"The fire has already incapacitated both tongue and throat," she said. "He would scream if he could. You must not expect too much."

Zhirek said to her: "I cannot be assured of his eternal pain."

"Then glance into the well, if you must, and see."

Zhirek leaned forward and did as she suggested. Minutes dragged by as he prolonged the vigil. But when eventually he straightened and came about, written on his countenance and in his eyes was the picture the well had given him.

As he had predicted, he fled the spot, though wrapped in the magician's cloud which had borne him there.

The witch beneath her unlit lamp, clawed runes in the green sand for her own reassurance. Fear and madness still hovered simpering and whispering in the starless sky. The fruit of the trees gave off a bitter smell.

There was a desert place, where even the powders and the dusts had ground away to nothing. This was the site Zhirek chose for himself, his exile.

Bone-white pillars of stone stood up at intervals, and in some were holes. Zhirek climbed the stone, selecting one of these fractures to dwell in. He sat down on the hot bare bone-floor and he bowed his head, and so he stayed for many years.

By day the sun beat in at him, by night the blue winds. He ate only what came to him, which was the air, he drank the dew, the infrequent rain. He lived because deprivation could not kill him, any more than a spear or a sea or a flame. But he became a blackened wire and his beauty left him.

Sometimes birds of prey would visit him. They approached because they believed him a corpse, a dinner laid out for them. He did not move or beat them off, and they rammed their beaks against the wall of his invulnerability and flapped away cawing.

He slept often, that fearsome sleep Death had granted him. And portion by portion, this sleep began to wipe his brain clean of everything. The intellect of Zhirek, which had caused him such distress, put constantly into this blinkered box, gradually dislocated itself from reason and so from its very self. Though, now and then, swimming in a pool of semi-conscious dark, Zhirek would fling himself against the memory of Simmu burned forever in the well of fire. The monstrous pain of this was sweet and dear to him; he did not over-use it, squeezing out its juices drop by drop. It was all he had, or all he had kept for himself. But at length even this taste was numbed.

Now, in the beginning, men had seldom come to that place, but decades went by, and men were venturesome. There was a year when caravans began to come and go across the bone-yard desert, and though their road was a distance from the stone pillar, at length some noticed that a thing sat in the hole there.

In the town beyond the desert, they expounded variously:

"It is a weird beast."

"It is a madman."

"No, it is a hermit, a holy man. We have seen the vultures fly to his cave and feed him at the direction of the gods."

From that observation it was a small step to suppose him gifted with powers. Inevitably, in bands of five or ten or more, they began to drift toward him across the stone land, clambering the pillar, peering in, bright-eyed, at the opening.

Zhirek, or what remained of him, looked at them with a dreadful uninterest they interpreted as blindness or inner vision. He returned no syllable to their entreaties and their veneration, which they interpreted as a self-imposed vow of silence. They brought him honey-cakes, wines, raisins and cold meats. The food, untouched, rotted on the ledge before him till others cleared it away.

Some months having elapsed, fruitlessly, the people ceased coming, but they spread his fame, his curiosity and holiness and wild appearance; and they invented for him miracles he had not performed, in order to make their tales more entertaining. One day a prince arrived from a far land, having heard the story of the hermit.

He travelled in a gilded chariot, this prince, under a canopy of scarlet. Thirty slaves loped either side of it, and young girls threw silks before him across the desert and all the way up the stone pillar—on which a track had long since been worn—so the slippered feet of the prince should not rest on common ground.

The prince nodded to Zhirek.

"I have had a dream," said the prince, "which concerns the ending of the world. The sun blackens and a new sun rises;

331

the mountains melt and the seas are poured away. What does it mean?"

But Zhirek did not answer this prince of men, and Zhirek's filmy eyes, which once had been the color of green water reflecting a blue sky, closed themselves like gates against him.

So the prince went back unanswered over the stones.

But fame is fame. After a hundred years, the demons themselves got word of the holy aesthetic in the desert, who would neither talk, nor move, nor eat, nor love.

When the moon rose, three of the Eshva stole to the pillar, and they began to dance under it. Neither did they say anything, having no need. Each rippling step spoke for them. And their dance led them up the pillar track to the very mouth of the cave where Zhirek sat bowed in his death-sleep.

No mortal could undo that sleep, but the Eshva breathed their perfumed breath on the eyelids of Zhirek and their long black hair brushed over his body, and presently he woke. Then they laughed at him with their eyes, and traced him over with lascivious fingers smooth as the paws of black cats. Two females they were, and one male, and beautiful as all the demons, but Zhirek paid them no special heed, for at that season his brain and senses were worn nearly featureless.

Then, fired by the moonlight, there shone a green ray from the throat of the masculine Eshva. Some remaining awareness roused in Zhirek, and the dilapidated and ancient stick that was Zhirek's remnant reached out one hand to pluck at the gem hung from the Eshva's neck. But all three Eshva shrank pliantly from him, and watched with a childlike innocent malice as he began to cry.

And he too, like a child, rocked himself, knuckling his eyes, and thus he wept and the rusty noises of grief rasped in his chest till the Eshva lost their pleasure in the spectacle and smoked away. And long after that, yet he cried and rocked himself, till the moon set and the stars faded and a red rose bloomed in the east.

When the morning was full, riders went by that way toward the town.

"What is that lament?" they questioned each other.

"It is the holy man in the cave," said one who knew the story. "Generally he is impervious."

Now a priest rode with them, and pompously he declared: "No doubt the hermit is weeping for the sins of the world."

But Zhirek was weeping, whether in rage or gladness he did not know, because he had been supremely cheated.

2

The fire.

Simmu, thrust into it, had been a second suspended, then plunged beyond all things.

The torment was immeasurable, the suffering so elaborate that in a fraction of time it had surpassed all limits of pain, ceased to be pain, become another state no less appalling, yet inexpressible and undefined.

Following his flesh, his thoughts were next to burn away. The immortal core persisted, that link which trapped the soul in the structure of a man, just enough of the body to hold him in the fire intact though almost obliterated.

But one other thing was burning along with hair and skin and bone and brain. The green Eshva jewel about his throat.

How long did the fire chew on him? It was said to be nine years. And then, with no sight or hearing left him, something suggested itself before the sockets of his eyes, and cadences rang in the cavities of his ears, a conversation like music, and quantities of miles below him.

"See, there the jewel is, burning, as I told you."

"It is the third burning. Each time the heat strikes it, it gives off a green hard note. But our prince will not honor his vow to the mortal?"

"Yes, but he will honor it."

These were the Vazdru, talking so melodiously below. And somewhere a dwarfish Drin tore his sable locks and groaned as his precious artifact, the faceted gem, spattered in the flames. It was the Eshva, the demon messengers, who flew up suddenly like black doves into the well of fire. Their water-cool hands grasped Simmu, all that there was of him, their hair fanned him. They bore him downwards.

He did not know where he was going. Shapes flashed through his sightlessness. The whispers of their silver minds were in his ears that had no hearing. His agony was horrible. He had forgotten the demons, although they were a comfort He went through three gates, and never saw them, into a shining umber city beneath the earth.

How he was, his blackened husk, goes unrecounted. It is possible to visualize it, unwise to set it down. His hurt shall be described no further.

Then, he felt—positively felt, though no feeling but the

hurt had been left him—the imprint of a hand upon his breast. Like frost-blighted leaves he crumbled, but never knew it, for the hand brought him balm and oblivion.

Azhrarn looked at what lay on the floor of his hall, under the windows of wine-red corundum. The jewel which had become his pledge, he had plucked off. It was like a dead coal. Even Drin-crafted handiwork could not endure that conflagration in the well.

The motives of the demons were both complex and simple. What intrigued them, they permitted liberties and rapture. What was fruitless or insolent or unwary, they eradicated. What bored them, they overlooked. Despite such factors, they were mobile, their choice not always steadfast.

Simmu had failed Azhrarn. Given Immorality and Simmurad to boot, Simu's ingenuousness had proved a fatal flaw. Yet, when Azhrarn met Death on the river bank that night, and put in his way the one weapon whereby Death might breach the city: Zhirek. It is not inconceivable that Azhrarn had flung more dice than merely Uhlume's. Zhirek was Death's pawn, but had also been a spoon to stir the pot of Simmurad.

The demon presence which Simmu had often yearned for in his citadel and which had never greeted him there—maybe it had been nearer in the conclusive days of the city than any guessed. Had Azhrarn been watching from the shade of a moonless night, or in some magic glass of Underearth, or through the eyes of a panther on the lawn? If so, what had Azhrarn beheld? Perhaps the Demon had meant to deliver punishment on what had failed and disillusioned and wearied him. But the punishment was delivered by another. And the punishment was complete. The fire was more terrible than any scheme Azhrarn the pitiless could just then concoct. To harm Simmu, had he wished to, Azhrarn could have done no more than this the fire had done. It had come to the point where the only avenue Azhrarn could take to display his omnipotence, and appease his vanity, was that of redemption. Besides, the demons were fascinated by justice, by what was opposite, however heinous or unlikely it might be.

Azhrarn called the Drin and told them what he wanted. They skipped with ravishment at his attention, and cringed in case they should get it wrong. Then they carried the leaves of Simmu away with them, those blighted leaves from which there feebly came the sound of a man's breathing, or a small twitching as of a man in slumber.

By a lake like black syrup, the smoulders of Drin forges throbbed on the starry air of Underearth. The stunted folk of Druhim Vanashta were renowned for their obnoxious whims and for their genius with metal, minerals and all items mechanical.

They laboured to construct a complicated image. It was of a man's height and a man's form. It was made in this way. To commence, a framework of bones was carved from the finest whitest ivory, and from the frame not a rib was missed, not the joint of a finger. The skull was burnished and enhanced with gorgeous teeth sculpted from the whitest of the white ivory. Then, about this skeleton was woven an anatomy of silk and silver wires astonishing to witness, and amid the curiosity of it were placed fabulous organs of bronze and fiber that a novel clockwork presently set in rhythm—permitting the heart to beat, the lungs to inhale. Next, over the carven bones and silken flesh was fitted a single skin, close as a glove, of the palest and most matchless vellum, and onto the enamel veins beneath were poured faint fragrant juices to colour from within. The image was unmistakably of demon kind. Its hair was black, but the black growing ferns of Underearth supplied it, and the black lashes of the eyes were ebony grasses from the lawns of Druhim Vanashta. For the eyes themselves, they were polished black agates, and the nails of the hands and feet were polished nacre.

It was marvellous this object, when it was finished. It looked alive, yet too perfect to be living, even to be a living demon perhaps. . . . The Drin wondered at their own cleverness. They stroked the image and mooned over it with admiration and amorousness. But they had no claim, either to what it was or to what it should be. In the end, they opened a box in which had been strewn a pile of cindery leaves, and they intruded this matter into the image by a vent they had left in the skull for the purpose, then sealed the vent and shook the image brutally and crudely, as if indeed to settle sugar in a canister, rather than a man's undying fragments in their case. This macabre ritual completed, the Drin hopped aside, as if their creation abruptly unnerved them.

Nothing happened for a moment. At that, the Drin began to upbraid each other horribly, each swearing another had omitted some vital part or magic from the work. They had fallen to purple-faced cuffing, kicking and biting, when the image, lying flat on the couch where they had laid it, sighed, and turned its head in sleep from their noise.

Azhrarn entered the workshop, and the Drin scrambled to prostrate themselves, squeaking. Azhrarn approached the couch. He studied the image which now contained the immortal surviving part of Simmu that was neither soul nor spirit but leaves of burned flesh.

"Little cunning ones," Azhrarn said sfotly, "you have done well."

The Drin slobbered and kissed the edges of Azhrarn's cloak.

Azhrarn put his hand lightly upon Simmu's shoulder—the Eshva image which housed Simmu's life, was entitled to his name—and Simmu's eyelids lifted. He blinked with the lashes of black grass, and with his radiant eyes of agate he focused on the Prince of Demons.

His agony had been subtracted from Simmu, and everything else returned to him—nearly everything. His senses and the sensual properties of taste and smell and touch and hearing and sight, all were there; but he was dumb, for the Eshva could not, or would not, speak. One other thing was also banished—memory. Amnesiac, he came alert at the infinitesimal pressure of Azhrarn's fingers, and in that instant, Simmu was born.

He was pristine. No vestige clung to him of the past, no sweetness and no pain. This was the initial awakening, the initial impression. And Azhrarn the Beautiful was the first thing he saw in his new, never-before-experienced world.

But it was Azhrarn who asked of him: "Say who you are."

The question taught. It was a lesson. It filled the silver brain within the ivory skull. The agate eyes revealed their voiceless reply: *A demon, and your subject. I am nothing more, but who would desire more?* And Simmu sank down before Azhrarn, his body so excellently made it was precisely as graceful as the bodies of those creatures that were its model.

Azhrarn mused. The completion of the spell lay with him and only with him. He lifted Simmu to his feet, and took Simmu away with him.

Once, Azhrarn had said to Simmu: "The time is mine to choose, and is not now." And now, unlooked for, the time had come. That it was a ritual and a magic thing made no odds. Some circle was joined, some lesion mended. For such as demons could not promise a thing and leave the promise unfulfilled; even their whisperings turned the sails of the earth, and their blackness, like a shadow behind glass, seemed to offer men a mirror by which to see.

When Azhrarn caressed the fern hair of Simmu, it became actually hair, and the lashes of grass brushing the cheek of Azhrarn, their blades also became hair. And the eyes filled with tears and though they were beautiful, they were eyes not agates. And when Azhrarn kissed the mouth of Simmu, it was flesh, and the body of Simmu was flesh and blood, that refined and wonderful flesh and blood of demon-kind—unhuman, better. And when Azhrarn possessed Simmu, and yet once more destroyed and yet once more reincarnated him through the death-like throes of ecstasy, then Simmu became, in every vessel and nerve and artery and muscle, in each inner mote and outer circumstance, animate, carnal and real. This final sorcery Azhrarn worked upon him, for even among mortals, then and now, love is a catalyst, and how much more could the Prince of Demons do with love, who perhaps had invented it. But Azhrarn was lord and king, not lover, to Simmu, for with very few was Azharan ever lover alone, and they were mortals.

But Simmu dwelt thereafter with the demons and roamed with them. Eshva, he inhabited the dusks of Undereearth and the moon-milk nights of earth itself. What in the beginning Simmu had almost been, now he was. And on the dancing-floors of midnight woods he strolled, calling the beasts wordlessly to follow him, hunting the foolishness of mankind, meddling, at ease in the burning Eshva dream of those who, at the commencement of his life, had adopted and nurtured him. And maybe even with those two, the Eshva women who had first cradled him with their glamour, maybe even with those he occasionally wandered here and there, probably all three unaware that once before they had similarly wandered.

Simmu, no longer apricot-haired, green-eyed, but demon-dark. No longer thrust now one way now another between the physique of male and female, for though male in his Eshva form, the demons, and particularly the Eshva, were pendulums, all love admissable to them, and their natures fluid, unhampered.

Yet about his neck he wore a green jewel, facsimile of the other, Azhrarn's gift, as often enough he gifted his people when they pleased him. Coveted by his brothers and the treasure of Simmu himself, this jewel winked and flamed through many many shadows. Generation after generation, murderers striding through forests, girls making charms and garlands, mages at complicated magics, glanced up at that sizzle of green, caught in the act by demon-kind in the person of Simmu.

For naturally, down endless millennia Simmu took his way, though immortality had ceased to confound him, for he was Eshva now. The truly immortal had never feared their state, neither demons nor gods nor any others of that plethora of enduring ones; it was merely a secondary aspect of their mystical condition.

One night, could it be, Azhrarn sent Simmu, Eshva messenger, to visit the mad hermit on his column of stone? Possibly the Prince intended some absolute joke, which only he might laugh at. Or possibly it was another of the Eshva who dipped and danced before the cave-hole, another gem about his neck, other mischief on his mind. That Zhirek was tutored by the happening, might have been due only to his wit, what there was remaining of it. For sure, he wept. And for sure, Simmu did not weep, save sometimes for entertainment, in the luxurious meaningless Eshva manner. Generally, Simmu burned instead, in the burning Eshva dream, all other fires forgotten. Thus it was in the Underearth, which was home to him at last—as it must always have been fated to be.

EPILOGUE

The Traveling House

Across the plain, out of the sunset, came an incredible sight. Men in the fields let go the scythes and stood gaping, women at the wells put down their dippers and pots in surprise. The dogs in the villages barked and the birds sheered up on sun-dyed wings. Such a show had not been glimpsed there for thirty years, not since the king had passed through, and even that passage of splendor paled beside the unlikelihood of this one.

A team of elephants of huge dimension and coal-black hide walked before. Their trappings were of gold and crimson bedewed with brilliants and bells. On the back of the foremost left-hand beast, in a golden seat, a big man lolled under a sunshade, apparently controlling the animals. Behind the elephants and attached to them by means of painted shafts and chains of bronze, rolled a kind of movable mansion with walls of carved wood, doors of red lacquer, colored windows, a roof of black porcelain and six tall towers with crystal cupolas. The whole edifice was mounted on a brazen platform equipped with some twenty great gilded wheels. To ensure a total lack of normalcy, the spokes of these wheels were dragons' heads of brass that puffed out scented smoke at each rumbling revolution.

The man in charge of the elephants paid no discernible heed to the outcry and gawping on all sides, nor to the yapping dogs and squealing children that here and there ran after the monstrous house on wheels.

But at one place, where a tavern stood in a grove of green poplars beside the road, some merchants, who had been sitting over their drink, hailed the man on the elephant.

"Come, take a cup of wine at our expense. You are an interesting apparition. What are you selling?"

The man on the elephant persuaded his team to halt.

"I sell nothing," said he in ringing tones. "I am the protector, and dare I say, the adoptive uncle or father, of the one who has the wares."

"More interesting still," said the merchant who had spoken before. "It sounds like a woman. Is it so?"

"I perceive your minds are running in a false direction. The lady, my, as it were, niece and daughter, who travels in this unique equipage, is the agent of a mighty lord, his intermediary, and the goods are his."

"Does she not then, sell herself?" inquired the merchant.

"Come," cried the man on the elephant, "have you ever heard of the House of the Red Doors?"

At that, an odd silence came down on the merchants, and indeed on the whole tavern yard. The sunset was fading to a dark pink afterglow, and the shadows, which all day had clung to the poplars, now spread their skirts over the ground, for in the provincial inn the lamps were not yet lit. Aloft, the leaves whispered like dry green papers. Yes, yes, the leaves seemed to answer, we have heard of the House of the Red Doors, and who has not? And the merchants looked slantwise and warily through the dusk at the gaudy mansion on wheels, now become mysterious and ghastly.

"A rumour is a rumour," said the merchants' spokesman. "And I do not think I believe it."

"As you will," said the man on the elephant. "But if you should alter your opinion, you may pay my mistress a visit, for we will rest tonight on the adjacent hill. And now," he added, "I wonder if any hay is to be purchased hereabouts for these elephants? Or if there are any persons of loose morals and crossed eyes?

An hour the merchants debated together. Their sojourn at this inn, which had threatened tedium, seemed to have grown all too momentous.

"I do not credit the stories," said one.

"But the house travels and has red doors, as in the tales. Moreover, the fat man fits his description—Yolsippa the Rogue, the showman, immortal tricky Yolsippa, whose horse rears at the strabismus."

"And who is she in the wagon house?"

"Well, if the rest is true, then she is Kassafeh, and she is the handmaiden of—"

"Hush! Hush, and be damned."

Meanwhile, the movable mansion lurked on the hill, a quarter of a mile off, its position clearly marked by two flaming torches set in the earth before it. And as the merchants quarrelled and made further noise, one of their number fell quiet. When the rest went in to supper, this one got to his feet, and with a nervous hurrying step, set off for the hill.

He was of middle years, a solemn man, spare of frame and clad in sober garments. Going uphill through the black night, he came to the elephants first, picketed in a meadow, which beasts trumpeted raucously at his approach. When he reached the torches, Yolsippa—if it were really he—was seated before the red lacquer doors, patiently awaiting him.

"Now what is it to be?" Yolsippa cried. "Some deceased magician whose bones you would question? Or some rich secret mausoleum you would find and pilfer? Or can it be some lover, newly dead, you would embrace again? Or a deathlike trance you require temporarily to tumble into, one which will fool the wisest physician—maybe in order to escape the tax collector?"

The sober merchant paled.

"How can you jest, if truly you serve the master you do?"

"I serve the lady," said Yolsippa—it must be he—"and she serves the personage we are talking of, Uhlume, Lord Death." The merchant staggered. "However," Yolsippa went on, "you had best be warned. Though my mistress can entreat her lord to oblige you, he may have business elsewhere and prove unavailable, not being, you will understand, at her beck and call. Still, state your business. Is it love, greed or curiosity you desire to solace?"

"If all this is a fact," said the merchant with horrified forcefulness, "then I will express my needs only to the witch in the house—Kassafeh."

Yolsippa shrugged.

"I have, in any case," said he, "an appointment with the pot-boy of the inn, who, though straight-eyed, has assured me he can turn his optics crosswise for three silver pieces." Then Yolsippa rapped on the doors of red lacquer, which at once flew open. "Now enter," said Yolsippa, and went off down the hill, leaving the gaping merchant alone.

A minute elapsed before the merchant gained sufficient courage to go through the doors.

The interior was quite inviting in itself, for rosy lamps burned up on every hand, revealing various wonders. Most exotic was the central apartment, with columns of carved cedar wood and painted walls and curtainings of lilac hue, while scented flowers spilled from golden vases. On the floor was a fierce tiger skin, with clockwork eyes which followed the merchant, and clockwork jowls which snarled. A loom stood nearby with a rainbow cloth half-finished on it. The

341

merchant cautiously approached the loom, and jumped with a violent agitation when the shuttle shot across it.

"Fear nothing," said a voice from behind the loom, "it is just a woman at her work."

Nevertheless, the merchant shrank back when she emerged, for now he was face to face with the legendary handmaiden of Death.

She was not as he dreaded she might be, a hag—or worse. She was young and lovely, her bright hair streaming about her a few degrees paler than her golden dress. Only her eyes were changeable and daunting, and, despite her words, she looked at him haughtily with them, so he thought it advisable to bow three times.

"And are you," he mumbled, "Kassafeh?"

"I am she," answered the maiden. "Now be seated, and inform me of your hopes."

The merchant sat on a couch of embroidered silk.

"Such magnificence," he cried. "Can it all be real?"

"It is quite real," Kassafeh said stiffly. "Nothing is illusion *here*." She seemed touchy on this point, and in order not to displease her the merchant quickly began to give her his reasons for calling.

"It is on behalf of another I disturb you," he said. "My aged grandfather, who has lived to a prodigious age, swears that in his youth he made a bargain with—with that master you serve. In honesty, I had always thought this boast of his a mark of his senility, but I have been forced to feign belief, since his fortune will pass to me at his demise, and I think it right, therefore, to humour him. Now recently, you may suppose, the elderly gentleman has become irked with life, and has been preparing himself to leave it. And quite cheerful was he, assuring me his place was certain at the court of— one you are familiar with. In fact, the old man told me the substance of his bargain. In exchange for enormous riches from an ancient sarcophagus, whose deathly guardians and curses only—ah—such a lord as yous might have means to subdue, my grandfather agreed to pass a thousand years in the Innerearth, in company with—someone of note. Being of a slightly supernatural bent, my grandfather, through dreams and trances, has frequently beheld the doings of the Innerearth, which apparently is a versatile spot capable of any illusory enhancement." Here the merchant paused and mopped his brow. "All this is well, and the tomb in readiness for my grandfather, and his wealth almost in my cof-

342

fers, when one night the decrepit fellow wakes from a dream yelling he refuses after all to die."

It appeared, the merchant went on to say, a new view of the Innerearth had been vouchsafed grandfather. Lord Death had taken a wife—a fright, she was, poison-blue with yellow sparks for eyes, and her right hand was a bone. The denizens of Innerearth cast themselves flat in squeamish homage before this horror, and she, proud over-bearing bitch, trampled on their backs. But there was more. One time, Death had had occasion to be much from home, and on his return he found this pest of a woman had snatched up the reins of his power. She was called Narasen, and had once been a queen. Now she said she had been cheated of her kingdom and would rule jointly with Lord Death over the Innerearth, nor would she vacate the premises after her thousand years were up. And to enforce her statements, she had already had her own palace (twice the size of Death's) quarried from the black granite of the region, and thereafter robbed the graves of half the kings of the world to ornament it. Peculiar immortal leopards roamed the rooms, biting the uninvited visitors. These beasts, it was related, Death himself had given her, as he had unwisely, in a moment of aberration, given her use of his magic power to open kings' monuments. Some excused him, saying it was a reward he let her have in response to a warning she had offered him, concerning certain fools who had styled themselves "Death's Enemies." Definitely she had abused all her privileges, and had even made oblique bargains of her own with human sorcerers, so now vegetable stuffs were being occultly passed through into Innerearth, from which she meant gardens made and parks laid out. And the slave labor for this enterprise would be supplied by the same unhappy force as had built her palace—the unfortunates that Death had personally claimed for a thousand years.

" 'And I am too old to toil on such nonsense,' my grandfather declared, with some cause," said the merchant. " 'Come,' postulated I, 'perhaps the dream is spurious.' 'Not so,' he screamed, laying about with his staff, 'for the woman who walked at Narasen's side, forever kissing her wrists and smirking, is the one who was his lordship's agent when I went bargaining, a hundred and fifty years ago—Lylas of the House of the Blue Dog.' And so," concluded the merchant, "my elderly relative has given up all thoughts of passing away, and being a phenomenally stubborn wretch, will probably persist several more decades."

"And what use am I to you in this?" said Kassafeh sternly. "I am not Lylas."

"If you serve whom you do, probably you might approach my grandfather and reassure him that there is no Narasen."

"But there is," said Kassafeh.

"Cannot then your lord quell the woman?"

Kassafeh smiled. Her eyes darkened.

"Uhlume rules the world, does he not? Why should he trouble that a woman supplants him in his lower kingdom, when all the earth is his?"

"But in my childhood the priests taught me," said the merchant uneasily, "that Death is the servant of men, not their tyrant."

"But," said Kassafeh, "all men know him."

The merchant shivered.

"It grows cold," he said.

"With good reason," said Kassafeh. "One comes."

The merchant leapt up. He saw how the flames in the lamps were flickering, how the tiger's clockwork eyes were shut.

"Honoured lady," he croaked, "I think I will be going."

And with that he bolted from the doors and down the hill, where even the elephants refrained from trumpeting.

Years before, Uhlume had found her, found Kassafeh.

Simmurad was drowned, and the sky elementals who had borne her away, had got tired of the affair, and left her on an upland somewhere, in a dismal rain with hardly a tree to shelter her. Yolsippa they dropped nearby, but from an uncivil height.

Here the two sat and wept and bemoaned their condition, and were a peculiar consolation to each other from simply being in the self-same plight. Even the tears Kassafeh shed for Simmu died, or were flooded out, by those she shed for herself.

When the rain ceased, they trudged downhill and through a landscape of woods and rivers. But when they spied a village or farm and pleaded for shelter, the pair were sent off with oaths, stones, dogs. Yolsippa, accustomed previously to these adventures, took up the burden again with complaining fortitude. Kassafeh, who had met them briefly while journeying with Simmu toward Simmurad, collapsed in paroxysms of despair and wrath.

She and Yolsippa were a disruptable-looking couple

344

through no fault of their own, but while Yolsippa readily forgave her her dishevelment, Kassafeh took exception to his.

"You hog! You flea-nipped rag!" she reviled him. "Could you not have brought a solitary gem from the city to secure our future?" (Her own had been sloughed during their flight—or stolen by the sky elementals.)

One dusk, as they dithered by a stream, Yolsippa puffing and blowing over a dingy fire, Kassafeh nagging at him, a cold and ghostly wind blew through the tall grasses, and the hearts of both gave a lurch.

"Someone walks at the edge of the trees," gasped Kassafeh.

"No, no," blustered Yolsippa, "there is no one. Look away."

Then a giant bird seemed to unfold a snow-white wing, and Death stood beside them. Death, magnificent, omnipresent and awful.

Kassafeh fainted; at least she dropped to the ground and tried to lose all her awareness, but could not quite do it. Death she saw through a haze of lashes and shadows. In insane terror she saw him, but she saw his beauty too. She evaluated, as in everything else.

Yolsippa grovelled. He told Death that he admired him, and would do whatever Death thought best.

Death said: "There are now no human Immortals on the earth, save only you. Did you suppose you could elude me? I am here."

"Your arrival is more delightful than the sun to us," gushed Yolsippa.

"I cannot end your lives," said Death, "nor is that my function, though I am no longer quite as I was, for now the sight of death pleases me, renovates me. But you. What am I to do with you, for I cannot rest till the problem is solved."

"All mankind palpitates in fear at your footfall, at your very name," said Yolsippa. "Do we matter?"

"Yes," said Uhlume, Lord Death.

"Then," Yolsippa suggested, courteously repressing his shudders, "let us be enlisted in your service. No doubt there is some tiny but useful way in which we might aid you. And if our names are linked to yours, men will know we have not escaped your powerful arm, will assume that we exist at your discretion. Indeed, we have no war with you, extraordinary sir. We were simply caught in the machinations of others. I, for example, was *tricked* into sampling the Elixir of Life—"

Kassafeh now recovered with rapidity from her faint. She sat up and stared with frightened boldness at Death. "Zhirek the magician was your agent and intermediary. I will be another. Since you have so much traffic with men on the earth, you will need such people. And, since I shall live forever, as you do, my choice is logical. Besides, I served a god before, and Death is, in his fashion, a god. I have experience for the post."

She did not know, and how could she, that she was offering to serve the same "god" she had once reviled and fled from, for the black god of Veshum's garden had been none other than Uhlume.

Uhlume looked down at Kassafeh. Perhaps he glimpsed Lylas in her place a moment, Lylas, who now went slinking at the heels of the blue woman, Narasen. How things had changed. Uhlume, the expressionless and inexorable, tarnished within by intimations of mortality.

"You sought," Uhlume said to Kassafeh, "a hero."

"What hero is greater than Lord Death."

It was true, and she meant it. It had come to her abruptly that here was the impervious and imperishable name on which to tie her own. Who would throw stones at Kassafeh, the Handmaiden of Death? Already, even as she trembled in doubt of his reply, she planned to ask for a fitting show to attend her, so his person should not be disgraced by her lack of it. None there were who did not understand Death had access to the treasure hoards of tombs.

Uhlume reached down to her his shapely black hand.

Kassafeh gazed at it. Then, heart pounding, eyes swimming, she took the hand, and he drew her to her feet. His touch could not slay her, but it could hardly fail to move her. She thrilled to him.

"I will instruct you," said Uhlume, "in your duties to me."

His smoke white hair brushed her cheek as he leant to her. Suddenly her emotion resolved itself. She gave him that migratory love of hers which had never yet found a home. The veracity of fear she could no longer offer him. Kassafeh—and Yolsippa too—had already lost much of the wooden waxen look of Simmurad, thrust out, as they had been to hardship and precariousness. Now, Uhlume tendered purpose, a reason for life, however macabre. Kassafeh, awash with adoration and fulfilment, raised herself and kissed the beautiful mouth of Uhlume, Lord Death, a thing which had never been done in all the long history of men. And Death, who had been levelled by events, in some sort, to the replica of a man, responded to her kiss with an obscure intensity of his eyes.

Yolsippa, noting the tableau, broke in with his usual indelicacy.

"And I, amazing lord?"

"And he?" Uhlume asked Kassafeh.

She, half lying in the circle of his arm, whispered: "Oh, let him come with me, if he is able. He can guide the elephants—that is, if you will permit me elephants?"

By night, the Lord Uhlume strode across the plains and hillsides of the world. He was often there now. He passed like a black note in the silence, the white notes of his hair and cloak played at his back, and sometimes a green-faced nightmare might scamper after him, though generally he walked alone.

Of course, he had not wed Narasen, but that she queened it in the Innerearth was true. Her palace had been built, and hung with thieved lamps of golden filigree. Those descending, now and then forgot Death, and ran to her, begging favors. Queen Death. The extinction of Simmu's sunlight had refurbished her own brilliance, as if she had fed upon his body, or his soul, and in some measure also, on Uhlume.

It was not, presumably, that Uhlume had not powers enough to quench her, merely that he had never turned to them. Maybe her challenge defeated him by its sheer improbable audacity, as from the first it seemed it had. Or was it only that to Uhlume, whose spirit spanned eons, the challenge had no permanent significance—the sting of a bee, a few million years—an instant—of rancour.

Whatever it was, it transpired that he surrendered that small kingdom, Innerearth, in favor of the other, greater one, the living world, where Narasen could not go. And here he walked, up and down, and round and about.

And sometimes, as the world's sun bled out its life, the Lord Uhlume could hear the faintest of sounds, that of a loom muttering somewhere in the deep jar of the dusk.

Painted by starlight, the plain had a marvellous softness and shady luminescence. Upon the hill, the lacquer doors beyond the torches stood open, and the silky lilac-red of the doorway smiled out into the dark.

Kassafeh rose from her loom. She did not kneel; her obeisance and her worship were all there in her eyes instead, which melted through amber and hyacinth to the blackest of blues.

No chair of bone for Uhlume in this house. It was Kassafeh who sat, and he, Lord Death, who lay down and rested his head in her lap. The fatigue of a thousand centuries had caught him up. Why not?

And as he rested there in silence and she with gentle fingers smoothed his forehead, the strange flat earth went on about its business through the night.

Attention:

DAW COLLECTORS

Many readers of DAW Books have written requesting information on early titles and book numbers to assist in the collection of DAW editions since the first of our titles appeared in April 1972.

We have prepared a several-pages-long list of all DAW titles, giving their sequence numbers, original and current order numbers, and ISBN numbers. And of course the authors and book titles, as well as reissues.

If you think that this list will be of help, you may have a copy by writing to the address below and enclosing one dollar in stamps or coins to cover the handling and postage costs.

DAW BOOKS, INC. Dept. C
1633 Broadway
New York, N.Y. 10019

Have you discovered . . .

JO CLAYTON

"Aleytys is a heroine as tough as, and more believable and engaging than, the general run of swords-and-sorcery barbarians."

—*Publishers Weekly*

The saga of Aleytys is recounted in these DAW books:

- ☐ **DIADEM FROM THE STARS** (#UE1520—$2.25)
- ☐ **LAMARCHOS** (#UE1627—$2.25)
- ☐ **IRSUD** (#UE1640—$2.25)
- ☐ **MAEVE** (#UE1469—$1.75)
- ☐ **STAR HUNTERS** (#UE1550—$1.75)
- ☐ **THE NOWHERE HUNT** (#UE1665—$2.25)

DAW presents TANITH LEE

"A brilliant supernova in the firmament of SF"—**Progressef**

- ☐ DELUSION'S MASTER (#UE1652—$2.25)
- ☐ THE BIRTHGRAVE (#UE1672—$2.95)
- ☐ VAZKOR, SON OF VAZKOR (#UE1709—$2.50)
- ☐ QUEST FOR THE WHITE WITCH (#UJ1357—$1.95)
- ☐ DON'T BITE THE SUN (#UE1486—$1.75)
- ☐ DRINKING SAPPHIRE WINE (#UE1565—$1.75)
- ☐ VOLKHAVAAR (#UE1539—$1.75)
- ☐ THE STORM LORD (#UJ1361—$1.95)
- ☐ NIGHT'S MASTER (#UE1657—$2.25)
- ☐ ELECTRIC FOREST (#UE1482—$1.75)
- ☐ SABELLA (#UE1529—$1.75)
- ☐ KILL THE DEAD (#UE1562—$1.75)
- ☐ DAY BY NIGHT (#UE1576—$2.25)

DAW BOOKS are represented by the publishers of Signet and Mentor Books, THE NEW AMERICAN LIBRARY, INC.

DAW PRESENTS MARION ZIMMER BRADLEY

☐ **SHARRA'S EXILE**
The newest Darkover book tells how the Sharra Matrix returned from the stars to threaten the whole of Darkover's domains. (#UE1659—$2.95)

☐ **STORMQUEEN!**
"A novel of the planet Darkover set in the Ages of Chaos ... this is richly textured, well-thought-out and involving." —Publishers Weekly. (#UE1629—$2.50)

☐ **THE SHATTERED CHAIN**
"Primarily concerned with the role of women in the Darkover society ... Bradley's gift is provocative, a top-notch blend of sword-and-sorcery and the finest speculative fiction."— Wilson Library Bulletin. (#UE1683—$2.50)

☐ **THE FORBIDDEN TOWER**
"Blood feuds, medieval pageantry, treachery, tyranny, and true love combine to make another colorful swatch in the compelling continuing tapestry of Darkover."—Publishers Weekly. (#UE1752—$2.95)

☐ **DARKOVER LANDFALL**
"Both literate and exciting, with much of that searching fable quality that made Lord of the Flies so provocative." —New York Times. The novel of Darkover's origin. (#UJ1684—$1.95)

☐ **TWO TO CONQUER**
A novel of the last days of the Age of Chaos and the ultimate conflict. (#UE1651—$2.50)

☐ **THE KEEPER'S PRICE**
New stories of all the ages of Darkover written by MZB and members of the Friends of Darkover. (#UE1517—$2.25)
